T0123318

Instant Karma

The second she touched Benjamin's head, his eyes opened.

He was fully alert in a second, his deep eyes a strange metallic color. "Karma," he murmured.

She drew back. He remembered her name? Nobody remembered her name.

"Do you need blood?" she whispered, leaning closer, even as the guard locked the cell door and disappeared down the hallway, leaving her alone with the enemy. Right now she was useless to the Kurjans, so if the prisoner killed her, they'd find a plan B.

"No." Benjamin sat up, looked around, and put his back to the cement brick wall. His impressive body seemed to take up all the space in the cell.

She shook her head, her lips trembling. "You must be badly injured or you would not have been captured. You need blood." It would hurt if he bit her, and he'd have to be quick to avoid touching her skin for long.

"I let them take me. I've been searching for you for three years."

Also by Rebecca Zanetti

Rebel's Karma

Rebecca Zanetti

LYRICAL PRESS
Kensington Publishing Corp.
www.kensingtonbooks.com

LYRICAL PRESS BOOKS are published by

Kensington Publishing Corp.
119 West 40th Street
New York, NY 10018

All Kensington titles, imprints, and distributed lines are available at special quantity discounts for bulk purchases for sales promotion, premiums, fund-raising, educational, or institutional use.

Special book excerpts or customized printings can also be created to fit specific needs. For details, write or phone the office of the Kensington Sales Manager: Kensington Publishing Corp., 119 West 40th Street, New York, NY 10018. Attn. Sales Department. Phone: 1-800-221-2647.

Lyrical Press and Lyrical Press logo Reg. U.S. Pat.& TM Off.

First Electronic Edition: June 2021
ISBN-13: 978-1-5161-1076-6 (ebook)
ISBN-10: 1-5161-1076-5 (ebook)

First Print Edition: June 2021
ISBN-13: 978-1-5161-1081-0
ISBN-10: 1-5161-1081-1

Printed in the United States of America

This one is dedicated to Jonah, Jessica, Jakob, and Alexandra Namson, because you're the best friends any family could wish to have.

Acknowledgments

Thank you to the readers who've been with the Realm since the beginning, and those who have jumped in with this new era, starting with *Vampire's Faith*. I have many wonderful people to thank for getting this book to readers, and I sincerely apologize to anyone I've forgotten.

Thank you to my loving family, Big Tone, Gabe, and Karlina; one of the few bright sides of this pandemic has been getting to spend more time with you as we isolated at home.

Thank you to my hardworking editor, Alicia Condon, as well as everyone at Kensington Publishing: Alexandra Nicolajsen, Steven Zacharius, Adam Zacharius, Vida Engstrand, Jane Nutter, Lauren Jernigan, Elizabeth Trout, Samantha McVeigh, Lynn Cully, Kimberly Richardson, Arthur Maisel, Renee Rocco, Rebecca Cremonese, Christy Phillippe, and Alex Gendler.

Thank you to my wonderful agent, Caitlin Blasdell, and to Liza Dawson and the entire Liza Dawson Agency.

Thank you to Social Media Guru Jillian Stein for the absolutely fantastic work and for being such a great friend.

Thanks to my fantastic street team, Rebecca's Rebels, and to their creative and hardworking leader, Anissa Beatty.

Thank you to Kimberly Detillier Rogers from my Rebecca's Rebels Facebook Street team, who came up with the name for this book.

Thank you to Writerspace, Fresh Fiction, and Social Butterfly PR for all the hard work.

Thanks also to my constant support system: Gail and Jim English, Debbie and Travis Smith, Stephanie and Don West, Jessica and Jonah Namson, Kathy and Herb Zanetti, and Liz and Steve Berry.

Chapter One

The smell of the earth, deep and true, centered her as she traversed the hastily created tunnel. It probably said something about Karma that she preferred darkness, muddy walls, and being underground to any other circumstance. Battery-operated lanterns had been dropped haphazardly along the trail, their artificial light dancing across the packed dirt walls, highlighting minerals she couldn't name as she descended quickly, the swish of her skirt the only sound she made.

She bent her head, trying to stay in the moment and not panic at the job to come. One she was no more prepared for than she had been for mating a Kurjan general nearly two centuries ago. Or was it closer to three?

Taking a deep breath, she turned the corner and faced the cell. The cell that had been dug just the day before, in case it might be needed.

It was.

She swallowed.

The male was sprawled across the ground, so large he could probably spread his arms and reach the cement blocks on one side and the steel bars on the other. If he'd been conscious. Bruises mottled his face and neck, while a wound bled freely beneath his jaw. Blood ran past his ear to pool on the dirt beneath him.

She couldn't breathe.

It really was *him*. Despite the bruises, blood, and dirt covering his face, she recognized him from more than three years ago. He'd tried to pull her into a helicopter with him after he'd attacked the Kurjan stronghold where she lived. He was bad, he was the enemy, and yet…he'd saved several kidnapped human females from the Kurjans. The Kurjans were an immortal species more powerful than any other. It had been a miracle that the male before her had succeeded in taking those gifted human females away from the Kurjan nation. He'd almost taken her at the same time, but she'd fought him.

Had he thought he was saving her? Had he hurt those human females? Were they now in worse danger than they'd faced when captives of the Kurjan nation?

She waited patiently, as she'd been taught. The guard would get to her when he had time. The medical supplies in her pack became heavy, so she set them down, stepping closer to the bars to study the male.

Benjamin Horatio Lawrence Reese. He was a vampire-demon hybrid, large even for his kind. At about six foot seven, or maybe eight, he was as tall as many Kurjans. The wideness of his torso tapered down at his waist, matched by the length of his legs. His boots had to be a size eighteen, and his hands were big enough to cause colossal damage. Oh, she'd been hit before, but one punch from him and she'd be dead.

He could never learn how much she already knew about him. How she'd been preparing for this day for three years—since he'd tried to take her from another Kurjan holding. Her home. With the Kurjans, since she'd mated centuries ago and thus had become immortal, even though she'd started out as a human female.

A see-through figure hovered behind the male.

Karma sighed. "Loti? I thought you'd moved on." She'd helped the Kurjan spirit accept his fate after he'd been killed in a training accident, or so she had thought.

The kid, his hair black yet see-through, rolled his eyes like any teenager. "I'm going now. Just wanted to say goodbye." Then he stiffened. "The guards are coming. Good luck." He wisped out of sight, and hopefully out of this world to the next one.

The air changed, and Karma stiffened as the guard made his way down the tunnel, his white hair glowing as he came closer. He was a Cyst: one of the elite soldiers and spiritual leaders of the Kurjan nation. A single line of white hair bisected his pale scalp, leading down to a long braid. His eyes were a deep purple tinged with red, and he spared her not a glance as he unlocked the cell and then stepped back.

She took a deep breath and entered, wincing as the coppery smell of blood assaulted her nostrils. Then she dropped to her knees and reached inside the pack for the materials that would clot the bleeding wound. The hybrid must've been badly injured in the skirmish if he was still bleeding.

A ghost popped up in the other cell, and she ignored him. He was wavering in and out of her sight and would soon cross over; there wasn't time to help him.

The second she touched Benjamin's head, his eyes opened.

He was fully alert in a second, his deep eyes a strange metallic color. "Karma," he murmured.

She drew back. He remembered her name? Nobody remembered her name.

"Do you need blood?" she whispered, leaning closer, even as the guard locked the cell door and disappeared down the hallway, leaving her alone with the enemy. Right now she was useless to the Kurjans, so if the prisoner killed her, they'd find a plan B.

"No." Benjamin sat up, looked around, and put his back to the cement brick wall. His impressive body seemed to take up all the space in the cell.

She shook her head, her lips trembling. "You must be badly injured, or you would not have been captured. You need blood."

It would hurt if he bit her, and he'd have to be quick to avoid touching her skin for long.

"I let them take me. I've been searching for you for three years."

God. The Kurjans had been correct. He really had been looking for her. He'd been caught twice and both times had asked about her, so it wasn't like he was keeping it a secret. "The baby? Rose?" Karma held her breath. When Benjamin's people had attacked the Kurjan holding, she'd gone with her instincts and forced him to take a toddler who had been kidnapped by the Kurjans—and she'd paid for that decision. "Is Rose well?"

Benjamin nodded. "Rose is fine. She's at Realm Headquarters with a nice family."

Relief and fear made an odd combination in Karma's body. "Realm Headquarters?" The Realm was the enemy of the Kurjans. Its people were evil, or so she'd been taught. She'd always wondered, because lies were everywhere. She held out bandages and antibiotics, although the wound beneath his jaw was already closing as he sent healing cells where they were necessary.

"I don't need those," he murmured, studying her with an intensity that shot tremors through her abdomen.

"I don't understand why you would come looking for me," she said, sitting back and keeping her knees covered with her dress. The Kurjan leaders had noted that this male kept showing up in different attacks, and he took ridiculous risks for a soldier with his experience. They'd been sure he was coming, based their plan on that knowledge, but she hadn't believed it. Why would this male put himself in danger for her? "You let them take you hostage?"

"Yes." Benjamin's voice was low and rough, hinting at demon ancestry.

She rested her hands on the thin material over her knees. "I don't understand."

A bone snapped loudly into place somewhere in his body, but he didn't even flinch. "Let's start here. I'm Benny Reese." He held out a hand the size of a frying pan, as if they were meeting at a village game instead of in a cell.

She hesitated and then slid her palm against his. "Karma."

His hold and shake were gentle, and he released her before the mating allergy could hurt either of them. She'd been mated centuries ago to a Kurjan, and no other male could touch her for long without both of them developing terrible rashes.

"What's your last name?" he asked. Another bone popped into place.

She jerked at the sound. "I do not have a last name."

"Oh." He looked beyond her at the steel bars securing the cell. "I was out for a while. Where are we?"

"In a temporary holding area where you will be kept until you are transported to a more secure location." She coughed. "For questioning."

His smile nearly knocked her over. Even the slight tipping of his lips turned his rugged face from dangerously hard to nearly boyish with charm. Amusement glimmered in his eyes for a moment. "Darlin', I've been tortured before. You don't need to trouble yourself about that."

She had bigger things to worry about than the life of this massive hybrid. She allowed herself one moment to stare into his unusual eyes. Oh, many immortals had metallic-silver eyes, gold eyes, even copper or purple. But his were a combination of all argent colors, mingling into a hard-edged glint, even with the humor lurking there. In another time, she might've thought him beautiful. She'd learned long ago that beauty could mask the darkest of evils.

Vampires were bad, demons were bad, and this male was a hybrid of both. When he decided to kill her—and he would at some point—she wouldn't stand much chance of surviving. Yet she still couldn't comprehend why he'd come for her. "Why are you here?"

"For you. To rescue you because I couldn't last time." He stretched out his arms and healed a broken finger in his left hand.

His words didn't make any sense. "Why?" Surely his ego wasn't such that he'd risked his life just because she'd rejected his help last time. She wasn't worth that.

He sighed. "I'd hoped to ease you into the truth, but here it is." He held up his right hand, showing a demon marking with a jagged *R* in the center. The *R* was a crest representing his surname: Reese. Demons mated with a branding and a bite—the marking was transferred from the demon to the mate during sex.

Her mouth dropped open, and she hurried to shut it. "You're mated?" Why did that thought nauseate her? How odd.

"No. The brand appeared when I touched you three years ago." His chin lowered, and he studied her, towering over her even as he sat. "When you shoved me away and refused to get into that helicopter with me." He didn't sound happy.

She snorted and then quickly recovered. "Impossible. I'm already mated." Well, she had been mated a couple of centuries ago, although her Kurjan mate had died shortly thereafter. Sometimes she forgot what he had looked like, and that was fine with her. "Your brand must have appeared for someone else."

"No." Benjamin looked down at the dark marking. "The mark hasn't faded a bit, and it's pulsing like a live wire now that you're near."

Oh, Lord. Her research on Benjamin suggested he might be insane. Dangerous and unstable? There was no way she could succeed in this mission. "Benjamin—"

"Benny. Might as well get cozy with me now." His smile held charm and determination that warmed her in an unexpected way.

For the second time in her life, she let her instincts take over. "Just leave. Take an opening and find freedom," she whispered tersely, her stomach cramping. "Forget about me."

"Not a chance." His gaze ran over her face like a physical touch.

Movement sounded down the tunnel, and she stiffened.

Benjamin tensed and set his jaw. "Get ready, darlin'. We're about to escape this place."

Chapter Two

Benny fought to send healing cells to the base of his skull while his body rioted at finally being this close to her. *Karma.* The name fit her. Her energy was soft and hesitant with a thread of diamonds through it—the world's strongest and most sparkly stone. Yeah, her strength was banked, and he had to wonder if she even knew it was there.

Her scent was sweetly natural. Like wildflowers lining an untouched river.

She scrambled away from him and stood as heavy footsteps sounded on the dirt floor of the makeshift tunnel.

He didn't much care who was coming—her draw was that strong. She looked as if she was in her twenties with smooth skin and long blond hair in a tight bun, but her deep topaz eyes showed a couple centuries of living. In fact, she looked just right in the long skirt and ruffled blouse that covered her from neck to wrists.

Like a lady out of the eighteen hundreds.

He wasn't sure how to act around a real lady. Not that his brothers' mates weren't ladies, but they were all from modern times. Not this female. Her eyes darted around, landing anywhere but on him.

Heat washed through the cell bars as two males approached on the other side.

The female pivoted and put her back to the wall, watching them. She held still, trying to make herself unobtrusive, looking as if she wanted to flee or vanish into the darkest corner. He continued to watch her, clocking the soldiers with his peripheral vision.

"Benjamin Reese," the Kurjan on the other side of the bar drawled, his voice low and rough.

Benny cocked his head and watched Karma. "I appreciate the help. I'm feeling much better now."

She jolted, and her gaze slashed up to him, her eyes widening.

He tried for his most charming grin, but with his size and current bruises, he probably looked anything but reassuring. "Honest. You're a great healer, and you did a good job. I'm so much better."

Confusion drifted across her face, and he noted several adorable freckles scattered on her nose. Her mouth lightly, barely, gaped open, and she looked toward the two males outside the cell and then back to him. Man, her bewilderment was cute…and sexy. Her tongue flicked out nervously to lick her bottom lip.

He groaned.

Concern appeared in her eyes, and she studied the wound on his neck, but she didn't speak. One of the soldiers smacked the bars, and she jumped.

Irritation clawed through him, and Benny turned just his head to view the two outside the cell. The first was a Kurjan, his white skin nearly glowing in the darkness of the tunnel, a stark contrast to his black hair tipped with red. His purple eyes looked intelligent, and he wore the standard black uniform of a Kurjan soldier, but he had several silver medals pinned to his wide chest. The guy was maybe six seven or eight. The male next to him was a Cyst, one of the Kurjans' elite soldiers and religious leaders. He was even taller and broader than the Kurjan and had one strip of white hair braided in the middle of his otherwise bald skull. He was pale as well, and his eyes were a purplish red. Many silver medals lined his chest.

So they'd sent the top dogs to deal with him. Well, a guy could get an ego from that. "Do you mind?" Benny growled, turning back to study Karma. His voice softened. "Sweetheart? Do you often help heal people?"

Her chin dropped, and she gave up any pretense of not being shocked. She faltered, and then her shoulders went back. "Benjamin Reese, this is Terre, one of our Kurjan leaders, and Jaydon, commander of the Cyst soldiers." The female sounded as if she were introducing guests at a formal gathering.

He grinned and waved a hand in the air. "Right. So, where were you born? Where did you grow up?" He had so many questions for her, and he'd spent three years wondering.

She shook her head, her jaw slack. "Mr. Reese? The soldiers are here to see you."

He lifted one shoulder and hid a wince at the pain that went through his chest. The beating had been a good one. "I'm not interested in them. I'd rather hear about you."

"How hard did you hit your head?" she whispered, taking one step toward him.

Good. He had a feeling she rarely approached anybody, and that was significant. Just what had she endured living with the Kurjans for centuries? They weren't known to treat females very well, and she definitely had a faded mating mark on her neck. But he had a theory about that, which might explain why *his* mark had appeared on his hand when he'd first touched her. It was unheard of, but still, it was there. "When did your mate die?"

She blinked. Once and then again. "Two centuries ago."

The triumph that filled him must've shown in his eyes, because she took a step back. Darn it. Though he could tell she hadn't been treated well based on her behavior in the presence of the soldiers, at least she'd been spared any sort of sexual abuse. A mated female couldn't be touched by another male, even if her mate was dead. He cleared his throat. "Is there anybody here you want me to kill before we go?" He'd gladly do it.

She just stared at him as if he'd frozen her in place.

He tried to smile to reassure her, and she turned even paler. "Has anybody harmed you, sweetheart? I'll take care of them before we blow this place." It was more than possible she'd been slapped around, and he'd gladly rip off the arms of anybody who'd hurt her.

"You're crazy," she whispered.

He nodded. "That has been said more than once, and often by my family." Probably because he said what he thought all the time, but tomato, tomahto.

"Damn it." The Kurjan soldier drew a firearm from his shoulder harness and pointed it at Benny.

Benny immediately put himself between the weapon and the female. "If you'd wanted my attention, you should've just said so."

The soldier fired.

* * * *

Karma's nerves were strung so tight she could barely breathe. It had been hours since she'd seen the prisoner, and she couldn't get his smile out of her mind. Even after Terre had shot him in the neck, he'd smiled at her as she'd exited his cell. What was wrong with her? The male was their enemy as well as being a vampire-demon hybrid. They were notoriously deadly and evil. She was not up to the job with which she'd been tasked.

Not that she had a choice. She'd never had one.

She deftly served supper to the five males in the dining room of the temporary headquarters, careful not to brush Dayne's arm as she did so. A tablet sat in his large hands, and he read through reports, ignoring everyone. He was the head of the Kurjan nation, and he was also Terre's older brother. Terre sat at the other end of the table, watching her as he always did. The look in his eyes sent chills through her, but she kept her face placid, sliding a plate in front of Drake, Dayne's son.

Drake didn't look up from the game he was furiously playing on a small console. His hair had grown long, and with his odd green eyes, the child looked almost human. "Thank you, Karma," he murmured, twisting his arm to press a button.

She paused. "You're welcome." The young teenager had always thanked her, almost automatically. It was silly to think his mother had had time to teach him manners before she'd died, but he had them nonetheless. Even now, at around sixteen years old, built strong and tall, he was absentmindedly polite.

Where had he come from?

She set the second plate in front of Drake's cousin Vero, who was a year younger than Drake.

"Thank you, Karma," Vero said, looking at her and smiling. His father had been killed, and his uncles had taken him in, although it appeared that Terre was acting as his guardian. Vero was a sweet lamb in a flock of lions.

She hustled to place a plate in front of Jaydon, the scary Cyst who had started taking his meals with the family. He was wiping off his bruised and cut knuckles, and he hadn't bothered to clean away the blood that saturated one sleeve.

Her stomach lurched. Jaydon and Terre had injured their hands by torturing Benjamin, no doubt. Was the hybrid even still alive?

She took the last plate off the tray and quickly tried to place it in front of Terre. He grabbed her skirt before she could draw away and jerked her to a stop. His knuckles were bloody and damaged. She sucked in a breath and settled herself.

"How was your day?" he asked.

"Fine." She knew better than to draw away. Once she'd attempted to evade him, and he'd held on to the material so tightly, her skirt ripped. He couldn't touch her skin or the mating allergy would attack them both, but he had found ways to torture her just by taking hold of her clothing.

He smiled, showing sharp canines. Oh, Terre was probably handsome to some, but she saw the darkness in his purple eyes. "What did you think of the prisoner?"

"I didn't think anything about him." She kept her eyes averted.

"I almost killed him this afternoon, but he'll survive," Terre bragged. "He does have a purpose, doesn't he?"

She nodded, wanting to edge away.

He forced her closer, wrapping his fist in the fabric, his hand right above her mound but not touching. "Our day is coming, female. You know not to disappoint me, right?"

The steak knife was so close. How shocked he'd be if she grabbed it and stabbed him through the eye. He'd kill her, but it'd be worth it. Except for the girls she'd leave behind. If nothing else, she had to save them before she left this world. The idea of being mated to Terre was too much to bear, and she had had enough of living in hell. "I'm not strong enough to take the virus that will undo my mating," she whispered.

He released her. "You don't have a choice. Be strong enough, or I'll break those girls of yours for amusement." He turned to his steak, obviously finished with her for now.

She turned and hurried out of the room and into the small kitchen, struggling to keep her calm facade in place. Her heart thundered and her ears rang, and trembling shot down her arms. The cook, busy stirring something in a pot, didn't look over his shoulder at her.

"Mama," Belle said happily from a blanket in the corner, where she and her stuffed animals were having tea with her twin sister.

Karma forced a smile and moved toward the three-year-old girls, her heart bursting. They were adorable children with light brown eyes, flowing black hair, and cute button noses. There was no doubt they were enhanced humans, although Karma couldn't pinpoint their enhancements. She had a feeling Belle might be psychic and Boone empathic, but she could be dead wrong about that. They'd been hers since they'd been kidnapped two years ago. A weapon to use against her. "Hi, girls. Are you being good?"

Boone, her hair in a braid, nodded seriously. "Of course. It's teatime." She craned her neck to look beyond Karma. "Is Other Mama here?"

Karma's stomach dropped. "No, baby. Your other mama isn't here right now." She pressed a finger to her lips.

Boone's eyes widened. "Sorry," she whispered. "Forgot the secret."

"It's okay." Karma tucked her skirts and perched on her knees by the teacups. "Your mama is in heaven, and sometimes she checks in with you, but she needs to be an angel now." Karma's human enhancement had been channeling, and she tried to use the gift to help the women and children in the camps.

When the Kurjans had kidnapped the twins in their search for enhanced females, they'd killed the girls' parents. The girls hadn't seen any violence, but they knew their parents were in heaven, and Karma had been helping to keep their memories alive as best she could. The twins didn't remember their life before, and perhaps that was good. Their mother, a pretty woman named Linda, had checked in several times, whether Karma had been open to her or not.

She had to get those girls free somehow. Their best chance here would be mating one of the Kurjans when they were of age, but that was no way for these bright lights to live. Their worst chance was one Karma couldn't think about—and didn't understand: Jaydon had a plan for a ritual that would kill them, and she had to stop him.

Cele stepped inside the kitchen, her chin up and her gaze regal. She'd been mated to a Cyst general for nearly a century, and she enjoyed her status. The female appeared to be in her early thirties with red hair and brown eyes. "Girls? Let's go."

Karma stood. "They can stay here—"

"No. Now." Cele gave a haughty smile. "We have to pack. It's time to move."

Then she really had no choice. Karma helped the girls pick up the tea set, determination settling hard on her shoulders. To prevent their deaths, she'd do anything. Even align herself with her enemy, Benjamin Reese.

It was almost time.

Chapter Three

Getting stabbed in the ear was so annoying. Benny sent healing cells to his inner ear, wincing as the ruptured tissue stitched itself back together. He'd gotten some information from the Kurjan during the torture session but not nearly enough. Terre had been very graphic about what he planned to do with the female, and Benny had tuned him out at that point. Then his eardrum had been pierced, and going temporarily deaf had helped.

Darkness had fallen, and above him, he could now hear movement. Maybe even a helicopter outside. Were they leaving? He couldn't let that happen until he had Karma in his hands.

The door at the end of the tunnel opened, and he stiffened, feeling her energy. There she was. Light exploded inside him, and he relaxed into it. How the female gave him a sense of peace, even from down the corridor, was a mystery he'd explore later.

A Cyst soldier accompanied her and opened the cell door, locking her inside with him again. Thus far, she seemed to be irrelevant to the Kurjans.

How little they knew. He wiped blood off his face and smoothed back his thick hair, trying to look presentable. "How are you?"

She looked at him as if he'd lost his mind. Yeah, he'd seen that look before…often. "How can you be standing?"

He popped his cheekbone back into place and went to work on his ribs. "I already healed my legs." Then he glanced down at the tray in her hands. "What did you bring?"

She removed a cloth napkin to show a steak on a plate. "I brought you something to eat."

"Protein will help. Thank you." He took the meat with his still-working hand and munched happily, letting the food energize him much faster than it would a normal immortal. Being a hybrid gave him extra skills.

She set the tray down and took the pack off her shoulder. "I have medical supplies."

He shook his head, finishing the meal. "I don't need anything." His other hand began to mend. Blood would help him more than anything, but he couldn't take hers yet. Not while she still held another male's mating mark. "I appreciate your help."

She kept her gaze averted. "Very well." Then she backed up until her rear hit the bars. She glanced over her shoulder and down the hallway before turning back to face him. She'd gone pale, and her hand trembled. "They're going to move you in about ten minutes, and I don't know where they plan to take you."

His clavicle popped loudly back into place. Man, she was pretty. Small and light in a big, dark world. "I thought I heard helicopters."

She swallowed, and her chin firmed. "Half of the camp has already flown away." While her tone remained neutral and her expression blank, he sensed an underlying thread of anger.

He stretched his hands out, making sure his fingers had healed from the many breaks Terre had inflicted with a hammer. "You're unhappy that they left without you?" When she didn't answer, he searched for another reason. "You're angry they took, well, friends of yours?" It made sense that she had friends in the Kurjan nation, since she'd been with them for so long.

She grew still. "Angry? I don't get angry."

Yet he felt that anger. "I'm empathic. Well, somewhat. Usually I don't take notice of people, to be honest. But you? I want to know you, and I'm tuned in." He cocked his head, studying her suddenly defensive posture. Just what was he dealing with here? He was a bull in a china shop usually. Today, he had to learn gentle. "There's nothing wrong with getting angry."

Her already straight spine straightened even more. "I am not angry."

Well then. "All right." Another helicopter took off. That had to be at least half of the camp. "How many soldiers are still here?" he asked.

"Plenty," she returned.

He studied her. "I'm going to make an escape. You're coming with me."

Hope flared and then quickly died in her eyes. "I'm sorry. I can't."

Why? What was keeping her here? He didn't have time to ask because three Cyst soldiers strode down the hallway. Two kept weapons pointed at him, while the third opened the door and gestured Karma out. The female left the tray but grasped her pack and walked out into the tunnel, casting a quick look over her shoulder as if to say goodbye.

Not likely.

The largest Cyst, the one at the door, motioned him forward. "Let's go, Hybrid. It's time to see your new home."

The soldier on the left snorted. "This is a palace compared to where you're going, Reese."

"Looking forward to it." Benny strode into the tunnel, his limbs loose and healed. The soldiers backed away, and he appreciated that fact, but his main focus was the female. She strode ahead toward roughly cut stairs. He didn't have much time.

The soldier behind him prodded him in the back with his weapon. In one smooth motion, Benny turned, grabbed it, and shot the other guy in the head. He went down instantly. The largest bastard manacled his arms around Benny from behind, partially lifting him off the ground.

Benny went with it, kicking up hard and beneath the chin of the other soldier, who got a shot off before dropping to a knee.

Pain pierced Benny's jaw, and his blood burst red across the cell bars. He kicked down, knocking the gun into the cell. Then he let his weight fall, grabbed the braid of the Cyst holding him, and threw the muscled jerk over his shoulder to land on top of the soldier on his knees.

They both crashed to the ground.

Benny ducked inside the cell, grabbed the gun, and turned to fire into the faces of both soldiers. The green lasers shot out of the gun and turned to metal upon impacting with flesh. Both males dropped unconscious for now. The bullets wouldn't keep them down for long.

He tucked the gun in his bloody jeans and turned down the corridor.

Karma stood at the bottom of the steps, her eyes wide with shock. Then she turned to run.

He was on her before she cleared the second step.

* * * *

Hard arms grabbed her from behind, and Karma struggled, fighting with all she had. Her head thunked against the stone wall before he could prevent her movement, and lightning flashed behind her eyes. The violence had been so easy for Benny. He'd taken down three soldiers, *Cyst soldiers*, without much effort. In fact, he'd appeared more methodical than emotional. How was that even possible?

She went with instinct, fighting him, trying not to throw up. Dizziness swamped her, and she couldn't think. He'd shot those Cysts so casually—one even in the eye. Yes, they'd live, but it took forever to regrow an eye.

He caught her up, his hands firm with only her clothing protecting her skin, and ran up the stairs as if he hadn't been injured and she didn't weigh a thing. Blood flowed down his neck, and she looked up to see part of his jaw and teeth visible with the skin and muscle torn away from his lower face.

Her stomach lurched. She hunched into herself as he cradled her against his hard-as-rock chest. This was a mistake. This was insane. "Put me down," she whispered, trying to curl into a ball.

"No." He cleared the stairs and turned the corner.

Panic caught her, and she wriggled in his arms, punching him as hard as she could in the chest. Then she struggled, unable to think, only needing to run. To get away. Her mind went numb, and her body fought on its own.

He shot three guards in succession, running past them and outside into the chilly autumn night. Then he fired up into the air, and the green lasers arced gracefully toward the stars.

Confusion muddled her pounding head. Had she given herself a concussion? The dark world swirled around her, and she had to close her eyes to try to balance herself. Why had Benny shot toward the sky? None of this was making sense.

Her head hurt. Badly. Even so, she opened her eyes, seeking escape.

The night lit up in every direction as explosions blew all around them. Heat blasted into her, and she screamed.

Benny held her tighter and started running full-bore toward the nearby forest. "Hold on, sweetheart. You're almost safe."

Safe? She couldn't think. "No," she whispered, the dizziness taking away her breath and forcing her to close her eyes. Or maybe it was the speed with which he ran. The wind buzzed across her skin.

Bullets hit the ground around them, spitting up dirt.

She opened her eyes again, seeing several helicopters to the left with Cyst and Kurjan soldiers firing from the sides. "We will not survive this." Then she noted the soldiers ducking as green laser shots burst out from the trees, several striking the nearest helicopter.

He dodged between two trees, his big body bending over her, protecting her, as bullets hit his back and his neck. He growled low but didn't slow his pace.

Then two soldiers appeared behind him to cover his retreat, returning more fire toward the Kurjans. "We have to go faster. Shut your eyes," he ordered, ducking his head and plowing through the forest so quickly the trees became a blur. The smell of blood competed with the strong scents of pine and dirt.

She had no choice but to obey, holding herself stiff, silently saying a prayer taught to her by her mother many, many years ago. One she'd all but forgotten until right now. Going with the enemy was a mistake, but once again, she was helpless. The twins had been taken away in one of the earlier helicopters, and she couldn't get to them. She couldn't save them.

Terror and pain welled up inside her, and she banished all emotion, attempting to go numb. Once again. At the same time, she tried to heal her head, letting the pain ease away.

The wind chilled her, while the immortal heated her, the contrast adding more confusion. He ran as silently as any predator, his movements economical, and energetic tingles popped in the air around them as he healed his wounds.

They ran for longer than she could count, and she drifted off, trying not to think of the girls.

"Start her up," Benny bellowed out of the blue.

She twisted in his arms and turned her head to see a dark, sleek craft in a small clearing. A large male with piercing pewter-gray eyes jumped in front of what turned out to be a helicopter. The low hum of its engines immediately vibrated through the air.

Benny leaped into the open door at the rear of the craft, and two males followed suit, the last one shutting the door.

Then they were rising into the sky, where the copter was soon blanketed by thick clouds.

Benny gently set her on the seat next to him, facing the other two across an aisle. "Are you all right?" he asked, bending toward her and studying her neck.

The interior light flipped on.

She blinked, wincing as her eyes and then her head protested. "I am fine."

He looked closer. "No mating allergy? Did you heal your temple?" He'd noticed she had bumped her head?

She tried to make herself as small as possible. "My head is healed, and I am not feeling the effects of any mating allergy." The two soldiers across from them watched her. They both had dark hair that reached their shoulders, incredible aqua-colored eyes, and muscled bodies.

Benny sat back, giving her space. "Karma, please meet Ronan Kayrs and Quade Kayrs." He pointed at the pilot. "That's Garrett Kayrs—their great-great-nephew—or something like that. The Kayrs family reproduces like jackalopes, and it's tough to keep their lineage straight."

Garrett looked over his shoulder, his eyes mesmerizing. "There's no such thing as jackalopes, and you know it."

"I've seen one," Benny countered instantly, resting his head back and shutting his eyes. More healing tingles emerged from him.

Garrett snorted and turned back to flying the craft.

Karma tried to take a deep breath, but her lungs refused to cooperate. Garrett Kayrs was the King of the Realm's nephew, and the other two males were probably more than a thousand years old. All of the males in the helicopter were members of the Seven, whose goal was to kill every enhanced woman and then destroy Ulric.

"Do you know who we are?" Ronan asked, his eyes looking more green than blue.

"Yes. I've heard stories about the Seven and you." She wasn't a good liar, so why bother? "Are you going to kill me?"

Benny opened his eyes and turned his head to face her. "Kill you? We just saved you."

Saved her for what? She didn't want to know, but she had to ask. "What now?"

"Now we see the queen," Benny said. "You'll like her."

The small interior swam around Karma, and she tried not to cry. The Queen of the Realm? She was the most frightening female alive on the planet. They were going to let the queen kill her.

She wasn't ready to die.

Chapter Four

Rain beat down on them as Garrett landed the craft like a pro, and Benny opened the door and kicked out the steps, wishing he'd brought an umbrella. The weather at Realm Headquarters in northern Idaho was unpredictable in the fall, and rain seemed to be a constant. He jumped out and noted the SUV waiting by the landing strip with armed Realm soldiers at the ready. "I don't think your uncle is happy to see us."

Garrett, leaving the craft running, leaped out of the pilot's seat. "Sure, he is."

Right. Benny motioned Karma out, wanting to give her space. The woman had gone starkly pale, and she seemed to need distance. "Come on out, Karma. You'll like the queen."

If anything, Karma turned even paler. Yet she took the two steps down, looking as regal as any member of royalty. Her hair was still in that tight bun, and Benny itched to release it. The one time he'd met her before, she'd had her hair loose, and it had been a stunning mass of curls. Of course, they'd both been pretending to be somebody else at the time. Who knew the mating mark would appear on his hand after touching her?

She stood in the rain and lifted her face, letting the water sluice over her smooth skin. The lights from the nearest hangar highlighted her classic bone structure and hourglass figure.

He'd always liked a woman with decent hips and ass. She was short for him at maybe only five nine, but she had those curves. Delectable ones. "This way." He turned toward the running SUV, his gaze focused on the nearest soldier. When they reached the overhang of the hangar, he relaxed as he made sure Karma stayed dry. "Hi, Max."

Max Petrovsky was one of the king's guard dogs, and Benny had always kind of liked him. Most immortals had a secondary eye color that emerged during dangerous or emotional moments, and Max's were a very cool pink. "Hi." He looked them over, gave Garrett a nod, and then set his feet. "You all need to be searched for weapons before I take you to the lodge."

Garrett strode forward and clapped Max on the shoulder. "We're armed, Uncle Max. No worries."

Max's nostrils flared, and he kept his gaze on Benny. "Benjamin?"

Figures Max would be okay with Garrett having weapons. "Just the usual. Gun at waist, in left boot, and thigh holster. Knives in all sorts of interesting places, and if you try to body cavity–search me, I might have to kill you."

Max rolled his eyes. "I'd rather shoot myself, Reese." His gaze gentled as he turned his attention to Karma. "How about you, miss?"

She slowly shook her head, standing in that completely still way she had. At least the eaves protected her from the weather.

The helicopter lifted into the air, and the ancient Kayrs brothers took off.

Max watched them go. "Good move. I don't think Dage is all that happy with his great-uncles, considering you all won't come clean about the Seven."

Benny shrugged. It was frankly a miracle that the king hadn't kidnapped Garrett and held him until he gave up the information, but Garrett was solid. He'd never tell. "Blood oaths and all of that. It's raining. Let's get going." The Seven had taken a vow of secrecy, and the King and his Realm knew too much as it was.

Max frowned. "I'm sorry, but your friend is going to meet with the queen. I have to check her for weapons."

The monster deep down inside Benny stretched lazily awake. "Oh, I don't think so. You touch her, and we really will have a problem." His blood started to hum with power.

Karma edged slightly closer to him as if unconsciously seeking protection. He stood straighter, willing and able to provide that for her. "You're okay, darlin'. Nobody is gonna touch you—I promise."

"Except the queen," she whispered, her voice shaking.

Garrett sighed. "Yeah, that's true. Maybe she'll chase Benny with the syringe first. That's always fun to watch." It was the first joke the kid had made in way too long.

Benny grimaced. Ever since the marking had appeared on his hand, for a Kurjan Soti no less, the queen had been relentless in her zeal to test his blood. He'd let her fill vials a couple of times, and now that he had Karma near, the queen would no doubt come at him again. "Just wait, Kayrs. She'll want your blood soon enough. You are a member of the Seven now, you know." While the queen didn't know the full truth about the Seven, she knew they existed, and she wanted to do all kinds of tests on them.

Garrett growled. "I'm not having blood taken until I get sleep and a decent breakfast."

Karma swallowed. "When it's over, I'd like to be laid to rest near a river, if that's okay." She clasped her hands together. "Unless I'm incinerated. Then maybe the ashes scattered by a river?"

Max's gaze went flat, and he froze in place. "What the hell?"

Garrett frowned and moved closer to Benny. "What exactly did you tell her?"

"Nothing," Benny said, eyeing the pale blonde. *His* pale blonde. "Honey, what are you talking about?"

She lifted her chin and strode toward the SUV, her skirt swishing around her ankles. "You don't need to lie to me, Benjamin. I'm ready to meet the queen." She paused, looking over her shoulder at Max, still safe beneath the eaves. "I do not have any weapons, but it's permissible for you to search me."

Max pivoted, and Benny stopped him with a hand on his arm. "You're not touching her." All the same, he did understand the need to protect the queen. Karma had lived with their enemy for a couple of centuries. "I'll search her. You can watch."

He moved toward the woman. "Put your arms straight out."

When she did so, facing away from him, he carefully patted her down, making sure not to touch her skin. The allergic reaction could still take place with the material between them, but if he went fast, it'd be okay. Every touch to her curves was torture, and he tried to hide his arousal. "Karma? You're not going to die tonight."

She didn't answer him. The woman didn't make a lick of sense. He'd have to sort her out after they got to the lodge.

He was quick, but by the time he'd patted down her ass, he was on fire. His blood burst through his veins, heating him even more, and his entire body had gone rock hard.

After the mating mark had appeared three years ago, he knew he had to rescue her. But that was it. He'd never contemplated taking a mate—and it appeared she was in agreement. He should be pleased.

The beast deep down inside him howled.

* * * *

Realm Headquarters was a surprise. The main building looked like a ski lodge, or what Karma figured a ski lodge would look like. She'd been escorted past a wide gathering room and down a lovely hallway to what appeared to be a comfortable waiting area, complete with a silent television on the wall. She sat in a thick, plush chair, her hands clasped loosely on her lap.

Benjamin sat next to her, shifting his bulk as if he couldn't get comfortable. "Why do you think you're going to die?" he asked.

She eyed the wide double wooden doors across the sparkling floor. Why was Benjamin acting dumb? "I know about the queen and her experiments," she said calmly. The Queen of the Realm was well known for torturing subjects in the name of science. The Kurjans had been graphic when depicting the atrocities the queen had performed on enhanced females as well as immortals in her quest for knowledge.

Queen Kayrs was a monster.

Benjamin groaned. "Well, she is a little obsessed, I admit. But if you just give her what she wants, she usually leaves you alone for a little while."

What if what she wanted was to hear Karma scream? To see how high her pain tolerance really was—an experiment Karma understood was one of the queen's favorite pastimes. "I am weak when it comes to pain," Karma admitted. "Before this happens, could you reassure me that Rose is safe?" Karma would always wonder if she'd made a mistake, helping Benjamin rescue the toddler from the Kurjans three years ago.

"Of course she's safe," Benjamin said.

To get through the next few minutes, Karma had to trust that he was telling the truth. "I would have liked to have seen her again."

Before Benjamin could answer, the doors opened, and a petite female rushed out. She wore ripped jeans, tennis shoes, and a T-shirt with what looked like a cartoon dog on it. A white lab coat hung on her slender frame, unfastened. Oh. It figured a lab assistant would prepare Karma for the experiments. It was late, probably after midnight. Perhaps she'd be left alone until the queen arose. No doubt the woman slept late.

Benjamin stood.

The lab tech went to him for a quick hug before stepping back. "Benny. It's so good to see you." The female's thick black hair was in a smooth ponytail, and her blue eyes sparkled happily. She truly was stunning.

The oddest and most out-of-place sense of jealousy attacked Karma.

Benny patted the woman's back. "You, too. Emma? This is Karma." He gestured to Karma.

Karma stood. "Hello." This Emma felt like a good person, although she was much too familiar with Benjamin. Maybe she'd help Karma end all of this quickly. To think the Kurjans wanted her mate bond destroyed by the virus the Queen of the Realm had discovered. Karma wouldn't survive that long.

Emma held out a hand, her eyes focused and intelligent. Seeking. "Karma. It's lovely to meet you."

Karma hesitated and then accepted the handshake. She'd forgotten other species shook hands as a greeting. When the tech released her, she stepped back, her knees against the chair.

Emma's eyebrow rose. "Honey, if you don't want to do this tonight, we can meet up in the morning. Maybe after you've slept?"

A side door opened, and a male stepped out of what appeared to be a conference room. Unrelenting power emanated from him. "That's fine, but I want her scanned first. Weapons, tracking devices, anything else." He had black hair, burnished silver eyes, and a body made for war.

Karma's knees weakened. On all that was holy. It was the King of the Realm. She'd seen pictures of him at Kurjan headquarters through the years. Was she supposed to curtsy? If she did, she'd fall on her face. Besides, her legs were frozen.

His expression softened. "Karma, I'm Dage. I apologize for all that you're about to go through." Amusement and resignation glimmered in his otherworldly eyes.

Karma couldn't speak. How could they joke about the atrocities that were going to be inflicted upon her? She wanted to rail at him, to yell and maybe attack. But why invite more pain? Oh, she'd been in the presence of power before, but the Kurjan generals paled compared to this leader. Primitive power cascaded around him, dancing through the room, no doubt coming directly *from* him.

Benjamin nudged her. "Go with Emma and get things started. We need sleep."

Dage lifted one very dark eyebrow. "That's fine, but I'd appreciate it if you came with me, Benny. Garrett is already in my den, and we need to have a discussion. If nothing else, I'd like to know why he looks like he hasn't slept in months."

Karma fought to keep her face calm. If Benjamin deserted her, she would be truly alone. Where could she run?

Benjamin rolled his eyes. "Fine. Let's get this over with, but I'm not telling you a thing about the Seven." He patted her arm. "I'll be back as soon as I can."

Confusion blanketed her. Why was he planning to return to her? Were the experiments on her to last several days? Maybe to see how fast she could heal herself? That made a sick kind of sense. She didn't look at him. Instead, she straightened her posture and followed Emma through the doors, hoping to find an escape route.

Though she didn't know how to fight, she could run. Somehow.

Her hopes were crushed when she walked inside a serene room that included a luxurious examination table, machinery on every granite counter, and what looked like a circular glass shower in the corner. Two guards stood at attention at the far door, both armed and huge.

There would be no escape.

Emma walked over to the shower. "This is what we call Grumpy Gus. It's a brand-new design, and the sensors have the ability to detect tracing powder, explosives, tracking devices, and any other threat to the area. If anything is detected, don't panic. It wouldn't be unheard of for the Kurjans to have placed a tracker inside you or to dust you with the tracking powder."

Karma faltered. "Grumpy Gus?"

Emma sighed. "Yeah. No matter how often I tinker with it, Gus still makes the weirdest clunking noise while working. This won't hurt. Just hop inside."

Karma looked at the guards, who were staring straight ahead, not at her. Taking a deep breath, she strode up the rubber incline and inside the glass cylinder. Her stomach lurched.

"All right. Just hold still for a sec." Emma took a tablet off the counter and tapped on it.

The glass circled around Karma, enclosing her, and then reopening. It all happened so quickly she didn't have time to panic, and the clunking noise wasn't so bad.

Emma smiled. "Hey, we didn't find a thing. The Kurjans must've had no clue Benny was coming for you."

Not true. Not even remotely true.

Karma strode back into the room, her head reeling. So the Realm hadn't been able to find it. Interesting. She tried to keep her posture upright. "When do I see the queen?"

The two soldiers looked her way and then went back to attention.

Emma laughed, the sound tinkling. "Karma, I'm sorry. I should've been more clear, I guess. I am the queen."

Chapter Five

Benny tipped back the very excellent Scotch he'd talked the king into handing over before agreeing to talk. "I do like the good stuff."

"I'm aware," the king said dryly, also pouring a drink from across the table. He looked at his brother. "Would you stop frowning?"

Talen kicked back and crossed his muscled arms. "This is my default setting."

His son snorted from next to Benny. "Oh, that's for sure." Garrett swirled the liquid around in his own glass.

Benny rolled his neck, double-checking that the bullet holes in his nape had healed. Though his torso had been made into a solid shield during the ritual that had made him a member of the Seven, his neck had not. He'd been shot way too much lately. He wanted to concentrate, but his attention kept wandering back to Karma. Should he have stayed with her? Emma was a sweetheart, and he'd figured the two of them would get along and maybe Karma would relax. "The queen knows to go easy tonight, right?"

Dage looked at his wristwatch. "Yes. I gave her an hour for preliminary work and then told her it was time to sleep. The woman would completely forget about the world and get lost in her research if she could. Even forgets to eat."

Garrett leaned forward. "Yeah, but she told me she's close to a cure for human cancer. That's impressive, Uncle Dage."

Talen shook his head. "Even our blood won't cure human diseases. I admire her for trying, but I just don't see it happening." His golden eyes softened slightly when he looked at his son. "I hope you're staying longer this time. Your mother needs your attention, and I have to remind you that she's an empath. Whatever is going on with you needs to be addressed."

Benny remained still. He'd been worried about Garrett for a while, but he hadn't pushed to find out what was wrong with him. Perhaps he should have.

Dage smiled, and determination filled his eyes. "In fact, I'd like to offer you a job, nephew."

Benny stiffened. Dage always tried to learn the inner workings of the Seven through Garrett, but he didn't speak. Garrett was an adult and had been for quite some time. Hell, the kid was an adult even back when he should've been a kid. The mantle of responsibility had landed heavily on him from day one, and becoming a member of the Seven was only a slice of his destiny. Even Benny had figured that one out.

Garrett took a drink of his Scotch and rubbed the whiskers across his chin. He looked twenty-five or so, and he would for a long time—although stress lines from lack of sleep definitely spread out from his eyes. "That's kind of you. What's the job?"

Benny cocked his head. Just how old was the kid? Mid-thirties, maybe? God, that was young.

Dage watched him carefully. "For the last three years, after other species learned about the Seven and how you all perverted the laws of physics and our people, I've been balancing our allies and enemies like an insane juggler. The shifters are closer than ever to coming after us, and the witches are one explosion away from blowing up my headquarters. I need a liaison between the Realm and the other nations, and I'm asking you to serve."

"It'd be an honor," Garrett said instantly. "My status as one of the Seven might not be well known, but most species have guessed it. Are you sure you want me?"

Benny sat back. "You have other vows, my friend."

Tension rose in the room instantly.

Talen leaned toward his son. "I want to know all of it. Now."

"What do you know?" Benny interjected, trying to protect Garrett from facing off with his father. Their relationship was excellent, and it often made Ben miss his own father. He didn't want the kid to suffer because he was a member of the Seven. "You come clean first, Kayrs."

Talen turned deep golden eyes toward him. The predator inside him was closer to the surface than in most immortals, and he did nothing to hide it. "The seven of you violated every physical law of this world, bonded your torsos into solid shields that can't be penetrated, and then created a prison world in some other dimension to keep an ancient Cyst captive."

Garrett grimaced. "Not in another dimension, Dad. The physicist we work with is really cranky about that. We move through dimensions to this place, but it's part of this dimension."

"I don't give a fuck," Talen said evenly, green sizzling through the golden hue in his eyes. "Now the two who were supposed to guard him, our ancestors, are back here. So I'm guessing this guy is going to return, too, and I want to know everything about him so we're ready to fight when he arrives."

Benny sighed. "You already know what we know. His name is Ulric, he's the ultimate Cyst, and he violated the laws first by making his entire body impenetrable. He did so by killing and using the blood of more than one hundred enhanced females. He wants all such women and girls dead, which is why we banished him. I think the Kurjans plan to save only the ones they want." His hypothesis made sense—although he was missing something. He'd always felt that.

"Is he back?" Dage asked.

Benny shook his head. "Not yet."

"Tell me about the final ritual," Dage said, his chin down.

Garrett didn't flinch or look away from his uncle. "The final
ritual involves the members of the Seven, the three female Keys,
and a location we haven't yet found. It's where we kill Ulric, by
using the blood of the Keys. That's all I know."

Not true. Benny tried to look casual. Garrett had left out the
most important part of the story: that little Hope Kayrs-Kyllwood
was the Lock. Something none of them understood. She was the
only female vampire to have ever existed. Considering she was
Talen's granddaughter, his only one, telling him the full truth
would make enemies of the Realm and the Seven. For sure.

Of course, Benny would trust Garrett with his life, but not
with Hope's destiny if the girl was meant to be a sacrifice. The
soldier definitely had his own motives for joining the Seven. That
showdown was probably coming soon.

Dage studied them. "What aren't you saying?"

Garrett shrugged. "Nothing. You either trust me or you don't."

Nicely done. Benny relaxed. The kid could play poker with the
best of them, and he also knew when to count on family. "I notice
the demon leader isn't here right now."

Tension and power emanated from Dage as he spoke. "The
demon nation is in peril. Half of them want to withdraw from the
Realm because of you degenerates, and the other half want to stay
in. Zane is juggling as much as I am right now."

Zane was the leader of the demon nation, and his youngest
brother, Logan, was a member of the Seven.

Benny sighed.

"Exactly," Talen agreed grimly.

* * * *

Karma sat on a very soft blanket on the examination table,
her legs dangling off the end, safely covered by her long skirt.
The news had made her lungs seize as if she'd been trapped in a
basement. The world closed in, but she kept her expression placid.

Her stomach cramped. Emma was the queen? Why would a queen be wearing worn clothing and working after midnight? Did she have such a compulsion to cause pain that she couldn't sleep?

The queen tapped on her tablet and then pulled a chair closer, sitting and resting the tablet on her lap. "If you consent, I'd like to ask you questions and then take some blood. I've never met a Kurjan Soti, or mate, and I've never studied the blood of one." Her eyes gleamed.

Karma fought a shiver. What sort of game was this? She studied the female, acutely aware of the two armed guards against the far exit.

The queen sat back, studying her. "You have every right to refuse, but I'm hoping you won't. I'm so close to finding a cure to many human diseases, and every iota of information helps."

Karma's mouth opened slightly, and she shut it instantly. This did not make sense. Why the falsehood?

The queen tilted her head. "Are you all right?" Concern softened her voice.

Karma tried very hard not to move. This was a trick, and she couldn't be taken in by it. Or was she supposed to? Were the Kurjans watching yet? She couldn't tell. "I am fine. Please commence your tests." Were the Realm soldiers going to witness her humiliation and pain? She wouldn't scream or cry, so they would be disappointed.

The queen pursed her lips. "I thought we'd talk, but I can take blood first if you're worried about it. A lot of people don't like needles. Benny is terrified of them, although he puts up a good show of being irritated instead." She chuckled and walked gracefully to the counter, opening a drawer and taking out a kit. Then she approached. "Are you sure you don't mind doing this tonight?"

Karma turned and looked at her. "Would that matter?" She failed to keep the desperation from her voice.

The queen retreated a step. "Of course it would matter. It *does* matter." She pushed the kit across the counter and returned to sit on her chair. "I'm not an empath, but I can feel that you're frightened even though you hide it well."

Was that the test? Had Karma passed it? She waited for the next move.

The queen frowned. "I know we've just met, but you can talk to me."

Karma kept her hands together. "What do you wish to discuss, Your Royal Highness?" Her tone remained neutral.

The queen chortled. "Your Royal Highness? For goodness' sake, please do not say anything of the sort in front of my mate or his brothers. I'd never live it down, and I have enough nicknames, thank you very much."

Nicknames? Karma looked at the soldiers and then the female. "Then how are you addressed?"

The queen sighed. "Please, call me Emma." She also looked at the soldiers. "Hey, guys? Would you please guard my precious body from the other side of the door? We want some girl time here. Grumpy Gus confirmed that Karma doesn't have weapons of any kind on her body."

Girl time? Was that when the needles came out? So the queen wasn't worried about Karma fighting back if the soldiers were out of the room? "Are you trained that well, Your...Emma?"

The soldiers instantly exited through the double doors, which shut quietly.

"Trained? What do you mean?" Emma asked.

It felt odd being up on the table while the queen sat on the chair a foot or so below. "Do you think I'll be that easy to subdue?" Karma had never trained to fight, but even a trapped kitten could claw deep enough to draw blood.

Emma took in a breath and then exhaled slowly. She held up her hands. "All right. I think we've gotten off on the wrong foot."

Karma frowned before she could stop herself. What in the world did that mean? "The wrong foot?"

Emma pressed her hands on her jeans. "It's an idiom. Okay. I hope you don't believe the guys when they complain about me chasing them with syringes. They're all just a bunch of babies."

Karma jerked. Had the female just called her soldiers "babies"? Her eyes widened. "You truly must be the queen." Yes, she had doubted it for a few moments, just because of the woman's clothing and casual attitude. "Nobody else would dare say such a thing." Even so, the king would most certainly not appreciate such talk. But he wasn't there, was he?

Emma curved her lips. "Such a thing? You mean calling them babies?"

Karma slowly nodded.

Emma snorted. Very unqueenlike. "If they don't want to be called babies, then they shouldn't act like such dorky wimps. I mean, seriously. They have you thinking I'm a wild woman with syringes. You're actually afraid to be in here. Props, by the way. You totally look calm and in control. It's impressive."

Karma couldn't find a response. None of this was making sense. "I have heard the legends about you."

Emma perked up. "There are legends about me? Like what?"

"That you like to conduct…experiments." Karma's stomach cramped.

Emma's brow smoothed out. "I do. I'm always experimenting. Dage says I'm obsessed, but he's just as busy, so pot and kettle, you know?"

The woman was talking in riddles. So much for the legends being false. Mayhap the female was insane, which would explain her cheerful attitude while discussing torture. Karma pressed a hand to her forehead.

"Oh. Benny said you were hit in the head. Do you have a headache?" Emma stood, her face softening.

Before Karma could answer, the door opened, and a tall teenager hurried inside. He looked to be about sixteen or seventeen, and he had huge hands, but he was gangly. Maybe he was younger than that. His black hair was cut short but still curled over his ears and managed to spike up in several areas, and his eyes were an intense blue.

"Mom," he burst out, handing her a notebook. "I think I solved the Terevosky Equation. What do you think?"

Emma took the notebook. "Hunter? Manners. Karma, this is my son Hunter, who should be in bed. Hunter, this is Karma."

Hunter smiled but didn't approach. "Oh. Hi. Nice to meet you."

Emma manacled the kid around the neck and yanked him close for a hug. She had to lean up to do it, but he let her move him. "Why aren't you in bed?"

He frowned. "Because I was solving the Terevosky Equation."

Emma smiled. "You're the smartest fourteen-year-old on the planet, buddy. But even you need sleep."

"Good point." The door opened, and the king stood in the entryway. "You're done tonight, love. Let's get some sleep."

Emma shot him a look. "Fine." She turned and smiled at Karma. "We can pick up again tomorrow, if you want. Benny will show you to your rooms."

Benny poked his head in, pushing the king out of the way. His gaze narrowed, and then his body relaxed visibly as he caught sight of her. He grinned and motioned her toward him. "Hey, darlin'. Looks like you survived just fine. Let's get you away from the needles."

"For now," Hunter muttered, earning a look from his mother.

All of these people were crazy.

Chapter Six

Benny led the way to the rooms he usually occupied when he visited the Realm, opening the door of the suite and allowing Karma to precede him inside. "I think there should be clothing for you in the master bedroom, should you want to shower and change." He followed her, letting the door shut. "I hope this suite is all right with you." He looked at the spacious living area with the stone fireplace and thought it was nice.

She partially turned, her long skirt and ruffled blouse making her look like a lady from years gone by. Her hair was still in the bun, and her face pale; the topaz of her eyes glowed. He'd love to see her in a bikini at the beach, with all of that smooth skin on display. The female was lovely—the very definition of the word. "I don't understand," she said.

He frowned, running through what he'd said to her. It all seemed to make sense to him. A knock sounded on the door, and he pivoted, putting himself between her and any threat. "What?" He pulled it open.

Max stood on the other side and shoved a tray piled high with dishes toward him. "Emma was worried you two hadn't eaten and sent this. Apparently she remembers last time you were here, when you ate all the cookies and I almost had to kill you." With a smart-assed grin, the soldier turned and strode away.

Ha. It'd be a good fight. Benny turned and carried the tray to the coffee table in front of the fireplace. "Come eat, Karma." He wasn't doing a very good job of caring for her. The female probably hadn't eaten in way too long. For that matter, neither had he.

She kept him in her sights as she crossed around the table and took the leather chair on the other side of the sofa.

Perhaps she needed some space after spending time in the lab. He could understand. So instead of sitting on the sofa closer to her, he took the opposite chair and lifted the coverings off the plates to reveal baked chicken, potatoes, green beans, and sourdough bread. The final plate held all sorts of different cookies. He smiled. "The peanut butter are the best, but the chocolate chip ones aren't bad."

She folded her hands in her lap, watching him.

The female had the oddest way about her. He handed her a plate. "You need to eat."

She set the plate on her lap and reached for a napkin. Utensils fell out as she opened it, and she caught them.

He lifted the bottle of wine and whistled. "The queen sent the good stuff. She must like you." He poured two very generous glasses and nudged one toward the female.

"I'm still alive," Karma agreed, taking a bite of the chicken.

Benny chuckled. "I can see that." He set his plate on his lap and took a deep drink of the wine. "It's good. Have some."

She took a sip, and color finally brushed across her high cheekbones. "It is good."

"It's a Jadot Le Montrachet, sweetheart. It had better be good." He took another bite of chicken. "How did it go with Emma?"

Karma stiffened. "I do not know what you expect me to say."

He paused with a forkful of green beans halfway to his mouth. "I expect you to say the truth."

"Oh." Her body seemed to relax, and she ate more of the chicken, chewing thoughtfully. "The queen was much different from what I expected. She just wanted to talk tonight. I'm sure the torture will start tomorrow."

He barked out a laugh. "The torture. Exactly. You have no idea." He munched happily on his chicken, pausing to look up at her eyes. Pain flashed in them for the briefest of seconds, and then she looked down. "Karma?"

She shook her head.

He set his plate on the coffee table. "Look at me." He put bite into his tone this time.

She jumped and then looked up, her eyes wide.

He didn't know how to deal with delicate or fragile females, and there was no doubt the woman staring so regally at him was both. She was also terrified. He rubbed the scruff at his chin. When had he last shaved? "If you don't want to give blood, you don't have to. If you want me to take you away from Realm Headquarters right now, I'll do it. Just stop being so afraid. Nobody is going to hurt you."

Even her scoff was delicate. "You brought me here for the queen to experiment upon. I doubt she'll just let us leave."

What the hell? "Experiment on?" Holy shit, he'd missed something. Something big. He moved to the sofa, sitting at the end close to her. She immediately shrank away, and his temper stirred even more. He swallowed several times to keep it at bay. "Honey? Emma draws blood from every immortal she can chase down. She studies it to help humans, and maybe us if a virus ever threatens us again. That's all. She conducts experiments in the lab, but not on bodies. I don't think I've ever seen her use even a mouse in a lab experiment."

Karma's mouth tightened. "I have heard the stories about her."

What was the correct approach here? Benny reached for a cookie and chewed, his mind spinning. "We should probably start there, then. Tell me about the stories."

"No." Karma looked surprised at herself for a moment. Perhaps she didn't say no often.

Just how bad was it in the Kurjan world for a Soti without a mate? Benny took another cookie and shoved down the anger inside him. "Okay. You certainly don't have to do or say anything you don't want." When she just sniffed, he had to grin. "However, I have to tell you, somebody has filled you full of bull…nonsense. The queen has never tortured a soul."

Karma's gaze flickered away and then back. "She doesn't tear the skin off enhanced females to see how fast they recuperate?"

Benny lost the grin. His gut chilled. "Hell no."

* * * *

Karma's mind frazzled, and it was difficult to concentrate. Male heat washed over her at Benjamin's nearness, along with that scent of wildness, citrus, and the woods that always clung to him. Her body grew sensitive so close to him—was it because of the bizarre mating mark? The fact that she'd caused his mark when she'd already been mated was unheard of. Until now.

She retreated into her calm facade. "It is well known that the queen tortures the enemy for fun. For her own research and enjoyment."

Benjamin sat back, his eyes a burning combination of metallic colors. "Let me get this straight. When I left you with Emma earlier today, you thought I was handing you over to have your skin torn from your body?" Because he was a hybrid, his voice was naturally low and hoarse. It lowered even more with his question.

She squirmed on her chair. Was there a correct answer? She was accustomed to fading into the background to keep herself safe, but right now, there was nowhere to go.

His gaze swept her face, and then he dropped his head into his hands. "All right." He lifted up, scrubbed both cheeks, and then pinched the bridge of his nose. "Okay." Then he pressed his thumbs to the corners of his eyes and shut them. "I see."

Was he having some sort of stroke? "Benjamin?" she whispered.

He lifted his head and let his hands drop to his black cargo pants. His fingers tangled and then folded together. He took a deep breath. Then another. "Where were you born?"

The question threw her completely out of the moment. "I was born in a small town in Sweden."

"When?"

She struggled to remember. "Late seventeen hundreds, in the spring. May first, actually." She hadn't thought about her birthday in centuries.

He handed her a peanut-butter cookie. "Your name is interesting, considering you're Swedish. Isn't Karma a Hindu name?"

She nodded. "The Vikings traded with the people of Constantinople and brought home spices. My mother heard the name from one of them. She liked it, and *Krama* means 'to hug' in my native language, so it's close to that, too."

His smile was too charming for her peace of mind. "When did you get mated?"

She took a bite, letting the delicious sugar ease her fear. "I was seventeen, I think." It was so long ago. "His name was Kraig, and he died that first year." She'd been a widow forever.

"You didn't go back home?"

"No. I belonged to the Kurjans by then. I've worked for them and helped throughout the years." She'd made some friends, and now she had the twins to protect. How was she going to help them?

"Did he hurt you, Karma?" Benny asked, his tone gentle.

She blinked. "Not really. My dowry was a good one, and I knew what my wifely duties meant. Mating wasn't much different. Of course, my family and I were humans—they did not know I had mated an immortal. Kraig took me away right afterward, so I never saw them again." Despite her gifts, she'd never seen any family member once they'd crossed into the beyond. Perhaps that was part of the rules she had never understood.

"Huh. What's your enhancement? Are you psychic?" Benjamin took another cookie.

Her body was weary and her mind fuzzy. She couldn't help relaxing against the chair. It was too much effort to lie to him, and it didn't really matter what he thought of her, so she told the truth for once. Not even the Kurjans knew about her gift. "No. I can sometimes channel those who've not crossed over completely. Not often, but it does happen."

His eyebrows rose. Oddly enough, he appeared intrigued. "You see dead people?"

Her face heated. Why had she just trusted him with such a private secret? Because it felt right, somehow. "Yes. You said you wanted the truth."

"I do. Always." He tugged on his ear. "Do you think the Kurjans always tell the truth?"

She finished the cookie. "No. I have seen them tell falsehoods."

He handed her another one—this one oatmeal with raisins. "Is it possible they lied to you about Emma? That they lied to all of the enhanced women or anybody thinking of escaping from them?"

She chewed and thought about it. Her body was almost too tired to worry about that right now. "I do not know."

"That's fair." He tipped back his glass and finished his wine. "Tell me how to convince you, and I'll do it right now."

She wanted to beg him to take her away from there. To challenge him to see if he'd do as she asked. That was not the plan, however. She searched for words to use. "Promise me you won't let the queen torture me."

"The queen would never do such a thing," Benjamin said, pouring them both more wine. "However, if it makes you feel better, I vow to you on the souls of my ancestors that I will not allow anybody to torture you. You don't even have to give her blood tomorrow if you don't want to do so."

Could she believe him? Did she have a choice? She required direction and had none. Were the Kurjans watching? If so, she had to do this correctly and follow the plan. "All right." She looked around. "Are there two bedrooms in your suite?"

"No. You take the bedroom. I'll take the couch." He tossed his napkin on his plate.

She coughed. He was a deadly warrior and she a servant. What was he talking about? Was this another test? "I shall take the sofa and you the bed. You're too large for this furniture."

He grinned. "I'm too large for most furniture. Now, take the bedroom, Karma. I'm not going to argue with you about it." While he usually appeared relaxed, there was an iron-steel determination just beneath his casual attitude.

She immediately stood and grasped her full wineglass. "Very well. I shall see you tomorrow."

He held up his hand to show his marking. "We do need to talk about this tomorrow."

She grew still.

He waved that hand. "I don't expect you to mate me, and I'm not mate material anyway. But this does mean I'm responsible for you, and I want you to let me help you. We'll get you settled wherever you want with a good life. It's totally up to you."

She truly had no words, although it made sense he didn't want to mate. She should feel relief; the hollow sensation in her belly did not make sense. "Good night, Benjamin."

"'Night." He gathered the plates and dishes together.

She swept by him and entered the master bedroom, shutting the door. Pain immediately slashed into the right side of her head, and she pressed the heel of her palm to her eye, biting her lip to keep from crying out. Sucking back a sob, she tripped past the bed to what must be the bathroom. She scrambled for the light, pushing her face toward the ornate mirror and lifting her hand.

Blood dribbled from her right eye. She wiped it away, looking closer to see if the implant was visible. Her eye looked normal, but her eyeball and her ear throbbed from the activation of the device. The Kurjan tech had said it wouldn't be detected and then would be activated about three hours after any test the Realm performed. So Grumpy Gus had done what the tech had promised.

She winced at the continuing pain in her head.

The Kurjans were now watching…and listening.

Chapter Seven

Midmorning, a soft knock on the bedroom door pulled Karma out of her whirling thoughts. She'd showered and dressed in the available clothing, but it was not working. The jeans did not feel right, although the shirt was flowered and soft. But it was short-sleeved, and much of her skin was exposed. She thought about donning the skirt she'd worn the day before, but it was stained with dirt and blood.

She felt as if sharp knives spun inside her head, sticking directly into the back of her eye after ripping through her right eardrum.

"Karma? It's Emma," the queen said, her voice quiet through the door.

Karma jumped off the bed and looked around. She'd tidied the monstrously sized bed and hung up her towels in the bathroom. She hurried toward the door and opened it, steeling her shoulders.

Emma stood with a handful of clothing in her arms. Today the queen's dark hair fell around her shoulders, and her eyes were brighter after a night of sleep. Concern glowed in them, however. "I thought about the clothes we left for you and what you were wearing last night. It seems you're more comfortable in skirts and all, so we ran to town earlier to see what we could find." She rolled her eyes. "Let me rephrase that. I asked people to run to town because Dage is over-the-top protective right now with two members of the Seven here at Realm Headquarters. He's being a pain in my ass."

Karma took a step back. Fear thundered in her ears. "You're speaking of the King of the Realm? Your mate?" Did the woman like being beaten?

Emma snorted. "Yeah. Him." She pushed the clothing into Karma's arms. "Find something to make you comfortable, and then come on out for breakfast. I'll set your table by the window. I thought we should talk."

Karma stumbled back and let Emma close the door. Was the queen truly insane? She turned and set the bundle on the bed, rifling through it with pleasure. A lovely floral skirt with matching burgundy-colored tights fit perfectly, and she pulled the softest blue cardigan over her shirt and instantly felt more like herself. Once she'd laced up her boots, she double-checked her braid and then strode outside to find the queen at a small table by the window.

"Come on over." Emma gestured her to the table, where plates of food smelled delicious. "I wasn't sure what you liked, so I made scrambled eggs, hash browns, bacon, biscuits and gravy, and pancakes." She reached for a carafe. "Coffee or tea?"

"Coffee, please." Karma sat, her aching mind spinning. The queen was serving her? That wasn't right. "Did you say you made breakfast?"

Emma held the carafe gracefully. "I sometimes like to cook to let my mind wander. I'm nowhere near as good at it as most of my friends or my sister or Max, but I try." She finished pouring and nudged sugar and cream across the table. "Here you go."

Karma poured a little cream and took a sip, nearly humming at the delicious taste. "Wonderful."

Emma leaned in, her cup already in her hands. "I have to confess, Max made the coffee. He's a genius with it, and the butthead won't share how or why."

Karma sucked in air. "You speak disrespectfully of the soldiers. Is it only when they are absent?"

Emma chuckled, although her eyes remained serious. "No. I told Max he was a jackass just an hour ago, and believe me, I read Dage the riot act when he said I couldn't go into town today. Are you not allowed to speak your mind in the Kurjan stronghold?"

"Not like that." Karma cleared her throat. "It was kind of you to find me additional clothing. I am much more comfortable in a skirt." Whenever she wore jeans, she felt vulnerable for some reason.

Emma shrugged. "You do you, girl. If you want to wear skirts, wear them."

How in the world was this female a queen? "I don't understand you," Karma confessed. She'd read many romance novels through the years, since the Kurjan soldiers considered them silly and allowed them in the camps. The women in them were strong and impressive. Maybe there was more truth in those slices of escape than she'd thought? If so, where were the sheiks with the ripped abs? Thinking about it, she took a bite of the eggs. They were delicious.

Emma dug into her food. "I talked to Benny earlier today and then figured we should have our own discussion."

"Where is Benjamin today, if it's okay to inquire?" Karma asked.

Emma looked up. "All right. First things first. You can ask, say, demand, or yell anything you want to while you're here. Heck. While you're anywhere except, apparently, the Kurjan Headquarters. Right now, Benny is sparring with Talen in the gym, working off some steam. Then they'll probably grab breakfast and start arguing about the Realm and the Seven. After that, they might spar again, depending on how well the argument goes." She grinned.

Karma's head ached, and while she wanted to do her job, she didn't want to get Emma into trouble. "I see." The Kurjans could now see through her right eye and hear through her right ear.

Emma nudged the pancake plate closer. "I put huckleberries in the pancakes. Have you had any before?" When Karma shook her head, Emma nearly hopped with excitement. "They're exquisite, and you can only get them here or in Montana. They only grow wild, and they're a lot sweeter than blueberries. I hope you like them."

Karma dutifully took two pancakes. "Thank you."

"Karma?" Emma's voice softened. "The Kurjans lied to you. I don't hurt people. Never have and never will. I'd like to think of myself as a healer who uses science and has the best equipment in the entire world."

Karma met Emma's blue gaze evenly, her chest settling. "I thought about this last night and realized it is entirely possible the Kurjans lied about you." She didn't care if they heard her since it seemed to be the truth. "I apologize for thinking the worst."

Emma patted her hand. "That's not your fault. How would you know?"

That was true. However, she still had a job to do. For once, she longed to see a spirit or a ghost hovering nearby, but the space around her was clear. So much for seeking input from others. "In that case, I would like to be exposed to the virus you discovered, the one that will negate my mating bond." There. She'd said it, as she'd been ordered to do.

Emma's eyebrows rose. "That's your decision. Guess you want to mate again, huh? Awesome!"

* * * *

"Now, wait a minute." Benny stormed into the queen's lab, his hair fresh from a shower and his clothing nice and clean. He still had a few bruises from his sparring hours with Talen, but they were slowly mending. Hopefully Talen's broken jaw was doing the same.

Emma leaned against a far counter, once again dressed in jeans, a T-shirt, and lab coat. "Morning, Benny. I heard you caused quite a ruckus earlier today."

Karma sat on the examination table, looking sexy and alluring in another long skirt with flowers on it. She'd twisted her thick hair into an intricate braid, making his fingers itch to untangle the sunshine-filled mass. "Good morning, Benjamin. What ruckus?" Then she jolted as if surprised she'd asked a question.

He took a deep breath and tucked his thumbs into the jeans Emma had provided for him earlier. They fit perfectly and didn't have one hole in them. "Good morning, ladies." All right. He needed to calm down so he didn't frighten Karma again. The idea that she'd asked a question warmed him. "Dage asked me to train the younger soldiers, but apparently he should've given me more direction."

Emma snorted, and she leaned conspiratorially closer to Karma. "Benjamin stripped them naked, hung them upside down, and fired honey at them from a squirt gun. We still have bees around here, even though it's fall."

Karma gasped, her eyes wide. "Benny. Why would you do that?"

He shrugged. "Training means dealing with the unexpected. They should've known that."

"The honey was mixed with superglue," Emma exclaimed before bursting into gales of laughter.

Karma chuckled and then covered her mouth with her hand. The mirth showed in her pretty eyes, and damn if Benny didn't decide right then and there to make her laugh every day. She moved her hand. "Do you like it when people think you're crazy?"

He grinned. "It doesn't hurt." Plus, it allowed him to snoop around a little bit. They'd gotten some very shaky intel about an anti-Seven group working within the Realm that not even the king knew about. But despite his investigations, Benny hadn't found anything...yet. For now, he got back down to business. "I take it the two of you had a nice discussion and now you know that Emma isn't going to peel off your skin?"

Red bloomed across Karma's smooth cheekbones. "Yes. I was misinformed."

When she sounded all formal and hoity-toity like that, he really wanted to kiss her. Full-on, deep, and wild. Instead, he grinned. "God, you're cute."

She blinked.

Apparently, the female wasn't used to compliments. He'd have to change that during their short time together. "You're also very pretty, and you smell like the freshest breeze off a warm lake."

She froze.

Emma looked up. "You flirt good, Ben. Who knew?"

He stood straighter and smiled. "I have hidden talents, Queen. Now, we're going to discuss what's happening here."

Emma looked from him to Karma and then back. "I figured you'd have a thing or two to say. Do you want me to give you some privacy?"

"No," Karma said softly. "You both have said I have freedom here or insinuated that fact. If so, I wish to take the virus and negate my mating bond. My mate died two centuries ago, so I'm a perfect candidate, correct?"

Emma nodded. "Virus-27, as you might not know, was created by the Kurjans to kill the vampires. We found a cure for it, but we also have been able to tweak the little bug to use it to our advantage. We've found the longer the mate has been gone, the weaker the bond. So far, we haven't tried the virus on anybody whose mate is still alive."

Karma hadn't known the Kurjans had created the virus, but at the moment, that fact did not matter. "If I take this virus, then the bond will disappear?"

Emma drew air into her nose. "We think so. We've successfully used the virus with demon mates, shifter mates, and vampire mates. However, Kurjans are a different species, and I've only gained a few samples of their blood through the years to test. I can't guarantee the results. You need to know that the virus can be deadly, and there's a chance your system will reject it, or a chance that you will become infected in a way I can't predict or possibly cure."

Karma appeared to weigh the words and then softly answered. "I understand your concerns, but I wish to proceed anyway."

Benny had no right to dictate to her, but the protectiveness sweeping through him had his jaw tensing. Even so, he kept his tone gentle. "Karma? For a moment, just consider the danger." The female was far more delicate than he'd realized when he'd met her three years ago. "You could keep the mark and live a good life, although you wouldn't get to have, well, sex." That sort of life was unthinkable to him, but she'd gone without for a couple of centuries, so who knew what she thought? Of course, maybe abstinence had made her crazy. She seemed sane, though. Perhaps she was good at self-pleasuring.

The idea smashed through him, landing in his balls. He shifted his weight to keep the jeans from killing him. "Just a thought," he managed to croak out.

She looked him right in the eyes. "I have no plans to mate again, and yet, I'd like the freedom to choose. It'd be nice to shake hands with somebody without getting a rash."

Why did it warm him that she didn't want to go off and mate somebody again? Benny looked at Emma. "If she takes the virus, will she still be immortal?"

Emma's shrug was anything but casual. "I can't guarantee that, Ben. Everyone I know who has taken the virus has gotten re-mated fairly quickly, so we don't have a trial to compare to. I know immortality lasts at least for a little while, maybe a year. After that, I just don't know. It's possible an enhanced human's chromosomal pairs, which have increased to grant immortality, will unravel again down to those of a mortal human. Or it's possible the pairs will stay strong, even without the mating bond. I truly don't know."

Benny exhaled. "All right. Well, if her chromosomes start to unravel, I'll mate her." That only made sense, considering the mark

REBEL'S KARMA

63

he wore was for her. At her soft gasp, he winced and focused on her. "I mean, if that's what you want. If you wish to be human, that's okay, too. Although why anybody would want to be human is beyond me." Could he really allow her to be human, get old, and die?

If that's what she wanted, he didn't have a right to stop her. Especially since he couldn't mate and still do the job he planned to do. "Karma?" he asked.

Emma held up a hand. "You need to know that the second I inject you, there's no turning back. There's no way to stop the virus once you have it. So, you have to be perfectly sure. It'll do its job until it runs its course, and if all goes well, you'll be fine."

Benny winced. "No risk there." It wasn't his decision to make. "Karma?"

She remained perfectly still. Pretty but pale. Now that he looked closer, he could see soft lines next to her eyes where the delicate muscles were pinched. "I'd like to take the virus," she said.

He moved toward her, ducking his head to peer into her eyes. "Does your head still hurt?"

"Yes," she whispered.

"You can't heal it?" The marking on his palm burned hotter now that he was close enough to touch her.

She shrugged.

Well, what the heck. He reached out and rubbed his thumb across her eyebrow, trying to pull the pain into himself. Agony flared in his head, behind his eye, and then detonated in his ear. He blinked several times and pulled away. "That's a hell of a headache."

Her eyes went wide, and the pupils contracted. "You took the pain away."

He took a couple of steps back. "Well, yeah." That mating mark had some power.

Chapter Eight

Karma's limbs felt weak. Jittery. Rubbery. She allowed Benjamin to escort her back to the suite of rooms after spending most of the afternoon in the lab. The queen had injected her with Virus-27, and the Kurjan plan was going as they'd directed. She walked to the sofa and sat, shivering as rain clipped against the sliding glass door.

Benjamin flipped on the gas fireplace and took a furry blanket off the adjacent chair to settle over her. "How are you feeling?"

"The same," she admitted, her muscles aching. "Thank you for taking me out of the lab. I couldn't stay in there any longer."

Benjamin leaned against the stone fireplace. "Emma will be along to check your vitals every hour or so. If you need to sleep, feel free. Besides Em, nobody will bother you." He stood tall, looking dangerous despite the concerned glint in his patina colored eyes.

Weariness rustled through her, and her skin prickled. "What's your secondary eye color?" she murmured. She'd heard vampires and demons had secondary eye colors that emerged during stressful situations.

His eyebrows rose, and he sat in the chair. "They say my secondary color is kind of a blackish green. I've never looked in the mirror, but I've been told." He shrugged, and the muscles across his chest played nicely. "Never thought about it, really."

Was it true that the color emerged when a male mated? Her palms dampened, and a trickle of sweat slid between her breasts. It had been so long, but she now remembered what being ill felt like. What a fever actually felt like. Interesting. She was kind of enjoying how mellow she felt at the moment. Almost safe, in a cozy cocoon. "Why have you never taken a mate?"

He grinned. "Not sure anybody would have me. I'm not exactly a settle-down type of guy."

She smiled. Oh, he definitely was not. There was a wildness in him—a pure, primitive energy—that sped up her heart rate, even without the fever. "You're a soldier. A warrior." Her gaze dropped to his large hands resting on his jeans. Oh, what he could do with those hands.

He kicked back and stretched out his legs. "Are you hungry? You didn't eat much of the soup at lunch."

"No." She'd vomit if she tried to eat. So she concentrated on his rugged face. His skin stretched over strong bones, all angled to create the masculine handsomeness of years gone by. The tough and primal look of a predator. Beautiful and deadly. The shadow along his jaw only added to his maleness. "You're beautiful, Benjamin." Yes, that statement would get her beaten when she returned home, but she didn't care. Not right now, anyway.

He snorted. "Darlin', I think your fever is taking over."

She laughed before she could stop herself.

He sobered, and an intense look flashed in his eyes before a heated crimson crossed his cheekbones. "Now, that's a pretty laugh. The sweetest sound I've ever heard."

What a kind male. Darkness edged around the room as her vision narrowed. So she kept her gaze on the soldier. "If you ever do mate, I assume you will find somebody modern and strong. Brave and tough."

He cocked his head. "Like you?"

She smiled, her eyelids dropping to half-mast. "That's funny. I'm none of those things." She plucked at the pretty material of her skirt. "I am not even comfortable in pants, so how could I be tough? One can't fight in a skirt." If she ever got free, maybe she'd work on becoming strong and even wearing jeans.

He leaned forward, and his delicious scent came to her. "Do all of the Kurjan Sotis dress in such a manner?"

"Yes. We have not changed much through the ages. Once in a while there is a new mate who might wear current clothing, but that usually changes as she settles in." She looked down at her skirt. "I like skirts. Is it true your women train to fight?"

He nodded. "Sure. Emma can probably take on a whole group of shifters at this point, but I don't see it ever happening. I can train you, if you like. Once you feel better."

The idea of her learning to fight was laughable. She could never be like those romance heroines she loved so much. She'd never have the courage to ward off a group of bikers with a plunger like the last heroine she'd read about. She shook her head. "That is a silly thought, Benjamin." But a sweet one.

He grunted, but she couldn't interpret the meaning of the sound. "Did you ever try to escape?" he asked.

She looked up, her head starting to hurt again—this time at the base of her neck. "And go where?" Two centuries ago, there was nowhere to go. Now she knew nothing of the outside world, hadn't even known that fireplaces could be ignited with a switch until just a moment ago. She was still working on using contractions in her speech, although that was becoming easier.

He watched her. "All right. Well, that's the answer, then. We have to teach you independence. I'll have a few million transferred into a bank account for you, and we'll start there. You can always have more if you want."

The words were not flowing in a manner that made sense. The fever was robbing her of comprehension. "A million what?"

"Dollars, baby. Are you even caught up on modern television or movies? Games? The Internet?" Benny wavered in front of her eyes.

Figures edged in, several who hadn't crossed over into the beyond. The ghosts were here.

She swallowed, her throat suddenly parched. "We are not allowed modern entertainment. I like to read, though. We often sneak in books, but not many are modern. The Kurjans don't mind if we read romance novels, however. Those heroines are amazing. I also read a novel about vampires who sparkled in the sun, and I truly enjoyed it. We all did, but I believe it was left behind during one of our recent moves." She wanted to sparkle. Who didn't? "Wouldn't it be lovely to sparkle, Benjamin?"

His face seemed to morph in every direction and then settled back in place. "Covert Ops would be difficult if I sparkled, but I guess everyone deals with obstacles. You sparkle to me right now."

With that kind thought wafting through her head, she pitched to the side and let unconsciousness take her completely.

* * * *

"Get out of my light," Emma barked, shoving Benny in the gut. "Dage? Get him back."

The king grabbed Benny around the waist and pulled him toward the fireplace. "Let her work, Benny. Trust her."

Benny let the king pull him because he could still see over Emma's head as she checked Karma's vitals while the woman lay still as death on the sofa. He'd bellowed for help the second Karma had gone over, and the guard at the door had radioed for the king. "One second we were talking, and the next she was out cold." After turning so pale he could see a blue vein running along the side of her temple. "What's wrong? How bad is it?"

Emma finished making notations on her tablet and settled the blanket more securely over Karma. She stood, her blue gaze worried. "She's out, that's for sure. Her temp is around 108, which is close to the danger zone for a mate but not quite there yet.

However, if it keeps rising, we need to get her into an ice bath. Right now, her body is fighting the virus."

Dage released Benny and stood ready at his side. "Her reaction is more extreme than what we've seen before."

Emma pushed a wayward curl out of her face. She'd put her hair up in a ponytail the second she'd arrived. "Yes. I've seen temperatures rise, but nobody has lost consciousness like this before. To be honest, I had hoped Karma's reaction would be mild since her mate died so long ago." She shoved the infrared thermometer into her black bag. "I don't know enough about the Kurjans and their genetic composition or chemistry to make a diagnosis here."

Benny's hands shook, so he shoved them in his pockets. Karma lay covered by the blanket, looking pale and still. Small and defenseless. He growled, long and low.

Power crackled along Dage's still form. "Should we take her to the infirmary?"

Emma studied the prone woman. "There's nothing in the infirmary that will help her, Dage. I have morphine in my bag if she appears to be in pain, but there's nothing that can stop the reaction going on inside her right now. Once the virus is in, it's in until it runs its course."

"There's a cure, though," Benny interjected.

Emma glanced at him. "There's a cure for immortals who contract the virus, but we've genetically engineered this version so it will negate the mating bond. There is no cure. I explained that to you."

Benny scrubbed a rough hand through his hair. "I didn't really think there was a risk to her, since we've seen the virus work on everyone else."

Emma shook her head. "Just a few samples, really. I can count them on one hand, and maybe we got lucky. I don't know, Benny. More importantly, the Kurjans aren't like the rest of you. They're taller, built differently, and are harmed by the sun. Or at least, they were harmed by the sun until they found some sort of protection."

Dage stepped forward. "I don't suppose either one of you got a chance to ask her how they managed that?"

Benny growled, fire ripping through him. "I'll ask her when she wakes up. She will awaken." He didn't like feeling helpless; he wondered if hitting the king would help him deal with his frustration.

Dage held up a hand. "Calm down. I was just thinking that maybe her reaction has something to do with the fact that her mate, who changed her biology, could not venture into the sun. Could there be a weakness there we had not considered?"

Emma grabbed her ponytail and tugged in exasperation. "I don't know. I've experimented with the Kurjan blood we've had on hand, and it hasn't reacted differently in a test tube than did vampire or demon blood. But test tubes obviously don't create the same environment as the enhanced human female body."

Benny moved around the queen, shoved the coffee table out of the way, and knelt next to Karma. "Fight this, sweetheart. You can do it."

She didn't move.

He gave in and rested his hand over hers, trying to give her some of his strength.

Fire burned his hand and ran up his arm, while an ugly red rash swept along her smooth skin from wrist to neck. Blisters formed instantly.

"Crap." Emma jumped off the chair and landed on her knees next to him.

Benny's mouth opened, and he snapped it shut, glaring at the raw blisters on his forearm. "I just hurt her."

Emma took out a cream from her bag and liberally rubbed it over Karma's rash. "It's the mating allergy. Apparently it's strong right now. I'm hoping that's a good sign?" She finished and handed the tube to Benny.

Benny didn't want to feel better. "If her mating is stronger rather than weaker, as evidenced by this fucking rash, then I'm thinking it is *not* a good sign." Had he gone and allowed her to end her life? What had he been thinking? They'd rushed into this because of his egotistical idea that he'd give her a bunch of money and teach her to be independent and have a fun life. He was an asshole.

Dage peered at the rash over Emma's shoulder. "If her body is fighting the virus, the mating allergy should be weaker, right?"

"I don't know," Emma whispered. "It seems that her mating bond is beating the virus right now. I'd give her another dose, but that would most likely kill her after negating the bond. If it can be negated." She looked at Benny. "Are you sure her mate is dead?"

"Yes. She said he's been dead for at least two centuries."

Emma reached for the thermometer and pulled it out, aiming the red glow at Karma's head. She read the screen and stood. "She's at one hundred fifteen. We have to get her into an ice bath. Now."

Chapter Nine

Karma drifted in and out of consciousness. Different things touched her. There was something very cold, something hot, something furry, something prickly, something hard. So many somethings, so many surfaces.

So many dead people all around her. Where had they all come from? She wasn't feeling well enough to help them all right now.

Linda hovered at her side, her black hair almost down to her waist, her light brown eyes filled with concern. "Karma? Where are my babies? You promised you'd protect them. Where are they?" Her voice echoed as if she were stuck in a chamber of some sort.

Karma tried to answer her and provide some reassurance, but her voice refused to work.

Linda came closer and grabbed Karma's arm with fingers that burned with the cold. "Where are my babies? You have to find them. You have to take care of them."

The frozen pain burned through Karma's veins, and she cried out. "Stop. Please, stop," she begged, trying to pull away.

"Karma. Hold still." The voice was firm and the pressure on her shoulder wide. A big hand held a furry blanket to her.

She obeyed instantly, seeking the voice. She knew it. Breathing in, she caught a scent. Citrus and wild forest. "I can't do it," she whispered.

"You can and you will." Minty breath brushed her ear as the voice grew closer. "Hold still and let the virus do its job."

That wasn't what she'd meant. "But—"

"Nothing. Take a deep breath in. *Now*," he ordered.

She breathed in, letting her lungs expand fully. That was not a voice to ignore.

"Good. Do it again," he said.

She breathed in and out, trying to take in more of his scent. More of his strength.

"Good. Now imagine the virus breaking the mating bond of a male you didn't want. You've carried that with you for too long, and it's time to be free. Stop fighting it," he ordered.

"Bossy Benny," she mumbled.

His laugh lightened something inside her. "Now," he said, his tone gentler this time.

"Yes, now," Linda whispered on her other side, no longer trying to hurt her. "You have to do what they say. Let the virus win. Please. For our babies. Yours and mine—our girls, Karma. Our sweet, kind, innocent twin girls."

Karma dug deep, imagining those bonds with Kraig unraveling as easily as a well-worn skirt. She watched the ribbons untie inside her, separating for all time. When the last wisp of the bonds trailed off into nothingness, she sighed.

"There you go," Benjamin said. Something firm and soft and delicious tickled her ear.

Had he kissed her?

She forced her eyes open and jerked her head as a soft light tried to pierce her brain. Crying out, she shut them again.

"Slower," Benjamin said.

She slowly started to open her eyes, but a massive vampire soldier hovered near her.

He leaned toward her. "I'm Franco. Tell Jayleen that it's okay. I want her to be happy." Then he dissipated.

She opened her eyes, focusing on Benjamin's face, which was very close to hers. His eyes were a fierce green rimmed by black that cut through the green with jagged edges. "Wow," she breathed. Never in her life had she imagined eyes like that.

He leaned back slightly. "You with me?"

"I don't know," she said, trying to move her arms beneath the heavy blanket.

The queen peered over Benny's shoulder, her eyes tired and her hair all over. Fine lines of exhaustion spread out from her pink mouth. "You were right, Hope. She had to *decide* to break the bonds."

A very pretty teenager slid up next to Emma. She had curly brown hair and stunning eyes so blue they looked violet. She and the queen were about the same height. "I had a dream. Some woman named Linda told me what to tell you. Do you think it was fate?"

Emma tapped her lips. "Who knows. I guess the other people who took the virus negated the bonds on their own, since they all wanted the bonds gone. Interesting, right?"

Benjamin rolled his eyes, and they returned to their customary metallic conflagration of colors. "Emma? Back up, would you? I don't want to talk science right now." His gaze softened. "Karma? Baby? Are you back or what?"

Karma drew her hand up to press against her eye. Her arm was bare. She frowned and took stock. "I am naked beneath these blankets."

"Yes." Emma leaned farther over Benjamin. "We had to put you in an ice bath. Several, actually."

Several ice baths? Karma wiggled her toes. "How long was I...out?"

"Three days," Benjamin said grimly, sitting back on his chair.

Three days? Karma gasped and then looked around. She lay in a hospital bed in a modern infirmary with soft green walls and counters with medical equipment. A machine beeped just beyond her head, and an IV trickled liquid into her arm. "Oh." Then she coughed. "Tell Jayleen that Franco says it's okay."

Emma's eyebrows rose. "Huh?" She cut a look at Hope.

Karma tried to concentrate. "Sometimes spirits talk to me. Did that make sense?"

Emma slowly nodded. "Yeah. Jayleen's mate, Franco, died a century ago, and she's been thinking about taking the virus but has been struggling."

That made sense. Karma's heartbeat felt slow still. "Well, Franco came to me and said to tell Jayleen that it's okay. She has his blessing."

"That's nice, but let's concentrate on the living right now." Benjamin felt her forehead quickly. "The fever is gone." Then he put his hand back on her head. "Let's see what else is gone."

Emma slapped his shoulder. "Give it a day, for goodness' sake. We don't know that it's all out of her system."

"I felt it unravel," Benjamin said, his eyes intense. "Can't explain it, but I felt it. There's no mating bond left."

Karma held perfectly still. No pain emanated from his touch. No rash. Relief filled her a few seconds before dread and fear slammed hard. Tears filled her eyes.

Alarm flashed in Benjamin's gaze, and he removed his hand. "What's wrong? Did that hurt? Is the allergy back?"

"No." A couple of tears slid down Karma's face.

He looked at Emma over his shoulder, but she seemed confused as well.

Emma's brow furrowed. "Are you sad the mating bond is gone? I'd thought you didn't really know or like your ex-mate. I didn't expect that you'd be sad."

"I did not truly know or like him," Karma affirmed, feeling small and vulnerable. And naked.

Benjamin patted her shoulder and studied her eyes, obviously trying to dig deep. His expression cleared. "Oh. I get it."

Karma tried to breathe again. Having him close was disrupting her system. "Excuse me?"

Wisdom darkened his eyes. "Even though you didn't want to be mated, that bond was still a protection for you. A shield of sorts—no other male could mess with you. Touch you. There's safety in that."

Her mouth gaped open. *She* hadn't even figured out the source of her tears yet. "Are you psychic?"

"No." His lips firmed. "I don't tell many folks because it's kind of wimpy, but I'm a mite empathic. I feel everything. Usually I shield well, but I think I've got you."

Now the fear took a different form. Hopefully, he could not read her that well. God knew what he'd do if he discovered she was working for the Kurjans, that they could see and hear him right now.

Benjamin smiled. "You're a free female. Congrats."

Oh, she was nowhere near free. "Thank you," she whispered, the lie cutting her deep.

* * * *

Hope Kayrs-Kyllwood left the infirmary after passing on the weird news from the lady in her dream and walked through the lodge to the playroom, dodging outside to a small alcove containing chairs and a fireplace. She flicked the switch to ignite the fire, letting the heat take the chill out of the rainy afternoon. The lake spread out before her, a dark gray beneath autumn clouds.

She sat and kicked her legs out, putting her feet near the fire. Then she looked at the clock on her phone for the zillionth time that day.

Where was he? He should be back by now.

A couple of guards strolled by, and both smiled at her before continuing along the cement path beside the lake. She reached for a blanket from the cupboard next to her and settled it over her lap. Then she snuggled into the furry plushness of it and waited for her best friend.

She didn't hear him arrive. One second the path was clear, and the next Paxton stood there. Giving a happy cry, she launched herself out of the chair and into his arms. "Pax!"

He chuckled and easily caught her, feeling even bigger than he had last time they'd hugged. "You didn't get any taller these last six months."

She smacked his chest and stepped away, taking inventory of him. "You did. Again." He'd been tall for years, and now, at six and a half feet, he was probably as tall as her dad. But her dad was all muscle, and Pax was still gangly, although his chest had filled out with some muscle. His green eyes sizzled, and his black hair had grown to his shoulders. She grinned. "You need a haircut."

He laughed and took her hand, leading them back into the alcove. "It's chilly. Let's sit by the fire."

She rolled her eyes but followed suit, retaking her seat and settling the blanket over her lap. "Not you, too."

He sat to the side of the fire. "You had a bad cold, Hope."

She should never have Zoom called with him while she'd been sick last week. "It was probably allergies."

He shrugged. "Even if it was allergies, you shouldn't have gotten sick. Vampires and demons and whatever else you are don't get sick. It's worrisome."

Had her goofy best friend just used the word 'worrisome'? "Dude. Did you get a new vocabulary or what?"

Pax grinned, flashing twin dimples. At sixteen, he was even cuter than he'd been as a chubby toddler. "Sorry. For the last month, it was only Uncle Santino and me in the wilderness watching the ecosystem of lizards. I've started to talk like him. It won't last long."

Who cared? It was amazing to see Pax happy and safe with his uncle, although his Uncle Santino was more of an absent-minded professor than a soldier. Pax's mom had died years ago, and his dad had been a jerk who'd hit him. "I'm glad you two had fun, although six months is a long time." She'd missed Pax so much, especially since their friend Libby had moved away three years ago.

"I know. I missed you." There was a new intensity to Pax's eyes, and it did funny things to her stomach.

This was her best friend. He'd always been good-looking but a little chubby, and now he was filling out with muscle, so it made sense that he'd be attractive. But they were just friends. She fiddled with the silver butterfly ring that he'd given her for her birthday years ago. She'd finally grown into it.

He caught the movement and took her right hand. "You're still wearing it."

"Of course," she whispered, her throat suddenly dry. "You're my best friend. Well, you and Libby."

He kept her hand and looked up, his gaze searching. "What about Drake?"

Hope had never lied to Pax, and she wasn't going to start now. "I don't know. I feel like we're good friends, and I'd love to see him again in a dream." It had been three years since she'd seen Drake, and she didn't know why it had been so long since she'd been able to create a dream world where they could meet when they were both asleep.

Pax released her hand and leaned back, watching her. "He's a Kurjan. You can't be friends." Even so, his expression was thoughtful.

"Sure, we can." Her voice rose. Why couldn't she get into the dream world to see Drake? Then she paused. "You know, last time I talked to him…"

"No," Pax said. "Definitely not."

She perked up. "It has to be you, Pax. You were in my bedroom last time I dreamed and met Drake in a dream world. Even before the dream worlds went away, you were usually around. You're the connection."

"No." Pax sounded as tough as any demon soldier now that his voice had deepened.

"Pax." She reached for his hand again. Her parents had met in dream worlds, so it made sense she could also meet friends in such worlds. The only problem was that the worlds had been destroyed during one of the Seven's rituals, or something like that. "You have to stay over tonight. You haven't since that one night when I saw Drake, *the last time*, and we have to see if your being here makes a difference."

"You want me to stay the night?" He sounded hoarse now.

Heat ticked from her chest up into her face. "Yes. Come on. We used to stay the night together all the time before you moved in with your uncle."

His jaw hardened, and for a moment, he looked like his vampire father. "Things have changed, Hope. If I'm staying in your room, I ain't sleeping on the floor."

Her mouth gaped open. Paxton did not just say that. Not her Paxton. "You want the bed?" Why couldn't she breathe?

"You know exactly what I mean," he said, meeting her gaze levelly.

She couldn't speak. Where had this over-the-top immortal bullshit come from? Pax had always been beyond that. "So you're saying you want to fuck me, Pax?"

He drew back.

Oh, two could play at this game. She leaned forward. "That's what you're saying, right? I mean, if that's what you want, shouldn't you have the balls to just say it?" He wasn't the only one who'd grown up a little bit in the last six months, even though he was still the only boy she'd ever kissed—and that was three years ago. Triumph filled her when he looked away.

Until he looked back. "Yes. I want to fuck you."

Now she drew back. "Paxton Phoenix!"

"You started it," he returned.

She sat straighter in the chair. "I did not. You did."

He sighed, looking more like her Paxton again. "It'd be more than fucking between us, and you know it." Then he leaned over and turned the fire higher. "Have you been dating anybody now that you've turned sixteen?"

"No." She'd been busy. "You?"

"Not really." Then he cleared his throat. "I'm always thinking about you."

Chapter Ten

Karma felt quite decadent in the butter-soft boots the queen had provided for her. Even though they were of a modern style, they looked perfect with the long pink and blue floral skirt she wore today. She stood at the glass door leading to the patio of Benjamin's suite, happy to be standing again.

It was her first day out of bed, and already, she was tired.

Rain pattered gently outside as if tuned to her mood, and the lake shimmered a light gray color that was more dreamy than chilly looking.

Her body felt no different with the mating bond destroyed, although the bite mark on her neck had disappeared. Oh, she was still tired, and her limbs were heavy, but the queen had assured her those weaknesses resulted from the high fever she'd endured and would soon dissipate. The queen was definitely one of those romance heroines Karma had read about. They really existed.

A knock sounded on the door, and she partially turned to call out, "Come in." It was an oddity, having the power to allow people into her space, one she had not yet become accustomed to.

There was no reason to get comfortable.

The door opened, and a tall woman, a very tall one, walked inside. She had sandy-blond hair, generous curves, and deep chocolate-colored eyes that looked...worried. "Hello?"

Karma turned from the view outside and strode toward the fireplace, double-checking that the woman was alive and not a spirit here to visit her. "Hello. Are you looking for Benjamin?" The woman studied Karma, her stance somewhat hesitant. She wore dark jeans and a light yellow sweater. "No. I'm looking for you, I think. I'm Sarah. Sarah Pringle Petrovsky." Karma paused. "I am Karma. If I ever had a last name, I do not remember it." She ran through the other woman's names. "You are mated to Max Petrovsky?" The hulking soldier was frightening, that was for sure. Was that why this female appeared scared? "Yes." Sarah hesitated.

Karma gestured her toward the chair on the other side of the coffee table. "I apologize for my manners. I haven't entertained in many years." She took the opposite chair. What in the world did this vampire mate want with her? "Is there something I can do for you?" Was this female going to ask about Virus-27? Did she want to be infected so she could run from her mate? Karma was the last person in the world who could help right now.

Sarah sat in the chair and perched at the edge, her legs so long, her knees poked up. "Benny suggested we meet, and I'd already planned to find you, anyway."

Karma settled her hands in her lap. "Shall I request tea or lunch? Are you hungry?"

"No." Sarah pushed back in the chair. "Thank you, though." She chewed on her lip. "I meant to see you earlier, but I was visiting friends and just got back last night. This morning I had classes—I'm one of the teachers for the Realm kids."

"Oh." Karma warmed to her. "You teach cooking?"

Sarah frowned. "No. Lately I teach physics and tactical warfare, and I'd like to start teaching philosophy soon."

Karma exhaled. A female taught such subjects? The Realm was a much more interesting place than she had thought. "I see." Yet she did not. "I am not familiar enough with those subjects to discuss them."

Sarah fiddled with her earring. "I know. Sorry. I'm just nervous."
Karma tried to make sense of the situation as the rain increased outside. "I do not, I mean *don't*, understand."

Sarah sighed. "You saved Rose, and I wanted to thank you. But then I got nervous. Was she your child? I mean, I know that her parents were human and she was found in an orphanage, but did you adopt her and then give her up three years ago to keep her safe?"

Karma tried to keep up with the tumble of words. Her breath caught, and she leaned forward. "Is Rose well? Have you seen her?"

"Yes." Sarah straightened her shoulders. "We, Max and I, adopted her when she was brought here. We've been trying to have kids for a while, but immortals can take centuries to procreate, right?" She chuckled. "Except the Kayrs family. There must be something in their gene pool."

Karma's chin dropped. "You and that Max adopted Rose?" Oh, Sarah seemed nice enough, but Max was a killer. She knew one when she saw one.

"Yes."

Karma bit the inside of her lip. "I did not adopt Rose. I only knew her for a short time before Benjamin rescued her."

Relief flashed across Sarah's freckled face. "Oh. Okay. Well then, thank you."

A scream sounded down the hallway outside, and then giggles erupted. The door opened, and Max strode inside with Hope Kayrs-Kyllwood over one shoulder and a pretty blond toddler over the other. They both were thrashing and giggling, with a squeal or two thrown in. Max dropped to his knees and tossed them both safely on the sofa.

Karma's mouth dropped open. The deadly soldier's face was gentle, and with amusement dancing across his blunt features, he appeared charming.

The little girl launched herself at him. "Get Daddy! Hope, get Daddy now!" Her little fingers dug into the warrior's neck.

"That tickles," Max complained, leaning forward and pressing a kiss on her upturned nose. "Calm down for a second, Rosy. You have a nice chat with your mama, and then I'll take you sailing later this afternoon if the rain stops. But you have to wear your pink coat."

The little girl sat back and crossed her arms, her small face scrunching up. "No coat."

The soldier smiled and tugged on her ear. "Little girls who don't wear coats end up getting colds, and then they can't eat ice cream."

Rosy, her chubby cheeks a lovely red, frowned. She seemed to think about it. "Okay. Coat."

"That's my girl." The tenderness in Max's tone couldn't be misinterpreted.

Rosy tilted her head, mischievousness in her smile. "Can Burt come?"

Max sighed. "Last time we took him, he jumped in and I had to swim after him." He looked over his shoulder at his mate. "Never met a dog that couldn't swim on its own to the shore."

Rose giggled. "My doggie is funny."

Karma straightened. When Rosy had been with her, she'd talked about a doggie all the time. "You got your doggie?"

Rose's eyes sparkled. "Yep. I knews I was gonna have him. Had dreams about him, and we gots him."

Max sighed. "She named him Burt the Babykins. We've shortened the name to Burt—usually." He smacked Hope on the knee and stood, turning to face Karma. "Are you feeling better?"

Numb, she could only nod.

"Good." He turned and brushed his hand along Sarah's arm before pressing a kiss to the top of her head. "Sarah, you should come sailing with us after class. The weather is going to turn soon, and we'll have to get out the ice skates."

Delight brightened Sarah's already pretty face. "That sounds like a plan. Maybe we should get Garrett out on the water. I'm worried about him, Max."

Max ran his knuckle along his mate's cheekbone. "So am I, *Malaya*. I'll see what I can find out." With a tug to her ear, he prowled to the door and left the room. In his wake, the energy in the room calmed, and three sets of eyes turned to study Karma.

Hope smiled. "It's nice you're feeling better."

Karma couldn't look away from the toddler. She was absolutely adorable. Her thick hair was in two ponytails, and she was dressed in jeans and a soft-looking green sweater that had bunnies on it.

Rose looked shyly at Karma. "Hi!" she shrieked.

Sarah laughed. "Inside voice, baby."

"I know!" Rose screamed, launching herself at her mother. "Inside voice!"

Sarah caught her easily and settled the girl on her lap. She laughed. "Sorry about that, Karma. We're going through an interesting phase."

"A loud phase," Hope interjected, curling one leg beneath the other on the sofa. "Although it's better than the phase where she would only eat blue foods. Turning bananas blue was just gross."

"Gross!" Rose agreed loudly.

Hope laughed, turning toward Karma. "Anyway, Rose wanted to meet you, and we wanted to thank you for saving her and bringing her to all of us. I babysit her when Sarah has class and I don't, and it's like having a little sister. A loud little sister sometimes." Her blue eyes sparkled.

"Sisters!" Rose yelled.

Sarah cuddled her close and snuggled her nose into the girl's hair. "I'd like for this phase to be done, but I'm worried about the next one." She lifted her head, delight in her eyes. "Okay. Not worried. But definitely curious."

Karma's arms ached for her girls. Were the twins safe right now? Were they asking for her?

Hope laughed. "I hope the next phase is her picking up her toys. That'd be a fun one."

"Toys!" Rose agreed. Then she looked at Karma. "Karma!"

Delight filled Karma. Maybe the little girl somehow remembered her. How wonderful would it be to introduce her girls to Rose. They would all be great friends. But that was not to be. Even now, the Kurjans were watching Rose through Karma's eye. Would they try to retake her someday? They'd have to go through the Realm, Sarah, and Max. All of a sudden, Karma was thankful Max seemed so dangerous. "I'm glad you've found a good home, Rosy," Karma whispered.

Rose smiled and bounced on her mom's legs. "We're going sailing. Wanna come?" Her voice lowered to a normal decibel. Then she frowned. "But you hafta wear a coat. Daddy's rules." The sweet little girl rolled her eyes and shook her head as if life was just too much right now.

Humor bubbled up through Karma, and she laughed. Finally, her mind could be at rest about the toddler. She was safe, and she was obviously loved. "While sailing sounds fun, I believe we're flying out in a couple of hours." Benjamin had said they needed to leave the Realm before he punched the king, and she believed him.

Rose's lips pouted. "But you haven't met Pax yet. He's my bestest friend."

"Hey," Hope protested, grinning.

Rose smiled, her eyes glimmering with mischief. "You like my sister. Pax my boyfriend."

Sarah cuddled her even closer. "You are way too young for a boyfriend, girlie. Pax can be your friend, but he's too old for you, anyway."

Rose settled into her mother's arms. "Paxton is pretty."

Hope snorted. "Don't tell him that. He thinks he's all tough these days."

"Who is Paxton?" Karma asked, remembering the implant in her ear too late.

"He's a demon-vampire hybrid," Hope said, shifting on the sofa. "He's our friend, and for some reason, Rose thinks he's the greatest thing on two feet. If you ask me, he's gotten a little, well, male this year." She rolled her eyes much better than the little girl had. "Boys are a pain, right?"

"Right," Karma agreed, thinking about Benjamin. He'd been treating her like glass while obviously trying to build her confidence at the same time. If he told her one more time that she was strong and capable, she might just smack him and prove it. If he thought she was that wonderful, he wouldn't be trying to make her independent before he left her somewhere with a pile of money.

Sarah leaned forward. "Karma? You just seriously went somewhere in your head. You okay?"

Karma sighed. "I was thinking about males being *males*. They're too much."

Sarah smiled. "I think they only get worse with age. It's too bad you're not staying another night. We have a girls' poker game tonight, and we often spend a little time complaining about our mates. Emma is on a tear these days because she's close to another medical breakthrough, which makes her obsessed, and she forgets to eat or sleep. Then the king gets all bossy, and I swear, his solution is to toss her in the pool."

Hope shrugged. "It works for them. Plus, Em likes to swim."

Karma enjoyed listening to these tales. She'd had no idea life could be unrestricted and free. "I like that you can voice your opinions with your mates."

Hope's eyebrows lifted. "Why wouldn't we be able to?"

The fact that she could even ask the question gave Karma hope. Real hope. Perhaps the world could change for everybody—even the Kurjans.

Chapter Eleven

Benny set the helicopter down right outside Seven territory while watching the silent woman in the passenger seat. They'd stayed at Realm Headquarters until he thought Karma was well enough to travel. Then he couldn't wait to get the heck out of there. Dage didn't like having the Seven in his territory, and that was fine with Benny.

Right now, Garrett snored in the backseat after being up all night partying. The family had been pissed at his departure, but he hadn't given them a choice. Something really was going on with the youngest Kayrs, but Benny hadn't figured out what yet. Right now, Karma came first.

He let the engines on the bird die down. Almost immediately, a cover emerged from the mountainous rock to enclose them, safely hiding the helicopter from the sky.

She watched the other side fasten to the ground. "That's incredible." Even her voice showed awe.

He grinned. "Yeah. We've been here for a few years, so we've been able to build what we wanted. For a while, our headquarters kept getting blown up. So far, we've been lucky here."

She looked down at her clasped hands.

He reached over and placed his fingers over hers, trying to give comfort. "You're safe here, sweetheart. There's no need to worry about the Kurjans or the Cysts or the virus any longer." He squeezed and then released her. "If you don't want to stay here, I'll take you somewhere else. Once I'm sure you're good on your own, I'll let you be." There was no question the woman wanted her freedom. He didn't blame her, although the more he was around her, the more he wanted to stick with her.

But she deserved more than a life saddled with someone like him. Now he just had to convince her of that fact. "I thought it was really impressive how you fought off the virus and then let it take care of the bonds. You have a lot more strength than you know."

The look she gave him was both adorable and disbelieving. "Right. I almost died."

"You did not." He rolled his eyes. "Why don't you think you're strong?" Part of his plan was getting her to see her own power.

She wrung her hands together.

"Is it possible you don't see the real you because you've been living with assholes the last two centuries?" He asked the question as gently as he could.

"Anything is possible, Benjamin," she said quietly, sounding as if she might be starting to believe it. "Although I can't even dress like a modern woman without feeling uncomfortable. It's not as if I can fight in a long skirt, you know?"

Garrett jumped out of the back of the craft. "I'm going to run to my cabin. You two have a nice day." He easily strode through the open archway and disappeared into the trees.

Benny stared at the trees for a minute. He needed to get Garrett alone to see what had crawled up his ass—and soon. For now, Benny opened his door and circled the craft to open hers, lifting her down with his hands on her waist. Instant desire slammed through him, heating his body as if he'd jumped into a hot spring. "This way." He released her and opened the door to the outside, where a golf cart was hidden beneath the boughs of a pine tree.

She followed and sat gracefully in the passenger side. "This is your headquarters?" For some reason, she now sounded hesitant, as if she didn't want to be there.

"Yes." He sat and turned the key before pressing on the gas pedal. "We took our cue from the Realm, years ago, and built a nice little subdivision here in the Utah mountains for the Seven. We have a central lodge and our own homes, which has been nice since a few of us have gotten mates. Which we were not supposed to do."

She looked toward him, steadying herself with a hand on the metal dash. "You weren't supposed to mate?"

"No." He'd given her as much time as he could before starting to question her about the Kurjans and the Cysts, and he hated for this time to end. "The final ritual will kill many of us. So taking a mate doesn't make sense." That fact hadn't stopped several of his brethren from taking the plunge, anyway. "Ronan, Quade, Ivar, Adare, and Logan have all mated." At this time, he was in the minority. "Only Garrett and I haven't mated, and Garrett seems to have another destiny in store for him. So the sacrifice comes down to me."

"Sacrifice?" she whispered.

It was only fair to give her the full truth. "Yeah. I'm the only unmated one who can give up his life without regret. I'm telling you this because of the mating mark, just in case you had expectations. I'd be honored if you did, but I don't have much of a future ahead of me."

She shook her head. "Why you?"

That was quite the question. "Exactly. I don't know. I mean, we all planned to sacrifice our lives during the final ritual, because that was the deal. Each one of these guys fought the idea of matehood, and each one fell on his face and took the chance anyway. I won't do that to you. You've already lost one mate, and who knows if you'd survive taking the virus again. I'm not worth that."

"You're not worth that? Are you insane?" she asked.

"Some would say," he agreed, glancing at the face of his phone. "Oh. Mercy has dinner waiting in the main lodge for us. It will probably be a more comfortable place for us to grill you, just so you know. I've held off as long as possible."

Karma jolted. "Grill me?"

He coughed out a laugh. "Not like a steak, sweetheart. But you have lived with our enemy for centuries, and we have a lot of questions for you. I wanted to wait until you were more comfortable and everything, but we probably do need to get on it." He turned and winked at her. "Don't worry. You can handle anything we throw at you."

"You're going to throw things at me?" Her brow wrinkled.

He let the laugh loose this time. The woman truly had been sheltered. "You're a fun one, Karma. You really are."

* * * *

Karma was accustomed to hiding her feelings and masking exhaustion after working long hours for the Kurjan nation, so she naturally slid into the familiar role as Benjamin led her into what he called the main lodge of the Seven. It was much smaller than the one at the Realm but built with wide logs that had been finely cut. The main room appeared to contain a few sofas and not much else. In the dining area, she sat at a round table that would comfortably seat twenty people.

Had the Kurjans caught Benjamin's mention of the mating mark on his hand? She couldn't worry about that and instead studied the area.

The table was of hand-carved cedar, and the chairs matched with the addition of bright red cushions. Oil paintings decorated the walls, but she couldn't get close enough to see signatures. Glass French doors comprised the final wall and appeared to lead out to the forest and a mountain range. She'd have to look at the area in the daylight.

Benny held out her chair, and she sat, feeling more comfortable when he sat next to her. "All right. Here we go. We're missing three members of the Seven as well as their mates, so it'll be a smaller group than usual tonight." He gestured toward a green-eyed demon who looked familiar. "That's Logan Kyllwood and his mate, Mercy O'Malley."

Mercy had shoulder length, curly brown hair, one blue and one green eye, and her smile was contagious. "Hi. This is my sister, Haven." She manacled a blonde around the neck and yanked her so close their heads smacked. "We only found out we were sisters about five years ago. I'm a Fae. She's part demon and part Fae, which makes her a little crazier than me."

Haven shoved Mercy away and smiled. "I am nowhere near as crazy as Mercy. Trust me." She had one black eye and one green and luxuriously thick blond hair. She patted the muscled male next to her. "This is my mate, Quade Kayrs. I think you already met briefly?"

Quade just nodded at her, his gaze seeking. Curious and intense.

All right. This wasn't so bad. She'd been afraid she'd have to meet everyone at once, and as much as she wanted her girls to be safe, the less information she could send back to the Kurjans, the better. Six people for dinner wasn't so many, and thus far, no ghosts had visited asking for favors.

Until the French doors opened and two more males stalked inside. One was Garrett, and he didn't look any more peaceful after his run. The second looked shockingly like Logan, except his eyes were a darker green.

Logan motioned with a tilt of his head. "You've met Garrett. This is Sam, my older brother."

"Hi," Sam said, taking the seat next to his brother. Garrett sat over on the other side of Quade, immediately reaching for the platter of steaks in the middle of the table.

"Hi," Karma said quietly. She had been ordered to ask questions, but she didn't want to betray these people who'd been nice to her so far. She also didn't want to betray Benjamin. But if she didn't do her job, the twins would be harmed. "Are you a member of the Seven, Sam?" She already knew that he was not.

"Nope. I'm just visiting my brother." He poured wine from a bottle and passed the glass on to Quade.

It was good that he'd lied. The Kurjan nation already knew he had a role to play in the upcoming ritual, but they didn't know what that was. At least, that's what Terre had told her while training her for this obscenity. She smiled. "It's nice to visit family. I've missed mine for so long."

Sam smiled, looking even more like his brother. "It definitely is nice to see everyone."

Benny took the salad bowl, dumped piles on their salad plates, and passed them along. "Please tell me that Logan cooked, not Mercy."

Mercy threw a roll at Benny, which he easily snatched out of the air and placed next to his salad. "I made the salad, Logan grilled the steaks, and Haven baked the potato dish and dessert. Start being nice, or you don't get any huckleberry pie." She rolled her eyes. "Ignore his manners, or lack thereof, Karma. If he doesn't learn them soon, he's going to find another snake in his bed."

Benny gave a mock shudder. "That's just cruel of you, Mercy. Logan, control your woman."

Logan snorted and reached for the wine. "You deserved that garden snake in the bed, and you know it. Besides, I'd rather have her evil genius directed toward you than me." He leaned over and kissed Mercy on the cheek. "Isn't that right, baby?"

"Yep." Her smile at Benny was a little evil.

Karma had never seen such interactions. There were some Kurjan mates who seemed to feel love, but even they didn't have this much, well, fun. For the very briefest of moments, she let herself dream. What would it be like to belong here? With Benjamin? She'd heard of females enjoying the act of love, and by the way her body reacted to his nearness, she might find simple pleasure with him. It was too much to hope for, but still, heat slid into her face.

Quade chewed on a roll and then cleared his throat. "Have the Kurjans created a plan to set Ulric free?"

Karma sipped on the red wine. It was full-bodied and warming. "I have no idea. You must understand that I'm not privy to the soldiers' plans." It was unthinkable, actually.

Mercy poured herself more wine. "That makes sense, since you're not a soldier. Don't worry. Do you know how many women they've managed to kidnap over the last few years? We've stopped several attempts, but I know we haven't rescued them all."

Karma tried to remember anything that would help, but she'd been kept in the dark. "I really don't. Sometimes I hear about shipments, but that's all. Before you ask, I have no idea where kidnapped females are being taken or held." That was also the truth. Terre had made sure she had no information just in case the Seven tortured her.

Benny slid an arm over the back of her chair, and his protective warmth surrounded her. "It's okay, Karma. Do you know why they're trying to kidnap enhanced human females?"

"I am not privy to the plans of the soldiers, but I do understand that some are to become mates." Karma cleared her throat. "I don't really know what's to become of the rest."

"There's one plausible explanation that we haven't talked about." Garrett looked up, his gaze tortured. "What if somebody wants to replicate the ceremony Ulric performed so long ago? They might attempt to create another impenetrable Cyst general." He looked at Karma. "Who's in charge of finding enhanced women, and who's in charge of the Cysts right now?"

Numbly, Karma tried to think through the issue. Such cruelty wasn't possible, was it? "General Jaydon is in command of the Cyst soldiers, and he's also the one in charge of finding enhanced females."

Benjamin cocked his head and studied her. "What else? I can tell there's more."

Karma squirmed on her chair but gave him the truth. "Jaydon is quite proud that he's one of Ulric's direct descendants and shares the same genetics."

The dark swear word Benny said made her jump. She set down her fork. So much for dinner.

Chapter Twelve

Benny paced a track on the back deck of his quaint cabin, trying to let the sound of rushing water soothe him. Nope. Not even close. The woman slept quietly in the one bedroom, having gone to bed hours before. She was so close to him right now that his body felt electrified.

At dinner, when she'd all but curled into his side, his body had started a slow burn that was just getting hotter. He wanted her with a ferocity he could never appease, and that was a pisser. Oh, she was a home-and-hearth kind of lady—no way was she into carnal pleasure and a sweet goodbye. All he had to give right now was sex, and she deserved more.

His phone buzzed, and he yanked it from his pocket to check the screen before answering. "Logan? What the hell? It's past midnight."

"I need to see you. Main computer room. Now." Logan disengaged the call.

Benny lowered his head and stared at the now-blank screen. Was Logan fucking kidding? The kid didn't give him orders, whether or not he thought he was all grown-up with a crazy-assed fairy mate to protect. Benny had centuries on him. "Somebody's going to get a butt kicking tonight," he muttered, setting the cabin alarms and then jogging down the one street of the subdivision toward the lodge. Mercy had better not get in his way. He'd never hurt a female, but Logan was in for some pain. Right now.

He reached the lodge and shoved open the door before tapping the right area of the wooden wall to the left. It slid open and revealed stairs leading down. "You'd better be down here and ready," he threatened, taking the steps four at a time. He landed at the bottom and turned to find Logan, Garrett, and Mercy at the computer console.

Mercy was pale and wouldn't meet his gaze.

He stopped. Dread dropped into his gut. "What?"

Logan typed into the keyboard, gesturing toward the widest screen on the wall. "I was alerted at dinner that there was a computer glitch, but I ignored it because we've been having problems that occur right after helicopters land near the bunker. I just took a moment to look, and boy, we have a new problem."

An alert came up, and then a holographic view of the entrance to the lodge. It showed the time, hours ago, when Benny had escorted Karma in to dinner. The screen started to blink, a red warning crossed, and then a buzzer rang.

Logan typed more, and the screen narrowed to Karma's face and then went deeper, showing something red and glowing inside her head.

Benny whistled. "What is that?"

Logan typed and the device circled out of her head and across the screen. "As far as I can tell, it's a visual and audio device that transmits everything Karma sees and hears. It's connected to her right eye and ear canal. It's also a homing device, just so you know."

Benny shook his head. Well, this was why they had secondary precautions, wasn't it? And third. "No. The queen scanned her from head to toe. The Realm's technology is the best in the world. The universe, actually." His gut clenched, and his hands heated. This couldn't be true. The sweet and innocent girl from centuries ago couldn't be spying on them. Bile burned his stomach lining.

Logan shrugged. "The Realm is good, but the Kurjans have been catching up technologically for the last fifty years."

Mercy leaned closer to the screen. "It's possible the device was dormant and then somehow activated a specific time after she was rescued. Maybe they figured she'd be scanned upon arrival."

"Or," Garrett said thoughtfully, "maybe somehow they have it programmed to activate after a scanning. That's what I'd do." He grinned. "This is why we're paranoid, man. It's a good thing."

Yeah, Benny had thought the precautions were stupid, but he'd been outvoted. Thank God. He was going to puke. "I've been so gentle with her—she seems so *breakable*."

"Maybe she had no choice," Mercy interjected.

Benny just stared at her. "Even if she didn't have a choice, she's good at lying. I honestly had no idea she was holding anything back. She even asked questions at dinner."

Garrett winced. "We have to go back through everything we've said to her and note everything she's seen since you rescued her. All of that information is in the hands of the Kurjans right now."

"Including our location," Benny said grimly. "It's a good thing we came here first." This was on him. He'd been obsessed with finding her since the marking had appeared on his hand, and now he'd put his entire family in danger. "It figures fate would mess with me like this." Only he would carry the mating mark for the enemy. Yeah, that fit. "It appears sweet Karma and I need to have a talk."

"Wait," Mercy said. "They'll come for her, right?"

Logan crossed his arms. "Yeah, but as long as it seems she can still get information from us, they'll wait. We're safe for the time being." He scratched his neck. "In fact…"

Benny crossed his arms. "We can feed them any information we want." The chains of decency that had been holding him back snapped clean away. "Oh, yeah. It's time for payback."

Mercy swallowed loudly, her eyes dark. "I really don't like the tone of your voice."

"Karma's going to like it even less," he admitted, feeling like a dumbass. Anger crashed through him, and he turned, punching a hole in the wall. Pain ripped through his knuckles and felt *good*. Real. "I was nice to her. Acted like a perfect gentleman. I even fucking stopped fucking *swearing*," he bellowed. "Could I be any more of a moron?" He would've beaten the shit out of anybody else if they'd done something so stupid. At least he'd gone with Garrett's plan and brought her *here*.

Garrett watched him impassively with an empty bottle of Jack next to him. As usual these days. "Listen. This might not be her fault, and you know it. Just ease up. Let's figure out how to use what we've learned to our advantage."

Logan lifted the phone to his ear. "Let's call in Quade and Sam. They're the best strategists I've ever seen."

Benny extended his fingers, gratified to find that one had broken. "All right. Let's do this."

* * * *

Morning brought nicer weather. Karma dressed in a light lilac skirt that reached just above her ankles. Maybe she'd slowly make her skirts shorter until she felt more comfortable revealing her legs. Brown boots and a white sweater completed the outfit. After she'd braided her hair and pinched her cheeks, she strode out to find Benjamin on the deck with a table already set for breakfast. She hurried outside. "I should be making breakfast," she offered shyly.

His smile held so much charm it was hard to breathe. While not classically handsome, he was tough and strong. Masculine. Yes, that was it. Benjamin Reese was all male. "Come sit down."

She did so, carefully spreading the napkin across her lap. Though this escape from the Kurjans was temporary, she felt free. She smiled and focused directly on his intelligent eyes, noting there was more green than usual in those depths. "This is kind of you, Benjamin." Oh, how she wished she knew how to flirt. Then her gaze caught on the windy river just beyond the grass yard behind him. "Your home is beautiful."

His smile deepened. "You're beautiful."

The compliment struck deep, warming her until her fingers tingled. She didn't know what to say. "Thank you." For so long, she'd been just like a piece of furniture that nobody really noticed. She reminded herself that was good. Less notice meant less getting hit. Even so, the feeling of being appreciated as a woman was pleasurable. She reached for the coffee to pour two cups. "What are we doing today?"

He dished out scrambled eggs and toast. "I thought I'd show you around. The area is pretty in the autumn, so we can explore outside. Then I can show you the headquarters and our computer room. It's pretty impressive." He sounded proud.

Oh no. She couldn't let the Kurjans see the Seven's military setup. Benjamin must be trying to impress her. He wasn't thinking clearly. "I would have thought the computer room was private." Perhaps she could help him.

"Yeah, but you're one of us now. I mean, with this and all." He held up his hand, palm out. The marking—an *R* with jagged barbs around it—looked even darker than the last time she'd seen it. His marking.

Panic heated her throat. The Kurjans would have just seen the mating mark. There was no way to hide that from Terre now. What would he do? "I don't understand."

"Well now." Benjamin tossed his napkin on the table and plucked her right out of her chair while hardly stirring from his.

She yelped and stiffened, landing on his hard thighs with a whoosh of surprise. "Benjamin," she whispered.

He smiled and settled her on his lap. "I'm thinking we should explore this marking and the whole situation. Oh, I know I said I couldn't mate, but you've been so sweet, you're hard to ignore."

Sweet? Ignore? She perched as stiffly as she could. She had never, in her very long life, sat on a male's lap. His thighs were hard. Very. The arms around her were steel ropes. The scent of him, masculine and citrusy, cascaded over her along with heat generated by his dangerous body. "This is inappropriate," she whispered, warmth flashing into her face.

"Who cares?" He leaned in, his nose barely touching hers.

Her nipples hardened against her plain bra. Her lungs just up and quit working like outdated kitchen appliances. And her sex softened and pulsed. "I care." Did she? Her body was on fire, and she liked it. Really liked it. What were these feelings? Oh, she'd had sex centuries ago. She'd been attracted to males before. But this was...intense. Direct and needy.

His nostrils flared. "Oh, baby. I can scent your arousal. Free and wild...like a summer storm."

She reeled. They were out of her realm of experience, and she wanted more. Curiosity and something deeper, something that ached inside her, had her placing her palm against his heart. The sheer rock wall of his chest excited her. "Benny," she whispered.

"There you go." He tugged the band off her braid and tangled his hand in her hair, releasing the rows to let her curls free.

She protested, trying to stop him. "Wait. My hair." Having it bound was necessary in the Kurjan nation, and it also gave her a sense of protection.

"It's beautiful." His voice thickened as the mass tumbled around her shoulders. "God. So soft. Captured sunshine."

She blinked, moved by his tone. Her breath panted out. Her gaze dropped to his firm mouth.

His lips curved into a smile. "I knew we were on the same page." Gently and deliberately, he tangled his fingers at her nape, twisting her hair until he controlled her head.

Her eyes widened.

He tugged back, elongating her neck. Then he licked from her clavicle up to her jaw, pausing over her mouth. Tingles cascaded from his tongue, shivering through her.

She held her breath, her entire body jolting with shock.

Then he kissed her. A gentle glide of his mouth against hers. Not enough. She moaned, struggling to get closer. To take his mouth. He held her in place with one hand. Then he smiled against her, his lips firm and the taste of fresh coffee wafting her way. "Patience, baby. You need to learn some." The dominating tone did something unexpected inside her, spinning her out of control and making her pant with need.

She swallowed, holding still. She had no choice. But she could speak. "Either kiss me or let me go." Her voice was breathy and didn't sound like her. At all.

Surprise flared in his eyes and then was quickly banked. "Ask nicely."

The words took a moment to penetrate. Ask nicely? She wanted him. Right now. But he had put her on his lap, and he had started this. Every inch of her wanted to ask nicely. She might be as useful as discarded furniture, and she might not have one ounce of control in this world, but a very long time ago her mother had told her she was stubborn. It turned out her mama had been right. "No," she whispered. "Kiss me or let me go."

The green rippled through his eyes like a shark through the ocean. Then he kissed her.

Chapter Thirteen

Benny took her mouth because he didn't want to let her go. She felt just right in his arms and on his lap, and that pissed him off even more. He'd wanted to kiss her from the first day they'd met, and until the night before, he would've gone slow. Gentle. Kind.

Not now.

Now he gave her all of him. He was demanding and rough, taking her mouth the way he wanted. She tasted sweet and wild, and he got lost, forgetting all about his vendetta. About his plan. About anything but the soft female in his arms and the raw need she aroused in him.

She moaned softly into his mouth and curled into him, dragging her hand through his hair to clutch and yank. Slight pricks of pain, shockingly erotic in the moment, cascaded over his scalp.

He tightened his hold and went deeper, pulling her even closer against his body. Even so, he brushed a hand up her side, feeling each rib, settling against the curve of her breast. The heavy weight of it was so close, and he would've torn that innocent sweater off her in a second if he thought she'd let him keep going.

He didn't want to have to stop.

Ever.

The entire world could've blown up, and he wouldn't have given a damn. He lost himself in her, letting the roaring that filled his ears drown out the desperate demands of the beast at his core. The one that wanted him to strip her naked and sink so deeply into her that neither one of them would ever get free. He was tasting the sun, and those deadly flames ripped through his bones, through his blood, and straight to his cock. There was no other feeling like this one.

He couldn't get enough. Never would there be enough.

She wiggled her little butt against his groin, and the beast howled in triumph. Keeping her mouth, holding her hair, he shifted his weight and pushed her with one shoulder to straddle him. Her hold on his hair tightened, and she swung her other leg over his, grinding her core against him.

Oh, holy fuck.

His hand shot up the back of her sweater on its own, the pads of his fingers brushing her soft skin. Her impossibly soft skin.

She drew up her knees as if trying to sink into his body and grabbed his neck with her free hand, kissing him back with an intensity that detonated parts of him from the inside out, one at a time, each culminating in a fiery explosion that guaranteed he'd never be free.

He caressed her rib cage and then along her leg, sliding that long skirt up her smooth thigh. His cock jumped to attention, trying to get inside her, a roaring monster that also wanted to be free. His thumb scraped her inner thigh, and she gasped, writhing against him.

His tongue swept her mouth and she let him, dueling with him, as caught up in the fire as he.

He brushed the outside of her panties, finding them wet. She trembled, pushing into his hand, her nails raking the back of his neck as she held on.

What had he unleashed? He gave her more, losing himself in the moment. In her. Twisting his wrist, he angled his hand and tapped her clit, still outside her panties.

She stiffened and drew in a sharp breath. Then she lifted herself slightly, her eyes dazed with a glimmer of shock. "Benjamin." She licked her lips and moved against his hand again as if seeking something. The hand in his hair pulled tight again.

He flicked her clit.

Her entire body shuddered, and her eyes widened.

Gently, he slid two fingers beneath the band of her panties and then his entire hand, pressing his thumb square on her throbbing clit while sliding a finger inside her. "Feel good?" he rumbled.

She held perfectly still except for the tremors taking her body and nodded.

"Say it."

"It feels good." Confusion clouded her eyes, competing with need, but she didn't move away. "I haven't felt this before."

He pressed harder, and she arched into his hand, sucking in air. "Lose the innocent act, sweetheart. I don't need it." More than that, he didn't want it. Oh, there was no way she'd been sexually active since losing her mate, but she'd kissed him like she knew what she was doing.

Or maybe she was as caught up as he. It was possible, so he remained gentle. Well, gentle for him. He lightly pinched.

She gasped and dropped both her hands to his shoulders. "Benjamin." It was a moan. "I don't, I mean, I—"

He curled up with the finger inside her, and she stopped talking. Keeping his gaze, she let her weight lower onto his hand, forcing his finger deeper.

"Oh," she breathed.

His cock was about to burst out of his jeans. "What do you want, baby?"

She licked her lips, and he nearly came in his pants. "I don't know," she breathed, tension coiled so tight in her that he could feel it.

"I do." He kissed her again, capturing her lips and taking over. At the same time, he plunged two fingers inside her, deep, and scraped his thumbnail over her clit.

She writhed and then cried out, her body undulating as an orgasm swept through her. He moved his fingers, crisscrossing them, forcing her to ride out the waves until completion. She came down, her body shuddering, her wetness coating his fingers. She blinked several times, her eyes even wider and her mouth set in a small *o*.

He removed his hand, and keeping her gaze, he licked his fingers clean. Instantly, he was obsessed with her sweet taste, wanting more. Now.

Crimson swept over her high cheekbones, making her eyes even more mysterious than before. They were dazed. It was all he could do not to strip her bare right then and there. But the Kurjans were watching…and listening. For the briefest of moments, he'd forgotten. Completely.

She came back to reality and slowly released his shoulders.

He smiled, right into the camera. "That was a nice start, wasn't it?"

* * * *

Karma couldn't breathe. She couldn't think. Even as Benjamin placed her back in her chair, her focus would not return. So that's what a good climax felt like. She'd had no idea. Was Benjamin magic? Or was it because of the mating mark on his hand? No, that couldn't be it. Her mate, years ago, had held a mark for her. She didn't remember the few times they'd engaged in sex feeling like that. It surely had not.

"Eat your eggs before they get cold." Benjamin dug into his breakfast as if the world hadn't just shifted.

How could he be so casual? Was this normal behavior these days? She could not believe that. Her hand trembled, but she grabbed her fork. Everything inside her wanted to run fast and hard to a dark corner so she could huddle and think. To mull through what had just happened. Did he think less of her? Shame felt like a heavy balloon in her chest that expanded to her belly. The Kurjans had seen what happened. Wait a minute. Her eyes had been closed. Had she made noise? If not, they did not know. Oh, surely they knew, or suspected, but maybe not. Maybe they thought she'd just kissed Benjamin and closed her eyes.

Even though she was confused, she hated the thought that Terre knew what had just happened. That he'd shared in that.

This was hers. And Benjamin's. Even though the moment had obviously not meant anything to him. Tears pricked her eyes, and she belatedly wondered if the device in her head would short-circuit from the water.

Probably not. Unfortunately.

"There now. Don't do that." Benjamin looked up, his gaze darkening.

She shoved emotion away as she'd learned to do through the years. The tears disappeared.

He watched her like a bird of prey, emotions crossing his rugged face that she could not decipher. Then his face softened. "Are you all right?"

The tears threatened again. But she would not discuss this with the Kurjans listening. "I am fine." She had to change the subject. "There seems to be a nice path along the river. Do you walk it often?"

His gaze became shielded. "Sometimes. Do you want to scout the path?"

Scout? What an odd expression. "I like to walk." If she asked too many questions, she'd raise his suspicions. If she didn't ask any, the Kurjans would be angry, and Terre had threatened to harm her girls. She did not know how to proceed. She was not a spy, for goodness' sake. Her orange juice sparkled in the sun, looking delicious, and she lifted the plain jar that served as a glass. How quaint.

"You could mate anybody now, Karma." Benjamin drank some of his coffee, and his throat moved as he swallowed. Even that looked strong and dangerous. "Thank God you don't have to mate another one of those pale, wimpy, limp-dicked Kurjans again, right?"

She coughed on the juice, setting it down and wiping her mouth. There was no way to answer that insult to the Kurjan males. "I had not thought about it," she lied. There was no question Terre planned to mate her when she returned. She'd hoped to grab her girls and run first, but the opportunity had never arisen. It was as if he knew she wanted to go, even though she'd always been polite around him. "I did not think the virus would work."

Benjamin waved a hand. "But now that it has, you're lucky. I can't imagine how awful it was for you with a loser Kurjan. I've heard their dicks are like miniature hot dogs. How sad for their females."

Her mouth dropped open. She reached for her toast, an inappropriate amusement teasing a smile from her. The insult would have Terre furious, but that wasn't her fault. The statement also wasn't true, but she was not going to discuss such matters with Benjamin. "What else do the rumors say about the Kurjans?" Surely Terre would want to know that.

Benjamin put more eggs on his plate. "No dicks, sucky lovers, shitty fighters. I'm sure you already knew that. Oh, and the Cyst are really the leaders of the nation. Dayne and his dumbass brother are just figureheads."

Her stomach rolled over. That was not true. She had to at least look as if she was trying to correct him. "The Cyst are a good fighting force as well as the spiritual leaders of the Kurjan nation. But Dayne and Terre lead everyone." Dayne did, anyway. Terre was his right-hand male.

Benjamin laughed, the sound arrogant. "That's funny. Dayne and Terre. I heard that Dayne is obsessed with becoming a Cyst, and that Terre prefers to be told what to do by females. That he's a sub who likes to be treated like a puppy." Benjamin held up a hand when she gasped. "I make no judgments. If a guy wants to be led around by a leash and have his ass beaten with a crop, it's his deal. Right?"

Leash? Crop? "What in the world are you talking about?" she whispered.

Benjamin nudged her plate closer to her. "Eat up. You're going to need your energy." Then he resumed eating. "I think it's called puppy play or something like that. Obviously you're not caught up on current kink, but that's okay. I mean, you don't have any interest in leading a wimpy male around on a leash, do you?"

She could only shake her head.

Benjamin exhaled. "That's good. I also heard that he likes real dogs to, well, you know. Do him."

Had Benjamin lost his mind? "I have never heard of such a thing," she whispered. Though she did not know Terre's proclivities, he did not seem interested in animals. In fact, he was all too interested in her. "I do not believe your research is accurate, Benjamin."

He just shrugged. "It doesn't matter, right? It's not like you're going back to them." He smiled, flashing his teeth.

"Right," she said, looking back at her breakfast. She'd lost her appetite. Again.

Chapter Fourteen

Terre threw a knife across the room in fury. A young soldier had to duck to avoid being hit, standing back at attention quickly. Dayne laughed, watching the wide screen on the wall of the communications room. "He's just trying to impress her, brother." Oh, Benjamin Reese was going to die a slow, painful, screaming death. Terre refused to look at the Cyst general chuckling by the doorway. Jaydon leaned against the wall, his wide chest blocking the view of the exit. To Terre's left, Drake played a computer game, working on his manual dexterity before combat training started outside.

Drake looked up and studied the screen. "You will have to kill that male for speaking such an insult to your intended."

"Oh, don't you worry. He'll take those words back while drowning in his own blood," Terre gritted out.

"When is she coming back?" Drake asked, looking at Terre but still playing the game with one hand. Impressive.

"Soon," Terre growled. "Why?"

Drake stared back to the screen as Benjamin Reese ate what looked like eggs. "She's the best cook we have, and she's always nice. I don't like leaving her in the hands of the enemy."

Neither did Terre. "Stop laughing, brother." He and Dayne were evenly matched in a fight, and Dayne only led their people because he'd been born first. By one year. If he screwed up, Terre would cut off his head and take the mantle of leadership. However, Dayne had an impressive ability to perceive the entire picture, while Terre knew he became too focused. That made him a better soldier and Dayne a better leader.

For now.

"This is ridiculous," Terre muttered. The bastard had kissed Karma. At the very least. Fury heated his limbs. "Karma is not smart or strong enough to gain us intel, brother. I've been trying to tell you that for three years." He would've fought harder, but he'd needed her to gain access to the Realm Headquarters and the virus so she'd be free for him to take as his mate. He'd waited long enough.

Dayne took notes on a tablet, watching the screen. "We don't require her to be smart or strong. The hybrid is bending over backward to impress her, not seeing her as any sort of threat, which she is not. So his guard is down, and we'll gain invaluable information about the Seven. We already have their location, and we've been searching for years."

Terre held on to his temper. "She won't be able to keep up the pretense for long."

Dayne shrugged. "I disagree. We have the perfect motivation for her with the children. Might I remind you, brother, that she considers them hers. If you mate her, they'll be yours."

Terre snorted. "Hardly. I'm sure we'll have many sons for her to nurture. We don't need human girls underfoot."

Drake looked up. "She cares for those girls. I'd tread carefully. Karma seems sweet, but she has a side to her that looks quite dangerous."

Terre narrowed his gaze. "Do you have a little crush, nephew?"

Drake returned to his game. "She reminds me of a feline. Maybe a cougar. They purr for you but can rip your throat out if displeased." He expertly worked the controls. "Besides. My path is set, so I wouldn't worry about it."

Dayne looked over his shoulder at his son. "Speaking of your path, have you gained access to the Kyllwood girl's dreams again?" "Not yet." Drake leaned forward as the game intensified. "Hope controls the dreams—for now, anyway. But I do feel a shift in the universe that I can't explain. Something tells me I'll be seeing her soon." He spoke with a casualness far beyond his years.

Terre studied his nephew with new eyes. The kid's loyalty was definitely to his father. If Terre ever took out his brother, he'd have to make sure to end Drake at the same time. His nephew's fighting skills were already being noted by the battle-scarred soldiers around them.

The door opened, and Terre sighed. His other nephew strode inside. Terre had taken guardianship of the kid when his twin had died, but the experience had not turned out as he had hoped. Vero was a year younger, an inch shorter, and about a minute slower than Drake when it came to combat. Of course. "What?" Terre asked.

Vero halted and then hurried forward to hand over their newest model pistol. "We've tweaked the mechanism to eliminate three seconds from the internal reload sequence." His black hair lacked red, and his eyes had a tinge of blue through the green. A Kurjan with blue in his eyes. It was unthinkable.

"Good." Terre took the gun. His brother never should have mated that enhanced female years ago—she'd been a gypsy with blue eyes. Killing her had been a pleasure once Terre's twin had died in a battle during the last war. "Shouldn't you be training?"

Vero shuffled his feet. "Yes."

The kid would rather work with guns than shoot one. Terre couldn't believe he'd come from Talt's loins. "I will be displeased if you don't do better than you did yesterday." While he had no idea how well the kid had done, it probably wasn't well enough to discuss.

Drake beat the game and flipped off the console. "I'll go with you." He gracefully stood and loped toward his cousin.

Vero puffed out his chest. "I don't need protection."

"Didn't say you did," Drake said.

Terre grabbed Drake by the arm before he could pass. "Have other kids been picking on your cousin?" He'd beat Vero later for that, but now, family came first.

Instead of answering, Drake slowly looked down at the hand on his arm. The seconds ticked by.

Terre released him when Drake refused to speak. "I asked you a question."

Drake looked up then, and his eyes were a soft purple. "Of course nobody has been picking on Vero. I made sure the last guy who tried limped home to his mama while bleeding from the eyes. Family is family, right?" Without another word, he turned and walked out the door with his cousin on his heels.

An unwelcome chill scattered down Terre's spine.

* * * *

Benny led Karma along the river walk after showing her the lodge and the computer room Mercy had hastily set up the night before. It looked impressive and would actually be full of booby traps within a day. "This is probably our only weakness. I mean, the river."

Karma walked along, her skirt against her ankles. "It's lovely."

Benny eyed the wandering water, the grassy banks on the other side, and the trees that surrounded everything. "I know. We wanted to create a better defensive position, but the females insisted on keeping it peaceful." He shrugged his shoulders as if the whole situation was beyond him. "Nobody knows where we are, so it doesn't much matter, right?"

She tripped on the trail.

He grasped her arm and helped her to stay upright. The sweet wildflower scent of her was killing him, and his balls had no doubt turned a lovely shade of bright blue. When she'd come apart in his arms earlier, it was all he could do not to take it further. Only the fact that she was lying to him and spying for the Kurjans had stopped him from kissing her again. Now he was pissed and aroused, which really was a terrible combination for an asshole like him. He kept her hand. "Let's hold hands."

She tried to pull away. "I don't think—"

"Oh, don't think." He yanked her closer, and her hip bounced off his. "What's it like living with the loser Kurjans?" How much would she admit?

She picked her way along the rocks and stopped trying to reclaim her hand. "It was fine."

Fine? Even he knew when a woman used the word "fine," she didn't mean it. What was she supposed to say if interrogated? How much would she give away with them listening and watching? "Karma? I really need to ask you some serious questions. The others wanted to do this all together around a conference table, but I thought you and I should have some privacy. I'll cover you."

She swallowed. "I really do not know of anything useful to you."

Right. He led her along the bank to a wooden swinging chair Mercy had made Logan install to make the place appear more permanent than it really was. "Let's sit."

She perched on the swing and turned to face him. "Are you angry with me?"

He sat and blanked his expression. "Of course not. Why would you ask that?"

She chewed on her pretty pink lip, her stunning eyes turned toward the river. "I don't know. It's just a different feeling from you, I guess."

He took her chin and drew her face back toward him. A blush washed over her cheeks, and he watched, intrigued. "Do the Kurjans know we have Ulric?"

She gasped. "Excuse me?"

He kept her in place with just a finger and thumb on her delicate chin. While he was at this, he might as well really screw with the Kurjan nation. "You heard me. Ulric, the badass Cyst who killed a hundred enhanced females just to make himself stronger. The loser bastard with no soul. Do they know he's no longer in the prison world we set up? Do they know he's here and we have him in custody?"

She shook her head, her eyes wide. "No. They think Ulric is still trapped on a prison world and is trying to make his way home. Ulric has been released?"

Benny chuckled. "Well, he escaped, anyway. We sure didn't release him. But we caught the bastard again."

She looked down and only glanced back up when he tightened his hold on her chin. "Wh-Where is he?" she whispered, almost as if she didn't want to ask the question.

Benny sighed. There was an excellent chance she was just a pawn in this whole situation, and his anger needed to be directed at the Kurjans, not her. For now, anyway. "You don't need to worry your gorgeous self about that, sweetheart." He sounded just condescending enough to make her eyes narrow. Good to know. Her eye could still narrow with the device implanted. "We have him somewhere he'll never get free—not here. Until the final ritual, of course. Then he goes to hell."

Karma breathed out, looking more than a little stunned. "How did he get free?"

Benny traced her jaw with his thumb, torturing himself. Her skin was soft, and her bone structure had the delicacy of days gone by. The female hadn't had a choice in her life from day one, and he couldn't be angry with her for the demands made on her now. But he had to play his part until the queen finished studying the scan of Karma's head to make sure there wasn't a bomb hidden in there. "I don't worry about the physics of everything. My job is to be ready to take out the enemy, and believe me, I am."

She studied him as if he were a puzzle she couldn't solve. "I'm sorry you have to fight."

Now, that was sweet. "I like fighting," he admitted. "It took me three years and a lot of fights to find you, and it was well worth it."

She grabbed his arm, her small fingers digging in. "Why, Benjamin? I just don't understand why you would put yourself in danger and even get tortured to find me. It does not make sense." Her soft words pierced right through his impenetrable torso to his heart. The female really didn't see her own worth. His ears burned as he realized he'd been using her just as the Kurjans had for centuries. Enough of that. He'd still feed her some information, because he had to, but he was no longer angry with her. So he grinned. "Honey? Fighting the Kurjans is like doing yoga for the day. They're wimps. And torture? Come on. That Terre and Jaydon the creepy Cyst were as good at torture as a dog would be at water skiing. Honest. I was mostly bored."

She scoffed and then caught herself. "Oh, Benjamin."

Okay. He might have to insult them some more, just for fun. The day was looking up.

Footsteps pounded, and he glanced over to find Mercy running toward them full-on. The wild-assed fairy grinned and threw him a phone. "It's Hope Kayrs-Kyllwood. Says some chick named Linda won't stop bugging her about getting Karma to return to her people."

Benny frowned and caught the phone, then handed it to Karma.

"Hello," Karma said, placing the phone against her left ear—the one that didn't have the device attached to it. She listened intently for several moments. "I understand. Yes, she's a ghost, for lack of a better term. Why? I don't know. Thanks." She disengaged the call.

Benny lifted an eyebrow.

Karma shrugged. "I told you, I see dead people. This one has business still with the Kurjan nation." She bit her lip again. "Apparently she found another conduit in Hope. I'm sorry about that."

Oh, there was more to this story. "I see," Benny said. No, he didn't, but he would. How could he get her to open up with the Kurjans listening? Time to shake them up a little. "Honey? I think we should mate. I know it's soon, but the Kurjans will forget all about you if you're mated."

The color drained from her face. "No," she whispered, her voice tortured.

Well. That was a little insulting.

Chapter Fifteen

This was insane—and kind of fun. Paxton Phoenix jumped from the tree onto Hope's roof, angling his body at the right moment to avoid the cameras and sensors set strategically around the property. The night-op glasses he wore showed both, although he already knew where most of the cameras were placed. He'd been sneaking into Hope's room at night as long as he'd been able to walk.

Of course, back then, Hope's parents and probably all of the demon nation had known he was there.

Now they didn't.

He shook off a feeling of unease and a sense of disloyalty at the thought. Hope's dad had always been more than cool with Pax, and three years ago, he'd even made sure Pax had a safe place to live with his uncle. But things had changed. Pax grasped the overhang and flipped over, swinging inside Hope's room to land easily on the floor.

She sat on her bed, her legs crossed, watching the window. "Nice."

He grinned and shut the blinds against the meager moon. It had to be past midnight, and most of the world was already asleep. "Thanks." Her room was as familiar as his own, even though he hadn't visited in over six months. "Where's the ghost?" He'd come the second Hope had texted him about the problem, although he'd never dealt with a real ghost before. Only the ghosts of the past that lived in his head.

She looked around, her eyes pinched. "She's gone. I called Karma earlier today and sent the message along. The ghost just kind of hovered around after that, but she finally disappeared a few minutes ago. Maybe because you got here?" Hope rubbed her blue eyes. "I can't start seeing ghosts, Paxton. There's just too much coming at me right now." The blue design that scrolled up her neck and over her exposed shoulder glowed for a moment. The design of the prophets.

He moved without thinking, kicking off his boots to sit on her bed and take her hand. "You're the strongest person I know. Take a breath and let it out."

She obeyed him instantly, then took another breath and blew it out, and the color returned to her face. "I've missed you."

His chest warmed. "Ditto." It didn't seem possible, but she was even prettier now than she'd been last year. Her eyes were so blue it hurt, and her hair was a little longer, curling down her back. Calling it brown didn't do the lush strands justice. They were brown, gold, and red, an ever-changing mass of color that made his fingers itch to run through it. "Is the prophecy mark bugging you?"

"No." She rubbed her neck. "It's just there. Feels heavy."

There were three prophets on the planet, each one determined by fate, and identified by the marking. They were the spiritual leaders of the Realm, but Hope had never wanted the calling. So far, her parents had shielded her from having to do anything about it.

Paxton intended to do the same, whether she liked it or not. She was in danger, more than she knew, and he'd give his life to protect her.

She sneezed.

He jerked.

She sneezed again and then winced before placing a hand over her ear. "Don't give me that look. It's just a little earache."

"An infection?" he asked.

She nodded. "Yes. I'm taking human antibiotics. Can you believe it?"

"No," he said honestly. Immortals didn't get sick. Hope was the only female alive with vampire blood in her, and combined with her demon, shifter, witch, and who knows what else ancestry, she should be stronger than anybody else. Instead, she seemed to be susceptible to human illnesses. It was unthinkable. "What do the doctors say?"

Hope shrugged. "Same as usual. They don't understand it. I'm an anomaly, remember?"

"If you say you're a freak again, I'm going to lose my temper," he warned her.

She grinned. "So what? Last time we sparred, I kicked your butt."

Yeah, and he'd let her. While he continued to get taller and stronger, she'd stopped growing a while ago. He'd soon be a foot taller and probably a hundred pounds heavier than Hope, at least once he started putting on muscle. "I remember," he said instead.

She yawned widely and covered her mouth with her hand. "Sorry. My mom gave me an antihistamine, and it makes me tired."

He patted her hand. "You should sleep. You don't think you're gonna start seeing ghosts everywhere, do you?"

She hummed thoughtfully. "No. I think I saw that one because she really wanted Karma's attention. It was probably a one-off."

"Good." He had enough to do keeping her safe from corporeal enemies.

She rubbed her ear.

He nudged her in the shoulder until she lay down and snuggled under the covers. "Go to sleep so you can get better. I'll watch for a while and make sure the ghost doesn't come back." Without waiting for her answer, he pushed off the bed and sat beneath the window, listening for footsteps from the patrolling soldiers by the lake. He'd memorized their schedules, but the demon nation was well known for changing routines quickly to make things difficult for the enemy.

He wasn't the enemy, although some would disagree if they knew he was trying to circumvent their security.

Footsteps sounded outside. Yep. Right on time. He crossed his arms and rested his head back against the wall, closing his eyes. His legs were stretched out and crossed at the ankles, but he could be up and across the room in a second if Hope needed help.

Her breathing evened out, and he slowly relaxed. The room was as much home to him as his own, but it felt weird to be there without their third friend, Libby. Libs was a cougar shifter, and her people had left the Realm after learning about the Seven and that the Realm was allied with them.

The alliance was a mistake and a big one. The shifters were correct to oppose it.

He drifted into a light sleep, still at the ready in case something happened.

The sand beneath his toes was a mellow pink that felt warm. He looked around the beach, where waves rolled peacefully in. He was dressed in cutoff jeans, a black tank top, and nothing else. What the heck?

"Paxton?" Hope said from behind him.

He turned to see her sitting on a boulder, swinging one leg. The sun highlighted her pretty hair, and she wore jean shorts that showed off her tight legs, a white tank top that curved very nicely over her chest, and the ring he'd given her. "What's going on?" He wanted to be irritated, but instead, he felt nice and mellow.

Her shoulders lifted in a shrug. "We're in a dream world. I didn't know I could bring you in." Her gaze dropped to his clothing, and she laughed.

He looked down, too. "Jean shorts? Seriously? Give me something else."

She blinked and then black swim trunks covered him. "Better?"

"Yeah." He heard movement from the direction of the water and turned, putting himself in the path of whatever was coming.

Libby waded angrily out of the ocean, her sandy-blond hair plastered to her head and her tawny eyes furious. "I'm a cat, damn it. I hate the water." She stared down at the pink sand. "Wait a minute." Then she paused, and joy crossed her feline face. "Pax!" She jumped for him.

He caught her, hugging her tight. "Libby. I've missed you." Oh, they video-conferenced every week, but it had been nearly three years since they'd been in the same space. Libby had grown even curvier now that she'd turned sixteen.

"You, too." She hugged him back, and when he released her, she made a beeline for Hope, who'd hopped off the rock. They hugged. Still having an arm around Hope, Libby turned them to face Paxton. "So this is a dream world. Very cool." Then she frowned. "Why did I get dropped into the ocean?"

Hope winced. "Sorry about that. When I saw Paxton here, I wondered if I could bring you, too. I guess my aim was off."

Pax tried not to laugh, but he couldn't help it. "I like this world." The trees behind Hope were aqua-colored, the sand pink, the sky a light blue, and the sun a brighter orange than usual. And both girls were wearing short shorts and tank tops, so this was pretty much a dream come true for him. For any guy who liked girls, which he did. A lot.

He looked around, and to the right, an outcropping of rocks led up to where a green book lay open on a tree trunk. "Hey. That's your book. Want me to get it?"

Hope looked and then shook her head. "You can't. The second you get close, it moves. I don't think it's time for me to read the book yet."

The thing had been around since Hope was born, and she always said it was her book. Because of some big ritual that was supposed to happen in the future with the Seven, Ulric, and the three female Keys. Pax wasn't going to let it happen, though—Hope would not *be sacrificed like that. Could he get back into the dream world without her, he wondered, now that he'd been granted access? If he could, he would try to read the book. He was sure it held the truth about what was going to happen.*

"So. What now?" Pax asked. "I guess we could swim."

Libby cut him a look. "Cat. Water. No."

He laughed, happier than he'd been in a long time. This was their place and their friendship—like it used to be.

Until two figures walked out from between the aqua trees and jumped down the overhang to the beach. Pax's body rioted, and he subtly settled his stance. "Drake. What a surprise."

"No kidding." Drake had grown tall like most Kurjans. He was just a little older than Paxton, but he'd always be taller. He smiled at Hope. "Apparently your powers have increased."

She blushed. She actually blushed. "I guess so." Tilting her head, she looked at the trembling kid standing beside Drake. "Um, hello. Who are you?"

The kid looked at all of them and then stood perfectly still. He was a Kurjan with shoulder-length black hair, not an ounce of red in it. His eyes were an odd shade of blue and his stance uncertain.

Drake looked to his side. "This is my cousin, Vero."

Pax's throat heated the way it did when he wanted to punch something. "You're bringing in flocks of Kurjans now?" he snapped.

Hope looked curiously at the kid. "This is a new one on me. I just sent out the call to Drake."

Drake nodded. "Vero and I were hanging out at my place and fell asleep watching a movie on the sofa. Apparently your call includes anybody in the vicinity. That could be dangerous. You're going to have to be a lot more careful with calling out now that you've gotten so strong."

"What is it about turning sixteen that gives us more power?" Libby asked, subtly pivoting and putting herself within striking range.

Pax did the same. Apparently, Libs had been training. He liked that. Between the two of them, they could handle both Drake and this new kid. Oh, Hope could fight, too, but she'd been sick. And as far as he knew, she still hadn't gained the extra strength most immortals had.

Drake's eyes were a mix of green and purple that looked cool. "So. Five of us. I wonder what this means?"

Hope stepped closer, and Libby tensed. "I think it means this is up to us. All of it. We can create peace where our parents couldn't. Don't you see? This is a good thing."

They weren't the Power Rangers. The Kurjans were the enemy, and while Pax liked how kind Hope was, she just didn't get it. Peace couldn't be found with people who wanted war. The Kurjans had been beaten in the last war, and they would not, could not, let that defeat stand. Plus, Ulric was coming back, and he wanted to destroy all enhanced females. Including Hope's mom. "Hope. Take a step back," he ordered.

Libby nodded.

Vero looked back and forth. "I like the idea of peace." Then he stared at the pink sand. "This is so weird."

"What about you, Drake?" Paxton asked softly. "You want peace?"

The Kurjan turned his full attention on Paxton, his gaze curious and his expression oddly calm. "Peace has different meanings to each of us, I think. The road to get there will vary, and you and I both know we won't be on the same one. We can't be."

Hope frowned. "Of course you can be."

Pax smiled, showing Drake his teeth. "No. He's right. We understand each other."

Hope's brow furrowed. She just didn't get it. That was okay.

Drake matched his smile. "Yes, hybrid. We definitely understand each other."

So Drake knew Pax was a vampire-demon hybrid. Good. It wasn't fair to beat the hell out of a guy if he didn't know exactly who you were. This was perfect. Any doubts Pax had had about his uncle and his group wanting to destroy the Seven before they could screw up Hope's life just disappeared. His uncle was a purist when it came to messing with the laws of the universe, as were his friends. They thought the Seven were too dangerous to be allowed to continue to the final ritual that might destroy the fabric of the entire universe. The showdown was coming soon, and Pax was determined to save Hope from the Seven, because she was what mattered. There was way too much at stake here. Even if she ended up hating him, he had to protect her.

Drake returned his attention to Hope. "Do the Seven have Ulric? Is he back in our world?"

Hope tilted her head. "I have no idea."

So, the bastard was looking for information. Who'd created this situation? Drake or Hope? Paxton shoved away the uneasy feeling in his gut.

Vero coughed. "Why do you all hate Ulric so much? The Realm is wrong. He doesn't want to hurt anybody. He's our religious leader, and we want him back."

"No," Pax growled. Even if the kid believed his words, he was wrong. Ulric was evil, and Pax's group would handle him without the Seven's help. They were almost as bad as Ulric.

"Pax?" Hope asked, looking over her shoulder. Man, she had good instincts.

He softened just slightly, taking in her sparkling blue eyes. "There can't be peace, Hope. Sorry." Then he clapped his hands, loudly.

Jerking awake, he hit his head on the wall of her bedroom.

She sat up, her hair wild, her eyes angry. "There can, too, be peace."

He stood, more determined than ever. It was time to report back to his uncle about Drake. "'Night, Hope. See you tomorrow." Then he bounded out the window, once again avoiding the cameras.

Chapter Sixteen

Karma paced the guest bedroom of Benjamin's lovely home by the river. The colors of the walls and bedding were calm and peaceful, so she doubted Mercy had decorated the room. Perhaps Haven had, but that still didn't feel right. Karma hadn't met the other two females yet, but they should be arriving soon. Would they like her?

Not that it mattered. She wasn't going to stay long enough to get to know them, even if they did want to make friends.

She'd changed into a silky tank top and shorts set provided by Mercy. It was green and decadent, and since nobody could see her, she decided to be comfortable right now. Oh, she couldn't look down at herself because Terre would see her form through the implant, but the material still felt delicious against her skin.

Benjamin had offered to mate her. Back in her youth, the goal of girls her age had been to secure as good of a husband as possible in order to provide for and protect their children. These days, women could live their own lives.

In any era, Benjamin would still be appealing. He was strong and kind, and he could kiss like the heroes she'd read about in bootlegged romance novels. Plus, she liked him.

Though something was off with him and had been since the morning when she'd let him touch her. Had that been a mistake? It certainly hadn't felt like a mistake. Perhaps once she'd gone back to the Kurjans and rescued her girls, she could find him again. She'd probably have to kill Terre to escape.

Did she have that in her?

To protect her girls, she did. Any mother would protect her children, and she felt a burning determination deep in her breast. In her heart. For now, she needed sleep. The Kurjans were only going to give her a couple more days to collect information, and then they'd come for her.

She slipped into the bed, her body heavy. When they infiltrated the location, they'd try to harm Benjamin and his friends. It'd be a fight, and people would get hurt or worse.

How could she prevent that?

Linda popped up by the side of the bed.

Karma yelped and then sat up. "What are you doing here? Are the girls okay?"

Linda's eyes were wide and too dark. She hovered, slightly see-through in the moonlight shining through the window. "They're coming. I just saw it. You have to—"

Explosions ripped through the peaceful night outside. Karma caught her breath, and before she could jump out of bed, her door crashed open and Benjamin barreled through.

He had her out of the bed and in his arms in a heartbeat.

"Benjamin." She grabbed the material of the T-shirt stretched tightly across his chest as he ran through the house and into the master bedroom, kicking it shut with one boot.

More explosions made the ground beneath them quake. A painting fell off the wall onto his sprawling bed, but he kept running into a well-appointed walk-in closet that was mostly empty of clothing. Then he set her on the dresser in the middle of the space, looked around wildly, and grabbed the lone tie from a peg. Without a word, he wrapped it around her face and covered her eyes before she could protest.

Then she was back in the air and against his chest. She had to grab on again to keep from falling. He moved a few feet and then must've reached the rear of the square-shaped closet. The sound of his hand slapping the wood filled her ears. Oh, God. He knew about the implant. He had covered her eyes. Something quietly slid to the side.

He lunged inside and ran down unseen steps; it felt as if he was taking them four at a time. Cool air brushed her, and she held on for dear life, acutely aware of her lack of clothing. She blinked behind the blindfold but couldn't see anything. The door snicked shut behind them. She held on tighter as he jostled her. "Where—"

"Shhh," he muttered, the sound curt.

She swallowed. "They're here for me, Benjamin. Maybe if you let me go, there won't be a fight."

"I'm not letting you go." The words were uttered as fervently as any vow she'd ever heard. "Don't speak again, or I'll gag you."

She bit her lip. So he knew about the device in her ear as well. She had no doubt he'd do as he said, but she had to at least try. "I don't want you or any of your friends to get hurt. Please just leave me and go." They had to have several escape routes, and he could be long gone before the Kurjans found them. "I have to go back."

"Not one more word, Karma. The only thing I have to gag you with right now is a sock, and it's been on my foot all day. Don't push me again, baby." He was running full-bore while carrying her, yet he didn't sound winded in the slightest.

The last thing she wanted in her mouth right now was his dirty sock. She'd tried to reason with him, and the Kurjans were surely listening to every word. "I can't see. Can I take off the blindfold?" It was imperative they understood she was blindfolded.

"No." He slowed down. "Sock it is."

"No," she yelped. "I promise. Not one more word."

He paused as if thinking it over. "All right. Last chance."

She pressed her lips firmly together to keep from making a sound. He moved her slightly and then stopped descending, so the ground must've leveled out. It became cooler and quieter, and the explosions in the distance sounded far above them. How far underground had he run? She didn't dare ask.

He ran for a few more minutes, paused, and pushed open what sounded like a door. Then he moved forward again, turning several times and finally moving into what felt like a smaller place. He ripped off the blindfold.

She looked around a cell with three rock walls and one of bars. "Benjamin."

"Sorry." He set her on a cot and hurried back out the barred door, shutting and locking it firmly. "I'll be back."

Then he was gone.

* * * *

"Talk to me." Benny ran into the control center inside the mountain. Screens were mounted on three walls, and the fourth held various weapons. The main weapons room was just beyond.

Logan looked up from a keyboard, still typing. "Attack from the river with secondary forces advancing from the east and south."

So they'd taken the bait. "Excellent. The river mines worked." Benny reached for several weapons to hide on his body. "I didn't expect them for a few days."

Logan looked over his shoulder, his eyes a startling and pissed-off green. "Neither did I."

Benny paused. Oh. Logan would've preferred to get Mercy out of there and to Realm Headquarters first. "Understood."

Mercy glanced up from another set of consoles. "We have movement in the air—looks like three attack helicopters." Then she lowered her chin. "And I'm ready to fight. I wouldn't have gone to the Realm."

Garrett emerged from the weapons room fully armed. He growled low. "We weren't expecting a fight yet. We have half of our force away. To say we're outnumbered would be a gross understatement."

Mercy looked at the big screen. "Incoming."

Benny studied the air support through the night vision camera. "Is that a—"

The missile exploded with a loud roar. The entire mountain rocked back and forth, and Benny had to brace his feet to keep his balance. "Holy shit."

Logan typed furiously, focusing the camera closer in. "What are they doing? We're in human territory. They can't just take out a mountain like this. There's no way to hide that."

"Agreed," Benny muttered. The Kurjans had blown up the Seven's mountain headquarters before, but those had been off the grid. This one wasn't, and even the Kurjans knew better than to attack like this and alert the humans to their existence. The entire immortal world, allies and enemies alike, would retaliate against such a foolish move. "Apparently my offer to mate Karma didn't go unheeded." Anger morphed through him, tensing each one of his muscles. This was personal.

Mercy studied him from her position. "Yeah. They definitely jumped the gun on this. The only reason they'd do so would be personal and not strategic. Ideally, they'd want Karma to gather more information for a few days as they prepared for an assault. They haven't had enough time to really study the area."

Quade and Haven ran inside, both ducking falling shards of rock. "Why are they here already?" Quade asked, tucking Haven close. His eyes were dark with anger, and blood trickled from a cut on his temple.

Benny winced. "We might have underestimated the fact that Karma is now unmated and free to mate again. Or I could be wrong about that." He should've asked her more questions, but it wasn't as if she would've been able to answer with the Kurjans listening. He grabbed night vision goggles from the shelf. "I'll go. We just need one prisoner to question."

Garrett stood. "I'm with you to the north. Could use a good fight."

Logan stood and reached for a gun. "Quade and I will take the east." Before Mercy could stand, he shook his head. "You're better logistically than the rest of us. I need you here with Haven and Karma in case we have to run fast. Keep an eye on the cameras."

She rolled her eyes but claimed his seat, while Haven drew up the defense plan on the farthest screen. "Remember, there are live mines out there now."

Benny allowed adrenaline to flood his system. Then he turned into the weapons room, secured an earbud, and ran up the back stairs while Quade and Logan went the other direction. He climbed easily and pushed open the rock portal to the forest with Garrett on his heels.

Smoke filled the air along with the crackle of fire. The makeshift lodge was toast. He moved through the trees silently, angling around the spot where the first ground force had been visible on the screen. Well, the second ground force. The first had been taken out in the river with the mines that had been activated the second he'd walked Karma by and admitted that it was a weak area. Yeah, he'd lied.

Sam dropped down from a hidden spot in the boughs of a fir tree, and Benny halted. "What did you see?"

"Full-out assault. We're gonna have to take one of them prisoner and fast." Sam gestured toward the most likely area to create their ambush. "If the copters stop blowing missiles and land to let the forces out, we have to retreat. There are too many of them." Sam wore head-to-toe black and blended into the night perfectly. With his green eyes covered by night glasses, Benny wouldn't know he was there if he hadn't made it obvious.

A light shone down, and then figures rappelled out of two helicopters.

"Move," Garrett muttered, ducking his head against the light. "They've hacked into our cameras and have eyes on us. Run."

Benny turned and barreled through one of the many trails they'd set up around the compound, careful to zig and zag in the way they'd memorized. A soldier ran after him, and instantly a bomb went off. Heat flared against Benny's back, and he circled a tree, coming back to the enemy. "Cut all cameras," he ordered tersely.

"Affirmative. Cameras cut," Mercy returned. "We're taking more missiles on the mountain. If they continue the assault, we need to evacuate within five minutes. Avenues A and C are damaged, so I think B is our best shot. If they get to B, we'll have to take D, and that's the least secure."

Benny growled and held his gun, waiting for sound. The lights from above swung around, and he ducked against a tree, out of sight.

"Clock is ticking," Mercy said in his ear. "Return to base in five minutes whether or not the capture is successful."

"It'll be successful," Benny growled, aware of Sam moving on his left and Garrett on his right. "I want a Cyst, not a Kurjan soldier. Period." Their white hair would glow in the night. "Take off their hoods to double-check."

"Affirmative," Garrett said quietly.

They fanned out, and Benny caught sight of a three-soldier pack edging toward the mountain. He signaled and circled around to the rear, careful to stay out of the spotlights crisscrossing the forest.

A Cyst soldier leapt between two trees and took him down to the wet pine needles.

Chapter Seventeen

Karma held the rough bars and tried to peer down the hallway. She felt naked in the silky shorts and top. "Hello?" Had she heard footsteps? She chewed on her bottom lip. Maybe Benjamin hadn't known about the device in her head. Perhaps he'd just blindfolded her because the underground headquarters were a secret. But then he'd put her in a cell.

Yes, he knew.

Footsteps came closer, and Haven stood on the other side of the bars. She pushed a cardigan and heavy socks with walruses decorating them through the bars. "It's cold down here."

"Thank you," Karma said, instantly sliding her arms into the cardigan. It was longer than her shorts, and she buttoned it up, feeling almost better. The color was a pale yellow, and the material was heavy and warm. Then she ducked to pull on the socks, her heart warming along with her body. "I appreciate it."

Haven leaned back against the opposite wall, watching her. The woman had pulled her sandy-blond hair up in a ponytail and wore dark jeans and a pretty green sweater that matched her left eye. Her other eye was a deep black. Fascinating. Did all Fae have dual-colored eyes? Haven and Mercy were the only ones Karma had ever seen, so the oddity might be limited to their family. "Do you need anything else?"

Karma slid her hands into the soft pockets and tried to meet the woman's gaze. "Not unless you want to unlock the door."

"I'm afraid I can't do that," Haven said, not moving. The woman had an alertness about her that was intriguing. Her face was angular and her nose pert. She was very pretty, even late at night without any makeup. "Benny shouldn't be long, and I'm sure he'll let you out."

"What a liar." A human male popped up next to Haven, his form wavering. His time to cross over was coming soon, whether he was ready or not. "She's always been a liar, and she's possessed by a demon." His face was contorted and furious, and spittle flew from his too-thick lips. Was that a clergyman's collar he wore? "Tell my daughter she's going to hell."

Karma watched him calmly. She'd learned a long time ago that the ghosts couldn't hurt her or anybody else. Usually she'd ask if he wanted her to pass on a message, but he was obviously one of the bad ones, and whatever he had to say wasn't necessary. Karma had no doubt Haven was not going to hell. So she concentrated on the female who had kindly brought her warm clothing. "What is happening?"

Haven studied the bars. "We're under attack from the Kurjans and the Cysts. It was to be expected since we have you, but we really thought we had more time. Do you have any clue why they came at us so quickly?"

Karma shook her head. The plan was for her to gain as much intelligence from the Seven as she could, and she'd barely had any time. Did Terre know that she was having difficulty being a spy? Had he lost confidence?

Haven rubbed a slight bruise on her wrist. "Darn rock got me. Seriously, though. The Kurjans don't know that you've taken the virus, so why would they need you back so badly? As far as they know, you can't be mated again, and you haven't had time to gather intel, so why the rushed timeline? I don't get it."

Out of all the people who might question her, Karma had not expected Haven. "I really don't know," she admitted. "I'm useless to them if I can't be mated again." Of course, the Kurjans knew she could be, and for some reason Terre really wanted her. But she couldn't tell Haven that—just in case Haven didn't know about the tracker. The woman was excellent at bluffing if she'd figured it out.

Haven wiped dust off her chin "Well, I guess that's a mystery. Don't worry, though. We won't let the Kurjans get you again."

"Right. That's why I'm in a cell." It was silly to keep playing this game, and Karma didn't have the patience for it. "Do you have any idea what Benjamin is going to do with me?" He obviously knew she'd been spying on the Realm, and that was probably considered treason. Would she be put to death? Dread dropped into her stomach, and her knees weakened.

"I don't know," Haven said. "He just put you in here to keep you safe."

That didn't make sense, but right now, what did? Karma edged closer to the bars. "You're mated to Quade, who was away from this world for so long." She held her breath. Oh, there was no harm asking her question. "Quade is not modern, just like me. Has it been difficult for you?"

Haven tilted her head. "Difficult? No, not really. I mean, he steals the toothpaste way too much, and he's a little bossy sometimes, but have you met an immortal who isn't? I love him, he loves me, and we work it out." She grinned. "Sometimes things get a little wild, but what fun is life without wild?"

Life was fantastic without wild. Karma would be just fine without wildness. Right? This might be her only chance to gain knowledge. "Is the Realm killing enhanced females as the Kurjans are?" The rumors were that the Realm liked to torture first. While she hadn't seen any sign of that deplorable behavior, she had to ask.

Haven's eyebrows rose. "Of course not. Did the Kurjans tell you that?"

Slowly, Karma nodded. After being at the Realm Headquarters and then with members of the Seven, she couldn't help but see that the females were treated with as much respect as the males. Their lives were not at all as Terre had described to her throughout the years.

It was no surprise. She had to get her girls out of that world and into a better one. She'd taken the responsibility to love and protect them, and there was no choice now. If she could only tell Benjamin the truth without the Kurjans hearing or seeing it and thus putting the twins in danger.

Something roared high above, impacted, and blew the earth apart. Haven cried out and ducked. Karma grabbed the bars and hunched her shoulders, trying to stay on her feet.

The wall behind Haven split, and shards of rock rained down. The earth kept shifting and quaking. She ran to the bars and quickly used a keypad to open the lock before yanking the door open. "Come on. We have to get out of this tunnel." Grabbing Karma's hand, she turned and pulled her down the hard dirt passageway as rocks fell from the roof to land and shatter on the floor.

A rock sliced Karma's forearm, and she flicked it off, running with Haven. Panic ballooned through her. They burst out of the tunnel into a round room with screens on three walls.

Mercy looked up from a computer console as rocks rained down around her. Blood dotted her chin, and her eyes were wide. "They hit us simultaneously from two sides. I've given the soldiers two minutes to make a capture and get back here. We have to prepare to evacuate. We're going with Avenue B, Haven. Get your mind around it."

Haven took a deep breath and blew it out. "Okay. I'm there. It isn't like I haven't gone on the run before. What's our destination?"

"Point Zero," Mercy said, turning to type quickly on a keyboard. "Setting self-destruct now."

Karma's legs shook. "Self-destruct? Wait a minute." Were they going to blow up the entire mountain? The Seven Headquarters?

Just because of her? "Hold on. Wait until Benjamin returns." Why she was counting on him to be the voice of reason was beyond her.

Mercy gasped, looking at the screen. "Oh, crap."

Karma stared at the biggest screen. She could make out two helicopters turning around and heading toward the mountain. As one, they fired missiles directly at the mountain. The swishing sound was instantly followed by a burst of fire out of each.

"Brace!" Mercy yelled.

Haven wrapped an arm over Karma's shoulders and tugged her down to the floor. The explosion was massive. The entire floor wobbled as if water lifted beneath it. Karma was thrown against the far wall, and more explosions cascaded through her head.

She rolled over, gasping.

Mercy approached her, ducking to avoid the falling rocks. "Haven, we can't wait for Benny. Faith and Ronan are approaching through Tunnel B. We have to do this now." She pulled a syringe out of her back pocket and used her teeth to rip off the plastic tip.

Fear made her weak, but Karma tried to scramble backward, away from Mercy. Haven grasped her by the shoulders and held tight. Before Karma could fight back, Mercy plunged the needle into her arm, and warmth spread out from it.

"What did you just—" Karma's voice trailed off. The room swam around her, and she fell back against Haven, her head going numb.

Then unconsciousness drifted through her, starting with her toes. By the time the fuzzy darkness reached her head, her vision and hearing had both gone. "Benjamin?" she whispered as unconsciousness tried to take her. Sounds grew muffled, and her eyelids closed, but her body still felt the pain of a rock slicing across her ankle. "Ow."

"We have to hurry." A male voice—a new one.

Gentle but steel-hard arms lifted her into the air, and even though her eyes were closed, nausea rolled through her belly. The male holding her was careful but moved quickly, barely jostling her. How odd. Just a few days ago, her skin would have been crawling with the mating rash. Never in her life had she thought she'd be free of that marking.

Then softness. A gentle blanket and a comfortable bed. Well, this was all right. She smiled slightly, ready for a nap. Whatever they'd given her felt warm and smooth through her veins. Much better than the sedative the Kurjans had used when they'd put the implant in her head. That had burned to her toes. This was nice. She settled in. Maybe she'd dream about her girls.

A cry of pain centered her attention.

"Faith. Are you okay?" the male voice asked.

"Yes. Just a rock landing on my shoulder. We have to hurry. Can you spread a tarp over her somehow, Ronan?" The female sounded in control of the situation. How strange.

A low growl sounded close by. "We don't have a tarp. There isn't time for the surgery. Make her comfortable, and let's get out of here."

"We can't just leave her," the female said as the scent of bursting wildflowers brushed Karma's senses. Kind of like her own scent but with spice.

In fact, the female in charge smelled like the meadows of Karma's youth. Even though she should be scared, she couldn't help but relax more. Then a firm bracket centered her head. A bright light pointed at her face and heated her skin as if she were sitting in the sun. "What—" she whispered weakly.

"She's not out," the male said.

A small pinch to her upper arm caught Karma by surprise. More warmth flowed through her blood, dragging her completely into the darkness.

Then she was out.

Chapter Eighteen

Benny clapped both hands against the Cyst's ears as more figures emerged from the trees and engaged Garrett and Sam. The Cyst punched Benny in the throat, and he barely turned in time to keep his trachea from being shattered. "Fucker." Using his legs, he rolled them over and reached for the knife in his boot, slashing.

His earbud crackled. "Ben? Faith and Ronan just arrived through the east tunnel, and they say we can't go out that way. It's falling around them as they run. We'll have to leave Karma here and return for her later. There isn't enough time for the plan now." Mercy's voice was breathless, as if she was running.

"No," Benny grunted, stabbing the Cyst in the neck. Dark red blood arced, landing across Benny's neck and burning instantly. "We can't let the Kurjans take her now that her mating mark has been neutralized."

The Cyst yanked the knife free of his neck, and his eyes morphed to a furious purple. He flipped it around in his hand and lifted up with his hips, plunging the knife into Benny's gut.

The blade bent in two and flew in different directions.

"Damn it," Benny growled. "That was my favorite knife." He punched down, breaking several of the Cyst's teeth. "My torso is impenetrable, dumbass." Most of the Seven's initiation ritual was focused on fusing together each male's torso to protect his heart.

The Cyst punched up, right into Benny's groin. Pain ripped through him, and he gasped, his balls on fire. A body careened out of the trees and manacled Benny around the waist, shoving him off the Cyst soldier. He flew headfirst into a tree, and his ears rang. He turned to punch out, nailing a Kurjan soldier beneath the jaw. "Mercy? I'm not messing with you. Do not leave Karma alone." A Kurjan punched back, hitting Benny in the ear. His head rang.

"Sorry, Ben," Mercy said, not really sounding sorry. "The mountain is exploding, and the surgery is impossible. There's not enough time. We have to make a run for it. We found her once—we can do it again." The sound of typing came over the COMM unit. "There are three more forces heading to your position. Logan and Quade are engaged on the other side of the mountain. You have two minutes—then we have to go."

Benny kicked the Kurjan in the gut and flipped to his feet. "Mercy? Listen to me right now. I'll buy Faith enough time to do the surgery. Just get to it." He waited until the Kurjan rushed forward and then went with a series of hard punches to the face, neck, and gut that had the soldier backtracking while trying to avoid blows.

"You're crazy. You'd have to lead them away from the mountain and then somehow get back in time," Mercy said, cutting off communications.

"I'm on it. Get that device out of her head," Benny barked.

The Cyst rose from the ground and approached, blood still pouring from his neck.

Benny hastily punched the Kurjan in the eye, temporarily knocking him out. Then he pivoted to kick the Cyst beneath the chin. The soldier's head snapped back with a loud crack. He fell, his blood pooling on the wet pine needles. Benny grabbed him by the braid. "I have one," he coughed, spitting up blood. Probably from the punch to the testicles.

Sam staggered out of the trees, bleeding profusely from his left eyebrow. "Two down. Not for long."

Garrett flipped the remaining Kurjan over his shoulder and then stabbed him right through the neck, impaling the guy on a prone Cyst he'd apparently already taken out. "I'm good. Let's go." The youngest Kayrs soldier bled from his neck and ear, but his eyes glowed a furious metallic gray. His shirt was torn, and so was his bottom lip. "We need to move." He ducked and grabbed the shoulder of the Cyst soldier Benny held by the braid. "Let's drag him. He's too heavy to lift."

Benny handed him over and paused. "I'll lead them away for just a couple of minutes. Go help with the surgery."

Sam turned and led the way through the trees, scouting the area. Another missile hit the mountain with a loud whistle, and trees flew in every direction.

A sliver of bark sliced across Benny's cheek and he winced but didn't slow his pace as he ran conspicuously in the opposite direction with the Kurjans already pursuing him. The thought that Karma was undergoing head surgery under these conditions was crazy. He had to give Faith time—she'd been the best human neurosurgeon alive before mating one of the Seven.

He scaled a tree and then leaped from branch to branch, fighting the urge to let out a Tarzan-like yell. The Kurjans fired their weapons from below while the helicopters hovered just above the treetops.

This might've been a mistake.

Even so, he kept going from tree to tree and then finally dropped to the ground in the densest part of the forest.

A Cyst leaped at him, and Benny stabbed him in the eye, quickly pivoting and running back the way he'd come. This was all the time they could afford. Dodging and weaving, he took out two more Kurjans on the way back, and then opened the rock wall to run down the steps, which were dotted with blood.

Benny hit the weapons room and kept going into the main room, jumping over an unconscious Cyst soldier. "Is it done?" he asked as he turned toward the makeshift operating room.

Garrett was instantly in his face, both hands on Benny's shoulders. "Listen. Faith is the best neurosurgeon alive, and that was before she became immortal. She saw the diagrams and pictures, and she said it'd be an easy surgery. Let her finish."

"I don't care." Benny threw his earbud across the room, shoved Garrett, and ran down the east tunnel, turning left and skidding into Ronan Kayrs.

Ronan grabbed him by the arms and pushed him back a foot. "Stop. Faith is operating now, and if you go barging in there, she's likely to slice something she shouldn't."

Benny squared himself and glared at the male who'd become his brother, through blood and vows, too many centuries ago to count. Ronan had black hair, a deadly body, and more painful experience in his aqua eyes than anyone should ever have. He'd lived lifetimes upon lifetimes by himself in a prison world far away, guarding Ulric and protecting the Realm. But right now, he was about to get his ass kicked. "Move."

Ronan studied him and then moved aside. "She's your female. If you want her brain damaged, that's your choice."

Smart aleck. Benny pushed open the door just as Faith, her brown hair up on top of her head and her body swathed in a white lab coat, snapped the lid shut on a brown metal box. Karma lay beneath a blanket, her head turned away. "Got it." Faith grinned, looking toward the door.

Benny barreled forward, reaching Karma. "Is she okay?" Her skin was pale, and her sunshine-filled hair splayed out over the thick mattress.

"Of course." Faith lifted Karma's wrist and counted her pulse. "She's just out from the sedative. I wouldn't attempt this surgery in these conditions if I didn't think I could do it, Benny. You know that. Great job getting me more time, though. You saved her."

Another explosion billowed through the night, and a fist-sized chunk of rock dropped. Benny caught it before the projectile could hit Faith's head.

"Thanks," she said, edging toward the door. "We should get out of here—right?"

Benny gently moved Karma's head so he could see her face. Her pink lips were slightly pursed, and she breathed evenly. "Where's the incision?"

Faith ducked as dust wafted through the space. "No incision. I took the device out through her nose, which was how they got it in. I'm looking forward to studying it."

"No. Is it in the box?" Benny released Karma and reached for the box.

Faith's eyebrows rose as she handed it over. "Of course. It's shielded and can't be traced in the box."

"That's nice." Benny walked to the corner and set the box down, letting the device tumble out. He made sure to keep the box between it and the rest of the room. The thing had connections in two places, where it had been attached to Karma's eye and one ear canal.

Faith opened her mouth, and he shook his head, motioning for her to stay silent and go.

Then he hurried toward Karma and lifted her, running to the door.

Double explosions erupted from two directions, and the roof began to cave in. "Run!" he bellowed. He followed Faith and Ronan through the computer room, meeting up with Garrett and Mercy, who'd shut down all the computers.

Garrett finished activating a box beneath the main computer console. "We're ready to blow. Logan and Quade called in and are already in Tunnel B, making sure we have a clear path."

"Let's go," Benny said grimly as the mountain began to fall around them.

Mercy looked over his shoulder. "Where's Sam?"

Benny jolted. "Sam was in here with you guys."

Garrett's eyes swirled with too many colors to count. "No. I thought he went back out to help you."

Benny's chest chilled. "No. Did he even make it in from outside?"

As Garrett turned to run to the weapons room, the entire wall seemed to morph before sharp boulders heavier than a dump truck began to fall. "Shit. Double shit."

Ronan grabbed him by the shoulder. "Check his comm."

Garrett yanked his earbud out of his pocket and shoved it in. "Sam? Come in." Garrett's face contorted with irritation, and he stared at the rock wall now separating them from the weapons room and stairwell. "Nothing. Come on, Sam. Talk to me." He frowned and bent forward as if to hear better. His face cleared, and fury burned in his eyes.

Dread made a lump in Benny's throat. "What?" he asked, sidestepping a falling piece of what looked like pure silver.

Garrett held up a hand. "Sam? Don't say anything and try to keep the earbud in. We're going to evacuate through Tunnel B, and then we're coming for you. Grunt to let me know you understand." The youngest Kayrs warrior's jaw hardened, and death shone in his eyes. There was Talen's son and the king's nephew.

Benny caught his breath. No wonder they thought Garrett would lead someday.

Garrett looked up. "Let's go."

Haven grabbed his arm. "Are you saying the Kurjans have Sam?" Panic colored her words, and she looked beyond Garrett to the blocked tunnel.

Garrett nodded. "Yeah. The Kurjans have him, but we'll get him back." He focused on Benny. "We're going to need Karma to level with us. You know that, right?"

"Yes," Benny said. "I promise she'll tell us everything she knows." There was no reason for her not to cooperate now that the device had been removed from her head. Better yet, it'd be buried in the rubble when the mountain blew, so the Kurjans would think she'd been killed. He turned and began running for freedom. They had ten miles to travel underground before emerging, then three hours of driving until they reached the helicopters that were hidden far away from here.

Then Karma would talk, whether she wanted to or not.

He set a pace that would keep her from being jostled too much but would allow him to move quickly.

Ronan ran up to his side. "Who's going to tell Logan his brother has been taken?"

Garrett ran by them both. "That would be me," he said grimly.

Another set of missiles impacted the mountain, and the walls blew inward. "If we survive this," Quade muttered, easily lifting Haven into his arms so they could go faster. "It's not looking good."

Ronan lifted Faith and swung her around to his back. The enhanced humans weren't as fast as the immortals. "We'll make it."

A missile ripped right through the tunnel behind them, spreading fire as it flew.

Benny ducked his head and ran as fast as he could. Then the world blew up.

Chapter Nineteen

Karma awoke midmorning just as Benjamin stepped out of a quieting helicopter, carrying her. Mercy paused next to them and looked up from a tablet in her hands. "The scans from the outpost came back clear, even after a secondary check. We're all good—no tracing powder or other devices attached to you while you fought hand-to-hand."

Karma's head ached. "We were scanned?"

"Yep." Benjamin strode between two majestic pine trees toward a lodge much larger than the one they'd just left. It was made of rough, hand-cut logs, and the sound of a rushing river bubbled through the air. "When we got to the helicopter, we went through a series of scanning devices before taking off. We're good."

Garrett reached the door before them and pushed it, hurrying inside. "We need to get a bead on Sam. Now."

Karma tried to concentrate. Memories of the sedative and the soft bed came rushing back. She pressed a hand to her eye.

"It's gone," Benjamin affirmed. "Took it out through your nose, and it's buried in a pile of rocks right now." He bypassed a bar and entertainment area to turn left and jog down a wide hallway, following Garrett into a computer center at least three times larger than the one they'd left behind. More screens covered the walls, and bigger satellite photos were taped to a fourth wooden wall. He set her down on a rolling chair.

Garrett sat and typed furiously, bringing up an aerial feed of a smoldering, crumbled, devastated mountain.

Karma gasped. "Was that your headquarters?" The Kurjans had decimated it.

"No," Benjamin said. "You're in our headquarters now."

She turned to look at him. He'd healed any injuries he'd sustained from the fight, but his torn shirt was bloody and his jeans filthy, with pine needles still sticking out from several places. "I don't understand."

He didn't answer. "Any sign?"

Garrett leaned forward, scanning the burning mountain. "No. The human wildfire forces have arrived and started dumping fire retardants on the blaze. The missiles were destroyed when the self-destruct sequence concluded, so it'll look like some sort of earthquake and a resulting forest fire. Hopefully."

Logan rushed inside the control room with Mercy on his heels. The hybrid's green eyes had morphed to deep black, and fury crackled along his skin. "Any sign of Sam?" he asked.

"Negative," Garrett said quietly. "I'm downloading the satellite feed and will rewind as soon as I have it. We'll find him."

"Shit." Logan snatched a coffee cup off a table and threw it across the room. The mug smashed against the wooden wall and shattered into pieces. "Sam is gone. What the hell am I supposed to do now?" He scrubbed a still-burned hand through his thick hair. "Zane will want to know. How can I tell the leader of the demon nation that our brother is missing because of the Seven? Because of me?" Red flushed high across his high cheekbones.

Karma edged closer to Benny, using the rollers on her chair to move quietly.

Garrett shook his head. "I don't know. Let's take this one step at a time. Adare and Grace are visiting with the demon nation right now, so we have somebody in-house. Well, they're with Zane's right hand."

Mercy looked up. "They're still with Nick and Simone?"

Karma listened carefully. According to her lessons, Nick and Zane were as tight as brothers, and Nick's mate, Simone, was a powerful witch. It was odd to know about these people whom she'd never met.

Garrett nodded. "Yes. So that's good. Probably." He glanced at his watch. "Ivar and Promise are headed to Realm Headquarters right now, even though Dage won't like the company. They'll use some sort of excuse to stay, just in case we need somebody at Realm Headquarters. This may mean the start of war with the Kurjans. I'm not sure if the Realm will back the Seven or leave us on our own. Hopefully Ivar can talk sense into Dage. I'd do it, but I'm going after Sam."

"Ditto," Logan said grimly.

Karma's mind began to clear. They'd gone through the locations of every member of the Seven except one. "Did Ronan carry me to a different room from my cell, and did his mate perform surgery on my head?" The constant headache was gone. Her eye felt whole again, and her ear didn't hurt.

"Yes," Benjamin said, bringing up a different view on a secondary screen. "Faith took the device out of your head. She checked your vitals when we stopped for the helicopter, and then she and Ronan headed off to try to calm down the shifter nation in Montana. Unfortunately, we just blew up part of their territory in Utah, territory they didn't know we were occupying."

Karma awoke fully. Panic seized her around the throat. "You removed my device?"

"Yes. You're welcome," Benjamin said, still studying the screen. "It's interesting that you know the names of the Seven and their mates so well. You failed to mention that earlier."

"I studied all of you before you rescued me." She jumped up and rushed him, grabbing his arm. "I need the device that was in my head. What do you mean, it was buried beneath the rubble? Please tell me you didn't leave it back in that mess." She had no connection to her girls without it. What would Terre do? Her stomach lurched and gurgled.

"Oh, it's back there. Hopefully the Kurjans will think you're dead," Benjamin said, again typing. The screen zoomed in to show trees on fire. "Wow. We really did some damage there."

Karma released him. What was she going to do? The betrayal dug deep as reality struck her still-muddled brain. "That wasn't your headquarters. It was a falsehood? A trap?"

"Of course. The entire place was fake, because we were worried the Realm was tracking us. Once we found the device in your head, we planned accordingly since the Kurjans were obviously watching and listening." Benjamin turned to look at her. "You're still pale. Sit down."

She was so accustomed to taking orders, she sat immediately. Irritation climbed through her, but she remained seated, since the room seemed to be spinning. "You discovered the device in my head."

"Yes," Benjamin said, turning back to his screen. "We knew you were transmitting data to them, so we used that."

Used that? The memory of their kiss and what he'd done with his hand flushed through her, no doubt adding more than a dose of color to her face. "Apparently you used me, too," she said quietly, her chest aching.

What had she expected?

* * * *

It was hard to miss the hurt in the female's tone, but Benjamin didn't have a good answer for her. Of course they'd used her to mislead the Kurjans. However, that wasn't what she was talking about right now. He was flooded with memories of her soft moans and sweet taste as he took her apart—something he'd like to do again. "We'll talk about that later," he said, still scanning the ground for the spot where the Kurjans' helicopter must've dropped to pick up the soldiers and Sam. God, he hoped Sam was still alive.

"Yes, we will," she huffed, sounding like her spirit was returning. Good. That sedative had knocked her out longer than he'd liked. Why in the world was she still sounding peeved? Well, besides the fact that he'd let the Kurjans hear her orgasm. She should still be thrilled that the device was out of her head. What was he missing? He'd have to figure it out as soon as they got a bead on Sam.

Logan paced back and forth behind Garrett. Tension rolled off him in dark waves, prickling through the room and heightening the stress and anger of everyone else. The guy could really emote. Mercy typed as fast as Garrett did, bringing up a third satellite, this one bootlegged from the Russians. It was an older model but was positioned in the right area. Sometimes Benny forgot what a great hacker Mercy could be.

Logan turned toward Karma, took a deep breath, and lowered his chin. "Where would they take my brother?"

Karma sucked in air. "I don't know." She held up a hand before Logan could explode, reading him with impressive accuracy. "I'm not stonewalling. Their main headquarters is still in Canada, which no doubt you already know. Their fighting forces move around a lot so that they're not a target. I think they'd go somewhere temporary to, um, question your brother. It'd be at least a couple of hours from the battle zone."

Benny angled his body slightly between Karma and Logan. Oh, Logan would never lift a hand against a female, but he was freaking out right now, and Benny didn't want Karma's feelings hurt.

The protectiveness he felt for her was surprising, although the desire was not. Her marking from the Kurjan mate was completely gone, as was the recording device in her head. She was free. He could touch her without repercussions or witnesses, if she wanted.

The idea made his hands shake, and he smacked himself out of it. They had to find Sam first.

Karma cleared her voice, tilting her head to look past Benny at Logan. "They have dossiers on all of you. They'll know Sam is your brother as well as the demon king's brother. It would make no sense for them to kill him."

Oh, the little sweetheart. She was trying to reassure Logan while using logic and reason to keep him calm. Benny flashed her a smile. Some might call it manipulation, but with Karma, the words came from experience and kindness. What would she be like if that kindness was allowed to bloom with freedom? She probably didn't even realize how muffled she'd been by the Kurjans and their rules and hierarchy. "That's a good point," he said, wanting to encourage her. "What else?"

"Oh." She sat straighter in the chair. With her blond hair falling down to the middle of her back and her eyes clear of the pain that must have been caused by the device, she looked like a lady from days gone by. One of the fancy ones who wore tiaras and silk. "They would've already scanned him, so if he isn't tagged, they could take him anywhere."

Logan growled low but otherwise didn't move. "Any idea where?"

She sighed. "They like heat and the desert, so my guess would be southern Utah or even Nevada." She looked beyond Benny, and her eyes glazed over, talking to dead air. "How did you follow me here? Do you have some sort of homing device on me?"

Benny jumped and turned to find empty air. He slowly turned back to Karma. "Who are you seeing?"

"What the hell?" Logan muttered.

"It's Linda. She's a human who hasn't crossed over yet, and I see her often," Karma said.

"Why?" Mercy asked, standing up and scrutinizing the empty area with narrowed eyes. "I don't see anybody. Are you saying you can channel?"

"Yes," Karma said. "I've used the skill to help people who need a nudge, but sometimes spirits visit me just before they cross over. Often they want something, and sometimes I can help, other times I cannot."

"What does Linda want?" Mercy asked, turning to focus on Karma.

Karma's gaze darted around as if she was deciding whether or not to trust them. Not that she had a choice. Apparently, she reached the same conclusion, because she answered. "Linda was the mother of my daughters," she said quietly.

Benjamin turned to face her. "What?"

She swallowed. "Terre and General Jaydon killed Linda and kidnapped her twin daughters, who are enhanced females. They're around three years old now, and they're mine. I've adopted them." Then she stood and faced Benjamin directly, having to tilt her head back to meet his gaze. "I have to return for them. There is no choice here, Benjamin. None whatsoever."

One of his dark eyebrows rose. "The Kurjans are extorting you with those girls. Well, at least your behavior makes sense now. I couldn't figure out why you'd work for them while you were free." He rubbed the shadow along his jaw. "Okay, then."

Joy and hope leaped into her eyes. "You'll let me go back?"

"Of course not," he said, frowning. "But I'll get your girls for you."

"No," she said softly. "It's too much of a risk. I'll do whatever I have to in order to save them. Just stay out of my way." She wrung her hands together even as she faced him so bravely. "My best hope of getting the girls out is to play along with Terre. Any other approach, and he will harm the children out of spite. Trust me. I know what I'm doing."

Logan stepped into her line of sight. "How good is Linda's intel?"

Karma paused. "I do not know. I've never had a reason to gain information from a spirit." Her eyes darkened to nearly black. "Until now."

Chapter Twenty

Benny piled a heaping serving of spaghetti on his plate and strode across the deck to a seat next to Karma. "Stop trying so hard."

She looked out at the rushing river. For autumn, the day was surprisingly warm, so they'd chosen to get some fresh air while eating a late lunch. Or early dinner. She'd borrowed a skirt and sweater from Mercy, and the pale green wool brought out the delicacy of her skin. "I don't understand it. Ghosts are jerks."

Benny grinned. He'd never heard her say a bad word about anybody. "Maybe Linda is just scouting since you asked her for information. She'll be back when she has information for us. Right?"

"I don't know. I've never asked one to work at a distance like this."

Benny missed the cami and short set. The woman had a pair of legs on her—that was for sure. They'd been working all day to trace Sam's location, and she'd even tried to talk Linda into helping. Logan and Mercy were still in the computer room, while Haven and Quade had made sure everything was fine in the residences before whipping up a feast of spaghetti, bread, and some sort of canned bean thing that Benny had walked right past.

Quade and Haven joined them outside on the deck, sitting over at the table. Haven held a bottle of white wine, while Quade carried what looked like Jägermeister.

"Damn it, Quade," Garrett bellowed, stomping through the kitchen area and out to the deck.

Benny groaned.

Quade stood and moved away from the table. "What's your problem, nephew?" He looked innocent.

"Just wonderful," Benny muttered.

Haven dropped her head and shook it. Then she poured herself a generous glass of chardonnay.

"You need a few 'greats' before 'nephew,' you old bastard." Garrett barreled up to Quade and grabbed the tee stretched tight across his chest. "You checked out my house while I was in the main computer room, didn't you?"

Quade's eyes sparkled and his lips remained tightly pressed together.

Garrett shook him. "Say something."

Karma looked over at Benny and then turned back to watch the interaction. Tension rolled off her.

Did loud voices bug her? Benny placed his hand over hers on the table, and it was trembling. "It's okay, sweetheart," he murmured. "They're fine."

Garrett got into Quade's face and sniffed. "I knew it!"

Quade sighed. "I'm sorry. It's the good kind. I just happened to check, and it was there, and well…"

Garrett pushed Quade off the deck, and he landed with legs set. "That's my favorite, and my mom just sent it. You can only get it in Idaho since it's made there by a guy who retired from Crest years ago."

Quade shrugged. "It's peppermint and spearmint. The absolute best. I didn't eat the whole tube."

"Yes, you did!" Garrett leaped off the deck and tackled Quade. The two muscled males rolled toward the river over rocks, grass, and weeds.

Karma gasped and then looked at Haven, who was drinking her wine, not watching at all. "Benjamin. What is happening?"

Benny took a bite of the spaghetti. Yep. Haven had cooked dinner. She always used too much salt, but it wasn't bad. "Well, Quade has a slight addiction to toothpaste, unfortunately. We've tried to give him candy and mints, but it just isn't the same. Garrett gets the best kind, and I know he hides the tubes, but Quade is like a bulldog with a scent."

Karma watched the men throwing punches and then shivered. "This is over toothpaste? They're going to harm each other."

Benny took a drink of his beer, surprised that Karma had chosen beer instead of wine. She seemed like more of a wine girl, but good for her. He loved a thick beer. "If they get hurt, they'll just heal. Right now, Garrett needs to let off some steam, and Quade is always up for a decent fight. It's good-natured, sweetheart. They won't cut off heads or anything."

She eyed her plate of spaghetti, her lips trembling. "I don't see how violence will solve the problem."

Huh. "Don't you ever go to a gym and work out hard? Maybe take on a punching bag?"

She turned to him, her forehead creased. "Are you kidding?" Her hands swept along her skirt. "In this? How exactly would I punch a bag in a dress? Females wear dresses because they put us at a disadvantage." She swallowed. "And we look pretty."

"You don't have to wear a skirt," he said.

She sighed. "I know. I plan to start practicing wearing slacks and jeans, but I'm going to work up to it. Maybe start with short-sleeved shirts. A couple hundred years of wearing skirts is a hard habit to break. I just don't feel like me in modern clothes." Her jaw firmed. "Although that has to change once I get my girls home with me."

So, they were back to that. "I promised you I'd go in and get the girls as soon as we have a location. I have never broken a promise." She pressed her lips together as if trying really hard not to lose her temper. "You do not seem to understand the situation." Her hand felt just right under his, but he released her when she pulled away. "If you do find Sam Kyllwood, he will be located at a temporary stronghold for military soldiers. My girls are at a more permanent stronghold, out of the way. They're only brought along to control me."

The female made sense. "Why haven't you tried to escape through the years? I mean, I understand why you didn't a hundred years ago, but even being isolated the way you've been, surely you understand how life has changed for women. At least immortal ones."

She shook her head. "I have tried to escape three times, along with some of the other enhanced females. When a mate tries to escape, her mate deals with her. Usually harshly, and she's often sent back to a main headquarters somewhere cold."

His gut clenched. "What about if widows try?"

She shrugged. "It depends. Sometimes they're beaten, and sometimes they're sent elsewhere. I've received both treatments." The casual way she spoke demonstrated acceptance of a life she never should've known.

Anger burned through Benny's body, singeing his ears. "Tell me anybody who's put a hand on you, and I'll make sure they lose it before they lose their head."

"Our priority is my daughters, and I'm the only one who can get to them." Her jaw firmed.

The fighting males rolled right into the river.

Haven set down her glass. "Benny? Fish them out, would you? Morons."

Benny stood. Oh, he wasn't fishing them out. The way he was feeling, he'd beat them both senseless. "No problem." He jumped toward the river.

* * * *

Karma lay quietly in the guest bedroom of Benjamin's lovely home on the river. While the cabin at the false headquarters had been charming, this house was beyond her dreams. All wood and stone, perfectly luxe and beautiful. The wide windows let in the outside light from every angle, and whoever had decorated it had kept Benjamin's size and tastes in mind. It was masculine and comfortable with wide furniture and stunning oil paintings.

How surprising that the Seven had had a decoy headquarters just in case. She could understand why they'd taken her there, and it had fooled the Kurjans. Did the Kurjans know that fact yet? How strong was Sam Kyllwood? If his brother was anything to measure him by, Sam would be incredibly difficult to break.

Terre was a master at breaking prisoners, or so she'd heard. General Jaydon's skill at torture was legendary among the Kurjan people, as well.

Her heart hurt for the middle Kyllwood brother.

She took a deep breath, sat up in the humungous bed, and mentally called out for Linda.

"That's the first time you've ever called for me." Linda popped up on the bed and took a seat. Her thick hair wafted around her head, and her light brown eyes seemed almost translucent, even more so than her form. With each passing month, less and less of her body could be seen, and right now, Karma could view a beautiful oil painting signed by Haven Daly *right through* Linda's form. "What's going on?"

"I've been calling you all day," Karma said quietly. "Where have you been?"

Linda paused and her full lips dropped open. "You have? I didn't hear or feel you. But I was taking a rest—we need that, you know—and then I heard you. So here I am. Where the heck are you?"

"Somewhere in Wyoming at the *real* Seven headquarters."
Karma smoothed her hair back into the braid she'd woven for
sleep. It felt good to talk to somebody other than the Seven and
their mates, who were kind but not exactly on her side. "The other
headquarters was a decoy, and the Kurjans might believe me to
be dead. Do you have any news on the girls?"

Linda threw up her hands. The room chilled. "No. I have only
been able to see them through you. If you're not with them, I can't
know how they're doing."

"All right." Karma shivered and pulled the blankets up to her
waist. "We've never really talked about what you can do, because
I don't care. So long as you protect the girls as much as possible."

"I can't do that if you're not with them. You're the conduit,"
Linda said, her face dropping.

"I know, but are you sure?" Karma rubbed her cold arms.
"You've always concentrated on the girls and me. Can you go
anywhere you want in, well, ghost world?"

"Ghost world?" Linda rolled her eyes, and they kept going like
spinning tops.

Karma gagged and looked away. "Stop that. For goodness'
sake, I do not want to vomit. Stop it."

"Sorry." Linda sighed. "Sometimes I can attach myself to
people you've been around, but it has to be recent. I just tried to
find the girls, and I couldn't do it. They might be farther away
from here than you think, and oddly enough, spatial relations do
seem to matter."

Karma had never interacted with a spirit to this degree, and
perhaps that had been a mistake. Except she didn't want to spend
a lot of time with ghosts. They all left sooner or later. "I need you
to try to find Terre. He's spent enough time around me that you
should be able to locate him if he's somewhere near here. Right?"

"Maybe. I don't know. I can try," Linda said.

Karma studied her wispy form. "Are there other ghosts nearby?
Do you have interactions with anybody?"

Linda looked at her as if she'd lost her mind. "Of course not. There's not a special town with ghosts who refuse to cross over. Frankly, there aren't many channelers, either. I think most people ignore the gift, as you would like to do."

Karma couldn't argue that point. Normally, she'd love not to deal with ghosts. Many were just angry, which kept them from passing through for at least a little while. Sure, she'd helped some spirits say goodbye to this world in one way or another, but her ability to interact with them had been limited. What if she were free? Would she be able to help more spirits? She liked that idea, but it was probably not to be.

Unless she could get her girls free. That, she had to do. "All right. Please do me a favor and go see if you can find out where Terre is." She leaned forward and tried to calm the hope in her breast. "See if the girls are anywhere near him. Perhaps if you find Terre, you will also find the girls? It's doubtful, so do not be disappointed. But there is still a chance." She bit her lip. "Can you read documents?"

"Yes, I just can't lift them." Linda reached for the bedspread, and her hand went right through. "See? I've been practicing, but I can't get hold of anything real. Anything in your world."

Karma kept her voice low so Benjamin wouldn't hear. "Please stop procrastinating. We must discover if you can be of help or not."

A tear slid down Linda's face, dropping into nothingness. "What if I can't be of help? We don't know where the girls are." Her emotions wafted from her, lowering the temperature of the room even more.

Karma straightened her posture. "Then we shall find another way to get our girls free. Together, we should be unstoppable." Yes, they were a Kurjan Soti and a ghost who couldn't touch this world, but they loved those girls, and that would have to be enough. "Let's try this first."

"Okay." Linda shut her eyes and winked out of sight.

The room instantly warmed up again. Karma waited and then waited some more. Finally, she snuggled down in the covers and closed her eyes to get a little rest. Who knew how time moved in the spirit world.

Her dreams were fluid and calm until she was jerked upright by a loud whisper. "What?" She sat straight up, her brain still in a dream about dolphins.

Linda sat on the bed. "I saw Terre and Jaydon. We found them. We can do this before I'm forced to cross over, Karma."

Chapter Twenty-One

Benny burned for the stubborn female in his guest room. The way she'd stood up to him earlier about returning to Kurjan territory was plain and simply sexy as hell. Karma might've practiced meekness for the last century to survive, but the female had a will of iron. Man, he liked that. In fact, he liked her.

He tipped back another glass of Scotch and headed outside to stare at the moon so he wouldn't knock on her door. She was an innocent, and the things he wanted to do to her, with her, were anything but pure. She was an old-fashioned lady, and she wouldn't consider a short-term fling. In addition, she apparently had two little girls. He had no clue what to do with little kids. No doubt he'd scare the heck out of them just by being himself.

He rubbed his chest and took a seat on his sprawling deck, admiring the way the moon glinted off the sleepy river. It was fall, the river had slowed down, and he liked this place. Mercy had left after helping him with a project, and now he wished she'd stayed for a while to talk.

Ragged breath sounded, and he moved to the edge of the deck to see Garrett running along the river. The kid stopped. "Scotch?"

"Yep." Benny ducked inside for the bottle and another glass, joining his friend on the deck. "You've been running for the last four hours?" It had to be about midnight.

"Yeah. We couldn't find Sam, so I thought I'd take a break before Logan and I came to blows. We're not going to find Sam tonight." Even though his tone was casual, Garrett's eyes were tortured.

Benny handed over a full glass of Glenfiddich.

Garrett accepted and dropped into the adjacent wooden deck chair, his bare chest and black gym shorts sweaty. While the fusing of his torso wasn't visible from the front, the back looked like a massive tattoo of solid ribs. "Thanks."

Benny sat. "Kid, you need to tell me what's going on."

Garrett downed half of the glass. "I'm middle-aged for a human, Ben. Maybe it's time to stop calling me 'kid'."

Middle age for a human was still young, very young, for an immortal. "We're brothers now, and I've never had a younger brother until you and Logan survived the Seven ritual." God, it had been difficult watching them both barely make it through the devastating journey. "I'd like to keep the 'kid' for a while." Though he'd stop if Garrett insisted.

"You do you," Garrett muttered, taking another deep drink.

"Thanks." Benny grinned and sipped, eyeing the young Kayrs. He looked remarkably like his father. Talen had the same wide chest and ripped muscles, and they both had an air of being relaxed even when they were ready to spring into action. "Doesn't your dad have the ability to halt the enemy in battle?"

"Yep," Garrett said. "Before you ask, I'm finally developing it, which is pretty cool. Dad said he didn't learn how until he was older, so we've been working on it when we get together."

Must be nice. Benny missed his parents, even to this day. Although he had the Seven as family, as well as several nephews who drove him crazy once in a while. "Okay. Spill it." He leaned over and refilled Garrett's glass.

"It's so stupid," Garrett muttered, becoming a hulking form in the deck chair as a cloud shrouded the moon for a moment.

"Most things that really bug us are dumb," Benny agreed. "Doesn't make it any easier to deal with. You know what does?"

Garrett stared into the distance. "Sharing the problem?"

"Shit, no. Scotch and beating the crap out of somebody else." Benny kicked his legs out and crossed his ankles, relaxing into a philosophical mood. "You have Scotch, and you and Quade had a good fight, so if you're not better, you need to talk. That rarely helps, but what the hell. What is going on with you?"

Garrett tipped back his head.

"If you're going to drink my good stuff, you'd better start talking," Benny warned. Otherwise, they'd try the beating part again.

"I know. I'm having dreams, and they're driving me shitballs," Garrett growled. "I've thought about asking my sister about them since she's all about dream worlds, but then she'll worry and bug me about it constantly. Don't get me wrong. I love Janie, but she can be a little over-the-top sometimes. Plus, she's mated to the king of the demon nation, and I don't need Zane up my ass about this."

Benny nodded. "You know, all of that makes sense. So tell me about the dreams. I won't worry or bug you, and the last place I'd ever want to be is up your ass."

Garrett coughed, laughed, and spit out Scotch. Then he laughed some more. "Okay." Chuckling, he sipped again and settled back into the seat. "In this dream, I'm on a motorcycle, there's a female holding on behind me, and we're on a ride with a bunch of other bikers. She smells like melted sugar and honey, and I can't see her. I can feel her, and I can sense the danger coming for her, but I can't turn."

Benny watched the moon beat the cloud and shine down again. "What happens then?"

"That's mostly it. Over and over and fucking over," Garrett said. "I feel like there's a clock over my head counting down, faster than normal time, and I can't get to her. Then, at the last second, she's gone, and I'm cold. I failed."

Benny winced. "That sucks. You think Fate is giving you a heads-up?"

"I don't know. Fate doesn't usually talk to me, and I'm not psychic in any way, at least I never have been. I can't let go of it. Every night I have the same dream, and every morning, I feel her being taken away. Sometimes I'm furious with her for not fighting harder, and I'm always angry with myself for losing her. It's killing me." Garrett finished his second glass.

Benny thought through the problem. "What's your plan?"

Garrett growled. "What do you mean?"

Benny rolled his eyes. "Come on. I know you. You always have a plan. What is it?"

Garrett wiped sweat off his brow. "I've been researching motorcycle clubs to join—after we get Sam safely home."

"That's dumb. If you're going to join a club, it should be an immortal one. Didn't you and Logan go undercover as prospects with Bear and his Grizzlies a while back?"

"Yep," Garrett said.

"There you go, then." If Garrett was with Bear, the head of the Grizzly Nation, then at least he'd have backup.

Garrett reached for the bottle. "You seemed to have forgotten that the shifter nation hates the Seven to the point that it withdrew from the Realm just because the Realm wouldn't denounce us. The Seven screwed with the laws of physics when we created the prison world to hold Ulric, and we did it again when we fused our torsos. Shifters believe in the supremacy of natural law and won't forgive us."

Benny shrugged. "Bear isn't like most shifters. He's a rebel, and he's a friend of yours. Either he'll take you in, or he'll rip off your head."

"Your point?" Garrett asked dryly.

"Either way, you won't have to worry about the dream any longer." Benny clapped his hands on his firm belly. Yeah, he was good at this friendship stuff. "Problem solved."

* * * *

Sometimes it was difficult to determine whether Benjamin was joking or serious. Karma eavesdropped on the conversation for a little while, wondering why Garrett would want to join a shifter motorcycle club. Weren't shifters just like animals? Her feet got chilly on the cold floor by the screen door, but curiosity kept her still.

Finally, Garrett clapped Benjamin on the shoulder and ran down by the river again. The smell of Scotch trailed in his wake.

Benny watched him go. "Are you going to come out or stay over there by the cold doorway?"

She jumped. Part of her wanted to flee back to the bedroom; the other part wanted to be brave and modern. "I'm coming out," she said softly.

"Grab a blanket off the sofa first," he said.

She turned and fetched a soft faux-fur blanket and then padded outside on her bare feet to claim Garrett's vacated seat. She'd already donned a cardigan over her borrowed pajamas, and once she'd settled the blanket around her legs, she felt comfortable and safe. Then Benjamin handed her his glass of Scotch. "Thank you," she said primly. They had kissed, so sharing his glass was probably not a big deal.

"You're welcome." He snagged Garrett's glass off the deck, wiped the rim, and poured a generous shot. "Have you had Glenfiddich before?"

"No." She took a sip, and the spicy liquid exploded on her tongue and down her throat to warm her stomach. She coughed. "I like it?"

He chuckled. "I can get you something else if you prefer."

The warmth spread throughout her limbs. "No, thank you. I am enjoying this." She took another tentative sip. "It's warming on a cool night."

"Why aren't you sleeping?" he asked, sounding thoughtful as he stared at the darkened river.

She drank more. "I was talking with Linda, the female who gave birth to my girls. I asked her to see if she could either find them or Sam Kyllwood."

Benjamin stiffened and turned her way. "I forgot you can talk to ghosts. Is there a chance she can help?"

Karma's shoulders relaxed on their own. "Yes. Linda doesn't know where the girls are, but she found Terre, Dayne, and Jaydon. She's working on finding their location. All she could tell me tonight was that they were near a lake and it's dark there. It has to be somewhat close for her to have been able to find them. My guess is within an hour or two, based on the time it took her to find them and get back to me."

Benny sipped slowly, his eyes blazing through the darkened night. "Let me get this straight. She can't just whip back and forth? It actually takes the same amount of time as it would for us in a car? Or walking?"

"I believe so, and it's my understanding that she kind of latches on to a sensitive being in the process," Karma admitted, taking another drink. The Scotch was tasty. She hadn't liked beer; she was more accustomed to wine. There was always wine in the Kurjan strongholds, and she was partial to Chianti, although this Scotch could become a favorite. "She was going to try to reach Terre on her own, but I'm worried about her. Usually I'm the one doing the work for the spirit."

"Like what?" Benjamin asked.

She paused with the glass almost to her mouth. Nobody ever asked her questions. "Oh. Well, years ago, one human man asked me to send a letter to his fiancée, and I did. Another woman asked me to say a special prayer for her, and I did. Just a few months ago, a teenager asked me to email his parents from his account, and I did so. I had to get sneaky, but I managed to do it."

Benjamin's lips curved in a half smile. "That's sweet. What did the kid die of?"

"Cancer," she murmured. "He just wanted an email from him to them about how he wasn't scared and loved them. He said he'd save a place in heaven for them. We made sure to backdate the email and send it to an account the parents didn't check all the time."

"That's kind of you, Karma," Benjamin said.

"I've tried to help the females I've met in the Kurjan camps, and now I might not be able to help them any longer. I can't go back after I get my girls." The guilt felt heavy.

"Not your fault," Benjamin said. "You've done what you could, and I have no doubt there will be more people to help, wherever you end up."

Warmth, stronger than that from the Scotch, filtered through her body. Right beneath her skin. "You're the kind one."

"Ha," he said. "I've been called many things, but kind isn't one of them." He took another drink of his Scotch. "This Linda has been with you longer than most?"

"Definitely." She took a bigger drink this time. "Ever since the twins came to live with me, Linda has been there. She doesn't want to cross over until they're safe, which I understand."

"Where do people actually go? Do you know?" he asked.

She smiled. "Not really, but they don't seem scared, so I figure it's a good place. For most people, anyway." She sipped delicately. "Linda will try to find where Sam is, don't worry. At the very least, we know the Kurjans are close-by and don't seem to be moving yet. She said they were staying in tents somewhere."

Benjamin shook his head. "I never thought I'd get help from a ghost."

"I believe they prefer to be called spirits," she murmured. "May I ask you a question, Benjamin?"

He chuckled. "You can ask me as many questions as you like."

Could he get any kinder? "Are shifters animals?"

"Well, yeah. I mean, they shift into animals. Canine, feline, or bear. And it's a secret, but there are dragons. Few and far between."

Dragons? Fascinating. She'd had no idea. "That's not what I meant. Are they just animals? Not evolved?"

"Oh. No. They're just like you and me, but they can shift into animals. I've never known of anybody who could shift into an animal other than the ones I mentioned." He took another big drink. "Keep it a secret about the dragons. I'm sure I'm not supposed to tell anybody." Then he turned to her. "So. Wanna make out?"

Chapter Twenty-Two

For breakfast, Karma dished scrambled eggs onto her plate in the sprawling dining room of the main lodge and then sat on the deck, where Mercy was waiting for her.

"Did you get some of the watermelon?" Mercy asked, nearly bouncing in her chair. "I cut it into small pieces that we can throw at the guys if they tick us off." She grinned, but her smile didn't quite reach her eyes. Lines of stress extended from the edges, and dark circles were smudged below them.

Karma sat. "Did you not sleep at all last night?"

Mercy ate part of a cinnamon roll. "I slept a little, but Logan didn't sleep at all. He kept going through the satellite feeds, trying to figure out which way the Kurjans went."

Karma patted her hand. "We'll find Sam. I have Linda working on it, and she's determined." She hoped Mercy didn't think she was insane or lying. "I believe Benjamin called Logan earlier this morning to let him know about Linda. Perhaps the information she finds will help somewhat."

"I hope so. It's pretty cool that you can see spirits." Mercy perked up as Logan and Garrett strode out of the lodge into the meager autumn sun. "There are pancakes, too. I made them with huckleberries that were still left in the freezer. They're not as good as Haven's, but at least I didn't add salt to the recipe this time."

Karma looked toward the lodge. "Where are Haven and Quade?"

"They left at first light to reach out to the Fae nation. Haven is half-Fae, so she's taking my place handling diplomacy right now. I want to stay here with Logan until we find Sam." Mercy took another bite of the roll. "It's good for her to spend time with them. She was raised human rather than Fae."

Karma took a sip of her mimosa. The Seven seemed to drink a lot of alcohol, but she wasn't complaining. "You and Haven weren't raised together?"

Mercy shook her head. "Nope. We didn't even know of each other until after she mated with Quade. It's so awesome to have a sister. Did you have sisters?"

"No. I was an only child, which was rare back then," Karma said. Would she have tried to return to a sibling after her mate had died if she'd had one? If she'd had a sister like Mercy, then certainly she would've tried her best to reconnect.

Mercy looked over Karma's shoulder at the side of the deck, her eyes widened, and then she spit out her mimosa. She coughed wildly and gestured crazily.

Logan and Garrett both stopped short on the deck, their jaws going slack.

Karma slowly turned to see what had shocked them. "Oh my goodness," she whispered.

Benjamin Reese stomped across the grassy area by the river, his combat boots making deep imprints. He wore a too-tight long-sleeved blouse that was buttoned to his neck as well as a long skirt that forced him to shorten his stride.

Karma's jaw dropped. Was he ridiculing her? That didn't seem like Benjamin.

He paused in the grass and motioned Garrett and Logan forward. "Karma? I'm showing you that you can fight no matter what you're wearing. You've mentioned several times that a lady can't fight decently in a skirt or a long dress. I understand a skirt might be a hindrance, but so is a broken arm or self-doubt. You can fight in any situation, and I'm going to prove it to you."

She couldn't speak. The male looked absolutely ridiculous in the green floral skirt and too-tight white button-down shirt. "Where—" She couldn't finish the sentence.

Mercy wiped tears off her face and then laughed some more. She pressed a hand to her stomach and took several deep breaths. "The shirt was Ivar's—he used to be much thinner. And the skirt is a shower curtain I sewed together for Benny. How sweet is he? I mean, he is never going to live this down, and he doesn't care."

Neither Logan nor Garrett had moved.

Benjamin put his hands on his hips, where the skirt was tucked in. "Get out here, you two. I want to take both of you on. You're both on edge, and frankly, I'm tired of it. Let's do this."

Logan tossed his plate onto the table, and it clattered several inches. Garrett put his down carefully and then followed Logan over the steps to the grass. Both males cracked their knuckles and then spread out, going at Benjamin from different sides.

"Wait a minute." Karma finally found her voice. She stood. "Two against one is not fair." Especially when the one was wearing a skirt that kept tripping him up.

Benjamin bent his knees and angled his body to keep both of the other males in his sight. "Fights are never fair, sweetheart. That's your first lesson." With the river at his back, at least the other two couldn't circle around him from behind.

She started forward, but Mercy grasped her arm. "Let them fight. Benny went to a lot of trouble to put on that ridiculous shower curtain for you."

Nobody had ever done anything so sweet for her before. Not that Benjamin didn't look good in a skirt, because he did. He would've looked amazing in a kilt. But the shower curtain was truly abominable. The flowers were a terrible lamé gold with flecks of vomit-colored green. Three or four birds danced around in the pattern. They were blue, but they didn't look like any bluebirds

Karma had ever seen. "That is the ugliest shower curtain in existence," she whispered.

Mercy sputtered out a laugh and then covered her mouth. "I know. It's terrible, right? We have a lighter purple one in a guesthouse down the way, but I couldn't help myself when Benjamin asked for a skirt. It's probably going to rip in the fight, and I didn't want to have to buy a new one for the purple bathroom. Well, lilac, I guess."

Garrett charged first. Head down, he went for Benjamin's midsection. The second he made contact, Logan rushed forward, aiming for Benjamin's head.

Benjamin pivoted and kicked Logan in the balls as he went down to the ground. The second he landed, he clocked Garrett in the throat with a forearm and threw the younger hybrid toward Logan, who'd dropped to his knees, one hand on his groin.

In an impressive display of strength, all three males went from the ground to their feet in one smooth move. "Wow," Karma breathed.

Mercy reached for her plate of eggs and perched on top of the table, watching with excitement. "I know, right? This is going to be a good fight." She scooted over and motioned for Karma to sit next to her. "Come on. We can still eat while cheering them on."

Karma delicately sat next to Mercy on the table and placed her feet on a chair, careful to keep her knees together. Unlike Benjamin. He aimed an impressive sidekick at Garrett's chin while spinning around to punch Logan in the jaw.

"Whoa," Mercy said, wincing. "Nice punch, Ben!"

"Thanks," Benjamin said, flipping backward and landing behind Garrett to place him in a choke hold.

Garrett grabbed Benjamin's forearm, dropped his weight, and threw the hybrid over his head. Benjamin landed on his back, rolled, and came up into a tackle into Logan's torso.

"Great throw, G," Mercy called, taking a swig of her drink.

Logan and Benjamin butted heads, and the sound echoed through the morning. Logan swept left with one foot while grabbing Benjamin's head and throwing him toward the deck. Benjamin's head impacted with a cracking sound.

"Excellent toss, baby," Mercy said, pumping her fork in the air. "You got him good, Logan. I want to learn that move."

Benjamin backflipped to his feet and pivoted in a sidekick that caught a rushing Garrett in the gut.

"Oof," Mercy agreed, spooning eggs into her mouth. She swallowed. "That's gonna leave a bruise, Garrett. Well, probably not. Considering your fused torso." She took another couple of bites. "Your foot might be bruised, Benny."

Karma looked sideways at her new friend. "Are all Fae slightly, well, nutty?"

"Yes," all three males said in unison, circling each other for an opening.

Mercy snorted. "No. We just like fun. Come on, guys. Stop playing ring-around-a-rosy. Do something interesting."

Karma couldn't breathe. Her mind blanked. She gently grasped Mercy's arm. "I do not understand. You care about these males. Why do you want them to harm each other in a fight?"

Mercy set down her plate and reached for the mimosa glasses, handing one to Karma. "They're brothers, Karma. They won't really harm each other. Plus, they're immortal males, and they have stress, and this is a good way to deal with some of that." She looked Karma in the eyes. "And apparently Benny is trying to prove something to you. Maybe a couple of things."

Karma sipped the delicious drink and watched Benjamin throw Logan into Garrett. Both young immortals crashed into a large pine tree, and pine cones and needles rained down. "Are you able to fight?"

"Sure," Mercy said, angling her neck to watch Logan take Benjamin down to the ground with both arms around the knees. "I'm not the best at it, but I can hold my own if necessary. Logan does most of the fighting in our family, but that's just because he's better trained and also a protective jackass sometimes." She grinned. "I do love that hybrid."

This was a whole new world. "I've never seen the Kurjans or the Cysts train for fun," Karma admitted. "When they fight, they do so to maim or really harm each other."

"That sucks," Mercy said quietly. "Did you see that kick Benny just landed on Garrett's ear? In a skirt?"

Karma took another drink. "Yes. He lifted the skirt, kicked, and then lowered it again. I saw his black briefs." And his muscled thighs. Benjamin Reese had masculine legs. Strong and powerful. Jitters cascaded through her abdomen, and her breath shortened. Was there a chance he'd kiss her again?

As she watched him valiantly fight off two dangerous warriors while wearing a constricting skirt, her heart seemed to swell. Nobody had ever done something so kind for her. He was teaching her that she could survive on her own, without him, without anybody.

That was selfless.

She'd dreamed of him through the years, after their first meeting. Wondrous dreams. But nothing came close to the reality of the kind soldier. Yes, he was deadly, and there was no doubt he could be bossy. Yet the way he cared for her, his attempts to help her see her own value, were things she'd never expected. Not from any male—much less one of the Seven, who were known as the deadliest and most dangerous males around.

The more time she spent with Logan and Mercy, the more evident it became that Logan was actually strengthened by their bond instead of weakened.

The Kurjans had that wrong. She was certain of it. Perhaps that was why the Kurjans had lost the last war.

Garrett caught Benjamin with a shocking uppercut that threw Benjamin's head back with a loud crack.

Karma gasped and stood up. Was he all right?

Benjamin lowered his chin and set his stance. His eyes swirled with a dangerous glint. "Oh, kid. You should've known better." He kicked the skirt out of the way and crouched, leaping forward with an impressive amount of speed and power.

Garrett's eyes widened, but before he could move, Benjamin connected and partially lifted the younger warrior to throw him into the river. Garrett landed with a hard splash.

Logan jumped for Benjamin, but Benjamin twisted at the last moment, manacled Logan around the neck, and then kept spinning until he released the hybrid. Logan sailed through the air and landed on Garrett. Both young warriors went under the water.

Mercy snorted.

Garrett and Logan both stood, water sliding down their bodies, their hair matted to their heads. Fury and fire lit their immortal eyes.

Benjamin looked at them, paused, and then threw back his head and laughed. Long and hard, he laughed until he had to hold his belly.

Karma couldn't breathe. His strength was impressive, but that laugh. It warmed her from head to toe.

Logan smiled first, right before Garrett did the same. Then they laughed as well, helping each other across the rocks and slipping several times before reaching the shore.

Benjamin prowled forward to help them out of the water. "You're excellent fighters." He sounded both pleased and proud. "I just have centuries of experience on you. Man, that was fun. Let's do it again."

Mercy whistled, making Karma jump. "You've all goofed off enough for the morning. Come eat your breakfast so we can get back to work." Her voice was no-nonsense, and shock of shocks, all three males instantly pivoted to come back and eat breakfast. They'd obeyed her.

Karma tried to mask her surprise.

Benjamin ambled up, the plastic skirt he'd put on again swaying as he moved. He reached her and smiled. "See what I mean?" Numbly, she could only nod. "You're very kind, Benjamin." He scowled, but the sparkle remained in his spectacular eyes. "Geez. Be nice, Karma. Don't tell anybody that."

She burst out laughing, shocking herself. Oh, goodness. She was absolutely falling for this deadly male. The one member of the Seven who would not mate. She sobered. "I won't tell a soul. I promise."

He grinned, sealing her fate. Taking her heart.

Darn it.

Chapter Twenty-Three

It was another fruitless day of trying to find Sam's location. Benjamin's patience was stretched as thin as a spiderweb, and Logan's was worse. They'd agreed to notify both the Realm and the demon nations if they hadn't located Sam by the morning, and Logan looked like he was going to puke at the thought of telling his older brother that Sam was in the hands of the enemy.

They sat at a campfire outside the main lodge, working through the discoveries of the day. Benny looked to his side to make sure Karma was bundled up warmly in the blanket and jacket he'd found for her.

She stared at the flames, her legs drawn up beneath her and covered by the blanket. "I think Linda's been resting, and after that she'll be able to travel more. So I'm expecting her to check in again now that's it's dark. I'm hoping. She was determined to find their location, but she can't move maps to help her navigate, so she just has to keep looking."

Benny reached out and took her hand, unable to stop himself. "You're doing your best. Just take a deep breath and wait for her to arrive."

She sighed. "I've experimented a little through the years, and most spirits can't travel like this. She seems to be losing power each time, and I'm not sure how much longer she'll last here."

Garrett leaned toward the fire, his elbows on his knees. "We have it narrowed down to eight probable locations, but that's too many for us to scout on our own." He looked sideways to where Logan sat on the other side of Mercy. "Where's your mom these days?" Logan winced. "She's in Ireland at Witch Headquarters, and she's gonna be pissed I haven't told her about this."

Karma perked up. "Your mom is a witch?" Vampires and Kurjans were male only, but the rest of the immortal species had females as well. Hope Kayrs-Kyllwood was the one exception in the history of the world, because she had vampire blood in her.

"No," Logan said. "My mom is a purebred demoness, and she mated Daire Dunne, one of the witch Enforcers. Believe it or not, I have a little sister." He grinned. "She's almost as wild as our mom."

Garrett snorted. "Logan's mom likes to rob banks for fun."

"Just the safety-deposit boxes and accounts of criminals," Logan protested.

Karma sat straighter. "Wait a minute. Your father had to have been a vampire. Yet she's mated to a witch? Did your mother take the same virus I took?"

Logan nodded. "Our father died a long time ago, and Mom took the virus before she mated Daire. It all worked out in the end, although she's going to kill me if she ever finds out that Sam was taken by the Kurjans and I didn't immediately call her."

"That is not a lie. Your mother is intense," Garrett said.

Logan picked up his mug of coffee and stood. "I'm going to study those schematics of the mountain range to the south one more time. Just in case."

Mercy stretched to her feet, barely reaching Logan's chest in height. "I'll help."

Garrett also stood. "I'm going for a run, and then I'll be back to help. Maybe there's something I missed about the Nevada rock formation that's a possible location."

Benny remained in place. "Karma? Do you want to stay here by the fire for a little while to see if Linda makes contact? Maybe with fewer people around, she'll show?"

Karma squirmed. It was obvious she wasn't accustomed to people asking her opinion or what she wanted. The idea just pissed Benny off. Finally, she cleared her throat. "Yes. That's a good suggestion," she said.

Benny smiled. "We'll do that and then maybe join you all to look through more data."

The other three left, and Benny stretched out his legs toward the fire. "Do you want more coffee?" He glanced at her half-empty mug.

"I am fine," she said softly, watching the flickering flames. "That really was nice of you this morning—wearing the skirt."

He took another swig of the excellent coffee Karma had made. "Did you get the point?"

"Of course." She sipped delicately, and the firelight caressed her heart-shaped face the way Benny wanted to do. "I think I should like to train when I get the girls free. It's doubtful I'll have time before that." She turned toward him, her eyes a glimmering hue. "Maybe a few lessons before I go? It would be nice to know some self-defense."

He kept her hand in his while he searched for the right words. Too much of her life had been out of her control, and as much as he wanted to tell her what to do, he wouldn't. So he fought himself for the moment. "The coffee is wonderful. Thank you for making it."

She ducked her head, and a lock of her sunshine-colored hair fell onto her cheekbone. "I am happy to help. In fact, I truly enjoy cooking and baking. I've lived so many years underground. Being aboveground and growing herbs is a hobby I would like to pursue further."

He jolted. "Really? No kidding?" His heart leaped.

She laughed softly. "Yes. It's the truth."

Oh, thank God. "Then you're hired while we're here, if you don't mind. I love to cook, and we could have some fun creating dishes." The idea of having decent food enticed him almost as much as the female herself. Her sweet scent wafted his way. What was that? The scent of flowers growing beside a lake? It was all her, and he could wrap himself up in the smell and happily remain beside her.

She took a deep breath.

All right. He was starting to recognize her tells, and she had something to say. Something she was gearing up to communicate. He waited patiently, which was not one of his strong suits.

"Benjamin?"

"Yes?" He turned back to the fire to make it easier for her to ask or say whatever she wanted. The woman was shy.

She waited a beat. "I enjoyed the other morning."

His cock jumped against his denim jeans, and he bit back a groan. "Me, too."

"I was wondering, if it wouldn't be too much trouble—" She shifted restlessly next to him. "I would like one night with you before I return to the Kurjans. A real night. You and me as partners. Just once."

His ears heated and damn if his head didn't almost blow off his entire body.

* * * *

Karma couldn't believe she'd just been so forward with a male. But she wanted one night to feel such pleasure again before she returned to hell, just in case she failed to get the girls out. She was unencumbered by the mating mark, and she could do with her body as she chose. For now, anyway. "I know about modern women," she said softly. "That they have a choice and that one night doesn't have to mean forever." The idea intrigued her, as did ripped abs and prolonged orgasms like she'd read about in the books.

Benjamin made a strangled sound.

Heat flushed into her face, burning her cheeks. "I'm sorry to be forward." It was entirely possible that he didn't want her in that manner. Oh, he'd been interested the other day, but the physical part hadn't progressed very far. Perhaps she'd insulted him. "I also apologize if I've insulted you in any way. I am not saying you're easy." She'd heard the expression from the new mate of a Kurjan lower soldier, and it probably applied in this situation.

He sucked in air and made a gulping sound.

Oh, she could just die. She tried to pull her hand free from underneath his arm and firm palm, but he held her tight.

"Karma." He turned to face her, and his eyes blazed through the darkness. "We need to get a couple of things straight. More things. Besides the fighting-with-a-skirt problem that isn't really a problem."

Was it her imagination, or was Benjamin having difficulty speaking in complete sentences? Had he injured his head that morning when fighting with the other soldiers? She leaned in closer to check his pupils just in case he was concussed. "Are you all right?"

"No, I'm not all right," he sputtered. "You have me harder than a rock, and it's all I can do not to bend you over the nearest table and take what you've so generously offered."

"Oh." She sat back, her body relaxing. He did want her. She had thought so, but it was nice to have the idea affirmed. "Why do you sound pained?"

His flash of teeth didn't reassure her. "I'm pained because I'm hard and I want to do something about it." Then he took a deep breath, exhaled slowly, and did it two more times. "Here's the deal. Yes, I'd like a night with you. In fact, I'd like a whole lot of nights with you. I'm not easy, you're not easy, nobody is easy.

That's just a dumb word. We can do whatever we want so long as it's consensual. That's number one. Got it?"

She quite liked that line of thought. "That makes sense to me."

"Good." His hand tightened on hers. "I've been honest about not wanting to mate, even though I want you with a desperation that burns. Although, from what I've seen around here, if we do indulge, I may throw caution to the wind like the rest of these morons and mate anyway. I mean, with your consent."

Her mouth dropped open. "Um..."

He chuckled and brushed a curl off her forehead. "What I meant is that if mating is on the table, we should discuss it. I like you, you like me, and we definitely have chemistry. But I don't think you should mate somebody just because you think that's what you're supposed to do. You can do anything and be anything you want in this world."

Oh, she just could love him forever. "I know, Benjamin." She wasn't an innocent young girl.

He winced. "Also, I've been a warrior for hundreds of years and don't know a thing about kids. I wouldn't want to hurt your little girls or scare them or screw them up. It's probably much better if I stay away from them."

Could he be any sweeter? Right now, she wanted to concentrate on him. "I've lived a long time, and I've met a lot of people—alive and dead. If I mate, I will do so with my eyes open." It was nice to speak so frankly with him. "I'm not asking to mate. I want to engage in physical closeness with you."

"Sex," he said.

She felt her blush intensify. "Yes. Sex." Just the thought made her body light up like a rocket. "Although, is mating on the table?" She'd heard the expression years ago and liked it.

A muscle ticked right beneath his powerful jawline. "I don't know."

She liked him all the more for his honesty. He wasn't making false promises just to get her into bed. "I agree with the unknowing part but still would like intimacy with you."

Did he growl?

"Okay. One was consent, two was possible mating. Three is a bit more difficult." He looked away at the fire for a moment and then refocused on her, his concentration absolute and somewhat intimidating.

She frowned. "What is difficult? Are you unable—"

"God, no," he burst out. "I'm able. Very, very, very able."

"Oh." She fought a chuckle. "That is nice to know."

He shook his head. "You just need to understand what you're getting into. I'm not kind, Karma. I sure as hell am not gentle, either. I can try, and I will, but you have a watered-down vision of me."

"You are kind, and you are gentle," she said quietly. "I've seen you be both."

He breathed out. "Yes, you have. What I'm saying is that I've been trying to be both of those things for you since you've had a difficult life with very little control. I like control, and I have no problem taking it when necessary. You're someone who deserves to make her own decisions in life. You've earned that."

She bit her lip. "Couldn't we share control?"

He ran his thumb across her knuckles. "Family is everything to me, and I protect family with everything I have and everything I am. Even if it makes them mad or if they think it's unfair." He frowned, but the thumb on her knuckles continued to be gentle, making her shiver. "My motivations are good—to protect and defend. But sometimes I come on too strong. I don't think you could handle that."

Her chin lowered. If he was motivated by affection and protectiveness, she could handle it. "I don't think you'd hurt me."

"Of course not." He sighed. "I also wouldn't let you venture into Kurjan territory by yourself." He seemed to check himself.

"In fact, I'm not going to let it happen now, either. So we'll have to find another way to find your girls and get them to safety. We will, though."

She reached out and cupped his rugged jaw. There was only one way to rescue them, and he'd have to agree with her on that at some point. In fact, that realization made tonight all the more important. It might be her last chance to make her own choices. She chose him. Nerves stretched tight inside her—a combination of need and anxiety. Right now, she needed an answer. "I understand your three points. I have not changed my mind. Have you?"

Chapter Twenty-Four

Benny had never been one to hesitate, and the fact he was doing so now when she'd offered something he so desperately wanted shocked him. The immortal animal, the primal need deep down, had awakened and was ready to play. Ready to take. "How much have you had to drink?" he asked.

"Not enough to make me do something I do not want." She stood then, and the scent of flowers, almost gardenias but with a hint of spice, wafted his way. She flipped her hand beneath his palm to tangle her fingers through his. "Yes or no, Benjamin?"

Yes. Definitely yes. He stood, catching her off guard. Then he smiled at her small gasp of surprise. "You might be doing that a few times tonight." Without waiting for a response, he ducked and caught her up against his chest, turning and striding off the deck and into the darkness.

She slid her arm around his shoulders and snuggled into his chest as if she belonged right there. "You have the broadest chest," she murmured, lifting her head and letting her mouth wander beneath his jaw. "Were you this big and strong before you became a member of the Seven? Your torso is impenetrable, correct?"

Right now it felt like she had a direct line to his heart, and nothing about him was impenetrable. A warning bell clanged in the back of his head, but he gentled his hold as he strode along the river. "Yes and yes." The woman felt light and fragile in his arms, even though her mouth was doing dangerous things to his neck. Once he'd given her the go-ahead, she seemed to want to explore. A lot.

Her hand caressed his shoulder and dug in, tracing the muscle to his neck. Her sigh this time was one of pleasure—and it went right to his balls, tightening them up.

She was killing him, and she had no clue. Damn if that didn't make him want her more. She was genuine and inquisitive, and she wasn't hiding anything about herself. In fact, except for the device that had been implanted in her head, she'd been honest about herself the entire time.

He walked easily up the steps to his back deck and opened the sliding glass door. "There aren't any ghosts here right now, are there?" he asked. Their presence wouldn't stop him, but he wanted to be aware.

"No." She giggled, and the sound was charming. Young and free.

"Good," he growled, prowling through his house without needing the lights. He reached his bedroom and stepped inside, grateful the moon streaming through the window softly illuminated the bed in the middle. Setting her down, he dropped to his haunches in front of her. Even so, he was as tall as she was sitting on the bed. "Are you sure?" He had to ask.

"I'm sure." She slowly began unbuttoning her flouncy blouse with the pearl buttons.

"Me, too." He reached down and unzipped first one boot and then the other, sliding them off her small feet. Women from centuries ago had the darndest small feet. If he and Karma ever danced together, he'd have to be careful not to step on one. Gently, for him, he drew down her stocking, rubbing the pads of his fingers along the smooth skin of her ankles.

She was so soft and breakable—immortal or not. Then he leaned in and kissed her knee.

"Benjamin," she murmured, trembling. "I have to tell you that it has been a long time. I want to please you." She slipped out of the blouse, leaving her in a plain white bra with the cutest pink flower in the center.

"You please me by just existing," he said honestly. Yet the skirt really was a hindrance. So he pushed her back, grasped the waistband, and tore it off her legs.

She laughed out loud this time, and the sound grounded him. Calmed and reassured him. Then she sat up and pushed him in the stomach, and when he stepped back, she stood. "You undressed me. Now I get to undress you." Her knuckles brushed his abdomen when she grasped the bottom of his T-shirt. Jolts of need shot right to his groin. Humming, she slowly pushed the material up, her palms flat against his skin until she reached his neck. He ducked his head and let her continue until she stood up on her toes and pulled the material away. "Oh, Benjamin." She flattened her hands over his chest.

Yep. She was going to kill him. He shoved the animal inside him way down and let her explore. She deserved to play and have fun, even if his head exploded off his body. She unsnapped his jeans, and he helped her shove them to the ground while kicking off his boots.

"You're beautiful, Karma." Sliding his hands through her silky hair, he twisted it at her nape and pulled her head back, taking her mouth. He couldn't wait any longer. Never in his life had taking off his clothes been so erotic. Her lips were soft, and she tasted like chocolate-flavored coffee. She kissed him back, her nails digging into his chest, her open eagerness spurring him on still more.

He unclasped her bra in the back and slid it off her arms, keeping her mouth the entire time. Then he gently brushed his free hand across her nipples, enjoying the shudder that went through her body. He released her mouth to look his fill. She was small and firm, with light pink nipples that looked like candy. "You're perfect," he whispered.

She scraped her nails lightly down his flanks. "You're perfect. Benjamin?"

"Yeah?" he asked, palming her and nearly dying as her hard nipples scraped his palms.

"I would like for you to take over now," she whispered.

* * * *

She might as well be a virgin for all she knew about a male's body. Especially this male. Benjamin was all solid muscle and firm skin. The bulge in his black boxers was both intriguing and intimidating—much like Benjamin himself. She could feel him holding back, and though she appreciated it, he was making her nervous.

He stiffened and looked down at her. "You want me to take over?"

She leaned in and kissed him on the solar plexus. "I really do."

His hands went to her waist and lifted her, tossing her back on the bed. She landed on her butt and bounced, unable to stop the laugh that erupted. Who knew that intimacy with him would be fun? Then he pressed one knee on the bed and leaned down to kiss her navel.

She gasped, and liquid fire shot through her veins faster than a good port. Never in her life had she wanted anything as badly as she wanted his mouth on her skin. His hands on her body. All of Benjamin for her to enjoy. She dug her fingers into his thick hair, which was silkier than she expected. She tugged.

He looked up, crouched over her like a predator, and his eyes glittered. "I'm taking over." His voice had gone demon-rough and hoarse.

The trembling that took her fire-bombed every nerve in her body. Her legs shook, and her abdomen rolled. "Yes." Never in her long life had she felt so needy. So wanted.

His primitive smile should've given her pause, but the promise in his eyes only heated her more. He leaned down and nipped her hip bone before sinking his teeth into the material covering her private parts. He tugged her panties down her legs. With his teeth! Then she was fully nude before him.

"Beautiful," he murmured, caressing his way up her legs and then placing the gentlest of kisses on her clitoris.

Electric zaps zinged through her from his mouth, and she gasped, shocked by the intensity of the pleasure. Then he kissed her again, settling in, his wide shoulders forcing her legs apart. She caught her breath, waiting. What was he going to— "Oh," she breathed, the room wavering.

"Yeah. Oh," he said against her sex, licking her again.

It was decadent and so good. She wasn't sure what to do. "I've never done this before."

His chuckle shot vibrations through her lower body. "You don't have to do anything. Just relax and let me play."

She could do that. When he slid one finger inside her, she wanted more. A lot more. He nipped her, and she spiraled out of control, an orgasm taking her with a suddenness that almost hurt. "Oh. I'm sorry," she whispered.

He looked up. "Huh?"

"It was so fast. I mean, it has been forever. I'm so sorry it was fast." She spoke in a rush, not sure what else to say.

He chuckled, his eyes an odd combination of black and green with no pattern. "Then let's go slower this time." Humming happily, he rubbed his tongue against her swollen clit.

"You don't have to do this. I'm sorry about earlier." She was having trouble thinking.

"Stop apologizing. Anything we do is good." He turned his head and nipped her thigh before returning to her core, his mouth beyond talented. He was doing all the work.

If he didn't stop soon, she wasn't going to be able to think. "Benjamin. This can't be all about me," she moaned. "I am sorry."

Faster than a popped champagne cork, he flipped her over, bit her butt, and flipped her back. His mouth found her again.

She yelped. "What was that for?"

He lifted his head, his gaze intense, his chin...right there. Slowly, he scraped his whiskers across her tender flesh.

Lava poured through her, lighting her on fire. Even so, she kept his gaze.

He grinned. "Lesson four. From now on, anytime you needlessly apologize, I'm going to bite your butt."

She couldn't quite grasp his meaning. "That's crazy." Yet everything inside her that wasn't on fire for him wanted to laugh. To settle into all that was Benjamin Reese.

"Maybe, but I don't like any other forms of discipline for you when you're not being nice to yourself. So, a nip to the ass it is." He licked her, swirling that dangerous tongue over her clit.

She chuckled, but the sound was pained. How in the world did he make her need and laugh at the same time? Maybe she was as crazy as he. He went to work again, using his mouth, teeth, and fingers until she was writhing on the bed, nearly sobbing with need.

Then he pushed her over. Live wires uncoiled inside her, and she detonated, crying out words that didn't make any sense. She rode the climax, shutting her eyes, trusting that she'd survive. Finally, with a soft whimper, she relaxed onto the bed.

Only then did he stand and shove his boxers to the floor.

By all the gods on all the mountains. Benjamin Reese was well endowed. Very. She stared at him from beneath hooded eyelids. "I want to please you," she whispered.

"You do." Anchoring one knee on the bed again, he settled against her, his very hard shaft probing her softened entrance. Her heart softened right along with the rest of her. He had made sure she was ready for him. Had completely put her comfort before his.

She tangled both of her hands in his hair. "You're perfect."

He kissed her hard, going deep. "Yeah, I figured you were nuts. But you go ahead and think I'm perfect." Slowly, he penetrated her, taking his time but giving no quarter.

It truly was the most exquisite feeling in the entire world. "I had no idea," she said, her voice hushed.

He dropped his forehead to hers. "Me, either." For two heartbeats, they were completely connected and still. Then he began to move. Slowly at first and then with increasing speed, he powered into her.

She shut her eyes so she could just feel, holding his hair and lifting her knees to take more of him. He hammered wildly for several long moments until that wire heated up inside her again. She bit her lip, so close to paradise. Then she toppled over, crying out, holding on to him as the waves swept her away.

He groaned against her neck, pounding into her, prolonging her ecstasy. Only then did he shove inside her and jerk with his own release. Slowly, still inside her, he lifted his head and kissed her so tenderly that tears pricked the backs of her eyes.

She blinked, shocked. "I think I love you, Benjamin."

He stiffened.

She slapped her hand against her mouth. What had she just done in the haze of lovemaking? "Oh, no. I'm so sorry."

His jaw tightened, and as sure as the sun would rise, he flipped her over and bit her butt.

Chapter Twenty-Five

The sun was barely peeking over the mountain as Benny skipped another rock across the river. Clouds rolled in from the east, promising a heck of an autumn storm. Even now, the dew on the weeds had dampened his boots and the bottoms of his jeans.

"What are you up to?" Mercy jogged up the river, her leggings the same color as the turning leaves on the other side.

He double checked for threats. Nope. "Nothing. Just thinking."

Mercy stopped. "Does it hurt?"

He snorted. The fairy was the closest thing to a sister that he'd never wanted, and he pretty much adored her. She was crazier than he, which was kind of nice. Plus, with her one green and one blue eye, she was always interesting to look at, and that was even when she wasn't driving poor Logan insane. "Yes, my brain hurts when I think. Happy now?"

"No." She leaned down and fetched a smooth rock. "It's no fun messing with you when you agree. What's the matter?" She expertly skipped the rock across the entire span of water, her curly hair bouncing in the chilly breeze.

He looked around. "Where's Logan?" It was odd to see Mercy out jogging without her mate.

She put her hands on slim hips covered by a bright orange hoodie that kind of matched her leggings. "Why? Do you think I can't go jogging by myself?"

"Not usually," Benny admitted. "Where is he?"

She huffed and picked up another rock. "We saw you, and I said I wanted to talk to you, so he returned to the control room to search for Sam. Again." Her eyebrows drew together, and she threw the rock too hard. It splashed twice and then sank to the bottom.

Benny handed her another rock. "This is a good one. Don't worry. We'll find Sam." He'd left Karma sleeping peacefully in his bed, hoping Linda would visit her and be helpful. He wasn't counting on it, though. "What time are we calling Zane and the demon nation?"

Mercy grimaced. "By noon. We can't wait longer than that."

Man, this might mean war. Brother against brother, family against family, and mates caught in the middle. Benny plucked a smooth rock off the ground and zinged it across the water, skipping it at least ten times.

"Nice," Mercy said, side-arming her rock. It skipped eleven times. "Tell me what's going on in your head. I can smell Karma all over you, but I don't sense matehood. So you got some, huh?" She grinned.

"Watch it or I'll toss you in," he said, kind of meaning it. "She's a lady."

"Does the lady have moves?" Mercy danced around him, her eyes full of sparkle. "Are you in luuuuuv?"

He rolled his eyes. While he'd like to discuss what Karma had said about mating, he didn't want to break her confidence. "I like her, you know?"

Mercy's expression turned dreamy. "Yeah. Are you going to mate?"

He lifted a shoulder. "I'm not sure. She's never been on her own or had choices, and I don't want to lock her down before she has a chance to see some of the world. Plus, there's the final battle coming up, and you know not all of us are going to survive. She also has two little girls, and I'm terrible around kids. Probably. What if I scare them? Finally, I like her, but I'm not into the whole white-picket, forever, roses, and mushy crap." He wasn't enough for a female who wanted all the trimmings.

Mercy's expression softened. She moved toward him, stretched up on her toes...and punched him right in the eye.

He growled and stepped back, clapping a hand over his brutalized eye. "What did you do that for, you crazy fairy?"

"Fae," she said, huffing. "I did that because you're a moron."

He sent healing cells to his eye to make sure it wasn't truly damaged. Nope. It just hurt like hell. What had he been thinking to seek advice from a Fae? "That was unnecessary," he complained, removing his hand and blinking into the soft light of the morning.

She reached for a rock and straightened up.

He paused and watched her carefully, just in case she decided to throw it at his head.

A small smile played on her pixie-like face, and she skipped the rock across the river. Twelve times. "One, Karma is old enough, by far, to make her own choices. If she's dumb enough to choose you, then thank your lucky stars. Two, I am so tired of hearing about that final battle. If Ulric makes it back here, we'll all deal with him as a team. Third, you're half-crazy, which kids just love. Any little girls lucky enough to have you around would love their very safe and probably wild life. And fourth, what makes you think any of us want white picket fences or roses? Personally, I like metal throwing stars and tulips." She turned to face him, her stance set.

He took two very cautious steps back. It wouldn't be the first time Mercy had kicked him in the neck, but he just wasn't in the mood. "I have no idea how Logan puts up with you." He kind of meant it, but his voice was still soft because this was Mercy.

"I know, right?" She snorted and bounced back on her heels. "Do you want to spar?"

"No." He shook his head. The fairy was smart and could be mean, but she really wasn't that good of a fighter. He'd spend too much time making sure she didn't get hurt, and she'd end up punching him in the eye again.

Mercy ducked her head and then moved, coming close again. He tensed.

She reached for his arm and patted his sleeve. "Listen. You're a good guy, Benny. I think if you gave things a chance with Karma, you might find happiness. You deserve that, and I'd love to see you with somebody. You don't have to be alone just because there might be a battle a zillion years from now."

"Thanks." He smiled at her, keeping his thoughts to himself. The timeline was narrowing—he felt it in his very bones. Ulric would soon gain his freedom, and the final battle would happen before any of them expected.

It was definitely coming.

* * * *

Karma rolled over in the ocean-wide bed and stretched before wincing. Wow. She was sore *everywhere*. There wasn't an inch of her Benjamin hadn't laid claim to the night before, and she wore light love marks over her entire body. Including her rear end. Turning her face into a pillow, she laughed. He'd lightly bitten her butt several times during the night. Why did she apologize so much? It was probably something she needed to work on, once she got her girls free of the Kurjans. More than ever, she could see hope for her future. For their future. She would get Benjamin to train her a little bit before she went back, which would have to be soon. The Kurjans would be searching the rubble for her, because Terre wanted her. He'd made that clear.

"What is so funny?" Linda asked, her voice muffled by the pillow.

Karma jolted and rolled over, making sure she was decently covered by the bedspread. "Nothing. Do you have news?" She sat up, pushing her wild hair over her shoulder.

Linda studied her with soft brown eyes. "You and the big guy, huh?"

This was so weird. "Yes." Who knew? Her best friend was a spirit. She leaned forward a little. "I was nervous because I didn't really know exactly what to do, but Benjamin knew everything." Her entire body warmed. "It was lovely."

Linda hovered near the bed, more translucent than ever. "I'm glad for you. You said you were mated centuries ago. I take it you didn't enjoy yourself back then?"

It was hard to remember. "Not really. It was just another duty, and he died shortly after we mated." In fact, she'd had no idea how wonderful sex could be. She knew Benjamin had held back the night before. What would he be like fully unleashed? She tapped her finger against her lips. "I need to conduct research on the Internet." She was fully aware of the Internet and had used it illicitly a few times in Kurjan territory, but here she could probably research all she wanted. There were no restrictions.

Linda shrugged. "Or just keep playing with the big immortal dude. He seems to be up for exploration."

How true. "I told him that I loved him, and he panicked." Karma whispered.

Linda snorted. "Men are dorks who are afraid of love. Don't worry about that. You have to go with your feelings."

Yes, that was true. Karma smiled at her friend. Thank goodness she had one for now. "I have to contact the Kurjans soon. Terre will be looking for me, and I don't dare leave the girls in their hands for long. They're safer if I'm with the Kurjans." Even if the twins were used to extort her cooperation, at least she could ensure their safety for now.

Linda wrung her hands together. "I'm sorry you have to go back."

Karma straightened. "They're our girls, Linda. Yours and mine." Her heart hurt for the young mother. "I'm sorry you can't be here with them."

"Me, too," Linda said softly. "But you are here, and you'll be a good mother for them. I feel better crossing over, knowing that you'll love and protect them."

"After we get them free," Karma vowed.

Linda wavered, and most of her dark hair wisped out of sight. "I don't have much longer. The pull is too strong."

"Okay. Tell me what you know," Karma said, grasping the bedspread. "Did you see the girls?"

"No," Linda answered, looking around the quiet room. "The girls aren't with Terre and Jaydon."

Any hope Karma had held that she wouldn't have to go back dissipated. "I see."

Linda flickered out of sight and then returned. "Terre is frantically searching for you in the rubble, while his brother is hunting for the technology the Seven left behind. They do think that the area was the true headquarters and are unaware it was a setup."

Well, that was something. "We haven't seen any trace of them on the satellite feeds," Karma said thoughtfully. "How are they searching?"

"They know of the satellites the Seven are using," Linda said. "They search when they are outside your field of observation."

That was a fact Benjamin would need to know. "So the Kurjans are located close to the mountain in Utah?"

"Yes. I don't know their exact location, but Terre said something about it taking thirty minutes to reach the imploded mountain. He wants you more than you feared, Karma. He's obsessed, not even sleeping. His brother is thinking about knocking him out for a while, and Jaydon is on board with that. But Terre is making plans to take out Jaydon."

Karma smoothed the bedspread across her legs. "He is?" Why did the Kurjans keep turning against each other? When she went back to them, it would only be a matter of time before Terre turned against her. Unless she kept giving him sons. The thought sent bile through her stomach. "Do they have Sam Kyllwood?"

Linda nodded. "Yes, but I didn't see him. I overheard Terre and Dayne talking about the Kyllwood brother and discussing what to do with him. They don't want war right now with the demon nation, so it sounded like they might try to exchange him for something, but I don't know what. Of course, they're in no hurry."

No hurry because they were torturing Sam for information about the Seven and probably the Realm and the demon nation. While Benjamin and the others seemed to be holding it together, there was a level of tension throughout the headquarters that made the air seem heavy. They all knew what Kurjans did to prisoners, and the need to rescue Sam before he was further damaged was paramount.

Karma gathered the throw blanket from the end of the bed and slipped free, covering herself. "Anything else?"

"They don't believe that Ulric is on this planet or being held by the Seven. They have some sort of tie to him that tells them he's still on the prison world," Linda admitted. "They know Benjamin was lying about that."

Well, it was worth a try. "I'll inform Benjamin and the others about Terre's location." Karma hated for this interlude of happiness to end, but at least she'd had the best night of her entire life. That could never be taken away from her. "Were you able to use a human to travel there?"

"No," Linda sighed. "I'm burning my own energy and making myself even weaker. I can't do this for much longer."

Karma rubbed a spot over her heart. "Was there absolutely no mention of the girls by Terre or Dayne?"

Linda shook her head. "None. They're not concerned with the girls, so our children could be at any of the strongholds. Her voice grew hushed, and panic sizzled in her eyes. "We have to hurry."

Chapter Twenty-Six

Benny sheathed an ankle pistol in his left boot while scrutinizing the area on the screen. "The Kurjans have gotten good at setting up camp quickly, haven't they?" Learning from Karma and Linda that the enemy knew of the Seven's access to satellites, especially which particular satellites, pissed him off.

"We need our own satellite," Garrett said grimly, tucking a knife at his waist.

Logan circled several areas on a map. "If they've had time to plant mines, this is where I'd put them." He studied the printout. "Here, too." He made another circle.

Mercy stared at the printout. "There's a weakness to the east between those two areas of forest. If they haven't planted mines there, they'll have a couple of extra patrols stationed." She leaned over and tapped an area to the north. "This is where I'd go in. It's steep and hard to get to, so they won't have it covered as well."

Benny angled his neck to study the map. "Agreed." His adrenaline began flowing freely, and his body settled into battle mode. "We can get there in under an hour, and a full-day assault would be best."

Garrett rolled his shoulders, looking ready to do damage in his black cargo pants, black shirt, and combat boots. His eyes were a calm iron-infused gray. "Even though the Kurjans have developed the ability to go into the sun, we don't know how long they can fight during the daylight. Let's test them if we get the chance."

Benny eyed the storm outside. The rain had already started. "It might be sunny there, but I doubt it. We're not that far away." He hadn't given much thought yet to the fact that the Kurjans could venture into the sun. Research was the business of scientists. His job was as a soldier, and fighting he knew. "Sam could be in bad shape." There was even a possibility that he was dead, but it was doubtful. The Kurjans did not know that Sam was the keeper of the final ritual location, or they hadn't up until now. "You think Sam withstood the torture?"

"Of course," Logan said, reaching for another jagged-edged knife. His jaw was set, and dark emotion swirled in his green eyes. "Sam would never tell them about being the keeper of the ritual."

Yeah. That fact would probably get Sam killed. Garrett looked over at Logan. "Are you sure you don't want to let Zane know what's happened before we go?"

"I'm sure," Logan said grimly. "The three of us can infiltrate a temporary Kurjan stronghold."

Well, that was true. Benny rolled his shoulders back, loosening up. "Agreed. If we call in Zane, the entire demon nation will descend on the Kurjans and start a war none of us is ready for. The shifters have withdrawn from the Realm, the witches are close, and even many vampire strongholds are pissed at the king for accepting the Seven."

"And none of them really know what we're doing," Garrett agreed. "We can handle this. Sam will probably need medical assistance. We need to get Faith Cooper back here as soon as possible."

"I'll reach out," Mercy said, her face pinched. "You guys concentrate on the Kurjans and the Cyst. Those guys are so creepy." She double-checked the innocuous-looking skin on Logan's forearm. "I hope this new technology works as expected."

Benny winced. "When does anything work as expected?" They'd be lucky if they didn't blow themselves up.

Garrett rubbed his neck. "Good point. The Cyst concern me. They're gearing up fast, and they're gonna be ready to fight."

The Cyst were excellent fighters. "I'll fly," Benjamin said, truly missing the days when he could teleport. When Quade and Ronan had returned from the bubble worlds where they'd stood guard over Ulric, something had shifted in the world, and demons and hybrids could no longer teleport. Neither could fairies, and sometimes Mercy looked like she'd lost a part of herself. "Let's take the Bluehawk." It was faster and smaller than the other helicopters.

Garrett eyed him. "Fine, but let's not hit any trees this time."

It wasn't a decent flight if Benny didn't buzz trees. "Fine." He turned to stride out of the COMM room to let Mercy and Logan have a private goodbye. He stopped cold in the living area, where Karma waited, her hair piled on top of her head and her pretty green skirt looking out of place on this dismal day. It hit him then. He had somebody to say goodbye to, as well. "Hi."

She blushed a lovely pink. "Hi." After she'd reported on what Linda had said, Karma had returned to Benny's house to shower and prepare for the day. Her hair was still wet, and she had marks on her neck from his whiskers. "Please be careful."

"I will." He reached out to her, and she instantly buried herself in his arms, her face against his chest.

"Um, about what I said," Karma started. "I haven't had relations in a long time, and I may have been overcome."

Was that true? He didn't want to take advantage of her, but he wanted her again already. Would it be so bad for her to love him? He wasn't into love, but he'd protect her with everything he had. That meant something. He didn't know what to do right now. She definitely deserved better than him. "We can talk about that later."

She softened against him, her voice muffled. "I hope Sam is all right."

"He will be." The Kyllwood family was tough and had dealt with worse through the years. "I'll do my best to find the location of your twins." If possible, he'd bring a prisoner home with him so they'd have time to question thoroughly. "We'll find them, Karma. I promise."

She leaned back, her face pale. "I know. They must be so scared. Please tell them I love them."

Benny's throat heated and his lungs expanded. Fury tried to take him, and he banished the emotion. "Don't worry. I'll take care of them."

Karma released him and stepped back. "Benjamin? Please be careful." Worry darkened her pretty eyes.

"I will." It felt good to have somebody worrying about him, but this wouldn't do. What if they were mated and he didn't make it back from a mission? What if the final ritual happened much sooner than even he realized? Did a year of happiness make up for leaving her alone for centuries? Two years? Three?

She smacked him on the arm. "Worry about us later. Right now, just stay alive."

He rubbed his chest, right where she was making a place for herself. Then he kissed her goodbye.

Just in case.

* * * *

Benny slid beneath the boughs of a sweeping pine after his eighteenth mile of running. They'd had to set the helicopter down in a secure location far away from the Kurjan stronghold. Garrett and Logan kept pace beside him, both quiet and more than prepared for battle. He had one moment of unease. If he got either the Realm King's nephew or the demon king's brother killed, war would most likely erupt. One the earth had not seen before.

It was good he hadn't mated Karma the night before. If anybody perished on this mission, it would have to be him.

Logan hand-signaled them to stop. He wore specially made glasses with a light purple tint, ones that could detect mines in the ground as well as laser boundaries.

Benny stopped and moved toward Logan. "What?"

Logan handed over the glasses. "Land mines set in a pattern I can't read. They look like they were just planted anywhere."

Benny peered through the glasses, memorizing the locations of the faint purple blips on the screen. "There must be cameras near."

"You could say that." A uniformed Cyst strolled out of the trees, his gun pointed at Benny's head. It was General Jaydon—not a surprise. Within a second, more Cyst soldiers appeared, their white strips of hair gleaming in the meager sun. The storm hadn't moved this far east yet, so maybe the sun would help. So far, it didn't seem to be weakening the Cyst. "I'm surprised to see you here."

Were they? Obviously not. Benny pivoted in case he needed to kick more than one soldier at a time. "I didn't see cameras or sensors on the way in." He waited.

General Jaydon smiled. "Let's just say our technology is better than yours."

"Can't argue with that," Benny agreed. "Our sensors didn't detect you."

"Good. We've learned to use the metal deposits in the rocks to mask our signatures," Jaydon bragged. "You had no clue we were so close."

An unfortunately true statement. For centuries, the Kurjan technology had lagged far behind that of the Realm. That situation had changed in the last couple of decades. Benny lifted his chin in acknowledgment of the two soldiers Logan had claimed with a pointed look. He slightly tilted his head to the three on the left, while Garrett marked the two to the east.

Jaydon flashed a set of yellowed canines that looked sharper than a Bengal tiger's teeth. "I suppose we should have a sit-down now?"

Benny winced. "We appreciate the offer. But no." With that, he jumped up and kicked both Jaydon and a taller Cyst right beneath their jaws, snapping their heads back with loud crunches. Faster than they could recover, he was on Jaydon, taking the bastard to the ground.

The general countered with a punch to the neck that had Benny seeing stars. They rolled over the wet pine needles, punching and kicking, each trying for leverage. A knife slid smoothly into Benny's thigh, and he growled, ripping it out and punching the offending blade right into Jayden's rib cage.

The thing sliced through like butter.

"Sharp," Benny grunted, going for the eyes.

"Of course." Jaydon pulled the blade out, swiped at Benny's face, and shoved him off. Then he backflipped to his feet, barely landing before rushing forward again.

Benny levered himself up on one knee, swept around, and kicked the general in the groin with the blunt edge of his boot.

Jaydon dropped to both knees, his eyes wide.

Benny burst forward, reaching for the knife in his boot. He slashed down, and Jaydon blocked with both arms crossed together. They battled, each trying to cut the other.

A cry of pain came from behind Benny. It sounded like a Cyst soldier, so he didn't turn. There was a crashing sound from the trees, and several Kurjan soldiers came into view.

They were seriously outnumbered. Benny increased his attempts to slice into Jaydon's neck, while the general did the same, drawing out yet another blade so he had one in each hand. Both males backed up and jumped to their feet, circling each other.

Garrett went down on Benny's side and then rolled, coming up with fury in his eyes. He darted out of sight, and the sound of a body smashing into a tree echoed back. Pine cones and pine needles rained down, coating Benny's jacket. He dodged the slash of a knife and then pivoted, catching Jaydon in the gut with a roundhouse kick.

The general roared and kicked back, nailing Benny in the knee. The bone cracked, and Benny switched his balance to his other leg while directing immediate healing cells to the injury. He smiled. "This is more fun than I thought."

Logan tackled a Cyst to the ground between them, plunging his knife through the Cyst's throat.

Benny angled himself out of the way, keeping Jaydon within arm's reach.

Jaydon glanced at the prone soldier. "That's enough." Straightening his shoulders, he let out a whistle that had a couple of coyotes in the distance responding.

Benny frowned. "What the—"

Immediately, a series of darts hit him. The ones that hit his torso bounced off. The others dug deep with a heated burn that felt like live fire. He shook his head, almost in slow motion. "What have you done?" The forest swirled around him, and he dropped to his butt. They had drugged him? Seriously? "This is unheard of, even for Kurjans," he slurred, his head feeling as if it was under water.

Garrett landed by his side, facedown. Logan fell off the Cyst soldier he was trying to decapitate and instantly went into convulsions that looked painful.

"Bring them." Jaydon turned and strode through the trees, wiping blood off his neck as he moved.

Rough hands hefted Benny up, and two Kurjans put their shoulders beneath his and dragged him between them. The world remained blurry and his body useless as they traveled through the woods and down a series of rough rock formations into a mountain. They removed his earbud immediately.

The Kurjans threw him into what appeared to be a solidly built cell with bars on three sides and solid rock on the other. He landed on his face and painfully turned over to sit up. His body felt like it had gone through a woodchipper, and his nerves fired in pain. He leaned back and forth, relief washing through him as Garrett and Logan were tossed into nearby cells after their earbuds were also removed. They were both unconscious.

He coughed and tried to clear his head.

Sam Kyllwood, his face bloody and battered, stood across the narrow space in a cell facing Benny's. He looked at the other two and then at Benny. "Tell me this was intentional," he croaked, his voice demon-hoarse and rough.

Benny grinned, and blood dripped into his eye. "Of course it was intentional." Kind of. Well, not the getting drugged part. The Kurjans and their Cyst faction must have new drugs, because the Seven had been inoculated against all known sedatives. "We're here to get you out."

"Fuck," Sam said quietly.

Benny barked out a laugh. The cell bars morphed and bent in a bizarre parody of a circus funhouse. Then the walls swirled around, clouds gathered in front of his eyes, and his gut ached.

He passed out cold.

Chapter Twenty-Seven

Karma stared at the satellite feed as the three males were taken. "Are you sure the Kurjans don't know about this feed?" she asked. Again.

Mercy shrugged. "I can't be completely sure, but since I just hacked into it this morning, there's a good chance they don't know we're watching them. This is one of the Coven Nine feeds, and those witches are almost the best at concealing their technology." She grinned, but the happiness didn't reach her worried eyes. "I'm better. Most Faes are, to be honest."

Karma rubbed her stomach, where a pit the size of a boulder had lodged. "Why aren't you more upset?"

Mercy grimaced. "Benny didn't tell you the plan?"

Hurt spiraled around Karma's torso. "No."

"He was probably just trying to protect you," Mercy said, the sympathy in her eyes making Karma even angrier. "Well, we wanted one of them to be taken hostage so we could get to Sam."

Benjamin hadn't trusted her enough to tell her about the strategy, even though they'd engaged in coitus. Karma tried to hold on to her temper. "This attack backfired if only one of them was supposed to be taken hostage."

"I know," Mercy said, watching the spot where the males had disappeared into the mountain. "The drug surprised me—it must be a new concoction."

Karma stood up, unable to sit any longer. "Mercy, think about this." The Seven were overconfident, in her opinion. Of course, they needed to be strong and ready for battle, but they had underestimated the evil of the Cyst and the willingness of the Kurjans to go along with dishonorable plans. "The Kurjans and their Cyst faction now have three members of the Seven, as well as Sam Kyllwood."

Mercy looked sideways and down the computer banks. "I'm aware of that."

Karma had lived with the Kurjans for several lifetimes, and she knew them better than did the Seven. She was also figuring out she had a decent head for strategy. "I know from listening to conversations between Dayne and Terre that it is very difficult to survive the ritual to become a member of the Seven."

Mercy slowly nodded. "Yes. Only ten percent of the warriors who have attempted the ritual survived. We finally figured out that certain family bloodlines have a better chance of survival." She pushed several curls away from her eyes. "The Seven know how to fight."

"The Seven were just taken down by sedatives," Karma said, her heart racing. Her temples began to pound. "Nearly half of the living members are now in custody, including the one soldier in the entire world who's responsible for finding the magical place where Ulric's final ritual will be held."

Mercy swiveled her chair to face Karma. "Excuse me?"

Karma blushed. "I overheard you all discussing Sam, and don't worry, the Kurjans don't know his destiny. They don't know who he is, as far as I can tell. Well, except that he's the demon king's brother."

Mercy looked back at the screen. "All right. This was a good plan. They know what they're doing." Her voice quavered.

Karma took a deep breath to remain calm. "There is only one smart move for the Kurjans, and Dayne is a strategic genius." Terre just liked to hurt people, while Jaydon was obsessed with the idea of taking Ulric's place. "Dayne is in charge, so strategy will be employed for now."

Mercy's nostrils flared. "The correct strategy would be to try to gain information from the Seven."

Karma's stomach dropped. "Not for long. Dayne has to know we'll call in the demon nation as well as the Realm. The smartest move on his part is to kill the members of the Seven and perhaps negotiate for Sam Kyllwood's release, unless Sam has told them about his role in the ritual."

Mercy paled. "Taking out half of their members would put the Seven back eons. Maybe more, if it takes a long time to replace the fallen members." She stood and grasped Karma's hands. "You know the Kurjans. Would they do such a thing? It would mean certain war with the Realm and the demons."

Karma's lips trembled. "The Seven attacked first. They charged into Kurjan territory, and the Kurjans could claim they were just defending themselves."

"Doesn't matter," Mercy said. "There is no way the Realm and the demons wouldn't declare war over this. No way."

Karma leaned forward, desperation chilling her very bones. "The Kurjans don't know that. They won't understand, I think." She really wasn't sure what Dayne would choose to do. "If Dayne's loyalty truly is to Ulric, and I believe it is, he'll do what he has to for Ulric to succeed. That means weakening the Seven at any cost, even if it means war."

Mercy shook her head. "That doesn't make sense."

Karma grabbed Mercy's hands this time. "You don't understand. Ulric is their spiritual leader. Their prophet and their god. Dayne has lived his entire life preparing for Ulric's return."

Mercy bit her lip. "I'm not sure what to do. We could call in Zane, but that'd be a disaster."

Karma released her and sat back. "I do not know, either."

Mercy looked back at the Kurjan encampment, where very little movement showed. "I trust Logan," she said softly. "You trust Benny, and we both know Garrett is a badass. I'm sure Sam is in good enough shape to fight for his life, and now that his brother is there, he'll gain twice the strength. You've never seen those guys together."

Karma tried to pull faith from Mercy's words. "You're saying we need to let them continue their mission?" The males wouldn't survive the following night. She just knew it.

"We either trust them or we don't. I do," Mercy said reverently.

Karma couldn't swallow over the lump in her throat.

Linda popped up next to her, and she fought a yelp. The ghost looked the worse for wear, if that was even possible. "We have a problem."

"I know," Karma murmured. "They've taken the Seven hostage."

Mercy angled her neck to stare at the air around Karma. "That is so weird. I can't see or hear anything. Did she track the guys?"

Linda leaned forward, her eyes blazing. "I didn't see anybody, but I discovered General Jaydon's plans. He's going to duplicate Ulric's ritual and make himself invincible."

Karma swayed on her feet. Her head spun. "What?" Her voice trembled.

Linda's hair shook around her too-pale face. "Yes. He's going to murder a hundred enhanced females, and the way he made it sound, the younger the better. His obsession will get our girls killed."

Mercy cleared her throat. "What did she say?"

Linda struggled but soon disappeared from sight.

Oh, God. Now Karma really didn't have a choice about going back. She had to save her girls. "Nothing. Linda has been watching the encampment but didn't see the Seven." Karma was going to have to call Terre herself. He'd trade her for the Seven, even if he had to go around Dayne to do it. "It'll be okay, Mercy. Trust me."

* * * *

Benny woke up strapped to a chair in what appeared to be a cement-block building lacking any windows. A lone bulb hung from the ceiling, barely illuminating the room, while a heavy-looking wooden table rested again the opposite wall. He tested the bindings holding his arms behind his back and then the ones securing his ankles to the metal chair, which seemed to be attached to the floor. His head pounded, and the coppery taste of blood lingered at the back of his tongue.

"You're awake." The voice sounded young.

He turned his head to see a Kurjan teenager lounging on the dirt floor with his back to the wall, a game console in his large hands. The kid had long black hair, greenish eyes, and a bored expression. "Who are you?"

"Who are any of us?" The kid grinned and set the game aside. "You're one of the Seven."

"I am," Benny affirmed. "Even have the multiple cuts across my hand to prove it."

The kid nodded. "I saw. Those happened in the ritual, right? When you became brothers?" He cocked his head, the intelligence in his eyes obvious.

"Yeah. Deep enough to scar." Benny looked around for an escape route, but there was only one door. "Why no windows?"

"Who needs windows?" The kid glanced at his watch. "It's after dark, and clouds have covered the moon, so there's nothing to see."

Benny's chin dropped. "I was out all day?"

"Yeah. Those sedatives are a little strong." The kid stood and stretched his neck. He had to be a few inches over six feet tall— maybe more. He seemed to be around sixteen or perhaps a year older.

"Who are you?" Benny asked. "You should always give your name before you torture somebody."

The kid yawned. "My name is Drake, but I'm not going to torture you. It's not my thing." He slapped Benny on the shoulder and loped toward the door. "While torture is certainly part of the world in which we live, I'd rather do anything else. Life's too short, right?"

"I've found life to be pretty long," Benny admitted, testing the ties at his wrists again. Pretty damn solid.

"Well, that's probably about to change." Drake glanced over his shoulder at Benny. "It appears that you're the most expendable in the group right now."

"I figured," Benny said. It was odd to meet the next generation of the enemy. The kid was calculating and arrogant. "Where are my friends?"

Drake shrugged. "Garrett is with my dad, Dayne. Logan is with Jaydon, and Sam is unconscious again." He sighed. "You get my Uncle Terre, and I have to tell you that the scent of Karma is all over you. I'm guessing that since your mating mark is still dark, you didn't mate her. But you're definitely going to pay for touching her."

"Why is that?" Benny asked softly, the animal deep down swelling.

The door opened. "Because she's mine." Terre strode inside, the red tips of his black hair sharp and bloody-looking. His face was paler than the kid's and his eyes more purple than green. He was several inches taller than Drake, and his chest was broad and muscled. "A fact we are going to discuss at length."

Drake strode toward the door. "Good luck, Benjamin Reese. It was nice to meet you." Then he was gone.

Terre shut the door. "My nephew is bored by such banalities as torture. He's a strategic genius, however, and I have no doubt he'll someday be responsible for bringing down the entire Realm."

"I can see he's a thinker," Benny agreed, testing his ankles this time. Nope. Solidly in place. "I'm extremely disappointed that you resorted to using sedatives like you were big game hunting. The

Kurjans of old never would have admitted their fighting weaknesses in such a manner." True story. "It's just so wimpy of you."

Terre placed a black bag on the table and drew out a cattle prod. A short one with a wide head. "We're in a bit of a time crunch, unfortunately." He turned toward Benny and ignited the burning end. "Remember this?"

Benny lifted a shoulder. "Sure. Although I believe I didn't tell you jack shit last time we were together. In fact, if I remember correctly, I ended up escaping along with a very pretty blonde. What was her name?"

Terre's lips peeled back. "Right. I smell her all over you. Don't tell me it was just a one-night stand." Fury burned in his face, turning his way-too-white cheeks a blood-colored red. His movements were jerky and his breathing harsh. "Where is she?"

Interesting. It was telling that Terre's first question was about Karma and not the Seven. Benny forced a smile. "Unfortunately, the lovely blonde is buried beneath a ton of rubble. That'll teach you to bring down mountains."

"Liar," Terre said, almost conversationally. "I've been concerned about that, but her scent is fresh on you. Very." He casually placed the burning poker on Benny's knee.

Benny sucked in the pain and fought a growl as the smell of his burning flesh filled the too-small room. "She borrowed this shirt the night we spent together. Or was it daytime? You know, I think it was both." His voice remained level, although the pain in his leg was lancing down to his bound ankles. "Yeah. That's right. It was all day and all night." He met Terre's gaze evenly. "Why did you have to bomb our mountain and kill her?" If nothing else, he'd get Karma free of this bastard.

Terre smiled, and damn if his canines didn't look even longer. "She's not dead. I would know it, somehow. She's been teasing me for centuries, and I'm this close to finally having her. Just think of the sons that female will give me. Although she is certainly going to pay for sleeping with you—whether she consented or not."

Anger centered Benny even more. "You know, Terre? You're a complete douche. I'm going to enjoy killing you."

Terre lifted the prod away, and the swish of cool air over Benny's damaged flesh brought still more pain. A knock sounded on the door, and Terre paused, frowning. "I said I was not to be disturbed." The kid poked his head in, obviously not worried about the disruption. "Thought you should know. Karma is on the line and has offered to trade herself for the Seven. The techs are trying to get a bead on her location right now." He disappeared.

Everything inside Benny went cold and then raging hot. Damn it. What the hell was Karma thinking?

Chapter Twenty-Eight

Drake settled down on his cot, finishing his game. The Seven were impressive, and not one of the males had shown an ounce of fear at being captured. Of course, they were probably accustomed to being tortured. Someday he was going to make the Kurjan nation so strong that nobody would ever dare try to infiltrate a Kurjan holding. It was the only way to guarantee peace and prosperity for his people, and he'd do it. No matter what it took.

Sighing, he closed his eyes for the mandatory five hours of sleep he needed to train effectively in the morning. Peace could only be achieved through battle, a fact he accepted easily.

The sun warmed him with soft purple rays as the ocean rolled in, a lighter pink mixed with aqua this time. He looked around to see Hope Kayrs-Kyllwood sitting on a rock, watching him. She got prettier every year with her extraordinary blue eyes, thick, curly brown hair—and elfin features. In fact, her eyes were so blue they were almost violet, much like his people's coloring. Was it a coincidence? He didn't think so. "Hello."

"Hi." She wasn't smiling. "I believe you have three of my uncles in your cells."

He kept his expression blank. "Interesting. Why would you say that?"

She jumped down and stomped toward him, her bare feet leaving perfect indentations in the greenish-colored sand. She wore white cutoff shorts, a blue tank top, and sparkly earrings. Her toes were painted a lovely shade of pink. "I know you have Sam, Logan, and Garrett. They're my uncles, Drake." She put both hands on her hips and leaned up into his face.

God, she was beautiful. So he kissed her. She tasted like bubblegum and sugar, and she kissed him back, her eyelids closing. It was as close to heaven as he'd ever get. Then he released her, watching carefully. Cataloguing. Did she like the kiss?

She blushed and stepped back. "Well." Her voice was hoarse. "Where are my uncles?"

He shrugged, his mind reeling from the kiss. Oh, he'd kissed other girls, but this one was special. "I have no idea. Why would you think we have them?" The Seven were a danger to the world, and his people had no choice but to eliminate the threat so Ulric could rule again. It was foretold.

"I dreamed about them being in Kurjan cells," she spat, looking even more gorgeous when she was mad.

His hands itched to grab her and kiss her again, so he slipped them into his jeans pockets. He needed Hope to stay on his side for as long as possible. "I don't know anything about your uncles or any cells, Hope. The Realm and the demon nation have made enemies of everyone. So if your uncles are in cells, they could be anywhere." He had to fulfill his duties, and if lying to her was necessary, so be it.

She huffed out air. "You know they're part of the Seven, and I know that you know about the Seven. So stop playing dumb."

Surprising. She knew about the Seven? He glanced at the prophecy mark winding down her neck. "What else do you know?" he asked. "Do you see Ulric returning? Do you see a final ritual? What can you envision?"

She took a step away from him. "Most of that is murky." She hugged her arms around herself. "However, I do see that if you ever lie to me, I won't forgive you. Since you and I are supposed to change the world, you might want to remember that fact."

He had no problem lying to get the right result. It was nice for her that she lived in a different world and had the luxury of honesty all the time, but lives were at stake here. Important ones. *"I don't know a thing about your uncles, but I'll see what I can find out for you. I promise."*

Her stance relaxed. *"Okay."*

Then Paxton Phoenix walked down the beach, having appeared from around a series of rocks. The vampire-demon hybrid was finally starting to fill out, at least in the chest area. He'd grown to a couple of inches over six feet, and his black hair was shaggy around his ears.

"What is he doing here?" Drake asked, feeling a rare need for battle sing through his veins.

Hope watched Paxton walk toward them. *"He's sleeping in my room at home. It seems that the only time I can create dream worlds is when he's nearby."*

Well, that was interesting. Drake waited until Paxton had reached them. *"This is becoming a habit,"* he said quietly.

Paxton looked from him to Hope. *"Why are we here?"*

Hope pushed her hair away from her face. *"I don't know. I fell asleep, and here we are. Drake is going to try to help us find my uncles."*

Paxton's gaze narrowed on Drake. *"Sure, he is."*

Drake fought a smile. The hybrid was much less trusting than Hope, which was unfortunate. Years ago, they'd almost been friends. There was no doubt someday they'd be enemies. Such was the way of life, according to his research. *"How's life, Paxton? You still with your uncle and his nice group of lunatics?"*

Hope swung her gaze toward Paxton. *"What's he talking about? Your Uncle Santino has crazy friends?"* She rocked back on her heels. *"I know he's an odd scientist."*

Paxton looked at Drake. *"What do you know about my uncle?"*

Drake smiled. "More than you think we know. It's nice to be on the same side." The dream world began to fade away. Hope must be awakening. "If we have your uncles, I'll help them escape, Hope. No matter what. We'll see each other soon." He awoke on his cot with the covers pushed off.

He glanced at the clock. It had barely been an hour since he'd shut his eyes. He idly wondered if the torture was still going on. Then he went back to sleep.

* * * *

Paxton awoke, still leaning against the wall beneath Hope's bedroom window. "That's the last time I'm agreeing to do this."

She sat up in bed, and her hair flew forward onto her shoulders. After the summer, she still had golden highlights through the chestnut color, which brought out the violet hues in her blue eyes. "We can't save the world like superheroes if we avoid the work." Her voice was light and teasing with a hint of steel beneath.

"We're not going to save the world with the Kurjans." Paxton pushed to his feet. They were going to save the world *from* the Kurjans. It was okay that Hope didn't want to give up her grand plan, but he wouldn't lie to her just to make her happy.

She narrowed her gaze. In her cute yellow pajamas, she looked delicious and kissable. He'd thought about their one kiss whenever he'd gotten together with other girls, but nobody compared to Hope. Nobody ever would.

"Paxton? What was Drake talking about?" She reached over and tugged on the little chain to light the pink glass lamp by her bed.

"What do you mean?" He edged closer to the window, ready to head back home. It was getting too difficult to control his body with such a pretty girl so close. Sometimes being sixteen really sucked. He'd love to be in that bed with her.

"You know exactly what I mean," she said, her stubborn look pinching her face. "About your uncle, his lunatic friends, and the fact that you're on the same side now. You've never been on the same side as Drake. What was he messing with you over?"

Pax's own temper stirred. "What was he messing with me over? You. Of course. It has always and will always be you, Hope. Drake and I can never be friends, we can never be on the same side, and we can never agree on the future because of *you*."

Her perfect bow-shaped mouth opened slightly. "Me? Seriously?"

"Yeah," he said. How could she not understand any of this? For an incredibly smart and insightful girl, she sure was clueless sometimes. "I think Drake has a vision of your future that you might not like, regardless of your fantasies about the two of you finding peace for everybody."

"We will find peace," she said, blushing a little bit. "All of us. You, too."

If she thought he was going to hang around and watch her fall for a Kurjan, be with a Kurjan, she was nuts. Oh, there might be a good Kurjan or two out there, but Drake wasn't one of them. Paxton knew that to his very being, and not just because they both liked the same girl. How was he going to protect her when she kept wearing blinders?

"Nice deflection," she muttered. "Are you going to tell me or not?"

"Not," he said quietly. "I'll never lie to you, and I hope you know that. But I don't have to tell you everything, either." He was sure she didn't tell him everything, and that might be a good thing. He really didn't want to hear about her feelings for Drake or any other guys she might be dating.

She blew right out of her bed and marched up to him, her eyes ablaze.

He went from relaxed to charged in a second and actually took a step back. "What are you doing?"

She put her hands on her hips and glared. "We have never kept stuff from each other, and we're not starting now. I've always told you mostly everything I understand, even about the Seven. So here's one more thing—I'm the Lock. In the ritual to kill Ulric, there are Seven males, three female Keys, and a Lock. That's me."

He already knew that, but she probably didn't know that he knew. "I know," he said softly, unable to lie to her.

She blinked. "You do?"

"Yeah. What exactly does it mean?" He grasped her upper arms, careful not to hurt her. "What kind of danger or sacrifice does that mean? To be the Lock?"

She didn't look away. "I don't know. Never have. I'm not even sure if the members of the Seven know I'm the Lock. If my uncles know, then they won't let anything happen to me. If they don't know, then they don't know." She paused, looked down at her bare feet, and then lifted her chin to meet his gaze. "What do you know about it?"

"Just that you're the Lock," he admitted. "That you have to be protected from that final ritual and stay far away from it. Hopefully the ritual will never occur." He'd vowed to protect her the second he'd met her, and that had never changed. Even when they hadn't been telling each other everything. "When the Seven distorted physics and elemental laws to become the Seven and fuse their torsos, they gave up part of their souls."

"They did not," Hope countered. "That's not true. I've seen many members of the Seven, and they're fully souled."

He couldn't help grinning. "That's not a word."

"It is now. Trust me. They didn't lose their souls." She smelled like vanilla beans and orange spice.

He released her arms. "My uncle and some of his friends know about the Seven and the ritual, and they want to prevent it from happening. So do I. If anything happened to you..." He couldn't finish the sentence. He'd rather see her with some other guy, so long as she was happy, than to see her hurt.

She shook her head. "I like your kooky uncle, and I'm sure his friends are goofy professors also. They don't have to worry about me."

He didn't correct her about his uncle or the group. The truth was, Paxton hadn't figured them out yet, either. Unable to help himself, he ran one finger down the side of her face.

She caught her breath. "Wh-what are you doing?"

He wasn't sure. Then he leaned down and kissed her, slow and gentle. God. It was even better than before. How was he going to save her in the end? He'd give his life for hers, and something told him that was his destiny.

Unless he was wrong. Maybe she was his future.

He hoped.

Chapter Twenty-Nine

Benny landed on the dirt floor of his cell with a muffled *oof.* His ears rang, and the burns on his body pulsed in pain. Man, he hated being tortured. Blinking blood out of his eyes, he rolled over. "Who's around?"

"Me," Logan groaned, sounding as if his throat had been sliced.

"Ditto," Garrett said, coughing so hard he might as well just hack up a lung.

"I'm alive," Sam moaned from across the way. "Who got Jaydon this time?"

Benny forced himself to sit up while sending healing cells to his brain. Had Terre smashed his skull? Yep. A hammer could do some serious damage. "I got Terre, and supposedly, Garrett ended up with Jaydon. Right?"

"Yeah," Garrett moaned. "The bastard has fists like sledgehammers. But I did get in a couple of good kicks. His nose was broken when I was so kindly escorted out."

Vibrations from the multiple healing cells being utilized buzzed through the underground chamber. Benny's eye socket popped back into place, and he winced. "Sam, good to almost see you. Did anybody get any relevant information? Did anybody hear about the enhanced females or Karma's twin girls?"

Nobody answered for a moment.

"I didn't learn anything about the females or the girls, but I have some intel for later," Garrett said.

"Ditto," Logan added.

Well, crap. Benny couldn't risk staying another day to find the girls, considering Karma had just blown his entire plan to the crapper. "We have to get back home." While he'd heard that the connection had been cut before the Kurjans could trace the call, she'd still made arrangements to meet up with Terre if she could find transportation.

The bastard now knew that she was alive. So much for keeping her under the radar.

Logan leaned against the bars that separated his cell from Benny's. "I could take a couple more rounds. Let's stay and try for more information before we leave. We have to find out how many enhanced females they've kidnapped and where they're keeping them. I still want to know how much they have on the Seven and if they have a bead on Ulric. They don't believe that we have him locked down."

Sam sat on the dirt floor across the way, blood pouring from a cut above his eyebrow. "I have some intel from my time here, but I think they're as much in the dark about Ulric as we are. Supposedly his Intended is sure he's close to breaking free of the prison world."

Benny fixed his broken shoulder and then started mending the cartilage around it. "Yvonne, right? She has to be getting on in age a bit. If she dies, doesn't another Intended for Ulric take her place?"

"Affirmative," Garrett said, breathing heavily. Pain radiated from him along with the healing tingles. "Why are there so many damn Chosen Ones or Intendeds? Jamie was one, Hope is supposedly one, my Aunt Brenna was or is one..."

"Why are they always female?" Sam asked absently. "Shouldn't a male be chosen as something once in a while?"

Logan chuckled and stared across the way at his brother and Garrett, whose cells were side by side. "We're not as smart as females."

That was the truth. "Except for Karma, right now. Oh, she's smart, but she hasn't figured out that if anybody is going to sacrifice themselves, it is not going to be her," Benny growled. Then he told his brothers about her phone call and promise to Terre.

"What phone did she use?" Logan asked, wiping blood off his chin.

"Dunno," Benny answered. "She had to have done it away from Mercy, because I'm sure Mercy would've stopped her. We have phones in different places. Mine is in the kitchen drawer at my house, and we also have the box of burners in the weapons room. It doesn't matter where she got the phone."

"So long as the Kurjans couldn't trace it, I don't care," Garrett agreed, standing and weaving back and forth on his feet. "Looks like our timeline has been moved up." He gingerly picked at a scab on his hand, tearing off a long strip of what looked like skin. "Let's do this."

Benny rolled to his feet, tearing off the fake layer of skin along his neck. He folded up the piece, pinched it, and slipped it into the key slot of the old-fashioned cell door. "Fire. Hole." Two steps brought him to the far stone wall, and he bent against it, covering his ears.

The door lock blew apart, and the cell door swung open.

Garrett and Logan did the same with their doors, and Logan took an extra explosive strip off his leg to use on Sam's door.

Sam Kyllwood looked a little the worse for wear. There were dark circles beneath his eyes, and his cheeks had hollowed slightly. "When did you last eat?" Benny asked.

Sam shrugged. "Who cares?" His eyes were a darker green than Logan's, as well as being rimmed with a deep bronze color. "I don't need food or blood. Let's get out of here."

Benny wasn't going to argue. He surveyed the other two. Garrett had taken a worse beating from Jaydon than Logan had from Dayne. "I'm on point. Garrett, you have Sam in the center. Logan, you cover our asses." Without waiting for agreement or argument, Benny turned and jogged down the tunnel. "It's probably still dark out, so know the Kurjans will be at full force outside." He paused at the door leading out. "This is now an escape plan. Take no prisoners, and if the enemy is down, keep going. No time to decapitate."

Garrett kept close to Sam, who was a little too pale. "Does everybody remember the layout of the mines? We need to go in that direction."

"Affirmative," Logan said. "Sam, you stay on Garrett's six."

Sam straightened, and the bloody wound on his forehead slowly closed. "I've got this, little brother. Don't worry your pretty head about it."

Benny snorted. They all looked ready to go. "Now." He kicked the door open with his boot near the lock. The bang took the guard outside by surprise, and Benny was on him in a second, knocking him out and taking two guns and three knives. The night swirled around him for a moment. He took a deep breath and sent more healing cells to his brain. "All right. Let's go." He ran into the night.

* * * *

After a sleepless night, Karma walked along the different storage units of the Seven headquarters. Several were large wooden sheds that housed many vehicles and even an armored truck. The morning had brought a light rain, and after checking in with Mercy and seeing no activity on the satellite feed, she had gone exploring.

"Looking for something?" Benjamin asked.

She gasped and turned. "Benjamin!" Joy filled her, and she jumped for him.

He caught her easily and wrapped his arms around her waist. His soldier clothing was burned, dirty, and wet, but he appeared as strong as ever.

She looked up, her heart swelling. "You're all right. You're here." She hugged him tight, noting a bruise beneath his right ear. She looked him over as well as she could, being pressed so closely against him. Thank goodness he was all right. "I didn't hear you arrive."

"We couldn't be sure we weren't tracked, so we set down a hundred miles from here and ran," he said, his eyes darker than usual. His hold loosened, and then he let her go.

She released him. "Are you harmed? What happened? Did you find the girls?" Something was amiss, but she couldn't read his expression. Had he been badly injured? Out of instinct, she began to edge away.

He grasped her chin with two fingers. "I'm not harmed, we got Sam out, but I haven't found the girls yet." His voice lowered to a curiously dangerous tone. "Would you like to tell me what you were up to while I was gone?"

Her mouth dropped open, and heated tingles ticked through her abdomen. "Well, I, hmmm."

"Karma? I am not pleased." He did not sound pleased in the slightest.

Her body quaked. She tore her head free and turned away from the building to stride toward the river.

"Stop." It was a command, and her body immediately obeyed.

"Turn the hell around," he ordered.

She slowly turned, but she didn't cower. Nor did she run.

He watched her like a hawk she'd once observed that had been choosing which field mouse to strike. His jaw was set, and he took several deep breaths before continuing. "What were you thinking?" he calmly asked, his stance casual.

She jolted. "I was thinking of saving my girls." The truth seemed like the correct avenue with Benjamin.

"Did I, or did I not, tell you that I would find your girls?" The strain in his voice made her wince.

"Are you in pain?" she whispered.

"No," he murmured.

She shifted her feet beneath the skirt. "Then why do you sound so...bad?" She couldn't think of another way to ask him.

His chin dropped, and she could swear steam came out of his ears. "Bad? Why do I sound bad?" In fact, he sounded like he was trying to swallow glass. "I'm doing my best to keep my temper under control. I don't want to scare you...much."

At those words, her temper blew. "How dare you? You think I'm so weak I can't handle you in full temper?" She was not a wimp. Sure, she didn't know how to fight, and yeah, she was used to running and hiding when angry males were around, but still. The simple truth caught her. Benjamin Reese would never harm her. No matter how angry he became. "Besides. You kept the true strategy from me, so I can make my own plans. For now, let me have it. Go for it. Give me what you've got."

His eyes widened, and then, by all the saints, he lost his mind. "Fine. You want it? You've got it." He threw up his hands and prowled toward the river, his hair matted and probably bloody. "I was in Kurjan territory when I discovered that you called Terre. You remember Terre?" His voice rose, and he was full-out shouting.

"Yes," she said, tilting her head to watch him. Interesting. She really had no fear of him.

"He wants to mate you," Benny bellowed, his hands moving as much as his legs. He paced. "Like *mate you*, mate you. The guy is obsessed. Probably has been for centuries. If you ask me, he let you escape just so you could take the virus and be free of the mating bond."

She nodded. "Yes, I believe that was his plan."

Benjamin paused. "You knew?"

Again, the truth was the only way to go. Though he wasn't going to hurt her, lying to him might bring on more anger than she knew how to handle. "Yes. He has never hidden his desire for me, and he made it clear that I would take the virus when I escaped. He has my children, Benjamin. For the time being, he will win this one."

"I don't give two fucks about him winning anything," Benjamin yelled, the veins in his neck bulging out. "I care about you and those girls. If you don't start trusting me, we're going to have a serious problem."

Mercy and Logan walked along the river from the direction of the lodge. "Everything okay?" Logan asked, also still wearing his torn and bloody clothing.

"Hell no," Benjamin bellowed.

Karma grit her back teeth together. "Benny? That's enough. I understand that you're angry, and you have every right, but enough with the yelling."

The male was twice her size and could probably take on a cadre of elite Cyst soldiers without breaking a sweat. He could certainly kill her with one blow. But when she spoke, he immediately calmed down. "Sorry. I didn't mean to scare you."

"I'm not scared," she admitted, shocked that it was the truth. "But you are giving me a headache." The hybrid had a set of lungs on him.

"And you look crazier than heck," Mercy chimed in.

Benny ran a rough hand through his hair, looked at them all, and then glanced down at his bloodied clothing. "Right. Okay." Without another word, he moved toward Karma and tossed her over his shoulder before turning to stride along the river walk.

The air whooshed out of her lungs, and shock kept her immobile for several yards. Then she smiled. Against all reason, she chuckled. "Benjamin? What in the world are you doing?" Her braid hung nearly to his ankles.

"I need a shower. You're going to join me, and we'll have a nice chat naked." He sounded marginally calmer.

She lost the smile. "Naked?"

Chapter Thirty

Benny walked into his bathroom with Karma still over his shoulder. She'd laughed for most of the walk, and that sound had calmed him down fast. Then her soft chuckle had wandered through his entire body, making him ache much worse than he had earlier. Finally, he flipped her upright.

She grabbed his forearms to catch her balance.

He exhaled. "I'm still not happy with you."

The smile on her face as she looked up made it nearly impossible not to share her joy. "Okay."

He kissed her forehead. "Being carried makes you happy?" She was truly a mystery, wasn't she?

"No." She laughed again, her eyes sparkling. "I'm happy you yelled at me and I didn't get scared. It's nice to trust somebody. I'm also happy you made it back safely and saved your friend. Everything has worked out for now."

For now. He agreed. Yet she wasn't getting him. Not completely. "Listen. I'm sorry I yelled, and I'm glad you didn't get scared. But the bottom line is that you went against logic and safety when you contacted Terre behind my back. You knew I wouldn't like that. If I had been here, I would've stopped you."

"That's why I called when you weren't here," she said logically.

He paused. The fact that she wasn't frightened of him pleased him, but still, a guy could use some control. What a conundrum. He wanted her to feel free, so he had to fight every inclination he had to lock her down and keep her safe. "You're killing me," he admitted. Maybe he should go spar with Logan for a while. The kid had completely healed by the time they'd gotten back.

Of course, Logan was probably with Mercy right now. Benny didn't want to walk in on them. Ugh.

Karma sobered. "Benjamin? Did you find out anything about my girls?"

"No." He brushed a couple of wayward tendrils away from her face. "But I'm not done yet. I will find them."

She exhaled. "You don't know that. Terre promised to bring them to where we're meeting in three days. I'm supposed to call to get a location when I get free of you. That is the only way we're going to find them, and you know it. You have to let me go."

"Not a chance." If he let her go, she'd end up mated against her will by the Kurjan who'd happily burned Benny's knee nearly off. The guy liked dishing out pain, and something told Benny that he didn't care who was on the receiving end. "He'll hurt you. You know that, right?"

She swallowed. "I do know that, but I'm still hoping I can escape with my girls. I'm their mother now, Benjamin. That means I do whatever I have to do in order to keep them safe. To get them to safety. Surely you understand that." Her voice trembled and nearly ripped his heart in two.

"I do understand," he said, tearing his shirt over his head. It was bloody and damaged, so he tossed it across the room into the small garbage can. "It sounds like I have three days to find them." He could work with that.

She looked at his chest and licked her lips. "Yes. I told Terre it would take me that long to get there, but I was guessing. I've never driven a car, and I was thinking of borrowing one from you."

"Stealing," he said, shucking his pants. After one night with the Kurjans, he respected her even more. She'd survived for years with them, and she'd kept her ability to love. She must love those kids deeply. He'd never met anybody like her, and he had the feeling she could see right through him to the darkness at his center. But he couldn't help wanting her anyway. Badly. "I need a shower. Do you want to join me? If not, we'll talk over dinner." God, he hoped she wanted to join him, but he understood if she needed some space. He had yelled at her, and at the moment, they weren't exactly agreeing on anything.

"I could use a shower." She reached for the top button on her shirt.

He covered her hand. "I've got this." Her hand dropped, and he gently slid each button free, brushing his knuckles along her smooth skin each time.

Tension spiraled between them. He was done holding back with her. From the first time he'd touched her, years ago, he'd known they would end up here. She'd survived his temper and his bite, and now she could have the real him. He ripped the shirt off, making her gasp. Then he grasped the nape of her neck, taking control, giving himself what he wanted.

Her second gasp was one of need. Yeah, he thought so. His holding back on who he was and what he wanted wasn't good for either of them. "This is going to be my way, sweetheart."

Her smile was full of feminine challenge. "Is it?"

* * * *

Karma knew better than to poke the beast, but the freedom she felt with Benjamin was better than any aphrodisiac. She hesitated only a second before reaching for his muscled chest and scraping her nails over it. He was amazing.

His smile held warning as he grasped her skirt and smoothed it down her legs, partially bending over to do so.

Her breath caught. "Benjamin." Grabbing his rib cage, she tugged. "Turn around."

He paused and then did so, revealing his back. A tattoo of an intricate shield covered the wide span of muscle from his neck to his behind with his ribs lightly outlined and bonded together.

"The Seven marking," she murmured, her hands wandering over the incredible sight. Oh, it wasn't a tattoo. Instead, a shield had formed when he'd survived the ritual of the Seven. "It's beautiful."

"Forged in blood and bone," he said, turning. "I'm done holding back, sweetheart. I'm not nice or easy or casual. I'm just me. You in or out?"

"In," she breathed.

He smiled, and the masculine promise in his eyes set wings to fluttering through her body. Then he cupped her chin, his big hand warm against her skin. With a small movement, he tilted her entire face up. He paused, studying her. Claiming her with just his look. Then he took her mouth.

The second his lips touched hers, that electricity he always seemed to generate burned through her. Hot. Wild. Free. This time, he wasn't holding anything back. He gave her everything, hard and deep, consuming her until it was only the two of them and right now. Right here.

He shoved her bra and panties away, flipped on the shower, and then dragged her in before the warm water had turned to hot. His mouth took hers again, and all she could do was feel. He was rough and aggressive in a way she'd only imagined before, his dominance as natural as breathing to him. The control he always exhibited came out in another way, demanding something from her.

Surrender.

She felt freedom in that demand and leaned into him, letting the heated water cleanse them both. He pulled her up on her toes, his mouth moving from her lips to her jaw to nip and attack, holding her exactly where he wanted her. For the first time, she forgot all about pleasing him.

There was only the pleasure he demanded she feel. Blood thundered between her ears, making her head ring. Her clit fired hot and needy, and the hard wall of his body was unyielding against her softness. He held her in strong arms, so powerful and just what she needed.

He roughly caressed her body, down and back up, filling his hands with her breasts and lightly pinching.

She gasped and leaned closer, wanting that small bite of pain. There was no hesitation and no insecurity. He didn't let her stop and think or worry about anything. In the space of a thought, Benjamin took control of them both, and it surprised her how much she'd needed him to do that.

There wasn't time to be concerned. For now, her body melted into his, and she let him do what he wished. Need burst through her with a tornado's force.

"So beautiful," he murmured, licking along the shell of her ear.

She shivered and scraped her knuckles right across the hard ridges of his abdomen and then lower. She swallowed, hesitating.

"Don't stop now," he murmured, reaching around her to clamp both hands onto her butt. "I love your ass. Have since the first time I saw you in those jeans three years ago."

Now there was a reason to wear jeans. She'd been looking for one. He kneaded her, and she moaned as delicious ripples cascaded right to her sex. "You're beautiful," she countered, finally reaching for him. His shaft was long and thick, and she kept her hold gentle as she slid her hand along his smooth skin. So smooth. She could spend all day exploring his incredible body. Maybe she'd do just that.

He nipped the soft spot between her neck and shoulder, staking a claim. His fangs pierced her skin, more powerful than any lightning strike, sizzling right to her sex. As if he knew her body better than she did, he pressed a knee between her legs, forcing her to ride him.

The orgasm stole her breath, beating through her with a hammering force. She came down sighing his name, and he drove her instantly back up with his talented fingers driving inside her. Her breasts ached, and her nipples hardened even more. He rolled one nipple just as he pinched her clit, and she climaxed again, her legs going weak. He wrapped an arm around her waist, holding her still and forcing her to ride yet another cresting wave. She could only take what he was giving, and it was delicious.

Finally, she sagged against him, murmuring and kissing his chest. Had she ever felt this much alive? Oh, she'd lived for centuries, but had she really been alive?

He flipped her around and placed her hands on the smooth wooden bench that ran the length of the shower.

She blinked. "I'm not—" He grasped her hips with relentless hands, his cock probing her entrance. "Oh," she sighed, leaning back against him.

Slowly, ruthlessly, he pushed himself inside her, forcing her internal muscles to relax and take him. Overcome, she bent over onto her elbows, letting her head drop. So much. He was so big, and he was behind her and definitely in control. At the thought, her body quaked around him.

"No. You wait." He reached around and tugged a nipple, gaining her attention. "You wait until I'm ready." Then he released her, gripped her hips, and pounded.

Hard and fast, powerful and devastating, he powered inside her, pulling her back to meet each thrust. She built hot and fast, needing that final detonation. "Please," she whispered.

"Not yet, damn it." He twisted one hand in her hair and drew her head up, his other fingers digging into her hip. Her neck elongated, and he scraped his teeth down it. "You'll hold on for me. Because I tell you to." The hammering increased in force, and with his body over hers, she was truly his.

The fire burned through her, and her body gripped him until she could feel his heart beat inside her. Every breath was a painful sob, but she couldn't stop. Biting her lip, she tried to hold on.

He swelled inside her. "Now, sweetheart. Give me everything."

Her body obeyed him before her mind caught his meaning. She clamped down on him. Then she shattered, crying out his name and shutting her eyes. Spasms overwhelmed her, stronger than before, igniting her every nerve. She gasped and sobbed, taking more of him.

He ground against her, his powerful body shuddering.

She murmured something, her body shutting down. Exhausted. So tired. So happy. So complete.

He was still over her, and he kissed her ear gently. "You can say it again."

"I love you, Benjamin." It was the truth, crazy as it seemed. Now her elbows gave out.

He withdrew and lifted her by the waist, setting her beneath the spray. "I care for you, Karma. I vow to you that I'll protect you with everything I have. You'll be safe, and I'll get your girls back for you." He kissed her gently on the nose.

Well, it was a start.

Chapter Thirty-One

Benny set the platter of Chateaubriand in the middle of the round table and took his humungous apron off. "You're welcome. I cooked." Yeah, he was the best cook among the Seven. Although, after he'd seen what Karma did with a simple potato dish, he realized he had some competition. Cooking with her had become almost as enjoyable as the hours they'd spent in the shower and then in bed.

Okay, not as enjoyable. Not even close.

His body was loose and his mind clear, and he owed that to the sweet female fussing over the green beans. He grasped her around the waist, lifted her up, and set her in a chair. "Sit and eat. You need nourishment."

She slapped the hand at her waist. "Benjamin," she admonished, embarrassment in her voice.

He grinned and took the seat next to her. It was way too late for him to pretend he had any manners. "Pour the wine, would you, Logan?"

Logan poured Opus One for everyone, handing the glasses down the line.

Benny looked at his family, feeling at home with Karma by his side. Logan and Mercy were making googly faces, but it didn't gross him out like usual. Sam had already dug into the dinner like a starved wolf, and Garrett was eyeing the green beans. Shrugging, he reached for the bowl and dumped some on his plate.

Benny waited until Karma had served herself before filling his plate. "All right. Sam, you start."

Sam washed down the steak with a generous gulp of the expensive wine. His eyes were dark but the color had returned to his rugged face. He looked like a cross between Zane and Logan with his square jaw and green eyes. Intelligence shone in those eyes, and he did nothing to hide it among family. "The Kurjans are assholes," he said. Then he winced. "Sorry."

Benny took a drink of the wine. "Call it like you see it. What else?"

Sam chewed thoughtfully and then swallowed. "You know, I think Jaydon has grand plans to become Ulric two-point-oh. If Ulric makes it home, I wouldn't be surprised if Jaydon doesn't try to do him in."

"That'd be convenient," Garrett said grimly. "How accurate are the rumors about Jaydon?" He looked at Karma.

She delicately wiped her mouth with one of the cloth napkins she'd found somewhere in the pantry. "Very accurate. Linda overheard him talking about it. I think that's why there's been a rush on gathering enhanced females. He is definitely going to attempt the ritual that Ulric performed centuries ago."

Sam shook his head. "I'd be surprised if Dayne allowed it. When Ulric performed his ritual centuries ago, he broke all natural laws by killing one hundred enhanced females and using their blood to fuse his entire body into an impenetrable shield. The Kurjans want to keep enhanced females for themselves or for whatever Ulric ultimately has planned, right?"

Benny kept an eye on Karma's plate to make sure she was eating before he answered. "Yeah. Supposedly Ulric wants to do away with all enhanced females except Kurjan Sotis, but I've never understood why."

Karma shrugged. "I don't know. I've never heard his plans or what his plans are believed to be." She coughed. "I do understand that the only way Ulric can be killed is if he ingests the combined blood of the three Keys."

Mercy winced. "So gross. I'm one of the Keys."

Karma jumped. "I didn't know that. Do you know the other two?"

Logan reached for a roll. "Grace Cooper, Adare's mate, is a Key. We haven't found the third one yet."

"Maybe it'll take centuries to find the third Key," Karma said, her voice hopeful.

Benny wanted to agree, but in his gut, he knew it wasn't true. Sometimes the world sped up as if rushing toward a countdown, and he could feel it happening now. The ritual was coming. He was glad that during his explorations of her body, he'd discovered she did not have the birthmark of a Key. Thank God. He looked at Garrett. "You get anything?"

"Besides a migraine?" Garrett muttered. "Not really. Jaydon seems ambitious and likes to inflict pain, but it wasn't personal, you know? He's a sadist, but I think he could get off torturing anybody, not just the Seven. He didn't give up much during our one session."

Benny reached for a roll that Karma had made from scratch. The pretty lady liked to cook as much as he did, and he could see them doing that for years to come. If he didn't die, that was. The more he was around her, the more he wanted to keep her forever. "Logan? What about you?"

Logan twirled his fork. "Dayne wanted information about the Seven and what we knew of Ulric's ability to get home. He didn't buy the intel that we have Ulric in prison somewhere, so I'm thinking they have some line to him, somehow. He also wanted any information I had on how Quade and Ronan got back here after guarding the prison world." Logan snatched a roll off

Mercy's plate. "Oh, and he was generous with information about their new technology."

Benny perked up. "Their new ability to venture into the sun?" It was unthinkable, and yet if he belonged to a species that was weakened by the sun, or died in the sun, he'd spend every waking moment trying to find a cure. Or at least he'd have his scientists on the job.

Logan nodded. "Yeah. Yvonne, Ulric's Intended, actually created the antidote to sunlight. She looked at the weakness like a disease and built a form of vaccine, although it's temporary. For now. And the sun still weakens them after a time, which we already knew."

"I'd forgotten she was a scientist," Mercy said softly. "She has a birthmark, too, right?"

"Yeah. A birthmark indicating she is Ulric's Intended," Logan muttered. "Seriously. If I remember right, that chick is nuts."

Karma cleared her throat. "She's not nuts, but she is very determined. It's a quest for power that drives her—as well as a blind devotion to Ulric. They've never met, and she has built an image of him in her mind, in her heart, that probably isn't anything close to the real warrior."

Benny slid his arm over Karma's slim shoulders. The woman was smart and insightful. The truth hit him right in the solar plexus. She was also...*his.*

* * * *

Karma had never felt part of a group the way she did having dinner with Benny and his friends. She belonged and was treated as if she mattered and could contribute. More than ever before, she wanted her girls to have this type of experience. This kind of family. She sighed.

"What's wrong?" Mercy asked, her gaze concerned.

Karma shifted on her chair, snuggling even closer to Benjamin. He'd slipped his heavy arm over her shoulder, giving her a sense of being protected and wanted. "None of this changes the fact that I have to go back. All of you must know that."

"No," Benjamin said.

She reached for her wineglass. The Seven seemed to have excellent taste in wine. "Yes. There's a main headquarters for the Kurjans, but the group Terre and Jaydon lead is transient. The best soldiers are always on the move, and if Terre doesn't have the girls brought back to him, we'll never find them." It had been her life for the last century, and she'd love to put down roots. To garden. Something in her had always loved working with the soil, and the second she had a home, she would create a flowery oasis. The twins would love that. "Benny, you have to get on board."

He grinned. "Benny? Look at you being all modern."

She snorted. Benjamin fit him better, but she liked the nickname, too. Benny fit the guy who'd put on a dress to show her she could defend herself no matter what she wore. Benjamin had taken her to unbelievable heights in the shower. He was both. "Don't distract me," she murmured. How wonderful it was to have the freedom to say such things and know there would be no repercussions.

Except his gentle tug on her ear. "You said I have three days to find them," he reminded her.

She tried to remain calm. "Yes, but don't we need to plan in case they can't be found? In that case, I have to follow Terre's directions." She looked around the table for support. "My children are at stake. Nothing is more important."

Mercy's posture straightened even more. "I agree. If we can't find them, what choice do you have?" She looked at Garrett. "Can we wire her up?"

Garrett shook his head. "We can wire her, but I have no doubt she'll be scanned the second she arrives in Kurjan territory. We don't have devices like the one that was in your head, Karma. Ours are detectable, and any tracking dust would be easily found."

Logan poured more wine in Mercy's glass and then his own. "Even if it can be found, we should dust her anyway. It takes a few days to get rid of the dust. They'll know it's there, but we'll also know where she is."

"So they won't move her anywhere of importance until it dissipates," Mercy said, hopping in her chair. "Plus, we could dust her without consent, so Terre won't be pissed and think she worked against him."

"No." Benjamin slammed his fist on the table. Dishes bounced and landed with a loud clatter.

Karma jumped. "It's just a backup plan. Shouldn't we make it as good as possible?"

Mercy's eyes glimmered with sympathy and understanding. "There are two children at risk, Ben. If Karma wants to do this, to try to save them, you can't hold her back."

Benny looked at Logan. "Would you let your mate go?"

Mate? Karma turned partially toward Benjamin, the heavy arm over her shoulder hampering her movements. "We have not mated."

He turned his head, his gaze nearly black. "How long do you think Terre will wait to mate you?"

Dread dropped into her stomach. "Not long."

"Mating doesn't have to be consensual," he said, his face showing no give.

"I know," she whispered. "But there are bigger issues at play than my feelings. You have to understand that."

For the longest of moments, he just studied her face. An expression settled over him that she couldn't read. Maybe acceptance and determination mixed with…she just wasn't sure. "I'm not saying yes, but we can develop a contingency plan in case we don't find the girls within the time frame."

Relief flooded through her. She'd deal with her fear of what Terre had planned later. "It's not just the girls, Benny. I know the Kurjans have kidnapped more enhanced women, maybe even children, and they matter, too. We have to find and free them before Jaydon attempts his ritual." He had power, and he had followers, so it was entirely possible he'd be able to do so without Dayne even knowing about it. The Cyst often went on their own paths, temporarily living apart from the rest of the Kurjans.

"Fine, but make no mistake," Benny started, his gaze not leaving hers, "if you plan to go into Kurjan territory, you'll do so as my mate. My mark will protect you from Terre to a degree."

She gasped. "I can't do that. If I'm mated, Terre has no reason not to just kill me."

Benny smiled, and the sight was frightening this time. "Not if he thinks you have access to the virus. Give him a little hope, a little rope, and I'll make sure to strangle him with it."

Karma swallowed, her mind reeling. This was a side of Benjamin she'd never witnessed, and his determination was intimidating. And intriguing. He'd also had no problem making such a declaration in front of everyone else. So much for privacy. "I don't know."

"I do," he said, his tone unrelenting.

Mating Benjamin? For real? Her body heated and then flushed. Goodness.

Chapter Thirty-Two

After another night spent in wild copulation with Karma, Benny was about to lose his mind. It had been two nights and two more days, and he only had one day left to find her twins. She'd told him story after story about the girls, and while he had no clue what to do with children's feelings, he knew how to protect and defend. That he could definitely do for them. The female had been correct that the contingent of Kurjan soldiers moved around. He'd almost had them the day before, but they'd moved on.

Satellites weren't as helpful as he'd hoped they'd be.

"We could reach out to the Realm for help," Garrett said from his computer console in the main room. "I can't guarantee they'll assist us, and it may take them more than a day to get up to speed, which won't help us any." He kept his voice calm, but a thread of anger wove through each word. "I'll back your play, Benny."

"Ditto," Logan said from a computer down the way. "If you don't want Karma to go, we'll stand by you."

Benny appreciated the support, but he had to make a decision on this. Karma and Mercy were downstairs in the gym working on self-defense moves.

Garrett turned around in his chair. "I don't want to get my head snapped off my neck, and this is none of my business, but I don't think you should send her in mated."

Benny rolled his neck and forced himself to think calmly. "Explain."

Garrett poked at a hole in his T-shirt. "From everything we've gathered, Terre has a shitty temper. The second he senses that she's mated, he might kill her. Or beat the hell out of her with a bat or something that won't give him the mating allergy." Garrett scrabbled a hand through his unruly hair. "That's not all."

"What?" Benny growled.

Logan partially turned. "If you mate her, no way will you let her go."

Benny stared at the young warrior. He wasn't wrong. "I know."

Garrett held up a hand. "Again, I'll back you, no matter the consequences. But I have a mom who'd walk through fire for me, Logan has one who would happily blow up an entire island for him, and I assume your mama was a warrior, too. Karma's a mother. In my experience, there's nothing she won't sacrifice to save those kids."

That was one of the many things Benny admired and truly liked in the female. "Terre will rape her. How can I let that happen?"

Garrett steepled his fingers beneath his chin and his eyes burned. "You've been training her nonstop. She can fight."

"She can't fight," Benny said quietly, glancing toward the door to make sure Karma wasn't there to hear him. "It's been only three days—she'll be no match for Terre or anybody else. Even Mercy, who frankly isn't the best sparrer, is having to pull her punches wearing cushy gloves." The idea of Karma being harmed was like a dual kick to the solar plexus and the balls.

Logan's eyes swirled with understanding. "If she's hurt, we'll help her heal after we get her back. Again, this is up to you."

Karma bustled into the room with Mercy on her heels. Both women were winded, and Karma's blouse hung with the bottom twisted as if they'd grappled on the ground. "We were sparring, kind of, and I have an idea." Her eyes were bright and her voice rushed.

Benny couldn't keep himself from reaching for her. "Go on."

"We can't mate." Her lips turned down, and her face turned pink. "I appreciate the offer, but one, I don't want to mate for convenience or any other rational reason. I want love and passion and crazy, over-the-top possessiveness. Like Mercy has."

Mercy grimaced.

Benny sent her a look. The last thing he needed was Mercy working against him. "We have passion. I'm definitely possessive."

"I want love. The whole wild experience of it." Karma placed her hands on his chest. "And two, we have an idea. Maybe a good one."

He couldn't give her the words. She meant so much to him, but what was love? He didn't want to sing in the rain, and he sure didn't want somebody telling him what to do or changing who he was or needed to be in the future. "What's your idea?"

She hopped once. "A rash. A big, ugly, itchy rash all over my body. We can tell Terre that it's a side effect of the virus, and it takes a while for the mating bond to dissipate. That should get me at least a little time before he, well, you know."

"Tries to rape you?" Benny growled, unwilling to use euphemisms.

"Yes." Karma turned pale. "Even so, I'm going, Benjamin. If the worst happens and I can't kill him, then I'll deal with what happens after I get my children to safety. I miss them. Terribly. It's like there's a hole in my soul, and I'm so afraid they're scared or hurt. It's torture worse than anything Terre could possibly do to me."

How could Benny argue with that? "You're immortal. How are you going to get a rash?"

"Poison ivy," Mercy said, plopping onto Logan's lap and wrapping her arm over his shoulder. "It grows wild across the river, and we can rub her from head to toe with the stuff."

"That's a decent plan." Logan clicked his tongue. "Healing cells fix allergic reactions within seconds, but if Karma refuses to use her cells, she could claim the rash was a reaction to Virus-27. The Kurjans don't have a sample of the virus, so they don't know much about it."

Karma expression brightened even more. "It's a fantastic idea, because Yvonne will want to test me immediately. She's desperate to know more about the virus, so maybe Terre will take me to her right away. We want that, because her location is stable and more than likely where the kidnapped enhanced females are being held."

Garrett stiffened. "If that plan is going to work, we can't cover you with tracking dust. They won't take you to Yvonne until the dust dissipates, and if you wait that long, the rash will probably heal itself, even if you don't employ your healing cells on purpose."

"I know," Karma whispered.

Benny growled low and long. This was an impossible decision.

* * * *

Except for the constant worry about her girls, this had been the best week of Karma's life. Partly because of Mercy, but mostly because of Benjamin and his kindness—as well as his spectacular body. Even so, she was about to kick him in the groin.

"Again," he barked, grasping her arm and pulling her off the mat. "You have to kick faster and then turn."

They'd been training for three hours, and she was done. She'd donned yoga pants that made her feel exposed, but she could tell her timing was better in them, and she was going to make herself wear jeans when it was time to go. She had that confidence now. "There is no faster. I'm tired, Benjamin." It was time to stop avoiding the inevitable. "I have to make the phone call, and you know it."

He stood so tall and broad, an immovable object in a dangerous world. His eyes blazed a deadly hue, and his muscles stood out from head to toe, giving him the look of a panther about to spring. The lazy humor usually evident in his expression had fled, leaving this battle-scarred warrior in its place. His tension and fury colored the atmosphere of the entire training room. "We need some rules."

What was it with the soldier and rules? Karma tried to remain respectful and not roll her eyes. "All right. Rules."

"One, you don't heal the rash at all—no matter how much it bugs you." He looked as if he was about to pounce and then lock her away in a closet.

"Agreed." She understood his need to control the situation as well as his frustration that he could not. She felt the same way about her daughters. Linda had disappeared, most likely crossing over at last. Karma would truly be on her own. "Next rule?"

"Once we get them back, this is your last mission. No going into danger—no matter what happens between us." This was said on a growl that sent spirals of desire right to her core.

She cleared her throat. "Agreed. I have no interest in being a soldier, spy, or dignitary. Not right now." She didn't care whether that was a modern attitude or not. She wanted peace and fun and time to enjoy her girls as they grew up. Her adventures would consist of picking the right flowers to plant and messing around with odd recipes. She'd lived in fear much too long; now it was time for joy. Would that life include Benjamin? It was shocking how badly she wanted a chance with him, but she wouldn't settle for anything less than everything. Never again.

"Fine." If he looked any angrier, steam would probably blow right out of his eyes and nose. He drew a small black phone from his back pocket. "This is a burner. Crouch down, whisper like you're hiding from me, and be quick."

Her hand shook when she accepted the phone, and by the tightening of Benjamin's jaw, he noticed. "Okay. I had to memorize Terre's number before I escaped with you." She crouched down, following Benny's directions, and then dialed.

"Terre," he answered.

She cupped the phone. "It's Karma. I have a way out and will be on the road in an hour while they're training. I don't know exactly where I am, but I will seek a road name I can recognize."

Terre was quiet for a moment.

She put her mouth closer to the phone. "Hurry up. I don't have much time before I must take them supper. I'll run right after I serve them."

"They've made you a servant." For some reason, Terre sounded pleased. "That's what you are."

"They're coming," she whispered, her voice naturally rising. "Promise my girls will be there."

Papers shuffled. "Go north and west, wherever you are. Head toward Seattle, and call me again when you're close for more specific instructions."

She kept her voice as level as she could. "Once I get close, I will require proof that you have my children. If you don't, I leave. Period."

"You've grown some balls while you were away." Terre chuckled, and the sound was chilling. "Very well. I will have those brats here. I'm looking forward to exploring this new side of you. Before I destroy it, of course." He clicked off.

She felt as if the acid in her stomach was eating through her body. She trembled and dropped the phone onto the mat. "He said to head toward Seattle."

Benny reclaimed the phone. "You don't have to do this."

"Yes, I do." She stood, accepting his hand when he offered it.

Mercy appeared in the doorway with a bag in her hand. "I collected enough poison ivy to turn you into one big blister, and I also cooked some of the leaves and extracted the urushiol to rub directly on your skin so the reaction will happen sooner than usual. It should take an hour or two, tops. This is going to be incredibly uncomfortable."

"I can handle it," Karma said softly, sliding her hand into Benny's.

Mercy's gaze dropped to their joined hands. "All right. What's the plan?"

Benny tightened his hold around Karma's hand. "Have Logan and Garrett search around Seattle for a Kurjan encampment, and somebody needs to notify Bear and the Grizzly motorcycle club. If we're going into his territory, he'll know it. The last thing we need is to get the Bear Nation pissed off at us."

Mercy set the bag to the side. "We can be wheels up in thirty minutes. Just let me know." Then she disappeared down the hallway.

"Bear is the leader of the Bear Nation?" Karma asked. "Is that a joke?"

"Bear is a smart-ass and took the name a long time ago," Benny admitted. "He's the leader of the Bear Nation, and he also leads a motorcycle club of wild-assed bears, where Logan and Garrett once worked undercover for a while. I think Garrett may join them again for a time."

She frowned. "Why are we calling them?"

"Out of respect, as well as the fact that they'll provide backup when we need to come in and get you." Tension rolled off Benny. "Unless they decide to kill us first. The shifters really don't like the Seven."

Life just kept getting worse. Karma looked at the innocuous garbage bag by the door. "I guess we should do this. I should."

Benny finally grinned, although the look was more of a grimace. "I'll help. Head to toe, right?"

Chapter Thirty-Three

The helicopter ride was made in the dark of a moonless night. Benny and Mercy made sure to rub the sappy oil and leaves all over Karma in the back of the copter as Logan and Garrett rode up front. Sam sat just behind them, sleeping with his head against the wall. Just as they started to land, Benny ripped off his gloves. "Does it hurt yet?"

Karma shook her head. "No. When am I supposed to start showing a rash?"

"Soon," Mercy said, wincing. "That pure oil is going to take effect way too fast for your peace of mind. Maybe we should've waited a few hours?"

The helicopter set down just outside Grizzly territory.

Benny waited until the blades had stopped and then opened the door. "Stay inside until I make sure Bear isn't going to just try to kill us." He jumped into the rainy night, instantly scenting grizzly. He turned to see Bear and two lieutenants standing near a log wood hangar. Sam leaped out behind him, his boots smashing the wet weeds.

Mercy sat at the edge of the doorway with a gun resting lightly on her lap.

Benny started forward, noting the lieutenants stiffening in response. He had known Bear for decades, and the guy looked better than ever, even though his square jaw was set hard and his honey-brown eyes sizzled with irritation. His shaggy brown hair touched his broad shoulders, and his clothing looked like it had seen better days. He waited until Benny reached him, flanked by Logan and Garrett. "The Seven isn't welcome in my territory."

Benny caught Sam moving out of the corner of his eye. The middle brother had angled to the south, just in case he needed to cover them. That was a good brother. "I know, and I don't want to be in your territory. I assume the Kurjans and Cysts aren't welcome, either. Have you found them?"

"Not yet," Bear admitted. "Nessa is back at the control center looking, and believe me, my witch is not happy the Seven is here." His gaze softened slightly when he looked at Garrett and then Logan. "Although she misses you two and can't wait to make s'mores again. You're going to have to visit with her, or I'll never hear the end of it."

Garrett grinned. "Your mate is a badass and one of my favorite females, and no way am I messing with her temper. S'mores it is."

Benny settled his stance. "I don't want to be here, Bear. You know it and I know it, but I have no choice."

Bear's gaze narrowed as he looked past Benny. "Who are the pretty ladies?"

Benny growled as the sweet scent of Karma grew nearer. Hadn't he told her to stay in the helicopter?

Logan grasped Mercy and pulled her in front of him, wrapping his arms around her waist. "This is Mercy. My mate."

Bear grinned and held out a hand the size of a Frisbee. "The fairy? Cool. I've never met a fairy."

"Fae," Mercy corrected, quickly shaking his hand. "Can I watch you change into a grizzly later? I've never seen a bear shift."

Bear's smile widened. "Definitely."

It was nice that crazy often found crazy. Benny drew Karma forward. "This is Karma. She wants to go into the Kurjan encampment in your territory to rescue enhanced females and her young daughters. That's why we're here."

Bear cocked his head and held out a hand. "This is your mate?" Puzzlement glittered in his eyes as they briefly shook hands.

"Not yet," Benny said, holding up his mating mark. "It's a long story."

Now shock showed in Bear's expression. "You're letting your mate go with the Kurjans?"

Karma stepped closer to the dangerous bear. "Nobody is 'letting' me do anything. The Kurjans have my daughters, and I have to rescue them. Now, are you going to help us or not?"

Admiration tilted Bear's full lips. "Well, then. I guess we help you." He leaned closer. "What's happening to your neck?"

She winced and rubbed her neck.

Benny angled his head down and made out the starting of blisters. "Looks like the oil worked."

Karma squirmed. "Yes. My whole body is starting to itch."

"That looks like poison oak?" Bear asked.

"Poison ivy," Mercy said proudly. "I extracted the oils to make sure it got in there deep and stayed. Those blisters are popping out all over. We did avoid her face so there wouldn't be any eye damage."

Bear stepped closer to her. "Are you in danger? I can free you right now." The words were delivered in a grizzly growl.

Karma shook her head. "It's all part of the plan. The less attractive I am to the Kurjans, the safer I'll be. The problem will be finding the girls and getting out." She blew out air and shivered as the poison took effect. "I have to figure out a way to find the enhanced females, as well."

"You're a brave one, Karma," Bear said solemnly. "All right. We'll definitely help you."

Benny kept his expression calm. He had been kind of hoping Bear would kick them out of Washington State. It looked like Karma was actually going to have to go through with this mission.

She slipped her hand into his again. "It'll be all right, Benjamin. Trust me."

* * * *

Every inch of her skin itched uncontrollably as the blisters took over. Karma parked the car at a small convenience store about sixty miles south of Seattle. She took the burner phone out of the console and looked around. She was in human territory. Where were the billionaire cowboys and hard-cut but handsome motorcycle club members? Perhaps those romance novels hadn't gotten all of it right.

She dialed quickly.

"Terre," he answered, his voice businesslike.

She searched for her backbone, feeling uncomfortable even though Benny was watching her through a scope. The soldiers had arrived a half hour before she did, just to get prepared. "I'm at the Miller Convenience Store for Campers just off I-90," she said, not having to fake the nervousness in her voice. She was still hoping to see some handsome pirates with long hair since she was close to the ocean. Nope. No pirates.

"Good." Papers rustled. "Drive twenty miles up Cross Creek Road, turn left at, ah, green mile marker seventeen, and drive another ten miles. Detour from this route in any way, and I'll kill those twin girls."

Her stomach clenched so hard, she almost cried out from the intense pain. That quickly, she forgot about human romance novels. "I want to see my girls."

"Excuse me?" Terre's voice cracked.

She shut her eyes and swallowed down bile. "Please, let me see them, Terre." She curled her other hand into a fist until her fingernails bit into her palm and centered her.

"Very well. Engage your video conference app."

She did so, and he slowly took form on the screen. If anything, he looked even larger and more dangerous than before, and his eyes were a swirling purple. God, she couldn't breathe.

He smiled, showing those bizarrely long canines. "Hello there. I've missed you."

She blinked. "I doubt that."

"I'll prove it to you when you arrive." He moved the phone to the side, and the camera caught the twins playing on a blanket with Yvonne sitting on a chair next to them, typing something onto a tablet.

Karma's heart leapt. The girls looked healthy and seemed to be happily playing with some stuffed animals, although they were quiet. Even subdued. She steeled her shoulders. No matter what happened to her, they were what mattered.

Terre came back on the screen. "Start driving. Now." He disengaged the call.

She set the phone down and rested her head on the steering wheel. This was too much, but she had no choice. Barely moving, she pressed a button on the dash, careful to keep her face hidden in case there were Kurjan cameras near.

"Hey, sweetheart. You did good," Benny said through the speakers. "We'll track you to the meeting spot, and then we'll follow you from there to the camp. Just drive slow and keep your wits about you. You're strong, and you're smart. Those bastard Kurjans have no idea who they're messing with."

Tears gathered in her eyes at the kind words. At the moment, all she felt was terrified. For her girls, for the enhanced women, and even for herself. Just how strong was that? "Thank you for the last week, Benjamin," she whispered, her throat clogging with those tears. "No matter what happens next, it was the best week of my life. I do love you. I always will." Before he could answer, she disengaged the call and turned off the telecom system of the car.

Then she lifted her head and began driving, making sure to stay on the right side of the road and follow the speed limit. It wasn't difficult. Why did the Kurjans only let males drive?

This was easy.

She followed the directions exactly, not seeing anyone flanking her from the forested creek side of the road. The Seven members, Mercy, and the grizzly shifters were out there somewhere, and the idea gave her some reassurance. But she had a job to do, and she would have to trust them all to do their own jobs.

The number-one priority was the twins.

Karma turned along the dirt road and drove until she reached a large clearing with mud-covered utility vehicles parked in a circle. The sun was meager, barely visible through the clouds, while rain continued to pummel the earth. The Kurjans would be at full strength, even without their new cure. She came to a stop and was instantly surrounded by vehicles.

Her door was ripped open, and Terre yanked her out.

She'd forgotten how tall he was.

"This way." He barely looked at her while dragging her past several vehicles to the center, where two Cyst soldiers were rapidly removing a camouflaged tarp from a helicopter.

"No," she said, struggling against him. If they got into the air, Benny would never find her. This could not happen. "Stop."

The engines started up; two Kurjan soldiers sat in the front of the craft, already waiting. The rear door of the hatch opened, and her two girls stared out. Their hair was wild around their heads, and both of them had wide eyes and looked scared. "Mama!" Boone yelled.

Karma paused. Every moment in her life narrowed to that one second. Then she rushed forward. The girls. Terre lifted her inside, jumped up, and shut the hatch.

Soldiers and bears roared out of the surrounding forest. One bear barreled right into the helicopter and bounced back to land hard and roll. The copter rose straight into the rainy air as the warriors began firing laser guns and flashing knives. Then the helicopter turned and rose so fast she nearly had to shut her eyes. The girls rushed to her, both landing on her lap. She put her arms around them, holding tight, her heart finally settling.

Then she looked around.

Yvonne and Jaydon sat on the far bench, while she and the girls sat in the middle on the floor. Terre unfolded a seat from the wall across from the hatch and sat, staring at her in the dim light. "You made that more difficult than I had expected. When did the grizzly shifters get involved?"

She held her daughters closer, putting her hands on their heads and pressing them close while being careful not to let her rash touch any of their bare skin. "Yesterday," she said, trying to remember the story. "The Seven discovered my call to you and knew where I was going, so they contacted the shifters—it's their territory."

Yvonne pushed her platinum-blond hair away from her stunning face. She was fairly young and definitely brilliant. It was truly a pity that she was spending her entire life waiting for Ulric. "You led us into a trap."

Karma carefully rolled her eyes, making sure Terre saw her. "Right. Like the Kurjans can't handle a few grizzly bears. I wasn't worried about that."

Terre's chest puffed out. Then he looked closer at her. "What the hell happened to your skin?"

"It's on fire," she said, not lying a bit. "Apparently many females have a reaction to the virus that negates the mating bond, and believe me, it's terrible. Supposedly the rash reacts much like the mating allergy and will infect any male that touches it for about two weeks. That's what the queen said."

"How convenient," Yvonne drawled. "Isn't that convenient?"

Sometimes Karma forgot how smart the woman was because she was so snide. "Not really," she retorted. "It itches worse than you can even imagine."

Terre leaned in and studied her face. "You lay with the hybrid. Why didn't he get it?"

"I most certainly did not," she said, heat filling her face at the lie. "He tried, but he was instantly infected with the rash. He deserved it." She almost choked on the words this time. What she wouldn't give to have Benjamin right there with her.

"Scan her," Terre ordered.

Yvonne drew a square device from her bag and leaned over, scanning Karma from head to toe. "She's clean. No tracking dust, either."

Terre smiled. "Good. They didn't want to keep you, either. The trap was about us."

Karma shivered at the look in his eyes. The Seven and the Grizzlies hadn't expected a helicopter. She truly was on her own now.

Chapter Thirty-Four

They weren't at the main headquarters in Canada, but the settlement was certainly a permanent one. By the number of Cyst soldiers patrolling in the rainy night, Karma could only surmise it was the headquarters for the main Cyst contingent. "How long are we staying here?" she asked as she helped the girls from the helicopter.

"As long as I wish," Terre said absently, accepting a tablet from a Cyst. "This way." He led her through the rain to a vehicle that took them to a lodge at the base of what appeared to be a ski hill. "It's after midnight. Put the girls to bed, and then we shall talk."

She was almost grateful for the order and that she could put her girls to bed, and that response ticked her off. She wasn't a servant, and she wasn't helpless. But right now, she was a mother, and her duty to her children came first. As they entered the lodge, she couldn't help but notice the different feeling of the place compared to the Seven's headquarters. This building was cold without any comfortable couches or a pool table, and the fireplace, which had no doubt been there before the Kurjans had purchased the mountain, was silent and dark. "Which way?"

"Wait." Yvonne set her black bag on a table and drew out a syringe. "I want to examine your blood while the Virus-27 is still present." Without waiting for consent, she took Karma's arm and tapped the vein. The needle pricked hard and went too deep, as if Yvonne enjoyed causing pain.

Karma remained silent as the blood was drawn and then pressed the cotton ball to her arm afterward. "No bandage?" she asked dryly.

Yvonne started and then looked at her, her gaze thoughtful. Then she took a quick swipe of Karma's neck with another cotton ball. "I'll see you in the morning for a full workup."

It was already morning or would be soon. Karma couldn't see a clock.

Terre pointed down the hallway. "Put them in the room at the end, and then return here for me. There's clothing there for you. Those jeans offend me."

Yeah, she was more likely to kick him in the face with the jeans giving her freedom of motion. Did he somehow realize that fact? She doubted it. She looked around for Linda to show her the way.

Linda was nowhere to be seen. Perhaps she had passed over.

Instead of answering Terre, Karma took both girls by the hands and bustled down the cold wooden floor to the room at the end, where she flipped on the light. The room was utilitarian, with two metal twin beds and not much else. Two bags had been tossed on the floor. She opened the first one and found pajamas for the girls.

"Potty," Belle said, her tawny eyes drowsy.

"I know, baby." Karma smoothed her hair back and then quickly helped the toddlers change into their plain sleep dresses before taking them across the hall to the bathroom. There weren't toothbrushes in the bag, but she found some travel ones in the medicine cabinet. After washing their faces, she took them back to the bedroom, feeling a cloud of fear over her head the whole time.

Boone yawned and hopped from one bare foot to the other. "Cold," she mumbled, her eyelids almost closing.

Karma lifted her into the first bed and then reached for Belle and placed her next to her sister. "You two share a bed. You'll stay warmer that way." When the girls snuggled down, she removed the blankets from the other bed to place over them. "There you go." Her heart swelled when she leaned down and kissed them both on their foreheads. "I'm here now."

Boone blinked sleepily. "Why did you go?"

"I had work to do," Karma said, sitting on the bed and wishing with everything she had that she could stay right here. But Terre would come looking, and she didn't want to frighten the girls. "I missed you both so much."

"Story?" Belle murmured, not opening her eyes.

"In the morning. Right now, it's very late, and you need to sleep," Karma whispered, kissing her babies again. She looked around the darkened room, but Linda wasn't there. Her earlier thought that the twins' birth mother had crossed over was confirmed. The pang to Karma's heart wasn't unexpected. "Did you do all right?"

"Yvonne is mean," Belle muttered. "Took blood."

Karma brushed back her hair. Yvonne was always experimenting on enhanced females and was far less kind than the queen had been. "You're safe now, sweetheart."

Boone snuggled into her sister's side. "Vero took good care of us. He's my friend."

Karma kissed them both again. Vero had always been a good kid; he lacked the Kurjan habit of striking first and asking questions later. She prayed he'd survive their rough world.

Both girls slipped into sleep, their breathing evening out. Karma made sure they were safely tucked in and then moved to the other bag, which held stuffed toys. Oh. So no clothing for her. Good. Now she didn't have to change into a dress. No doubt Yvonne had forgotten on purpose, knowing that Terre didn't like jeans.

At the moment, Karma didn't care. She tiptoed across the room and slipped quietly into the hallway, where she ran into Vero, Terre's adopted son. The kid had his head tipped back and held a tissue beneath his bleeding nose.

"Vero," she whispered, drawing him into the bathroom. "What happened?"

"Should've ducked," the kid said, shaking his head. "I'm fine. I'm glad you're home. Did the Seven males hurt you?"

She shook her head. "No. They were all quite nice, really. So was the Queen of the Realm. I think she'd make a terrific friend if life was different. The rumors about her aren't true." She had to at least try to convince the younger generation that the Realm was not evil.

Vero's eyes widened. "No kidding?" His speech came out muffled behind the tissue. "Can you tell me more later?" His eyes were a light blue, so different from most Kurjan children. Were the other kids still making fun of him?

Karma patted his shoulder. "We can talk all about it tomorrow. You need sleep tonight."

"I know." His jaw worked as if he needed to find control. "Terre is waiting for you in the large room. Make sure you duck if you need to." Without waiting for an answer, he slipped into the bathroom.

Karma exhaled slowly and walked down the hallway. Had Terre hit Vero again? She hated that male sometimes. All Vero needed was a safe place to land, and he wasn't getting that in the Kurjan stronghold. If there was a way to take him with her when she fled, she'd do it. Would he go? She actually wasn't certain.

She walked quietly into the main room, which held computer consoles, two screens, and hardwood furniture except for two plush leather chairs.

Terre sat in one of the leather chairs, his long legs extended to a coffee table as he read a tablet. He looked up. "You didn't change." He appeared more startled than angry.

She kept her expression neutral. "There weren't any clothes to change into. Is there a different room I should check for my clothing?" It would be a good idea to scour the entire lodge and memorize the layout and possible escape routes. Her arms itched, and she gently rubbed them, not wanting to break the skin and worsen the now-painful rash.

Terre frowned and set the tablet aside. "I gave orders for your clothing to be here."

"To whom?" She paused several feet away from him. "I can go ask that person." Oh, she already knew who'd forgotten her clothing.

"Yvonne," Terre said, dropping his feet to the floor.

Karma kept her expression wide-eyed and innocent. "Yvonne doesn't take orders. The Cyst generals call her by a royal title, and even Dayne defers to her wishes most of the time." In fact, Terre was the only one who treated Yvonne like any other female. No doubt Yvonne would take issue with him if Ulric ever returned and mated her as she'd planned. "Yvonne gets away with everything." Could Karma cause a problem between Yvonne and Terre? It wasn't a bad idea. This whole spy business was getting easier.

Terre studied her. "Your rash is getting worse."

"It itches terribly," she admitted, trying to keep the relief out of her voice. "You should have seen what it did to that lowly hybrid when he tried to touch me. I've never witnessed anything like it." She shivered, and it was cold enough in the room that she kept shivering until she made herself stop.

Terre swept his hand toward the bar. "Get me a drink and then come and talk."

She barely kept from telling him to stuff it. Instead, she strode to the bar set up at the far end of the room. Terre liked gin, so she chose the best bottle and made him a martini with two olives. Holding her head high, she strode toward him and handed it over before sitting on the hard wooden chair he motioned her toward. The plush leather one remained vacant on the other side of him.

He took a sip. "Yvonne wants to examine you more fully in the morning now that you've taken the virus." It wasn't a question or a request.

"All right. Is she in this building?" Karma asked, folding her hands on her lap.

"No. Her lab is next to this building. I'll escort you in the morning." He took another drink and then leaned closer to study the blisters on her neck. "Turn your head."

She did so without question, her left foot all but twitching with the need to kick up right beneath his chin. How surprised he would be.

"That looks terrible," he muttered, sitting back. "Yvonne said she'd try to find a way to speed up the healing process."

Oh, Karma just bet she would.

Terre finished the martini. "I had different plans for us tonight, as I'm sure you know."

No answer was expected, so Karma didn't give one.

He handed her his glass. "Another."

It was truly unfortunate she didn't have poison with her. She silently took the glass and walked to the bar as the front door opened and Jaydon strode inside, the rain still dotting his uniform.

He looked at her. "Make that two."

What a dick, as Mercy would say. Karma looked at the far table, the one near the doorway. It held maps and a couple of tablets. Perhaps there was information about the enhanced women over there. She'd have to find a way to examine those documents. She hid a small smile, made two gin martinis, and carried them to the males now sitting in the plush chairs. Neither thanked her.

Terre motioned for her to sit again, his gaze running over her body the way it had for decades. "Start at the beginning. I want to know all about your time at the Realm and any weaknesses in security you saw there." He took another drink of the gin.

"I didn't see any weaknesses," Karma said, hiding her revulsion. The blisters felt better on her body than did his gaze.

Jaydon settled his large bulk back in the chair. "You need to ask more basic questions. She wouldn't know a weakness. How many soldiers did you see?"

She tried to look ditzy. "I didn't count. The queen put me in a machine, and when I came out, she said that I wasn't tagged in any way. They didn't find the device in my head until I went to the Seven Headquarters, which you blew up." Being underestimated could definitely work to her advantage. "King Dage Kayrs and the Seven members were all very insistent in their questioning about the enhanced females you've kidnapped. About how many you have and where you have them kept."

Terre smiled. "I'm sure they want to know."

Karma leaned forward and frowned, letting confusion show on her face. "The Seven members also believe that Jaydon is going to duplicate the ritual the great leader Ulric performed centuries ago and then take his place. Can you believe that?" She widened her eyes just enough.

Terre stiffened. "That is just enemy propaganda." He looked at the general. "Correct? You'd never attempt such a travesty."

"Of course not," Jaydon said smoothly, his shoulders too wide for the chair. The overhead lights glinted off his mostly bald head, and even sitting, he emitted a sense of controlled command. "I want our supreme leader back even more than you do. The Cyst need him."

Terre's eyes narrowed, but he didn't speak.

Karma perched quietly, letting the suspicions grow. What would happen if the Cyst faction turned against the Kurjan nation? The idea was unthinkable, and yet...neither group trusted very well. Dayne was a born diplomat, who could smooth over any misunderstanding. Terre, on the other hand, wouldn't know diplomacy if it bit him on the chin. If Jaydon was attempting to become the new leader of the Cyst, Terre would object.

Perhaps she could start an internal war. Why not dream big?

Yvonne strode inside again, rain dotting her stunning hair and triumph on her angular face.

Dread dropped into Karma's stomach, and her knees trembled with the need to run. Hard and fast.

Terre looked up. "Yvonne. I thought you were going to bed."

The woman smiled, and minute wrinkles spread out from her eyes. She was clearly getting older. There was no doubt she was jealous of the females who had stopped aging once mated. "The blood tests will take all night, but I thought you should know that the rash is from a leaf. It's poison ivy." Her smile was catlike.

Terre turned toward Karma, his smile furious. "Heal yourself. Right now, or you won't like the results."

Considering the girls were just down the hall, Karma instantly sent healing cells to her skin. The rash had protected her from Terre, but she still sighed in relief when the blisters disappeared.

Yvonne laughed. "I can't believe you suffered for hours like that just because you didn't want to mate Terre."

Terre stood and grabbed Karma's arm, yanking her up. "Oh, that's nothing compared to the suffering to come," he growled.

Karma wrenched free and then kicked him square in the balls.

He lunged for her just as an explosion rocked the lodge, scattering the papers off the table. Then the entire world lit up outside.

Karma turned to run.

Chapter Thirty-Five

Pure panic and raw rage had Benny jumping out of the helicopter before the thing had neared the ground. He hit wet pine needles and rolled, coming up firing. Karma was in the hands of the enemy. By herself. The beast at his core roared in fury, and the mating mark on his hand pounded as if he'd just been branded with a hot poker.

She. Was. His.

If this was love, it wasn't at all what he'd thought. He turned and fired into the neck of the nearest soldier and then ducked as a series of knives flew over his head. Grizzly bears careened from the forest, the lead bear creating a zigzag pattern as he identified the areas of land mines without glasses.

Impressive.

Benny ran toward what appeared to be the main lodge with Sam and Logan flanking him. A trio of Cyst soldiers barreled out of the smaller building next to the lodge, firing rapidly. Ducking, he turned and tackled the first Cyst to the ground while Logan and Sam engaged the other two.

Garrett leaped over Benny's head to take down two Kurjan soldiers who'd run out of the main lodge.

The Cyst soldier beneath him punched Benny's neck and scraped his claws across Benny's jugular. Pain flashed, and his skin gaped open.

He punched down several times, cracking the soldier's nose and eye sockets. The Cyst wrapped both legs around Benny's torso and squeezed, twisting to the side and punching Benny in the hip, right below his shield. Agony flashed hot and deep inside his body, and he sent emergency healing cells to keep him moving.

"Get off me," he growled, grasping a knife from the sheath in his boot and stabbing it through the soldier's thigh. The hold loosened. He had to get inside the lodge before Terre could kill Karma. Benny knew enough from his research and few torture sessions with the asshole that he would kill Karma before he'd let Benny take her back. He twisted the knife up the thigh and planted the blade in the Cyst soldier's groin.

The guy let out a high-pitched scream and grabbed the handle, rolling to the side.

Benny struggled to his feet and contained his own pain in a box to be dealt with later. His right foot had gone numb, but he ran through soldiers fighting hand-to-hand and tried to dodge the lasers shot at him. Several hit his chest and fell useless to the ground. One whizzed by his still-injured neck and singed the skin.

He kept running.

Two Cyst soldiers dropped from a tree near the entrance to the lodge. Before Benny could engage them, an enormous grizzly bear took them out from the side.

"Thanks, Bear," he yelled, ducking his head and running faster toward the lodge. Smoke billowed from the side, and it looked as if fire was rapidly spreading throughout.

The front door opened, and Jaydon calmly stepped outside, weapons visible across his chest. He shut the door and smiled. "You're not getting past me."

"Wanna bet?" Benny ran full-bore for the general as the soldier yanked a small sword free and held it in front of his body. At the last second, Benny dropped into a slide and took the bastard out at the knees. Jaydon dropped, and Benny grabbed him by the shoulders and threw him into the door, smashing the entire thing inward.

Jaydon caught himself just inside and backflipped to his feet. "You'll pay, hybrid." Blood dripped from his mouth and fangs.

"Karma!" Benny bellowed, kicking shards of wood out of his way as he approached the general.

No answer came from within the lodge. Dangerous gray smoke billowed from the hallway, and the crackle of fire could be heard over the fighting and rain outside. Maybe Karma was in one of the other buildings. Roaring wildly, Jaydon lowered his chin and rushed Benny.

Benny pivoted and kicked the general in the gut. Pain ricocheted up his leg to his already-damaged hip, and he fell back into the damaged door frame.

Jaydon manacled him by the neck and lifted before dropping onto one knee. Benny partially turned in the nick of time to keep his neck from being broken. He shifted and elbowed Jaydon in the gut, groin, and finally neck. Then he followed up by flipping around, landing on his feet, and yanking Jaydon over his shoulder.

The Cyst soldier flew across the room to land on a hard wooden chair, smashing the entire thing to the ground.

Benny paused. The scent of wildfires by a river filled his head. Karma. She'd been there. He kicked another chair out of the way and stomped over to Jaydon, who was struggling to get up. Benny stole a knife from the back of Jaydon's waist and shoved it in the male's nape.

Jaydon gasped and went down.

Benny straddled him and gently pulled the knife to the left. "Where is she, General? Tell me now."

Jaydon groaned and struggled beneath him, facedown. He planted his hands and pushed up, nearly dislodging Benny. "She's gone, asshole," Jaydon grunted. "Terre killed her the second you landed."

Benny twisted back and forth, nearly decapitating the monster. "Last chance. Tell me, and I won't cut off your head."

Jaydon kicked up, bending his knee. The force of his boot hit Benny square in the back. Fortunately, his shielded torso protected his internal organs. Jaydon cried out as the sound of his foot breaking filled the room. Then he struggled wildly, nearly dislodging Benny.

Benny viciously wrenched the knife back and forth, effectively knocking out the big bastard. Fire rushed in from the other side of the room. He had only seconds to find her. Cutting off Jaydon's big-assed head would take too long. "We'll meet again," Benny growled.

Then he stood. "Karma!" he yelled.

There was no answer.

* * * *

Karma struggled against Terre's hold as he dragged her down rough stairs through a hidden hallway, his tablet in his hand. "Stop," she said, pushing against him.

He backhanded her and kept going.

Pain exploded in her face and through her skull. She tried to look behind her, but he'd closed the door against the fire. Her girls were up there. She fought him, punching and kicking, but he didn't relent. "The kids are up there. We have to get them," she hissed, trying to find purchase with her boots.

They reached a dirt floor, and Terre pulled her through a doorway and pushed her inside. She flew across a small room and caught herself at the far wall before turning.

Terre shut and locked the door by using a keypad to the right of the knob. Lights were already on across the ceiling, and he strode toward a computer console in the room next to another doorway that appeared locked. "Sit down and shut up." He leaned over and punched keys on a keyboard before grasping a phone from beneath the desk and dialing. A gun was stuck in the back of his waist. "Dayne? Where are you?"

She needed to get that gun.

Dayne's voice came in loud and clear. "At the south end right now. The explosion caused a cave-in on Tunnels North and South, and we're working to clear the southern one right now. Are you in the south cell?"

"Yes. I have Karma." Terre didn't even turn around to look at her.

Karma searched for a weapon, but there was nothing except the small computer station in the underground room. Maybe a rock would fall from the ceiling. She looked up but didn't see anything that looked loose. Gathering her strength, she rushed for the door and tried to yank it open. "What's the code?" she yelled, her chest thundering. The girls were upstairs by themselves. Would they know how to get out?

"Did you see Drake or Vero?" Dayne asked. "I haven't found either kid yet."

"No," Terre barked. "The main lodge was already on fire when we came down here. Are you sure I shouldn't open the tunnel door?" He glanced at Karma as another explosion rocked the night.

She pulled uselessly at the door and then dropped to the floor to see if she could scrape free enough dirt to go under.

Static came over the line, and then it cleared. "No. You're safe in that room until we finish with the tunnel. The room is surrounded by cement, so a fire won't get you. The top door is secure, and nobody will find the passageway. You have oxygen and whatever you need. I'll call you, brother. If you do need to unlock the tunnel door, you can do it with the keypad. It can't be unlocked from this end." Dayne disengaged the call.

Terre stood. "Get away from that door."

Karma turned around and struggled to her feet, tears clogging her eyes. "Open the door. The kids are upstairs, even Vero. He's yours, right? Please let me save them."

Terre stared at her, his long hair dark against his pale skin. "I care little about those children but will be very interested in the sons we create." He moved toward her, full of grace and anger. "It was a nice try with the rash, by the way." He grabbed her elbow and yanked her toward him. "You lay with the hybrid, didn't you?"

"No," she lied. "Let me save the kids, and I'll do whatever you want. We can mate the second we get to safety." She had no idea what he might have used for a code. It was probably random numbers, and that door was the only way to her children. Another explosion echoed through the night. "Please, Terre. If you want to have any sort of life with me, let me save them."

He shoved her back against the door. "Those aren't the children for us, and you'll do whatever I want already." His hold was painful, and he squeezed her arm harder, yanking her up. Then he kissed her, his mouth bruising.

Her mind settled, and she kneed him directly in the groin, tearing her mouth away. He partially bent over, his eyes wide, and she punched him in the left one. Then the right. She kept punching until he backed up, and then she kicked him right below the knee, just as Benjamin had taught her.

If she could just get him on the ground, maybe she could take the gun. She kicked again, and he grabbed her ankle, yanking her off the ground and then letting go.

She flew up and landed on her back. The air whooshed out of her lungs, and her head thunked on the dirt floor. Her ears rang and sparks flew behind her eyelids. The pain was immense.

Then he was on her. Straddling her and ripping her shirt. She screamed and raked his face with her nails, thrashing beneath him to get free. He tore off the shirt and then grabbed her by the neck, cutting off her oxygen. The room swam around her.

Something hovered to the side of her vision. She looked, and Linda was there, throwing all her force into a punch that actually landed on Terre's temple.

His head flew to the side, and the spirit hit him again, grunting with the effort. Her eyes were a wild topaz, though her hair was barely visible.

Karma pushed Terre and slid out from under him, grabbing the gun out of his waist. She backed away, and Linda hovered next to her, fading in and out. "How did you do that?" Karma gasped, her lip bleeding down her chin.

"Don't know," Linda said, her voice weak. "It's for the girls."

"Our girls," Karma said, lifting the gun and pointing it at Terre.

He stood, many, many inches taller than she. "You won't shoot—"

She fired several times, hitting him in the head, neck, and chest. Blood poured from his wounds, and he dropped to the ground, his brain taking refuge in unconsciousness so he could heal. Breathing heavily, she turned and fired at the keypad. It was her only chance.

Nothing happened.

She fired again, shooting the green lasers all around the pad and right through it. Finally, something clicked. Crying, she snatched Terre's tablet off the table and ran out of the room and up the stairs, her boots slipping on the rough wood.

It couldn't be too late. It just couldn't.

Chapter Thirty-Six

Benny kicked another door open in the main lodge as fire crackled around him and smoke billowed. He tried to cover his mouth and nose. "Karma," he yelled again.

"Benjamin!" A hidden door opened in the hallway, and she stumbled out, blood on her face and her bra dirty. Scrapes covered her bare arms, and her shirt was missing. She'd never looked so good. "The girls," she gasped, turning to the right and running through the smoke.

He followed her, grasping her elbow to steer her away from the fire licking up the east side of the building.

She reached a room at the end of the hall and pushed open the door.

He ran in behind her as the ceiling in the hallway collapsed, barely slamming the door shut before the fire could rush in. Heat smashed against his ankles.

"Boone, Belle?" Karma cried out, dropping to the ground beneath the smoke.

Two little girls crawled out from beneath the nearest bed, both in little shirts that covered them past their knees. They had long black hair and terrified brown eyes, and both rushed to Karma, crying. She gathered them in her arms as she knelt.

Benny ran past the bed and opened the lone window, looking around the night outside. Most of the fights seemed to be finished. "Let's go, sweetheart. Now." The fire was coming in, and the smoke was unbearable. He didn't trust this ceiling, either.

Karma grabbed the little hands of the girls and rushed toward him.

He whisked her off her feet and set her outside the room before she could stop him. Then he picked up both girls and handed one out. Karma took her, and Benny jumped out with the second one, landing on his knees and rolling to keep from hurting the fragile child.

The door inside exploded inward.

Benny jumped up. "Follow me. Stay right behind me." He kept the toddler in his arms as Karma ran behind him with the other twin. Avoiding a couple of skirmishes still going on, he ran to a couple of grizzly bears guarding a shifter helicopter that had just landed. A male opened the back door, and Benny handed over the girl before turning and lifting Karma and the other twin inside. "Go to the back and keep down in case anybody is still shooting," he ordered, ripping his shirt over his head and tossing it at her.

They did so, and he turned to guard them as the world burned around them all.

The main lodge exploded, and he ducked to avoid debris. Karma, his shirt safely covering her, perched at his side with the girls behind her, her gaze seeking. "Vero! This way," she called, gesturing wildly to a young Kurjan teenager.

The kid took a couple of steps toward them and then glanced at the forest, where another teenager stood, watching him. It was Drake, and for a second, their gazes met. Drake was braced to fight, but his gaze remained thoughtful. Many of the Kurjans were fanned out before him, protecting him. He said something to the younger kid, but Benny couldn't hear what it was.

"Do you want me to grab the kid?" he asked Karma. Kidnapping a Kurjan child would be a disaster, but he'd do it if she wanted.

Just then, the kid ran toward Drake. When he was safely behind the Kurjan line, he and Drake turned and disappeared into the forest. "He chose to go with family," Karma said softly, tears in her voice. "I wish we could've taken both of them."

"They're old enough to make their own choice," Benny said. Hopefully they'd make good choices in the coming years and not end up as his enemies. "Get your head down, sweetheart. There's debris flying."

She did so and he watched the remaining few skirmishes wind down. Most of the Kurjan forces had followed the kids or taken other escape routes, and the grizzlies lumbered off, blood on their teeth, to run home. Garrett and Logan bounded into the helicopter, followed by Sam and Bear.

Benny gave the pilots the heads-up to move. He grabbed a rifle off the mount and then sat with one leg hanging out, ready to provide cover.

Garrett clipped him in at the belt and secured the other rifle, facing in the rear direction.

They lifted into the air, watching the fire burn below them. The rain slashed inside, mixing with the dark smoke as it tried to choke them.

Then they were free. Away from the fight and into the clouds.

One pilot looked back, his brown eyes still bearlike. "Don't see any Kurjan forces in the air yet. Are we tracking?"

"Negative," Bear yelled, leaning against the opposite wall, his head back and tingles emanating from him as he healed a bloody hole in his neck. "We're done. Get us home and don't engage unless somebody comes after us."

"Affirmative," the pilot said, turning back to the front windshield.

Benny remounted the rifle above the hatch. Once Garrett had done the same, he slid the door closed. Then he turned and stared at the back of the craft.

Karma sat in his too-large shirt, her eyes wide and bruises on her neck. The twins sat on either side of her, safely secured against her body by her arms, their clothing wet from the run through the rain. Their eyes were wide and topaz colored. Soot covered their faces.

They looked like three terrified birds all holding their breath.

He smiled and not one of them smiled back. "We're safe," he mouthed, wanting to go reassure them but figuring if he moved, they'd freak. The little girls huddled as close to Karma as they could, their small bodies trembling.

Benny looked around. It wasn't as if they had blankets in an attack helicopter. "Bear? You have a tarp or anything in here?"

Bear slowly opened his eyes. "Where would I get a tarp?" He looked to the back of the helicopter. "Oh. No." Then he glanced around. "My shirt is wet, or I'd give it over."

The pilots both immediately took off their shirts, which were still dry. They tossed them back to Benny. He grinned and threw the warm garments back to Karma. "They're all we have right now, honey. The pilots are big bears, and these should warm you a little bit."

Her hesitant smile eased something in him that had hardened painfully when she'd been taken. She covered the girls with the shirts and settled back, her gaze never leaving him. Then she frowned. Edging slightly to the side, she yanked a tablet out of the back of her jeans. Her grin this time was triumphant.

Yeah. That was his woman. His. And those incredibly fragile creatures hanging on to her were her children. None of them belonged in the life he was leading right now.

How was he going to let them go?

* * * *

The small cabin given to them for the night at Grizzly territory was warm and safe. Karma finished settling the girls into a quaint queen-sized bed after a very quick shower to warm up all three of them. They wore clean shirts and she had on a clean tank top and short pajama set the bears had provided. The girls fell asleep within seconds, even though the storm had increased in force outside. The wind and rain battered the windows of the comfortable cabin Bear had given them for the rest of the night. Exhaustion weighed down her limbs.

Linda wavered by the end of the bed.

Surprise caught Karma, and she turned. "You're here."

The meager light from the attached bathroom seemed to shine right through Linda. Yet her smile was clear. "We did it, Karma."

Karma smiled, and tears filled her eyes. She had no idea what was going to happen next, but they *had* done it. The girls were safe. "We did."

Linda reached over and she touched Karma's hand. Karma flipped hers around and held her friend's hand. Her sister, really. The closest thing she'd ever have to a sister. They'd been united in saving these girls, and they both loved them completely.

"Thank you, Karma," Linda whispered, her voice sounding far away. "Keep them safe and love them. You're a good mother. Someday tell them about me, okay?"

"You know I will." The tears slid down Karma's face. "I promise I'll protect and love them. You're free, Linda. Don't worry. Our girls will have a fantastic life."

Linda smiled, released her, and then kissed both of her babies on the cheeks. A light surrounded her, she sighed, and then her form slowly disappeared.

Karma let her shoulders relax. Finally. They had done it. Together. She leaned over and kissed both girls good night again. "Terre should've known not to go up against two mothers," she whispered, meaning every word. "There's not a doubt in my mind that a mother's love is the most powerful force there is."

The girls snuggled down, both sound asleep.

Karma stood and padded barefoot out of the peaceful room to the main part of the cabin. Benjamin sat on a quilted sofa facing a crackling fire. His hair was wet, and he wore fresh jeans with a dark tee that stretched tight across his powerful chest. Her entire body heated and flashed wide awake.

He looked up and smiled. "Did they go down okay?"

"Yes." She hesitated.

He patted the sofa next to him, and she gladly went forward to sit. When he reached behind himself for a hand-stitched blanket to place over her legs, she fell for him all over again. "Thank you." She pushed her wet hair away from her face. "How did you find us?"

He reached for her hand and held it gently. "We figured there would probably be a helicopter if they got the chance. Did you see the first grizzly ram it?"

She nodded. "I thought he just was out of control."

"No. He had a tracker on his tongue, which he stuck to the bottom of the helicopter." Benny's voice was a low masculine hum. Healing tingles cascaded from him.

She leaned against him, trying to see how badly he'd been hurt. "You're healing. What is injured?"

"Just a few bones in my leg," he said quietly. "You have bruises on your neck. What happened?"

She wasn't ready to talk. "You first."

He gave her the time she needed, telling her of their ride to the compound and the ensuing fights. "Now you. What happened? I need to know so I can help you."

The reality hit her then. She'd left Terre to die in the rubble, because there was no way he'd been able to open that door with the keypad. "I caused Terre's death." Should she feel bad about taking a life? She didn't and might have to think about that later. Right now, she relayed the entire story to Benjamin.

By the time she was finished, he had her on his lap and was holding her tight. "You were so brave."

Nobody in her entire life had ever called her brave. "I was terrified and desperate," she admitted softly.

"That's brave, baby." He tilted her head back and kissed her, long and deep. "I'm proud of you, although I wish I could've killed Terre." He really did sound sorry about that.

She grinned. "Well, you did get to kill Jaydon."

Benjamin rolled his neck. "No, I didn't. I only had seconds to find you before that lodge collapsed, and my gut feeling is that he made it out. That guy isn't giving up his plans so easily. We might've bought some time for now, but he'll keep trying to duplicate the ritual."

So he'd chosen her over vengeance. She snuggled closer into his chest. "Thank you for coming for us." Her body was sore, but she'd never felt better in her life.

"Of course." He tugged on a strand of her hair. "I've been thinking."

Joy careened through her. "Yes?"

"I have family members that live all over the States, and some live in nice, quiet towns. Why don't you think of locating in one of those? You'd have family instantly, and a smaller town would be a good place for the girls to grow up." He rubbed his chin. "I'll get you a list."

She grew still, and her blood chilled. He was sending her away? "Would you be coming, too?"

"No, sweetheart." He kissed her gently on the forehead. "You and the girls need a safe life. Mine is anything but."

Oh. She hadn't considered that he wouldn't want to be a father. Of course, he didn't want to be a father right now. She and the girls were a package deal, and asking him to take that responsibility on was more than he apparently wanted. "I understand," she said softly.

Someone knocked on the door, and Mercy came inside. Her hair was wet and her eyes wild. "Excellent job stealing the tablet, Karma. I cracked it."

"Already?" Benjamin stiffened and released Karma. "Did you find the enhanced females?"

"Some of them," Mercy said. "They're at a temporary location north of Portland. Garrett needs a few hours to heal his head, and Logan does, too. He's contacted the other members of the Seven, and they're coordinating a strike plan for just before noon."

Karma gasped. "You're all wounded. You can't strike now."

Benjamin shook his head. "We have to go before they figure out we took the tablet. It'll be shock and awe, Karma. It's what we do."

It was crazy. Healing tingles were still coming from him.

Benjamin stood and drew her up. "Get some sleep. I'll go help plan the attack." There was still a crust of blood beneath his ear that he'd missed in the shower.

Karma watched him go. Terre had tried to destroy her spirit for years, and he'd failed. It had taken less than a week for Benjamin Reese to break her heart.

Chapter Thirty-Seven

The rain had lightened as dawn began sneaking over the mountains and the sun tried to pierce the still-thick cloud cover. Benny quietly opened the door to the cabin Bear had provided for him after a contentious night of planning a desperate op and arguing with Bear about strategy. Sometimes Bear just liked to argue, Benny finally decided. Mercy had brilliantly gone and awoken Bear's mate, Nessa, and her presence had calmed the shifter. As Nessa had commanded an elite witch fighting force before mating Bear, her insights had proven invaluable.

Benny wasn't entirely sure she'd changed jobs, in fact. But that was none of his business.

He kicked off his boots and moved to check the fire when a small sound in the kitchen caught his attention. He bypassed the fire and turned to find the two little girls rifling through the pantry. "Hello, urchins," he murmured.

They both jumped, and the slightly taller one pushed her sister down and then stood in front of her in a protective stance, her eyes wide. They were dark topaz, not merely brown, and there was no doubt both girls would be incredible beauties one day.

Benny paused. He didn't want to scare them, but his sheer size was a lot. He was big even for immortals, and the males the girls had been around in the Kurjan strongholds probably hadn't been the nice, nurturing types. Neither was he. Yet he crouched to his haunches, acutely aware that he still towered over them. "Are you hungry?"

The girl on her butt edged to the side. "Hungry?"

His heart just melted right then and there. So he grinned, keeping his voice quiet and gentle. "From here, I can see pancake mix. I'm sure there are huckleberries in the freezer, because bears are nuts for huckleberries. Seriously nuts. How about huckleberry pancakes?"

The sitting girl chewed her lip.

The one protecting her with her tiny body looked toward the exit and then back to Benny.

He sighed. "Okay. Let's start here. I'm Benny. You can call me Benny, Ben, Benjamin, or butthead."

The sitting girl burst out laughing. "Butthead," she repeated.

The other urchin narrowed her eyes and just studied him, obviously looking for a trap.

Benny didn't move. The more still he stayed, the more they seemed to relax. "If you don't tell me your names, I'll have to give you names. And I'm terrible at naming people. I had a dog once, and I named him Freddy the Farter."

Both girls laughed and then caught themselves.

"All right. I'm thinking Goat Nose and Frog Face." He nodded as if satisfied. "Yep. Good names."

The girl sitting slowly stood and moved to her sister's side. "Those aren't girl names," she whispered.

Benny shrugged. "Oh. Well then, how about Girly Giggles and Girly Goober?"

The serious one lifted her eyebrows, obviously wondering which one was her name. "No," she whispered.

Benny waited.

The other one reached down and took her sister's hand. It was like a punch to the gut for Benny, but he kept his expression curious. "I'm Belle, and she's Boone," the girl whispered.

Benny smiled and pursed his lips as if thinking it over. The girls held their breath in unison. "All right. Those are very pretty names. We'll go with those."

Boone studied him. "Benny, Belle, and Boone. All Bs."

He grinned. "Yes. All Bs. You're a smart one, aren't you? We'll have to form the Huckleberry Pancake B Club."

Belle perked up. "Club?"

"Sure," Benny said easily. "Everyone needs a club, right?"

Boone frowned. "But you're a warrior. We're just girls."

Ah, shit. He wished he could go back and bomb the Kurjan stronghold again. "Yeah, and girls are the strongest ones out there. Didn't you know that?"

Both kids shook their heads.

He nodded solemnly. "Honest. Sometimes people tell girls they aren't strong because they're actually afraid of how strong girls can be. Do you feel strong?"

They shuffled their feet in unison, and hand to God, it was adorable. Benny sent healing cells to the ankle that was still bugging him. "Well, you might not feel strong because you haven't eaten truly excellent huckleberry pancakes yet," he said, trying to sound wise and not like his ankle was breaking. "But you're both badasses. Totally tough. You survived a bombing last night. Definitely strong."

Boone clapped a hand over her mouth. "You said 'badass'."

He winced. Swearing around little girls was probably a bad idea. He sucked at this. "You're right. I shouldn't have said a bad word. I'm very sorry."

Belle's mouth gaped open, and she turned to look at her sister, her eyes even wider than they had been before. "He said 'sorry'," she whispered. Boone shushed her.

Benny's chest hurt, and he rubbed it. Maybe he should try a different tack right now. "Here's the deal, ladies. I was in a battle last night, and my ankle hurts and my stomach is really empty.

Huckleberry pancakes sound like a great breakfast, but I need help. Will you help me?"

Now they looked shocked. He didn't want to awaken Karma, but he was at a loss here.

Slowly, Boone walked toward him, still holding her sister's hand. "You're hurt?"

He let his lower lip pout just a little and felt like a total dumbass. "Yeah. My ankle and my stomach. I think breakfast would help."

Boone reached out and gently touched his arm, her body braced. "You gots hurt saving us."

Benny held perfectly still so he didn't startle them.

Belle grinned, showing two wide dimples in her cheeks. "We can help."

Benny smiled. "Great. Grab the pancake mix, I'll get the huckleberries, and we'll try to figure out this stove. It looks complicated."

Belle leaned over to her sister. "He really needs help."

Boone nodded wisely.

It was like another punch to the solar plexus. They were much safer away from him and his life, right? But he didn't want to let them go any more than he did Karma.

He sighed.

Boone patted him. "It's okay, Benny."

* * * *

If Karma's heart hadn't already broken the night before, it shattered into pieces as she listened to Benny and the girls making breakfast. He was sweet, he was kind, and he built them up with every sentence. From how smart they were to figure out the stove to how they picked the perfect number of huckleberries for each pancake. By the time they were sitting down and eating, the girls were chattering along in a way she'd never heard them do.

They were happy, and for once, they knew they were safe.

She joined them after a while, and the girls both looked shocked when Benjamin served her. She acted as if it was no big deal and accepted the pancakes, eating even though she wanted to cry. Then when Benjamin cleaned up the kitchen and all the dishes, and the girls looked on in surprise, she didn't know how to thank him.

Now, hours later, she checked on them in the queen-sized bed, making sure their napping was peaceful. Benny looked over her shoulder. "They're cute."

She quietly shut the door, turning to look at him. "This is a mistake. You going on a mission this close to the last one," she whispered.

He drew her away from the bedrooms to the crackling fireplace. "This is what I do. This is my life." He looked down at his clothing. "Can't you see who I am?" He wore black cargo pants, a dark shirt, and a black jacket with guns at his thigh, waist, and probably boot. A knife handle protruded from a sheath at his other thigh, and combat sunglasses perched on his head, even though a storm outside was now actively trying to destroy the earth.

"I see who you are," she whispered, trying not to wring her hands together. Maybe it was Benny who didn't see who he was or who he could become.

"Good." His jaw hardened, and he looked every inch the warrior he claimed to be. God, he was big and dangerous. "Go through the papers Mercy left and choose where you want to live. I'll have bank accounts set up for you and the girls, and we'll make sure to buy the right house before you go." Then he kissed her on the forehead and turned to stride out into the storm.

She looked at the closed door for a second. Then her head heated, and so much pricking heat swept her body that her lungs stuttered. She ran for the door, whipped it open, and hurried outside into the battering rain.

Benny turned halfway down the path. "What are you doing? Get out of this storm."

"No," she yelled, stomping down the porch steps to the tall grass. "You get out of this storm. You're crazy if you think this isn't a life we can handle. How dare you make such a decision?" She couldn't gather her thoughts, she was so angry. "You should not be going on this mission, and you know it. Yet you take the risk anyway."

He tilted his head to the side, and his jaw tightened in a way that wasn't comforting. "I told you to go back inside." This time, it was a low growl.

She squared her shoulders and lowered her chin. "I said no." It felt good to stand up to a male, and she knew she could do so with this one because he'd never hurt her. "You're being a moron."

His flash of a grin was a surprise. "You're not the first to say so. Karma, my life is dangerous. It's only going to get worse. The last thing I need is somebody worrying about me every time I step out the door, because usually I ain't going to the grocery store."

"I know that," she spat.

He looked around. "You and the girls will be safe here in Grizzly territory until I get back. Choose a place to live."

"No." She ran toward him and shoved him as hard as she could in the stomach. He didn't move an inch. "You don't get to dictate my life if you don't want to be in it. We won't be here at Bear's headquarters when you get back." Now she wasn't even making sense, but she couldn't stop the words pouring out.

His lips pressed together. "Honey? You're not going anywhere, and you know it."

She stomped her foot. "You know what? It's not me or the girls you're worried about. It's you. You're the coward, Benjamin."

His eyebrows lifted. "Stop trying to get me to lose my temper. It isn't going to happen."

Was that what she was doing? "I don't give two fucks about your temper," she said, meaning it. Yelling it.

"Then you're not as smart as I thought," he snapped, grabbing her arms and hauling her toward him. His mouth crashed down on hers. Hot and burning, the kiss tore through her with more power than the storm around them. She tried to hold on to reason and her anger, but the force of his kiss, of his hard body against her, burned both away until there was only Benny.

Only a passion that pierced so deep there was no turning away. He took control of her body, her mind, so quickly that all she could do was feel. Every nerve fired just for this moment and this male. Her nipples hardened to diamonds, and her clit pounded with a demand she'd never experienced.

He was raw muscle and deadly determination, and he made her crave both. Crave him. Hunger for him with an intensity that was too strong for her to do anything but sink right into him and let him take what he wanted.

When he let her go, her mouth tingled, and her mind fuzzed. His rugged jaw was hard and his eyes a blazing black with a rim of green. Otherworldly, powerful, and dangerous. For the first time, she saw the primal being he kept so carefully caged.

She gasped, trying to fill her lungs.

His hands much gentler, he turned her toward the cabin and gave her a light push. Then he was gone.

She put her hands to her lips and stumbled to the cabin and back inside. It took her a second, but she caught sight of a hovering spirit by the fireplace. "Whoa," she muttered. "I don't know who—"

The spirit turned, and it was Terre. Fury lit his face. "I'm going to kill you," he spat.

That was it. Just plain and simply it. She put both her hands out and shoved imaginary energy right at his face. "Go to hell right now, you bastard."

His face morphed in pain, and he wavered wildly.

Holy crap. She tried harder, and he screamed, pulled right into the fire. The tension dissipated as she vanquished him. She'd had no idea she could do that. It was crazy. She really was a badass.

A badass with a broken heart. The first tear slid slowly down her face, and she shoved it away. That was the one tear Benjamin

Dumbass Reese would get from her. Steeling her shoulders, she picked up the printouts of good places for her to settle down with the girls.

She'd make a perfect life for them without Benjamin. He'd made his decision.

Chapter Thirty-Eight

Benny leaned his head back against the side of the copter as the storm bounced them around. His knuckles were shredded, and he'd rebroken his ankle in the raid. What a raid. His brothers healed themselves on either side of him, injured and pissed off, but alive. The shifters had been excellent backup, and Bear was even giving them one more night to get off his property.

"Did you see those women?" Garrett muttered.

Benny didn't open his eyes as he healed himself. It was dark, anyway. "Yeah." They'd managed to save twenty enhanced females, and the two other helicopters were delivering them to Realm Headquarters for medical treatment and rest until Dage could relocate them.

"One gal said she was an accountant taken right off her farm in the mountains," Logan muttered. "She hadn't been fed in four days."

"We have to figure out how the Kurjans are finding so many enhanced females," Garrett said. "Dage is on it, but he doesn't know. None of them are safe. There is no doubt Jaydon is going to keep kidnapping women until he can complete the ritual."

"That's a worry for tomorrow. We'll come up with battle plans ASAP." Benny pulled his earbud out and stuck it in his pocket.

What time was it, anyway? Past midnight at least. "Did we lose anybody?"

"No," Bear said from across the craft as he healed a hole in his neck. "We've got some decent injuries, but everyone kept their heads on their bodies."

"Good," Benny said, opening his eyes to see Sam pop his shoulder back into place. Enhanced females weren't safe anywhere right now. Karma had called him a coward. Was she right? Was he afraid to take the chance? Afraid he couldn't protect her and those precious urchins? Afraid he'd be killed and leave them alone and Karma without a mate?

He was a member of the Seven, a brother to six, and he had a vow to fulfill.

If Karma was willing to take the chance, then maybe she was the brave one and he was a dumbass. He'd cooked breakfast for the girls without scaring them. Maybe he could figure out how to be around them, because he loved having them close. They did need protection.

A gust of wind hit the craft, and they spun sideways.

"Baby? Would you keep it on the proverbial road?" Logan called out.

Mercy looked over her shoulder from the pilot's seat, her eyes sizzling. "If you want to fly, feel free to get your cute butt up here and do so. If not, be quiet."

Garrett groaned. "Why in the hell did you give her flying lessons?"

Benny shrugged. "It seemed like a good idea at the time." Yeah, he'd fought both Logan and Garrett over it. True, Mercy was a little reckless and wild, but if they crashed, they'd probably survive. Maybe.

She landed just a little off the landing strip, the end of the helicopter taking out one of Bear's hangar walls. He jumped out first. "Logan? You're paying for that."

"I always do," Logan said, as he stepped out and headed to the pilot's door.

Benny grinned and slapped Garrett on the back. "We need to talk tomorrow." Then he turned and ran through the woods to his temporary cabin. He stopped short, yards away, at the sight of Karma sitting on a porch swing beneath the overhang, bundled up in the darkness. "What are you doing?" Rain poured over him, washing away the blood and the hurt.

She slowly stood and set the blanket aside. Once again, she wore a long skirt with a sweater, looking so pure and innocent that it hurt. "Waiting for you."

Waiting for him? Nobody had ever waited up for him. All his emotions coalesced, landing hard in his chest. His body was in motion before his brain caught up, and he was in her space, inhaling her sweet scent. "I'm not a coward," he murmured.

"I know." Pink tinged her high cheekbones. "I shouldn't have called you that."

"Oh, I was being a dumbass, and maybe I was afraid of the future. But it's coming for us whether we're together or not. The future can't be stopped." When realizations smacked him, they did so with a vengeance. "You're strong enough to face it with me."

Her head tilted slightly, and surprise lifted her eyebrows. "I know."

"So do I." He leaned down and kissed her, going gentle this time. She tasted sweet and like...his. "I want the future with you. No matter how long it lasts." Who knew. Maybe they'd have forever. "I'll try to be the right guy for the girls."

"I want a future with you, too. You're already the right guy." She flattened her hands across his chest, not coming close to spanning the entire width. "I'll make you happy, Benjamin."

"You already do. There's nothing else you need to do but be you." He had some work to do with his females, but he was learning how to be a patient guy. He leaned down and kissed her again, lifting her up to her toes to go deeper, his entire being settling.

She pulled away. "I'm not alone. I mean, I have—"

"They're mine, too." He swung her up in his arms and carried her inside, kicking off his boots and striding toward his bedroom. "You know what this entails? It's all or nothing, and I'm taking it all." The brand on his hand burned in agreement, shooting up his entire arm. The beast inside roared.

"You can have it all," she whispered, tangling her small hand in his wet hair. "You already do."

* * * *

Her heart might explode from love and need. Maybe a little trepidation. Benny's words were calm, but there was a primitive tension flickering around him, coming from him. She felt feminine and vulnerable, strong and desirable in his arms. He laid her down on the bed and lifted her shirt over her head in one smooth motion. Buttons popped and flew in every direction. Then her skirt and undergarments were gone, just as fast.

He pressed her back on the bed, and her hair feathered over the pillow. Then he looked his fill, fully dressed while she was naked. "God, you're beautiful."

She felt beautiful. Only for him. Maybe for everyone, but he was the only one she cared about. So she let him look.

"You're mine, Karma," he said, drawing his shirt over his head. The play of muscle and movement was all male. Strong and hard. His words were a vow with more than a hint of possession. Considering she was giving herself to him, all he spoke was the truth.

He removed his pants, and weapons dropped to the floor. His legs still carried bruises, but he didn't seem to care as he placed a knee on the bed and hovered over her, kissing her ankles, knees, hip bones, breasts and chin on his way to her mouth.

The kiss was raw and passionate...all Benjamin.

She tugged on his hair until he lifted his head, looking like a predator whose prey was about to flee. "You're mine, too."

The smile that curved his firm lips warmed her way beyond her body. If she had a soul, he'd just taken possession of it, too. "Yeah. Definitely all yours." His fingers found her, and as usual, she orgasmed almost instantly.

"Sorry," she breathed, coming down.

He flipped her over and sank his fangs into her butt.

She yelped, half-laughing, as he turned her back over. "I forgot."

He sucked a nipple into his mouth. "I didn't." He growled around her, and her body spasmed, needing more than she would've thought possible. Then his hands were everywhere. His mouth, his hands, his entire body surrounded her, taking her, forcing another orgasm through her.

She gasped. "That was fast. Sorry."

"You said that on purpose." He flipped her, bit her, and yanked her up onto her hands and knees.

She smiled, her heart thundering. "Maybe?"

He penetrated her, forcing her internal walls to yield, his grip firm on her hips. Her head dropped forward, exposing her neck to him. He grasped her nape, his unrelenting hand holding her in place. For him.

Her sex quaked around him, and her breath deserted her. She couldn't move.

"You're where I want you, baby," he rumbled in her ear, his breath hot. Desperately hot. She tried to move back, to take more of him, but he held her in place. "My way." Then he pushed all the way in, consuming her.

She gasped again and arched her back, barely able to do so with his commanding hold. It was everything. The mere idea that he held her in place, his hold unbreakable, gave her a sense of security she'd have to figure out later. All she could do right now was feel.

He pulled out, then powered back in, setting up a hard rhythm that had her breasts bouncing against the sheets. The warrior was in control, and she let him play, little sobs escaping as her need climbed higher and higher. Maybe too high. He was unstoppable, the pleasure he gave her edged with just the right amount of bite. Of Benny.

His fangs sank into her neck, and she flew into another orgasm, her body trembling. She whispered his name, overcome, the waves too powerful to stop.

A hot flash of deep pain centered in the middle of her back, spreading out from her spine. The mating mark. The intricate R would be beautiful right there. Another orgasm crashed into her, shooting from her core to her ears, quaking ecstasy in places she hadn't realized could feel pleasure.

Into all of her. The physical body as well as the rest of her that couldn't be seen. Not just her heart. More.

His massive body shuddered against her, and his fangs retracted. Slowly, lazily, he licked the wound closed. His heart thundered against her back, but his hold gentled. He withdrew and pulled her under the covers, spooning his big body around her. "I love you, Karma. All of me and all of you."

Tears pricked her eyes. "All of me and all of you." Could there be anything more perfect?

Chapter Thirty-Nine

Benny whistled as he entered Bear's rec room, surprised to find the place lacking in coolie cups and naked females. "No party last night?"

"No," Bear said from behind the bar. "Coffee?"

"Hell yes." Benny accepted the mug shoved his way.

Just then, Garrett, Logan, and Sam entered the room and hustled toward the massive coffeepot.

Bear watched them with resignation in his honey-brown eyes. "Once you four clean me out of coffee, you need to get going. So far, I've kept your visit under the radar with the rest of the shifter nations, and I don't need that kind of problem right now. Ever, actually."

Garrett finished his mug. "You're right. Thanks for your help. We're all packed up and will get going." He held out a hand for Bear to shake.

Benny straightened to his full height. "This coffee is crap, Bear. You're lucky we're drinking it." Yeah, he might've gotten spoiled by Karma's coffee the other day. Even so, he had a job to do right now, and he had no problem interfering. He was good at it. "Garrett's going to stay with you. He was a prospect in your MC a while back, and he needs to be patched in."

Bear dropped his mug on the counter. "What are you talking about? Garrett was undercover as a prospect, and besides, that was before he became a member of the Seven. Secrets never stay secrets, and most of the world knows your identities now, even if we don't understand this final ritual."

"He's right," Garrett said. "Ignore Benny, Bear. We're good."

"We are not good," Benny said, angling his body toward Garrett. "You're looking to join an MC, and this one is already an ally. Since you're on your own, you need to be with friends."

Logan looked at Garrett, indecision on his powerful face. Obviously Garrett had told him about the dreams.

Sam looked at his brother. "Mercy wouldn't like the MC life, and you know it. I'll stay. Make me a prospect and then patch me over fast, because I don't take orders well."

Garrett shook his head. "Sam? That's crazy. You don't have to ride with me."

Sam shrugged. "I'm searching for a place, as you know. Might as well do it covering your back and riding free. I love to ride."

Logan's expression cleared. "That would make me feel better—the two of you riding together."

Bear slammed his hand down on the wooden bar. "Hello? Remember me? The president of the Grizzlies and the guy who could shift and rip all of your heads off with one paw?"

Benny barely kept himself from rolling his eyes. "Yes, we remember you. We also all know that you're going to say yes, so could we just skip the argument? Why do you have to be so contrary all the time?"

"It's my nature," Bear snapped, looking more than ever like a real bear.

Benny sighed. "Listen. I could tell you that having the Realm King's nephew and the demon king's brother riding with you as you accept them into your brotherhood would be a good thing for your people. That having those two leaders on your side would be an advantage. But I'm not going to tell you that."

"Why not?" Bear asked, his chin lowered.

Benny grinned. "Because you don't give a shit about diplomacy, and we all know it. What you do care about is loyalty, and you feel loyal to these two. You know it, we know it, so let's just go with it."

"You have always been a pain in my ass, Reese," Bear growled.

"Doesn't make me wrong," Benny said reasonably. This was finished as far as he was concerned. He reached over and clapped Bear on the back. "Stay in touch." Then he headed out into the drizzly day and down to his cabin, to get his family.

Family.

He paused at the sight of the twins sitting on the front porch swing, rather forlorn expressions on their tiny faces. "What's going on, girls?"

Belle looked down at her shoes, and Boone just looked at him.

This might take time. He moved toward them and sat on the rough porch, still taller than they were on the swing. "What's up, Boondoggles?"

Boone snorted. "Mama says we can't get wet." She gestured toward the grounds. "*Everything* is wet."

Benny grinned. "True. All right, this is good. We need to have a little chat."

Both children focused directly on him.

He kept the smile in place. "So. Here it is. I want to marry your mama, and it'd be great if you two would help me plan a wedding. I don't know how."

Belle frowned. "Marry?"

"You know. Become a family. I'd be your dad." Unease settled in his gut. Facing these sweet girls was one of the hardest things he'd ever done.

Their faces cleared. Belle angled her neck to study him better. "You'd train us to fight?"

"Well, sure," Benny said. Was that all Kurjan fathers did? "But more importantly, I'll keep you and your mama safe and protected. Well, I'll teach you to protect yourselves, too."

Boone blinked. "Do you hit?"

He paused, his ears heating. "No. I don't hit. I'd never hit you or your mama. Has anybody hit you before?" He might have to go hunting after he got his family home.

Belle pulled on the bottom of her sweater. "Terre liked to hit, but Mama always got in the way."

Benny ignored the fire suddenly burning inside his throat. "He'll never hit anybody again. Your mama took care of Terre." Twice, actually. It had been an excellent story she'd told about his ghostly visit. "I won't hit you, and if anybody else ever dares, they'll regret it."

Boone studied him. "What if we burn down the house?"

Yeah, fire was probably on their minds still. "I wouldn't hit you, but I'd make you help rebuild it."

Belle smiled. "That's good."

He waited for the tougher sell. "Boone?"

She eyed him. "What if we get sick or throw up?"

"Then I'll clean it up and get you medicine." That one was easy.

"Okay." Boone's smile was smaller but there nonetheless.

He relaxed. "So. We're going home now, where we live with your aunts and uncles, who are also known as the Seven. You're going to love it there, and they're going to love you. For now, how about you help me pick a ring for your mama?" He had some pictures on his phone.

"Green ring," Belle said.

"Blue," Boone contradicted.

He smiled. "We can make that happen."

* * * *

Karma laughed as Benny swung her up in his arms to cross the threshold of his home in Seven territory. She loved the open floor plan with the expansive view of the river, although they'd have to figure out a way to keep the girls safe from drowning. They ran in behind them, chattering happily.

Benny set her on her feet and stared out the window. "The river."

"I know." She chewed on the inside of her cheek.

He looked down at the girls. "We can build a fence around the backyard for now, and we'll start swimming lessons in the spring." He jolted. "If that's okay with you."

She smiled. "Of course that's okay with me." It might take him a while to make decisions without checking in with her, and that was just sweet.

He tugged on her ear. "You doing okay? With everything?"

If he meant her still-tingling back, then yes. The marking was awesome. If he meant the fact that she'd vanquished a spirit, then probably. She'd had no idea she could send the obnoxious ones away that easily. Maybe she could develop the skill so it happened naturally. All of a sudden, she had so much faith in the two of them and in herself, and part of that confidence came from Benny. "I'm fantastic."

He glanced toward the girls. "There are two bedrooms past the fireplace. Choose which one you want to share and then we can start decorating." When they ran off, he looked at Karma. "They should share for a while, right? Since they're only around three years old?"

"Right." She looked around her new home. It was perfect.

He also looked around. "You can redecorate all you want. We're loaded. One of the benefits of living for so long."

Loaded? Fun.

The girls ran back in, having chosen the bedroom closest to the fireplace.

Benny cleared his throat, and they halted, their expressions sobering. Slowly, they walked up on either side of him, facing her. A giant of a male and two tiny little girls, all with softness in their eyes.

She tilted her head.

Benny gracefully knelt down on one knee, and the twins followed suit, looking adorable in new jeans and cute sweaters. One blue and one green.

Karma smiled. "What are you doing?"

Benny looked a little pale. Interesting. "We want to ask you to marry us."

Boone hopped up and down. "Yes. Marry us, and we'll be a family."

Belle leaned forward. "If you say yes, you gets a ring we ordered. It's pretty."

Karma looked at her little family. Her chest just up and exploded with so much love her body couldn't contain it all. They were hers. Eventually, there would be little hybrid boys to join the family since vampire hybrids only made boys. They were all going to have a life full of love, laughter, and adventure. She just knew it. "Yes."

The girls nearly bowled her over with hugs, followed by Benny, who picked all three of them right off the ground, holding them securely. "Life is good, baby."

"No," she whispered. "Life is perfect."

And it was.

Epilogue

"Benny, hurry up, would you?" Karma waited on the chilly front porch as her family finished getting ready inside. They'd taken to calling themselves the Three Bs Club. Oh, they'd offered to give her a B nickname so she could join, but she liked that they had their own thing. Plus, it was easy to talk the B Club into doing chores since they did so as a group. She smiled at her freshly decorated pumpkins and swished her pirate costume around her legs.

The door opened, and the trio walked outside.

Her mouth dropped wide open. "Oh my goodness."

"We're princesses," Boone yelled, rocking back and forth on shiny blue heels. She wore a very sparkly blue dress with a tiara atop her long dark hair.

"Yeah," Belle yelled even louder, dressed in a similar outfit that was bright green.

But it was Benny that captured Karma's attention. She fought a full-out laugh. "Benjamin."

He looked down at his sparkling purple dress and ridiculously high heels. "This is becoming a bad habit. Twice in a lifetime is enough." The tiara on his head tilted dangerously to the side.

"We're the Three Bs," Belle chirped. "We hafta dress the same this year, and we voted. Two against one."

Karma nearly choked on a chuckle. "What did Benny want?"

"To be cats," Boone said, hopping happily. "He lost."

Benny sadly shook his head, his eyes sparkling.

Her heart turned over once again, as it did often with her mate. They were about to trick-or-treat in the Seven subdivision, and he'd face all of the warriors in that dress that had no doubt been a shower curtain at one time. Yet he didn't care. It was all about making the girls happy.

Benny took a small hand in each of his. "We'll hit each house and then the storage buildings. I believe we have people stationed at each one."

She shook her head and took Boone's free hand. "How much candy did you buy, anyway?"

He shrugged. "Dunno. I had to buy enough that there would be some left when Mercy was done. We'll only eat a little each night."

"Yeah," Boone said right before Belle chimed in with her agreement.

"All right," Karma said, her stomach still rolling from the chocolate she'd eaten earlier that day. "Afterward, maybe we could sit on the porch swing for a while. Just you and me." The girls had found a new TV show with dinosaurs they loved, and she'd make sure it was on.

Benny grinned, leading the way. "I wondered when you were going to tell me."

She stumbled and caught herself. "You know?"

He whistled happily. "Please. I know your body better than my own."

That was true. "You're happy?"

"I'm so much more than happy I can't find the words," he admitted, his gaze meeting hers and showing her what love felt like. What it looked like. "We'll celebrate later. Girls? You're gonna have a baby brother."

The girls both looked up at him, not slowing their strides. There was candy at the end of the walk, after all. "A boy?" Boone asked.

"Yep," Benny said.

Belle looked at her sister. "Should we give him a B name?"

Boone looked up at Karma. "How about a K name? There should be a K Club, too."

"We're all in the R Club," Belle reminded her. "The Reese Club."

Karma smiled and looked down at her wedding ring. There was a massive diamond with an emerald on one side and a sapphire on the other.

Benny caught her gaze. "We'll have to get another stone. Can't wait to see the color."

"Me, either," she whispered. How could life be this amazing? Benny winked.

Yeah. That was how. "I'm so glad you came for me," she whispered, her voice shaking.

His gaze softened even more. "Oh, sweetheart. Of course I came for you. I always knew you would end up on my side. Yep," he said happily, leading them to the first doorway. "I've always had Karma."

Please read on for an excerpt from the newest Romantic Suspense novel in Rebecca Zanetti's bestselling Deep Ops series.

DRIVEN
Rebecca Zanetti

Prologue

Six months ago

Thunder sounded in the distance as the wind rustled dried leaves along the lake path. Angus Force stumbled over an exposed tree root and somehow righted himself before falling on his ass. Again. The mud on his jeans showed he'd slipped at least once.

Roscoe snorted and kept scouting the trail, his furry nose close to the mud. His snort held derision.

"Shut up," Angus said, surprised his voice didn't slur. He'd started the morning with his fishing pole and two bottles of Jack. Several hours later, it was getting dark, he had no fish, and the bottles were empty. The forest swirled around him, the trees dark and silent. He glared at his German shepherd. "Be nice or I won't feed you."

The dog didn't pause in his explorations. His ears didn't even twitch.

Angus sighed. "I should've left you with the FBI." Of course, the dog had a slight problem with authority and probably would have been put down at some point. Angus brightened. They had that in common. "All right. I guess I'll feed you."

Roscoe stopped suddenly.

Angus nearly ran into him, stopping at the last second and slipping on the leaves. "What the hell?"

The fur down Roscoe's back ruffled, and he stared straight ahead down the trail. He went deadly silent, his focus absolute.

Angus dropped his pole and the sack containing the bottles. Damn it. He hadn't brought a gun this morning. He'd been more concerned with having enough alcohol to get through the day.

He gave a hand signal to the dog and veered off the trail, winding through a part of the forest he could have navigated blindfolded. Soon he approached his lone cabin from the side, where he could see front and back.

Nothing.

Roscoe remained at his side, his ears perked, the fur still raised.

The woods around them had gone silent, and a hint of anticipation threaded the breeze. Roscoe sat and stared at the cabin.

Yeah. Angus remained still. There was definitely somebody inside. He angled his head and spotted a black Range Rover parked on the other side. So they weren't trying to hide.

His shoulders relaxed, and he waited.

Waiting was what he excelled at. Well, waiting and drinking. He'd become a master at downing a bottle of whiskey. Or several.

Ten minutes passed. Something rustled inside the cabin. Now he was just getting bored. So he gave Roscoe a hand signal.

Roscoe immediately barked three times.

The front door of the cabin opened, and two men strode out. Government men. Black suits, pressed shirts, polished shoes. The older one had a beard liberally sprinkled with gray and the worn eyes of a guy who'd already seen two much.

The younger guy was a climber. One who even stood like he was on his way to the top and had no problem stepping on bodies to get there. His shoes were expensive, and his blue silk tie even more so.

Angus crossed his arms. "You're trespassing, assholes." Was it a bad sign he could sound and feel sober after the amount he'd imbibed all day? Yeah. Probably.

The older man watched the dog. The younger man kept his gaze on Angus.

The older guy was obviously the smarter of the two.

The younger guy smoothly reached into his jacket pocket and withdrew his wallet to flip it open. "Agent Thomas Rutherford of the HDD." His voice was low and cultured. Confident. He was probably about Angus's age—in his early thirties.

"You're lost," Angus returned evenly.

"No. We're looking for you, Special Agent Angus Force," Rutherford said, his blue eyes cutting through the space between them.

"I'm retired." Not exactly true, which was probably why these guys had shown up.

The older guy cocked his head. "That's a tactical Czech German shepherd," he said thoughtfully.

Angus lifted an eyebrow. "Nope. He's a mutt. Found him last week in a gulley." Was he drunk, or did Roscoe send him an irritated canine look? Angus jerked his head at the older man. "You are?"

The guy also took out a wallet to flash an HDD badge. "Agent Kurt Fielding." Rough with an edge of the street—no culture there.

Angus crossed his arms. "There is nothing the Homeland Defense Department could possibly want with me." The agency was an offshoot of Homeland Security—one of the offshoots the public didn't really know about. The name alone made it easy to divert funds. "Go away."

Rutherford set his hands in his pockets in an obvious effort to appear harmless. "We'd like a few minutes of your time."

"Too bad." Angus would like another drink. They stood between him and his bottles. That was a bad place to be.

Agent Fielding had deep dark eyes with a hangdog expression. He finally looked away from Roscoe and focused on Angus. "We know you've been nosing around the old files of the Henry Wayne Lassiter case."

Heat flushed down Angus's spine. "The last person who said that name to me got a fist in the face and a broken nose."

"We're aware of that fact," Rutherford said. "Special Agent in Charge Denby still has a bump on that nose."

Yeah, well his former boss had known better. Angus shrugged. Fielding tried again. "We just want to talk."

"No," Angus said softly. "I know something is up, and I'm not going to stop until I find out what." He'd been a damn good tracker for the Behavioral Science Unit until the Lassiter case, and then he'd fucking lost everything. Maybe even his mind. "A source reached out and told me Lassiter isn't really dead." Yeah, he'd shot the lunatic, and blood had sprayed. But he'd been shot as well, and he'd passed out before he was able to check the body for a pulse.

Rutherford smiled, showing perfectly straight white teeth. The guy probably had them bleached. "We understand that an old file clerk contacted you, but you have to realize that we'd just forced Miles Brown into retirement, and he was trying to make trouble by calling you. He apparently succeeded. Lassiter is dead."

Miles had been a great record keeper, and the only thing his message had said was that there was a problem with the Lassiter file and for Force to call him immediately. "Fine. Then let me talk to Miles." The phone number had been disconnected.

Fielding winced. "Miles Brown suffered a stroke and is in St. Juliet's on the east side of DC. He has no family, so we put him up."

That would explain why Force couldn't get to him. "I'd like to see his office."

"His office was cleared out," Fielding said. "Per procedure. Nothing out of the ordinary there."

Right. Except that Miles had called, and there was a sense of urgency in his voice. "Yet you're here," Angus murmured.

Rutherford sighed. "We know you've been through an ordeal, but—"

"Ordeal?" Angus growled. "Are you kidding me?" He'd give anything for his gun.

Fielding held up a hand. "We're very sorry for your loss, but this is important."

Loss? Had the fucker really just said the word "loss" to him? Angus took two steps toward the agents, and Roscoe kept pace with him, low growls emerging from his gut. "Leave. Now." His sister had been murdered by the last serial killer Angus would ever put away. *Loss* didn't cover it. Not by a long shot.

Rutherford eyed the dog warily. "We want you to stop pursuing the issue. Lassiter is dead. Let him lie."

Angus snorted. Roscoe kept at attention but stopped growling. "Why are you here, then? If the case was really closed, you wouldn't bother." The psychopath had actually worked for the HDD.

Fielding shuffled his feet, his gaze dropping to his scuffed shoes.

Angus straightened. His gut churned, and his instincts flared to life. "Say what you need to say."

Rutherford looked toward Fielding.

Fielding sighed and glanced up again. "Let it go. We're not going to give you a choice."

Ah, shit. Lassiter really was alive.

Angus stood perfectly still, his mind focusing despite the booze. "Well, then. If you're here, I guess I have leverage." Enough to get an office and maybe a team he could put together—until the HDD figured out a way to get rid of him. He looked down at the dog. "Wanna go back to work, boy?"

Chapter 1

The swirl of red and blue lights bounced off the yellow crime tape in a back alley outside of DC. The bastard had dumped the victim near a pile of garbage.

Angus kept his face impassive as he ducked under the tape and flashed his badge to the uniformed officer blocking access. It felt good to be able to flash the badge, even though he worked better without it.

It would be the only good feeling of the night.

Agent Kurt Fields was the first one to reach him, skirting several numbered yellow evidence markers placed on the wet asphalt. The guy was pale and looked even more grizzly than before. "I heard the call go out, got the details, and figured you'd be here." His T-shirt was wrinkled and his brown shoes scuffed.

Force nodded, acutely aware of West and Wolfe at his back. They'd both seen some rough shit in their time, but this was something new. He needed West to run the office, but when he turned his head to give an order, West was already shaking his head at him, his gaze direct. No way would he be left behind.

Angus turned back around and started to focus, speaking as much to himself as to his team. "Everything is relevant. Any sign on a piece of garbage, any scratch on the building, any glint of something shiny."

Agent Fields shook his head, sliding to the side and putting his body between Angus and the scene. "You're not understanding me. This is not your case."

Fire ripped through Angus as if he'd been prodded with a hot poker. "It's Lassiter, which makes it my case. Period." He had to get to the body and make sure, but his gut never lied.

Agent Rutherford, his blond hair mussed for the first time ever, reached them next. "You're not supposed to be here."

"I still have some sources in Homeland Defense," Angus muttered, his hands itching for his gun. "Now get out of my way."

"It's not the same," Rutherford said, his eyes bloodshot.

Wolfe came up on Angus's left. "What do you mean?"

Rutherford shoved a hand in his perfectly creased dress pants. Who dressed up for a crime scene at two in the morning? "I've studied your old case files on Henry Wayne Lassiter. His MO was unique. This crime scene is different."

Angus swallowed. "Where's the note?" The bastard had always left him a note.

"No note," Fields said as techs worked efficiently around them.

"Look again," Angus said evenly, his gut aching so much he wanted to bend over and puke.

Rutherford planted a hand on his shoulder. "This isn't your case. Please leave before I have you escorted away."

Wolfe shoved Rutherford's hand off Angus before Angus could grab it and break a finger or two.

Angus probably owed him for that. "There are two options here. Either you get the hell out of our way so we can examine the scene, or we get in a fight, beat the shit out of the two of you, and then we go and examine the scene." His voice had lowered to a hoarse threat.

Wolfe tensed next to him, while West drew up abreast, his shoulders back.

They were ready to fight with him, if necessary. His team was good. Better than good.

Rutherford smiled. "I'm ready. You hit one of us, just breathe wrong on us, and we'll finally get you out of the HDD. You're done, Force."

West cleared his throat, his blue eyes dark in the night. "Give us a minute with the scene. If it isn't Lassiter, Force will know."

Rutherford began to shake his head.

"Okay," Fields said, stepping aside. He shrugged at his partner. "Why not? Lassiter is dead, right?"

"Right," Rutherford gritted, his gaze promising retribution.

The stench of puke, garbage, and worse filled Angus's nostrils as he stepped past the agents to go deeper into the alley. "Lassiter kidnapped women and tortured them until their hearts gave out," he told his team. "We'll need an autopsy on this one, but we probably won't know much about her heart."

"Why not?" West stopped short as the body came into view.

"That's why," Angus said.

West's breath caught. "Oh."

Yeah. Oh. A tarp had been erected above the body to protect it from the elements. She lay naked on the pavement, her eyes open and staring straight up. Long dark hair, milky brown eyes, petite form. Her arms were spread wide, hands open and facing up. Her legs were crossed and tied at the ankles with a common clothesline rope found in a million places.

But the signature was just similar. Not the same. What did that mean? Her chest gaped open, the ribs and breastbone spread, leaving a hole.

West coughed. "Her heart is gone."

Angus went even colder. The scene was...off. "He eats it. Says it makes them stay with him forever." Nausea tried to roll up his belly, and he shoved it down.

Wolfe came up on his other side, his movements silent. He didn't gasp, stall, or go tense. He just stared at the body, his jaw hard. He pointed to the victim's arms. "Burn marks?"

"Affirmative," Angus said crisply. "There will be both cigarette and electrical burns." Outside and inside the woman. "As well as whip marks, ligature marks around the neck, and knife wounds. Shallow and painful—not enough to let her bleed out." Yet the cuts made to remove the heart were rough—not smooth as Lassiter liked to do.

No. Yet the heart was gone.

West coughed. "Raped?"

"Probably," Angus said.

Special Agent Tom Rutherford approached from the far end of the alley, carefully stepping over water-filled potholes with his shiny loafers. "There's no note, and she's not blond. In addition, the cigarette marks are too large—almost like a cigar was used." Angus breathed in and out before responding. He so much preferred Fields to this guy. Lassiter had been very choosy about his cigarettes and never would have used a cigar. Too common. Angus dropped into a crouch, closer to the woman. Lassiter had also loved blondes. This close, the victim's skin looked dusky, not pale. Lassiter had liked them pale. "Are you sure there isn't a note?"

"No note," Rutherford snapped. "Told you it wasn't him."

Yet, everything inside Angus insisted it was Lassiter. He looked around, noting the alley had been cordoned off, blocking access to any nosy neighbors or the press. In a different case, he'd be fighting with Rutherford right now about the news media. It probably killed the guy that he couldn't chase the cameras yet. "Once you get an ID, track down her medical records."

"No ID," Rutherford said, glancing down at his phone. "Her prints came up empty."

Wolfe scouted the alley, his gaze sharp. "You think Lassiter did this?"

Yes. "I don't know. The MO is close but not perfect, and he was a perfectionist." Frustration tasted like metal in Angus's mouth. "If it isn't Lassiter, it's a copycat. This is my kind of case. I was the best profiler the FBI had."

"Until you drank the entire wagon," Fields said, his bushy eyebrows raising.

Something on the victim's hand caught Angus's attention. "Glove?" He gestured toward a couple of techs.

One tossed him a blue glove, and he slid it on, gently turning the woman's right hand over.

"Shit," West said, leaning down. "Is that what I think it is?"

Angus swallowed. "Yeah." A perfect tattoo of a German shepherd had been placed right beneath her knuckles.

Wolfe shook his head. "Looks like Roscoe."

"Could be a coincidence," West said, his lips turning down.

"Probably is," Angus stood. But he knew it was Roscoe. "Fields? I want this case. Lassiter or not."

West gripped his arm and pulled him to the side. He leaned in to speak quietly. "You sure you want this? Serial killers don't just change their MOs, right? Especially ones like Lassiter."

Angus nodded. "You're right."

"You're obsessive, and you're just getting your drinking under control. If this isn't Lassiter, and that tattoo is a coincidence, then why take on the HDD right now?" West released him, his gaze again straying to the poor woman on the ground.

Fields slid his phone back into his pocket. "The boss says no way. You have a full docket of work, and he said to get back to it. We'll call you if we need you."

Angus turned on his heel and shoved his hands in his pockets, striding down the alley. A light rain began to fall, cold and angry.

His team members flanked him.

Wolfe sighed. "We're not letting this go, are we?"

"Not a chance in hell," Angus said. "Call everyone in. We have a new case." He ducked under the crime tape, walking away from death.

For now.

Printed in the United States
by Baker & Taylor Publisher Services